The East Coast Swaggie

TED DAY

ABOUT THE AUTHOR

Ted Day is a retired metal fabricator who has spent his whole life living at Lake Illawarra. He's worked for a number of companies that provided maintenance services to business and industry between the Shoalhaven and Sydney.

Published in Australia by Sid Harta Publishers Pty Ltd,
ABN: 46 119 415 842
23 Stirling Crescent, Glen Waverley, Victoria 3150 Australia
Telephone: +61 3 9560 9920, Facsimile: +61 3 9545 1742
E-mail: author@sidharta.com.au

First published in Australia 2017
This edition published 2017
Copyright © Ted Day 2017
Cover design, typesetting: WorkingType (www.workingtype.com.au)

Day Ted
East Coast Swaggie
ISBN: 978-1-921030-31-4
pp464

DEDICATION

*This book is dedicated to all those people
who have a crack at writing their first book.*

ONE

The east coast swaggie

In the early hours of the morning, Sydney Harbour is a tranquil place to be.

While the city's lights are never turned down, the tall buildings on the southern shoreline are mirrored in the water, making a beautiful backdrop for the massive white sails of the Opera House and the Sydney Harbour Bridge. Coastal gulls with their never-ending chirping patrol the waterways on endless flights to nowhere.

An alarm clock rang to awaken the occupants of 13 Deep Water Crescent, North Harbour. Fingers probed in the darkness to turn the cursed thing off.

Jack B Kelly rolled onto his back and breathed out heavily, then turned toward his wife Kate. He asked the obvious question. 'You awake honey?'

'Yes,' was the sheepish reply.

Kate rolled toward Jack for an early morning kiss and a cuddle, and then threw off the sheet covering them to slide out of bed. The big red digital numerals on the wall clock said it all: 4.05 am. Friday, December 17th. Kate was a tall lady with a slim figure and nice long black hair. While most of us don't look too flash first thing in the morning, Kate looked a pretty good picture in her white shortie pyjamas all covered in little red stars. She picked up a small bundle of clothes from a bench on the bedroom wall and headed towards the ensuite and the awaiting hot shower. 'Come on Jack, out you get ... we don't want to be late getting down to the jetty, the others will be waiting for us. We've got to leave here in thirty minutes, okay?'

'Okay mate,' replied Jack then continued, 'Oh, by the way Kate …'

Kate looked back at Jack, who was still lying in bed.

'Gee you look a little bit nice this morning darling, perhaps you'd like to pop back under here for a little while.' He held the sheet back and put on a charming smile as a form of inducement.

Kate wasn't having any part of it, so with her own beautiful smile she answered, 'I look good every morning.'

'I can't argue with that.'

'As for the other, the answer's *no*.'

Jack said, 'Oooohhh honey, you just broke my heart.'

They both laughed as Kate disappeared into the shower.

It didn't take Jack long to get dressed in a simple outfit of blue denim joggers and a short-sleeved checked shirt. He looked an imposing figure at thirty-six years of age and one could best describe this man in the same way that Hollywood describes its leading males: tall, dark and handsome. Jack was armed with an infectious smile and glowed with a touch of ruggedness. He was a lean, fit man capable of mixing it with the best in rugby league, running and surfing. He worked out in the home gym, located in the bottom floor of the house.

Kate emerged out of the ensuite dressed and ready to go. Her clothes were a carbon copy of Jack's, except the shirt was one size smaller than it should have been, giving her that *wow* factor.

'Were all set to go, eh?' said Jack.

'Yes, and right on time too,' replied Kate.

She put her shoulder bag on; the radio was given the flick along with the bedroom light. As they walked into the hallway the lights came on automatically. At the end of the hall was the west side entrance, which took them to the side boundary fence.

They passed through a security gate and stepped into a well-lit laneway about one hundred metres long and wide enough to drive a car down. The Kellys and their neighbours shared this lane and they also owned it. At the street's end two security gates were fitted, but at the moment they were open, while at the harbour end the lane, which was on a downhill slope, married up with the private jetty. The boundary fences were of solid brick with pillars every six metres. On top of each pillar a light in the shape of a coastal lighthouse had been fitted. The little lighthouses of the lane shone brightly, doing what all lighthouses are designed to do: to show the way in the dark.

They approached the jetty, which was constructed at right angles to the lane. Two fibreglass vessels were moored there, one behind the other with their bows facing the east. The vessel that was parked behind the Kellys' place belonged to them; it was primed up and ready to go. The lights were on and the motors were idling over. Arriving at the jetty, Jack and Kate were met by two people standing by the stern of the vessel. Bill and Marree Scanlon were the Kellys' best friends. Bill was a detective with the Sydney Crime Unit and carried a bit of rank, while Marree was a medical secretary at St Vincent's Hospital.

'Morning everybody,' said Jack.

'G'day Jack,' replied Bill.

'How are you Marree?' asked Jack as he gave her a kiss on the forehead.

'I'm fine thanks,' was her answer. Kate and Marree had a little hug then Kate gave Bill a kiss on the cheek.

'Thanks Kate, I always knew you liked me,' remarked Bill.

Kate responded by saying, 'Now that is true Bill, but I really like you a lot more when you get me off those speeding fines.'

'Darn it,' said Bill. 'I'm being used by another beautiful woman — oh well, what can I do?' It was laughter all around.

Jack's father Jimmy came out of the main cabin. 'Morning Dad,' said Jack, followed by, 'Morning Dad,' from Kate.

'Get out a bit early mate?' asked Jack.

'Yeah,' replied Jimmy. 'Couldn't sleep. Still can't get used to your mum not being around … I know it's been two years but I can't help it. Anyway, life goes on, so all aboard everybody, the fish are waiting.'

Bill stayed on the jetty to cast the lines. When Jimmy gave the signal, Jack took the helm on the flying bridge and Jimmy claimed the co-pilot's seat, while Kate and Marree took their place in the main cabin.

Because there had been a spate of late night accidents on the harbour in the past six months, Jack had an aviation strobe light fitted to the top of the mast. He now turned this light on. His theory was simple: if your vessel was well lit-up in the dark, how in hell could someone run into you?

Bill received the signal to release the lines and did so, then jumped on board. Jack pushed the gear lever into forward and this magnificent twelve metre twin hulled Powermaran, not yet six months old, slipped away from the jetty under the idling speed of the twin 250-horsepower diesel engines. Once clear of the shoreline the motors were given a little more fuel until the speed reached fifteen knots. This would do until they reached the Heads and the open sea, about thirty minutes away.

Inside the main cabin, the Scrabble board came out and a game was underway.

The Powermaran passed the well-lit 200-plus year old Fort Denison that sat on a rocky outcrop in the centre of the waterway, its old guns still pointing in the direction of an enemy that never came. This fort was a stark reminder of Australia's connection to its British colonial past.

Meanwhile a twenty metre steel trawler was about to enter the harbour with a full cargo of fish, prawns and octopus. Captain Dan De-Urey owned and operated the trawler, and was at the helm in the wheelhouse.

His crew of two men and one woman were in the cockpit at the stern, asleep on a pile of fishing nets. The ocean was like a millpond and the air still. Captain Dan had spent the past twenty years fishing the ocean and was very familiar with what he was doing. Above the noise of the big working diesel and the smell of the saltwater-exhaust mixture, Dan's thoughts were ahead of himself. After unloading it would be a week off for everybody.

'You bloody beauty,' he said to himself as he lined up the harbour beacons and drove his trawler right through the centre of the Sydney Heads. In the darkness the seventy-five metre high sandstone cliffs were just an eerie dark shadow.

Back on the Powermaran, things were going well. The first game of Scrabble was over with Kate being eliminated, so she decided coffee and biscuits were the way to go. Up on the flying bridge, the navigation lights of the trawler had been spotted as it reached clear harbour water. Jimmy had the binoculars on it and estimated it to be about ten minutes away.

Captain Dan spotted the Kelly vessel, lit up like a Christmas tree with the strobe light on top. He also knew the dangers of night-time navigation and welcomed the effort that some people put in to provide extra lights. There was no doubt that the thoughts of both skippers were with the four people who lost their lives when their party boat was run over by a late night ferry, just last month. For all boat owners, navigating at night was like a dull, ever-present toothache.

Passing time was down to about two minutes now as the two vessels approached each other on their starboard sides.

The female deckhand on the trawler was beginning to stir. An attractive bottle-blonde in her early thirties, she maintained a good figure and nice face and was sporting quite a large pony-tail. She was dressed provocatively with her tight work shirt and denim shorts leaving nothing to one's imagination. She was also Captain Dan's girlfriend. She stood up and made her way to the wheelhouse and her lover.

Kate Kelly had prepared five cups of beautiful aromatic coffee and two plates of mixed biscuits. Up on the flying bridge, Jack and his dad were discussing their portfolio of racing horses. They had ten: five pacers and five thoroughbreds.

Jack had recently taken a keen interest in the training side of the pacers and had been giving Vic, their trainer/driver, a bit of a hand on Saturday and Sunday mornings After logging up the required amount of hours and participating in a number of trials, the trotting club had declared Jack an amateur driver and issued him with a trackwork and trial license.

The two vessels were now fifty metres away from each other as Kate climbed the stairs to the flying bridge with the coffee and biscuits.

'Geesus, that smells good Kate,' said Jack as he turned to acknowledge her presence.

Jimmy jumped off his comfortable seat to take delivery of the tray off Kate.

Back on the trawler, the bottle-blonde — whose name was Marilyn — joined Captain Dan in the wheelhouse. On seeing her he said, 'Hello baby, I was just thinking of you and there you are — what a lovely surprise.'

Marilyn slid in between the large wooden spoked steering wheel and Captain Dan, clasping him around the middle and giving him a nice big squeeze. Their affection for each other was undeniable and Captain Dan was vulnerable when it came to women. He would walk over broken glass barefoot to get his mitts on one.

Marilyn looked into his eyes and said in a seductive voice, 'I'm bored and lonely, Captain, and I'm looking for a bit of excitement.'

'Well you know what, you've come to the right place.'

He was under her spell in a flash and completely lost control. He grabbed her with both hands and they passionately kissed while their tongues explored the interior of each other's mouths. She reached behind her and pulled the main switch, dousing the trawler's lights. Now she had her man to herself.

Back on the Powermaran, Kate was descending the stairs back to the cockpit. Jimmy was about to get back into the co-pilot's seat while Jack watched Kate until she reached the bottom of the stairs, giving her a nice smile. He then turned back around to continue driving the boat.

'*Dad!* That trawler's disappeared,' yelled Jack with urgency. At the same time the Powermaran's perimeter alarm started beeping.

'Jesus Christ,' said Jimmy in a frantic voice.

Jack pulled a red lever and instantly a floodlight situated on the mast came on, revealing the trawler too close for comfort and coming at an angle. A collision was inevitable. Jimmy hit the continuous siren button while Jack gave the twin diesels full power and turned the rudder to extreme port in an attempt to get away from the fishing trawler.

Captain Dan's early morning kiss and cuddle was about to come to an end. Firstly the light, then the siren hit him as one and gave him the fright of his life. '*Holy fuck*,' he yelled as he threw Marilyn out of the way like a rag doll and turned the rudder hard to port whilst giving the engine full throttle, hoping for the best.

The two deckhands asleep on the stern nets jumped to their feet, but they had no idea what was happening or which way to run.

Back on the Powermaran, the sudden turn and increased acceleration soon had the coffee and biscuits all over the floor.

Kate lost her balance but Bill grabbed her in time to prevent her being hurt.

A dog's leg was put in place by both skippers as they brought their vessels' sterns away from each other, passing with a minimum of clearance. Disaster had been averted.

Bill watched from the cockpit as the monster trawler passed by with barely a metre between them, but it looked more like a ghost boat without its lights on.

Jack cut the engines and asked his father, 'You okay Dad?' He was ashen white and shaking.

'Yeah I'm all right now, but for a while there I thought we were goners.'

'Me too, but we got out of it, that's the main thing. I'll go and see what's happening downstairs.' He went down into the cockpit and asked, 'How's everything down here?'

'We're okay, just a bit of cleaning up to do,' answered Kate.

'What happened?' asked Bill.

'The trawler's lights went out, then it crossed over into our path.'

At that instant the trawler's lights came back on. Bill got angry. 'Look at that,' he said. 'He hasn't even bothered to slow down or stop and see if we're all right. Now that's not very neighbourly is it? Bugger it, let's go after him.'

'Right,' said Jack. 'Hang on.'

'With that he returned to the flying bridge, took his seat behind the steering wheel, restarted the engines, turned the Powermaran around and set off after the trawler.

Back on the trawler, Captain Dan was trying to explain the loss of the lights to the two crewmen without actually telling them the truth, when Marilyn interrupted. 'They've turned their boat around, Dan. They're coming after us.'

Captain Dan took control of the situation. 'You two go to the back and arm yourselves with those long boat hooks.'

He pulled a rifle out of a metal security locker that was in the wheelhouse and placed it beside the door on the inside, where it couldn't be seen from the outside.

The trawler, with its load of fish, prawns and octopus, sat deep in the water, making it slow and sluggish — while the Kellys' twin-hulled Powermaran was built for speed. At full throttle it would lift out of the water and race on top of it, so it wasn't long before Bill was looking Captain Dan in the eye as the two boats went abreast.

'Shut your motor down mate, I want to talk to you,' yelled Bill over the sound of the engines.

Captain Dan responded by gesturing with two fingers in the air. This infuriated Bill, who could get nasty and vicious quite quickly. He pulled his police badge out. 'Detective Bill Scanlon, Sydney Crime Unit,' he yelled. 'Cut your motor.'

Dan could see the police badge quite clearly as Jack brought the Powermaran right up to almost touching the trawler. Captain Dan made a decision to defy him. The two deckhands were making their way up, each carrying a long boat pole with a nasty looking hook on the end. Bill had them in the corner of his eye.

Captain Dan decided to play his ace card and introduced the rifle, but Bill was quicker. They weren't playing games now. He seemed to pluck his service revolver from nowhere, pointing it straight at Captain Dan and again ordering him to shut the motor of the trawler down.

The two crew members with the boat poles were now in a position to use them.

Bill pointed his revolver straight at them, viciously saying, 'Okay, drop those poles on the deck now and get to the back of the boat before you get hurt.'

Looking into the barrel of a gun had an immediate effect on the two crewmen, as they discarded the poles and bolted for the stern of the trawler.

Bill re-pointed the revolver at Captain Dan, who was lifting the rifle up. Again Bill showed him his police badge and yelled at him, 'Don't lift that rifle any higher or I'll shoot you, I'm a police officer. If you don't stop your boat I'll call the Marine Area Command and they'll stop you before you get to the harbour bridge.' He put his police badge away and then pulled out his mobile phone.

Captain Dan realised that he couldn't win. If the water police stopped him they would probably lock him up for a couple of days. The fish wouldn't get to the market, and he needed the money. Reluctantly he placed the rifle on the deck and said to Marilyn, who was at the helm, 'Shut it down sweetheart.'

Jack did the same and the two vessels stopped as one.

Bill boarded the trawler and asked Captain Dan to unload the rifle and lock it back up inside the security cabinet, which he did. Only then did Bill put his own revolver away before pulling out his notebook to begin a quick investigation. He took down all the particulars and listened to Captain Dan's explanation of the events, which he thought did not quite add up. Nonetheless, there wasn't any more to do.

Bill spoke to the four of them. 'Okay everybody, today we were lucky, tomorrow we or somebody else might not be. You will all have to attend a lecture on harbour safety — other than that you're free to go. And remember, we can't be too careful on the harbour when it's dark.'

When Bill was safely back on the Powermaran, Marilyn started the trawler's motor, pushed the gear lever forward and drove them off into the last minutes of darkness towards the Harbour Bridge and beyond. This would be a talking point for a while.

Everybody was talking at once so Jimmy thought to himself, *I'm outta here.* He climbed the stairs to the flying bridge, started the motors, turned the Powermaran around and continued on towards the heads.

The first signs of daylight were beginning to emerge as Kate remade the coffee and again handed out the biscuits. This time they would get to enjoy it.

The ghostly cliffs that Captain Dan saw as he entered the harbour in the darkness had now been replaced by clearly visible ones as daylight gathered a bit more strength. Jimmy followed the same course out that the trawler followed in, right through the centre of the Sydney Harbour Heads and into the freedom of the ocean. He gave the twin motors three-quarter power and under the guidance of the GPS they arrived at their favourite fishing spot, six nautical miles off the coast. The fish finder confirmed that the water underneath them was absolutely teeming with fish. Jimmy cut the motors of this beautiful fifteen metre craft that they'd designed themselves and had built to their specifications. The twin-hulled Powermaran was like a floating hotel room with all the comforts of home. It could sleep ten and was capable of reaching New Zealand.

The men began fishing straight away, while Kate and Marree prepared breakfast on the high seas. The ocean belonged to them, at least for the time being. But of course they knew that within the next hour they would be joined by more fishing boats, and that the common coastal sea breeze, the 'north-easterly', would come along and destroy the tranquil conditions that were now enjoying.

After breakfast it was all hands on deck as the ladies joined in the fishing and by mid-morning they'd taken their quota of fish, filling three boxes. Cleaning the fish was a laborious task but it had to be done, and the low-flying coastal gulls on their surveillance flights soon surrounded the Powermaran to pick up a free lunch. Two large ocean turtles rose to the surface. Jack took great pleasure in hand-feeding these wonderful ancient creatures. A dolphin circled the Powermaran at high speed, scattering the birds as it went.

'Hey Jack,' said Kate. Jack looked Kate's way, then she continued. 'Here comes the Spanish Armada.'

About one hundred metres away and coming toward them was a Sydney Harbour pilot boat, and not far behind were six tugboats.

'Wow, look at that will you,' said Jack as they stopped cleaning fish and watched the approaching flotilla with interest.

The pilot boat pulled up alongside the Kellys' Powermaran. John Steed, the Sydney Harbour maritime pilot, came over to the rail. 'G'day Jack, how they biting?'

'Ahhh pretty good John, we've caught our quota, now we're scaling and cleaning up. Then I suppose we'll be out of here.'

The six tugboats created a lot of turbulence and after they went by, the conversation continued.

'You're out a fair way John, what's happening?'

The two crewmen on the pilot boat joined their boss on the rail as John replied, 'There's a big mother coming, Jack. The tugs will soon stop but I'm going out to the ten mile mark where I'll board the ship and drive her in. We'll pass by here at eleven-thirty.'

'In that case we'll hang around to have a look then follow you in.'

Kate put six nice fish in a plastic bag and said to John as she handed them over, 'Have tea on us, mate.'

'Thanks Kate, snapper's my favourite fish.'

'Hey John,' said Jack, 'we're all going out to the trots tonight, you're welcome to come if you've got nothing on. Dinner's at five-thirty in the restaurant. We've got a horse going around so you might get yourself a winner.'

Richie, one of the crewmen on the pilot boat, was quick to chime in. 'What's the name of the horse?'

'Hope at Midnight, Richie, and only put half your pay on it this time,' answered Jack.

Everybody laughed except Richie, who was known to be one mad hatter of a gambler.

'Okay Jack,' said John Steed, 'I'd love to come, I've seen the publicity and I think it'll be a pretty good night. I'll probably be by myself as Cher and I aren't talking at the moment. I had a late night and I've not only been getting the cold arse but the silent treatment as well.'

Kate and Marree both laughed and clapped; John began to chuckle as well, then everybody was laughing.

'All right Jack,' said John, 'I'll see you all at five-thirty.'

And under the umbrella of laughter the pilot boat silently moved away from the Kellys' boat and continued on its way to meet up with a very large ship surrounded in mystery.

Usually when something big came into the harbour everyone knew about it weeks in advance so all the tour boats could cash in — but this time there'd been no publicity at all.

After scaling and cleaning the fish, Kate lit the barbecue and started cooking a few snags. Seeing as they were going to be here for a while, they might as well have lunch.

Bill and Jack grabbed a couple of cold ones to suck on while the ladies were trying out a new drink called Sydney Heads Sparkling. Jimmy decided a coffee would do him — after all, somebody had to stay sober, as the Highway Patrol worked out here too.

Bill was first to notice the mystery ship coming into view and as the tugboats moved into escort positions he said, 'It looks like showtime's about to begin.'

There were about thirty boats out now, spread over plenty of territory. Four police boats arrived and began moving boats well away from the path of this monstrous aircraft carrier. An officer with a loud speaker was delivering a message. 'Don't attempt to move your boat until the carrier passes you by two hundred metres, okay?'

Bill waved to him and said, 'Right you are.' Then he said to his friends. 'Looks like we're in the middle of a massive security operation, how about that?'

Three attack helicopters preceded the carrier, which was about to draw level with the Powermaran. John Steed blew the carrier's whistle. Jimmy blew the Powermaran's whistle and all the other boats followed; it sounded a bit like midnight on New Year's Eve.

The carrier looked magnificent as it powered on by in its ghostly grey colours. All the American sailors in their clone uniforms covered the full length of the deck, adding a visitor's personality by waving and waving. All the people on the fifty odd fishing boats were waving as well; what a sight it was.

This aircraft carrier was the USS *Zemits*, a nuclear-powered vessel rumoured to be able to disappear from radar. It was en route to the Middle East via Australia. Following the carrier were another three attack helicopters in a V-formation. That seemed to bring a conclusion to the marine procession as it slowly made its way towards the Sydney Heads and the entrance to the harbour.

By the time the Kellys and the Powermaran re-entered the harbour, the USS *Zemits* was halfway to the Garden Island naval dockyard. The tugboats could be seen pulling the stern to change its direction and it would be quite some time before the carrier would be safely docked and tied up. The replica of the *Bounty* passed by on its way to the ocean with a full complement of paying customers eager to get some feeling of what it was like to be on a historical sailing ship. Fort Denison was coming up, which meant the Harbour Bridge — the 'Coathanger' — was dead ahead; so was the Kellys' private jetty. Jimmy turned the Powermaran around so as to have the bow facing the east and gently brought the vessel onto the jetty's rubber cushions.

Bill was on the jetty in a second and secured the bow and stern lines. It was 1.00 pm when they unloaded the boxes of fish and placed them on the jetty; so far it had been a very interesting and eventful day. Kate and Marree gathered their belongings as Jimmy locked up the Powermaran then put himself on the jetty. Suddenly they heard somebody calling out.

'Help, help, get away from me! Leave me alone, help, help!' Other voices could be heard as well but they weren't loud enough to be heard with any clarity.

Kate said to Jack, 'There's something going on up the lane.'

Jack put down the box of fish that he'd picked up and said, 'I'll go and have a look.'

With that he took off to investigate. Just down from the top security gate there were three people. Two were standing up and another one was on the ground. As he got closer he quickly assessed the situation. The one on the ground was obviously one of Sydney's homeless, while the other two were a couple of young fellows. They were certainly harassing this old guy, who was cowering close to the brick fence with his hand up in defence. At the same time he was singing out, 'Help, help, get away from me, leave me alone!'

As Jack approached, one of the young aggressors hit the homeless guy's hat, knocking it onto the ground. He yelled, 'Go on, pick yourself up and get going before I give you a clip under the ear.'

The other young man was enjoying this lopsided competition, as he was giggling like a little girl. Jack could see that he was big and fit, so he'd have to remain alert to avoid those big fists if things got out of hand. The two young men were surprised as Jack intervened by saying, 'Is that any way to treat a senior citizen?'

'This is the only way to treat these dirty old men, we don't want them in Sydney,' answered the skinny guy.

Jack asked him, 'What's he done to you?'

Skinny's reply was, 'I think you'd better mind your own business pal.'

'Yeah, well I think you should pick his hat up off the ground and place it back on his head. While you're at it, say you're sorry,' answered Jack.

Skinny just ignored Jack and carried on. Jack didn't hesitate as he grabbed Skinny by the shoulders and rammed him into the fence, and at the same time turned to see what his mate was doing. He was closing in fast with a haymaker already on its way. Had this punch connected, Jack would have been out for the count. With such ferocity did this big young fellow throw his punch, that when Jack ducked under it the momentum turned the big young fellow sideways and he lost his balance. Jack was onto it and sunk a punch under his ribcage. It must have really hurt because the attacker screamed out loud. Although he was instantly wounded and shocked he still tried to launch a second attack — but it was cut short as Jack buried a second punch right into his belly, taking all of his precious air. He bent over like a half-shut scout's knife, holding his stomach. Spluttering and gasping for air, he harmlessly fell onto the ground.

By now the others had arrived from the jetty and were watching. Skinny had recovered from being rammed into the brick fence and was starting to get himself up when Bill approached him and said, 'I think you'd better stay down.' Skinny took that advice and didn't move.

The big young fellow was beginning to breathe like normal again so he moved into a sitting position with his head between his legs.

Bill pulled out his police badge and introduced himself. 'Detective Bill Scanlon, Sydney CIU. Do you have any ID?'

There was no answer.

Bill continued. 'Well, we can do this the easy way or we can do it the hard way. You show me your ID and you walk away, or I ring for a police car and they take you away. You can decide.'

They knew they had no choice so reluctantly they handed Bill their IDs. He wrote down their particulars and a story of the scene that they'd witnessed here — and then the two young men could go.

Jack intervened, talking to Skinny. 'You knocked the old fellow's hat off, so now you can go put it back on his head and say you're sorry. Go *on*, do it now,' he yelled.

Skinny walked over, picked up the hat, placed it back on the homeless guy's head and said, 'I'm sorry.'

That was good enough for Jack, but Bill had one last thing to say. 'You can go now — and remember, don't go around picking on harmless homeless people ... pick on the bad people in your neighbourhood.'

'Oh yeah, sure,' answered Skinny. And with that they disappeared out of the lane, turning right.

Jack helped the homeless guy to his feet and picked up his bag; what he had in it was anybody's guess. 'What's your name?' Jack asked.

'Ronnie Bottles,' he answered.

'Look Ron, we were about to have a cup of tea and we'd like you to join us.'

'Orrr, no thanks, I don't wish to be any trouble.'

'Ron, it's no trouble, come in, have a cup and a biscuit then you can be on your way, okay mate?'

It was always the same with homeless people — they avoided socialising with 'normal' people, especially from the upper end of town. If Jack hadn't showed up when he did, anything could have happened.

Ronnie was clearly reflecting on this when he replied to Jack's offer of a cup of tea and a biscuit. 'All right then, thanks very much.'

Inside the Kelly mansion, Ronnie Bottles was being treated like royalty and for him that was quite puzzling; you could smell him a mile away but the Kellys didn't seem to mind. Kate had taken off his big coat and stained tattered hat and sat him at the table while she went to make the coffee and tea. Over at the oven, Marree was warming up the scones. Jimmy gave him a nice big glass of cold lemonade, which he scoffed down in one big gulp. Then Kate gave him a strong cup of coffee. The hot scones, blackberry jam and cream went down well with Ronnie cleaning up six — while Bill and Jack weren't far behind him.

Jack noticed Ronnie's anxiety returning and said to him, 'Ron, before you go I've got something I want to show you.'

'Okay then.'

He followed Jack out the side door then down a path to the back of the house, where Jack opened the door to a one-bedroom unit they called the Motel.

'Now Ron, I'd like you to stay here tonight. You can give yourself a nice hot shower, you can cook your own tea ... there's everything in here that you could possibly want including a full range of clothes and shoes. Fit yourself out with anything that suits you and it's yours to keep. We'll wash your clothes and your big coat then tomorrow you can take them with you when you go, what do you say?'

It took Ronnie two minutes to decide what to do; he just stared at his feet like he was moulded in concrete. Then he said. 'All right Jack, thank you.'

Jack went back inside. Jimmy asked him, 'How'd you go?'

'Good, he's going to have a clean-up and put some new clothes on.'

'Gee, we won't know him in the morning,' said Jimmy.

Jack replied, 'Probably not.'

The day's fishing trip yielded three boxes of fish. One for the

Kellys, one for the Scanlons and one for the Salvation Army's homeless people's kitchen. Bill and Marree collected their belongings and a box of fish as they made their way to the car in their driveway.

Bill said to Jack and Jimmy, 'Well, by this time next week we'll have fish coming out of our ears, ha ha ... see you tonight.' And with that they were gone. Jack had one more thing to do: ring a colleague of his at the Salvation Army.

Donny King was a powerhouse worker for the homeless people of Sydney. He was also, as Jack described him, a pain in the neck sometimes due to his very individual nature, but there was no doubting his commitment to help people who were down on their luck. After a couple of rings Donny answered the phone.

'Hello Don, how's it going?'

'Not bad Jack, what's happening?'

'We've got a guest in the Motel you might be interested in. He's staying the night and leaving about ten in the morning.'

'Okay, I'll be there just before he's about to leave, I'll see you then.'

'Bye Don.'

Jimmy delivered Ronnie Bottles' big coat and clothes, now washed and dried, back to the Motel. He said goodbye as he handed the clothes over; he also noticed that Ronnie had cleaned himself up and was looking like a human being again. He'd even washed his long matted hair. As Ronnie sat on the lounge looking at the TV but not actually watching it; his brain was travelling at one hundred miles an hour. In the last fifteen years, this was the luckiest day that he could remember. *Maybe there is a god after all*, he thought, remembering that it took Moses forty odd years to find his way out of the wilderness.

In the meantime on the southern side of the harbour, Sydney

Harbour Pilot John Steed and his crew had returned to their base after bringing in the world's biggest warship to safely dock at the Garden Island Naval Base. John said goodbye to his workmates, then headed to the tugboat car park and his four wheel drive. He relaxed behind the wheel of the stationary vehicle as the western sun beamed through the open window. He leaned back into the comfortable seat, closed his eyes and went into deep thought. He wondered why, having such a prestigious job on Sydney Harbour — a job that left him satisfied, fulfilled and happy — did he now have this feeling of doom, gloom and depression overcoming him? He realised that he was happy at work but unhappy at home. Decisions would have to be made and soon.

Things hadn't been going all that well at home with Cher, his live-in lover of seven years. Maybe that was it. They'd been together too long. It might be time for a change. A sudden tapping on the windscreen ended his deep thought session; he opened his eyes.

'You okay chief?' It was Richie.

'Yeah Richie, I just closed my eyes for a moment, you know, thinking about today and all that. Look mate, I'll see you at the club, it'll be my shout.'

'I'll be waiting for you,' answered Richie as he walked away toward his vehicle.

At the Cruising Yacht Club, John and Richie had a couple of light beers before it was time to go. John lived in a white brick townhouse overlooking Bondi Beach. It was double-storey with twin garages and a large party balcony with views of the beach, coast and ocean — and all this within twenty minutes of the city centre. He cut a real charismatic figure as he walked up his driveway after parking on the street. Tall and thin, he looked like a British submarine captain out of World War Two in his dark blue uniform and officer-like cap with the letters 'Sydney Harbour Pilot' emblazoned in gold lettering across the front.

Upon entering the house, John put the fish that Kate gave him in the fridge, and then he turned on the widescreen television with the surround sound and relaxed in the lounge as best he could. It wasn't all that long when he heard Cher's car enter the garage. Her day's work was over. A short time later she entered from a door behind him. John's heartbeat increased considerably. Cher poured herself a cold drink out of the fridge as the early news began on the television, and naturally it was all about the aircraft carrier. John watched the highlights from his own interview.

Upon hearing John's voice coming from the TV, Cher came into the lounge room and watched from the doorway with her hands on her hips and her mouth still well and truly zippered up. As the interview came to an end she walked away.

Time was becoming a premium for John as he went for a short 'climate change' shower. Now, Cher was no fool — just because she wasn't talking didn't mean her brain wasn't working. His car wasn't on the street for nothing, he was obviously going somewhere. As far as the shower was concerned, well, he always had a shower at this time, but the sound of the electric razor made her blood start to boil.

That dirty bastard's up to no good. There's only one place he'd be going: the Cruising Yacht Club where that redheaded thing works.

She'd noticed the chemistry between them more than once and it made her livid to even think about it. Two weeks ago, John arrived home at three in the morning and Cher suspected that he was with her, so she decided to give him the silent treatment, that advice coming from her mother.

Cher watched John flit from the bathroom to the bedroom with only a towel draped around him. Now her heart was pounding. John dressed himself in a casual shirt and jeans with a belt that had a beautiful gold buckle. A pair of high heel cowboy boots finished it off. John was combing his hair when he heard Cher's footsteps approaching. She couldn't contain herself any longer. Now inside the bedroom with her hands on her hips in that defiant stance, she asked John in a sarcastic voice, 'And where do you think you're going?'

In an equally sarcastic voice John replied, 'Well, well, well, you have got a big mouth after all. You want to know something? It's none of your business.'

Cher responded in her saved up nasty voice, 'Well you needn't think you're going to that sailing club to meet your redheaded girlfriend.'

John replied in a firm voice. 'She's not my girlfriend. I told you what happened but you won't have it, so you have the problem, not me. You have been the love of my life for the last seven years and in that time I've never questioned your loyalty once. If I was with that woman that night … and I'll tell you again I wasn't … but if I was, I would have rode off into the sunset with her. My loyalty to you has been one hundred percent. If you're not happy with me then go back and live with your mother until you find yourself another bloke, because I won't be living like this for much longer.'

Cher was gobsmacked, her eyes were frozen. This was the first time that their relationship was being put to the test. And all it took was two bad weeks out of seven years. How quickly things can change. Cher recomposed herself then asked John in her normal voice, 'Can you just tell me where you're going? I'd really like to know.'

'I'm going out to the Paceway to watch the trotting races. Maybe I'll be able to find myself a beautiful chestnut horse with a white blaze that might want to talk to me.'

Cher replied, 'I doubt it. Who are you going with?'

'Jack, Kate, Bill, Marree and Jimmy.'

'When did you see Jack?'

'Today, about five miles off the Heads.'

'Is that where you got the fish?'

'That's right.'

'And then you brought the carrier in.'

'Right again.'

'Okay, what about me?'

'What about you? You don't talk to me for two weeks and now you expect me to ask you out? I've got a simple answer for you: kiss my arse.'

'No thanks,' replied Cher. 'You know I like to go out there occasionally, so you needn't think you're going without me.'

'Suit yourself, you can bloody walk and spend your own money.'

'What time are you leaving here?' she asked.

'Five o'clock.'

Cher looked at her watch. She had thirty minutes to get ready.

Frantic was the only way to describe her application to be ready by five. Everything she had to do to be ready on time was squashed into a thirty minute schedule, so it was amazing when at one minute to five, Cher walked out of the bedroom looking like a David Jones model. She wore a tight black modest skirt with a wide matching belt, black fishnet stockings and high heel shoes, while her long brown hair was brushed straight down, reaching the middle of her back. That curvy figure was topped off with a small red hat pinned on an angle with an imitation rose on the side.

John was taken aback when she appeared, *God she looks fabulous*, he thought. Normally he would have rushed over and hugged the living daylights out of her — and steal a taste of those big beautiful lips at the same time — but after the emotional torture of the past two weeks he wasn't about to give her any praise at all. Instead he left it by saying, 'Well, that didn't take long did it?'

'No.'

As they walked down the pathway to the road Cher took her man by the arm, as if to say, 'This is my super Sydney Harbour pilot; he's the one on TV and I'm so proud of him.'

Their next-door neighbour was in the front garden; when he spotted John and Cher coming down the path he came over to the fence. 'I see you had a good day today, eh John.'

'Yes, it'll be a day on the harbour I won't forget in a hurry.'

'You looked pretty good on the TV. You know, I reckon you could be become the Prime Minister one day if you wanted to.'

'Ah thanks a lot Harry, you're too kind. But who would want twenty million people whingeing at you when you do something wrong and then whingeing at you when you do something right? No thanks mate, I'm happy like I am.'

'Yeah you're probably right. Anyway, enjoy your night you two.'

John and Cher continued on to the four wheel drive and headed off towards the west of the city and Sydney's International Paceway and Trotting track, the cauldron of equine competition on the ribbon of light.

TWO

A night at the Sydney International Pacing and Trotting Track

Approaching the Paceway and Trotting Track from the city was the only way to see the layout of this night-time horse-racing track. Over the crest of a hill, the track appeared like a sunken bathtub about the size of an Olympic Stadium. There was a large spectator stand along with a variety of eateries, souvenir shops and a hall of fame.

Jack, Kate and Jimmy were the first to arrive and took their reserved seats in the Miracle Mile Restaurant, which was located high up in the main stand and gave sweeping views of all the action. TV screens were positioned to relay information and prices that would help in assessing the winning chances of the horses involved in the current race.

The Scanlons arrived next, followed by John Steed and Cher. They soon sorted themselves out with the ladies taking one end and the four men the rest. A waiter arrived with dinner being ordered along with drinks. Bill was studying the form guide and said to Jack, 'Our horse is in race five.'

Jack replied, 'Yes, that'll come along pretty quick once things get underway. Race seven is promoted as the Great Race, and it'll certainly be worth watching.'

John Steed asked, 'What do you think about our horse?'

Jack said, 'Hope at Midnight has had three good runs since a spell. Its form reads 6-5-4 and it should be at peak fitness for tonight's assignment. Dad was talking to our trainer Vic on the phone this afternoon.'

Now Jimmy was the centre of attention. 'Vic said that this race will suit our horse and the only thing that will stop him from winning will be bad luck. Speaking of bad luck, the horse has number ten, on the outside of the second line. He told me that he's going to drive him cold. To explain that properly, when the starter lets them go he's going to restrain the horse to the back of the field for at least the first half of the race. Coming into the bell lap he's going to drive the horse around the field fast and attempt to snatch the lead. If that move works out all right, then Vic reckons that there's no way anything can come from behind and run him down.

'So there it is fellows, take your chances. Jack and I are putting five thousand on Hope at Midnight. We're hoping to get four to one odds.'

The Miracle Mile Restaurant was about half-full when their meals arrived, and eating in earnest began straight away. Conversation around the table was good; the ladies were enjoying themselves talking about fashions, shoes and handbags, while the men were, of course, talking about that aircraft carrier. Two old ladies came out of the lift and sat down at a table marked as reserved, not far from the Kellys. Jimmy gave them a wave and they waved back.

John Steed remarked, 'A couple of old boilers, eh Jimmy?'

Jimmy answered, 'You can call them whatever you like, John. They wouldn't care.'

'So what do they do? Bring their pensions out here and splash it on the first horse they see?'

Jimmy was getting a bit irked by John's questioning but he kept his cool, saying, 'I don't think so, go and ask them.'

John had one more jibe. 'Well you'd have to think that they're a couple of old maids wouldn't you Jimmy?'

'No, I don't think that, and now I'm going to tell you why.

They're friends of mine, Margaret and Matilda Harmon. As you can see, they're identical twins. They've both been married three times and they've got an extended family of three children and eighteen grandchildren. They both divorced their husbands after an incident happened right where they're sitting now.

'Matilda's husband seemed okay but Margaret — that's the one in the white suit — her husband Dick was an abusive mongrel of a person. The more he drank the worse he got. Dick asked Margaret to place a bet on for him. The horse got beaten and he blamed her for it. He reckoned she put it on the wrong number. After looking at the ticket he went into a rage and yelled, "I said number two, you silly bitch." He got behind her and started shaking her while yelling at the same time. Margaret starting crying.

'Jack left his seat, grabbed Dick from behind and said, "Leave your wife alone." Dick took a swing at Jack but it missed. Jack hit him twice and knocked him down, while Matilda's husband got up and left. Jack came back and sat down.

'A little time later two ambulance officers arrived to treat Dick, who was still lying on the floor in Ga Ga Land. Shortly after a young policeman showed up.' Jimmy said to Bill, 'Would you like to add a bit here mate?'

'Sure,' said Bill. 'I'd just graduated from Goulburn City Police Academy and the sergeant at the trotting track asked me to go to the restaurant and investigate an incident that had been reported. The ambulance people had a male on a stretcher who was unconscious. I took down all the particulars that they had, then I went to talk to the gentleman's wife. I asked her what happened. She said Dick had been drinking heavily, got out of his seat, lost his balance and fell over. As Dick was being carried away I did an investigation around the tables and the answers seemed to be the same: an accident fuelled by alcohol. And that's the way I signed off on it.

'A week later I joined the Newtown Boxers Gym to keep my fitness up. I couldn't believe my eyes when I saw this bloke from the restaurant getting stuck into a punching bag. I sure wouldn't have liked to be on the end of those fists. I walked over and said, "I'm Bill Scanlon, I remember you from the other night, come and I'll shout you a drink." He looked at me like I had the plague and reluctantly shook my hand.

'In the gym lounge we had a fruit juice and some nice conversation. I said, "That incident the other night is dead and buried, but off the record what actually happened?" So Jack described what happened: when Margaret started crying he walked over to Dick and flattened him. I laughed and said, "Couldn't have happened to a nicer bloke." Jack introduced himself and you know what? we've been friends ever since.'

Jimmy said to John, 'Two weeks after that night in the restaurant, Margaret and Matilda's father died, leaving them an inheritance of six dress shops in Melbourne's CBD. They moved to Victoria to take charge of the business. The Harmon twins are worth 60 million dollars. They know they're in the final years of life so they've come home to Sydney to be closer to their daughters and extended family. So what do you think of your old boiler pensioners now?'

John replied. 'Maybe I'll I won't be so quick to judge other people ... in future I'll be keeping my mouth shut.'

The first two races on the programme had been run and won while the dining had been going on, but they didn't seem to care. Jimmy had already drunk two glasses of the amber beverage; noticing this, Jack said to Kate, 'If you want to have a guzzle tonight go for it, I'll stay sober and drive us home.'

She replied, 'Right-o, one bottle of Champers coming up.'

Kate called the waiter and ordered. He came back with three long-stem glasses, cracked the bottle and filled the glasses to the brim. Sipping of the beautiful liquid began with polite determination.

'All right,' said Bill, 'let's go downstairs and have a look at the action.'

Jimmy and Jack stopped to talk to the Harmon twins. 'Number ten in race five,' said Jimmy.

The twins did everything together but separately. They both ran their fingers down the form guide to number ten: Hope at Midnight. Margaret said, 'We backed that horse here two weeks ago. I think it ran third but we didn't touch it last week.'

Jimmy said. 'Tonight's the night — Jack and I are putting five thousand dollars on it.'

Margaret replied, 'All right, you talked us into it.'

Jack asked, 'Are you coming over for Christmas day?'

'Maybe, we might have the mob with us.'

'That won't worry us, the more the merrier. See you downstairs later,' said Jack.

Race three was in the finishing stages when they joined the large crowd on the concrete steps that led down to the dirt racing surface; they found some available real estate at the entrance to the home straight and sat down there. The winning post was three hundred metres away but with the gigantic electronic screen in place you could see all the action no matter where you were. A summer breeze was flowing across the track, making conditions perfect for open air entertainment. Banks of strategically placed lights shone on the racing surface, turning it into a ribbon of light.

The course announcer interrupted. 'Ladies and gentlemen, please give a big hand for Vince and his horse Strawberry, who will entertain you for the next ten minutes.'

A lone horse attached to a replica Roman chariot was making its way onto the racing surface, its driver dressed as a centurion with a beautiful flowing crimson cape. Vince and Strawberry made one complete lap before coming to a stop at the normal start position, right in front of the Kellys and their friends.

The lights on the racing surface were dimmed to candlelight. Vince shook the reins and Strawberry stepped away into a nice paced gait at a comfortable three-quarter speed. Vince placed the reins on a hook and now Strawberry was driving herself.

As they passed where they started, Vince began letting off fireworks. Large Roman candles were alight on the corners of the chariot, spewing out their golden flames before launching beautiful green-coloured balls high in the sky. A monster Catherine wheel the size of a car tyre was spinning on the side, while at least a dozen sky-rockets left the confines of the chariot, bursting into colour patterns at the end of their flights. Four large sparklers the size of baseball bats came alight, a grand sight in the dim arena. When the sparklers began to fade in strength, the side of the chariot burst into flames; this certainly was the 'Chariot of Fire'.

It seemed like the climax, and applause was maintained as another lap of the course was in progress — but halfway down the straight a dull thud was heard, followed by the whistling sound of a projectile being hurled into the air. A massive explosion followed, frightening the daylights out of everybody. Vince took the reins as the lights returned to full strength; he slowed Strawberry down to almost a walk and skirted the outside fence to give the spectators a close look at what he called the star of the show, 'The horse,' and who could disagree? Horses got spooked by loud noises, yet here was one that accepted the fire and flames along with loud explosions as if it was normal. Its pay would be its hander's affection, a feed bin of hay and an apple plus a couple of carrots when it got back to the stables.

The horses for race four came onto the racetrack and began doing their warm-ups. This race was for two year old pacers, the babies of the sport. In due course they were called to the start and lined up behind the standing start tapes. Of the ten, only three showed any interest in the proceedings, while the rest didn't want to be there. They were nasty and cranky, viciously kicking their hind legs and trying to connect to something like a human being, rearing up and turning sideways, going forward when they should have been going backwards — it was nothing short of equine bedlam. Now a large crowd had emerged to watch the start, but they really came to watch the entertainment that these young horses provided when learning to race, and they weren't disappointed. Eventually they formed some sort of a line and the starter pulled the lever.

'Racing!'

Two horses just stood there, three got away well to share the early lead while the rest were all over the shop — but at least they were going forward.

Exactly at that time, over at the northern turnstile a group of people were entering the racecourse. Two stood out: a man and a woman who were dressed to the nines. Both tall and good look-ing, they could have easily been mistaken for royalty. They joined the spectators on the steps, standing just in front of the Kellys.

The field of two year old baby pacers were coming around the top circle in two lines of what could only be described as poetry in motion on the ribbon of light. As they levelled up the lady grabbed her man by the arm and said quite loudly with the utmost sincerity, 'Oh darling, aren't they beautiful.'

The race progressed down the home straight, around the bot-tom turn, up the back then around the top circle again, where the horses would re-enter the home straight with the bell sounding, signifying that there was a bit over one lap to go. A young pacer made a mistake just as they straightened, causing a chain reac-tion: urgent yelling from some drivers who were being squeezed. Two pacers crashed to the ground then two more crashed into them, throwing their drivers out with one being flung into the air.

The immaculately dressed lady began screaming and screaming; it was as if the end of her world was near as equine pandemonium exploded right in front of her eyes. Six pacers missed the scrimmage and continued on as if nothing had happened. Red flashing lights came on while track attendants swamped the scene. All drivers were on their feet and the two horses that were lying on the track had their hobbles released, allowing them to get themselves up. Drivers and horses were moved to the inside track. Finally the red flashing lights stopped flashing, indicating the race was still on. The six pacers left in the race were approaching the circle with the drivers making their final runs for supremacy and the prize money.

The immaculately dressed lady who was holding her man even more tightly now than before said, 'Oh, nobody got hurt.'

He replied, 'Yes, they tell me it's exciting out here ... let's go find the bar.'

The City Of Sydney Brass Band entertained for ten minutes with a fine display of marching and playing their big instruments, and they were well received by those who stayed trackside to watch.

After the Brass Band finished their stint, the horses for race five came out onto the track to do their preliminaries. This is the race the Kellys and their friends were waiting for. At that moment there were joined by the Harmon twins, and Richie from the pilot boat popped up out of nowhere.

'Okay,' Jack said, 'this is our race; we'll have a look at the horses then go put the money on.' After doing a visual analysis of the contenders it was agreed that they all looked much the same — except for number one, Holy Terror, who had the look of *back me* written all over it. Big, strong looking and jet black in colour, this was the form horse of the race, having won its last three starts. The men went to the bookmakers and placed their money on Hope at Midnight in the final two minutes of betting, then they re-joined the ladies, who were now into their third bottle of champagne.

Jack and his dad wagered $5000, John Steed went for $2000, while Bill Scanlon and Richie put on $1000 each.

A hush came over the racecourse as the mobile barrier that had been parked in the back straight began to move off with the contestants in close attendance. It picked up speed as it came around the top circle. This field of ten horses thundered into the home straight nearing release point. The blue light came on.

'Racing!'

Number one, Holy Terror, was the 2/1 favourite for the race and the driver in the orange and black checks drove him to the early lead before being attacked by three other serious contenders in the first 400 metres, but he easily repelled them. The Kellys were more interested in Hope at Midnight, listed as number ten. Their hearts were in their mouths from the moment the blue light came on as they watched their horse being restrained out to last. 'The magnificent ten' was the only way to describe these horses as they passed by on tight reins in two lines of pacing unison.

Halfway around the bottom turn, Vic moved Hope at Midnight off the rails and joined the outside line. As soon as the turn was behind him he moved the horse into the fast lane and gave it full rein. Showing a scintillating burst of speed, Hope at Midnight hit the lead before the top circle, much to the delight of the Kellys and their friends. So far Vic's plan was working out and they led the field into the home straight to receive the bell. One more lap to go.

The course commentator was getting serious now. 'It's Hope

at Midnight the leader, after that lightning move down the back. Sitting on the outside in the death seat is Bundanoon, a length and half to Apre Ski, followed by It's Time. Back on the inside Shy Castles is receiving a nice economical run. Behind those Linton Son is travelling kindly, followed by The Wild Mustang, Birthday Cake, It's All Over Now and Bold Aussie is two lengths away last on the rail.

'They sweep up the back in the Catch Me If You Can Mobile Free For All and it's Hope at Midnight being held back, his main danger Holy Terror sitting on his back. Here's one steaming around the field — Bold Aussie wants to get into the action. Linton Son is following him for a nice three-wide tag into the race.

'Around the circle and into the home straight it's Hope at Midnight travelling like a winner, Bundanoon is still there half a length away and being aggressively driven. Halfway up the straight the favourite Holy Terror needs racing room, but it doesn't matter — they're all chasing Hope at Midnight.'

Hope at Midnight booted away and won by four lengths, much to the delight of the Kelly gang, who let off a big cheer as the horses crossed the finishing line.

A small presentation followed with Hope at Midnight being awarded a nice new rug and trainer Vic received six months' supply of petrol for the family car. Horse and trainer had their picture taken and now it was time to do a lap of honour. The Kellys were waiting when they came around the circle at slow speed. 'Good on you Vic,' they shouted as one.

Vic stopped to have a talk. 'G'day Jimmy, Jack, ladies. Things went all right for you?'

'Sure,' answered Jimmy.

Richie called out, 'Hey Vic, bring him over here, I want to kiss him.'

Vic started laughing and then the others joined in laughing

as well. The horse turned his head and looked straight at them; perhaps he was waiting for that kiss, or maybe he was checking the ladies out, who were now well and truly champagne-tiddly based on their girlish giggling. Vic and Hope at Midnight continued on while the men went and collected their winnings before re-joining the ladies.

So far they'd had a fulfilling night and were about to go back up to the restaurant and have supper when Cher said in a slurred voice, 'Johnny Steed, Super Harbour Pilot. Can you see what I see?'

John looked at her and she pointed to a horse on the track that was doing a pre-race warm up; it was coming around the circle and travelling in a slow pace.

She said, 'There's your horse.'

'I didn't know you had a horse John,' said Kate.

John replied, 'I don't.'

As the chestnut horse went on by Jimmy said, 'That's Paleface Adios, the Riverina champion.'

Everyone looked at Cher in confusion. She said, 'John was coming here tonight without me, and when I asked him why he said he was looking for a beautiful chestnut horse with a white blaze that would talk to him.'

John Steed went red in the face as hysterical laughter broke out; Cher had made their night. 'Yeah but I only wanted to talk to it,' John went on, 'we just saw Richie wanting to kiss one.'

Richie answered back straight away. 'I had a reason to want to kiss it, didn't I?' With that he pulled a wad of $100 notes out of his pocket and waved them in the air, laughing gleefully at the same time. What would he spend that $4000 on? A good guess would be his favourite hobby: wining and dining a variety of good-looking women at the Cruising Yacht Club on Friday and Saturday nights.

Cher excused herself, saying, 'I'll see you all up there.' She pointed to the restaurant, which was directly above them.

When she was out of sight Jack said to John, 'Cher's in a good mood tonight.'

'Yeah, that champagne never fails to get them to loosen up a little.' Kate and Marree were listening with interest as John continued. 'But I'm a bit worried about midnight.'

Marree interrupted. 'You mean Hope at Midnight don't you John?'

John couldn't stop laughing at Marree, who was insinuating that he was hoping Cher might be sexually responsive at midnight; it was the last thing on his mind after a rough two weeks.

'No, no, I mean what if the Royal Carriage is waiting with the Friendly Footman when we get home tonight?'

Kate said, 'What are you talking about? You're not making any sense.'

'Cher might turn back into a bullfrog. I mean, look what happened to Cinderella.'

They all had a good laugh at John's explanation, then Richie asked, 'Where'd the name of the horse come from, Jimmy?'

Jimmy's answer was a simple one. 'Hope at Midnight represents all those people that have had a bad year. They look to midnight on New Year's Eve, and when those fireworks start going off they hope that the next twelve months will be better than the last twelve. So, Hope at Midnight.'

'Gee that's nice Dad,' said Kate as she gave Jimmy a kiss on the cheek and a big hug to go with it. Then she grabbed John by the arm and said, 'C'mon, let's go find Cher.'

They all went back up to the restaurant and Jimmy shouted his favourite supper: apple pie and cream along with a beautiful Espresso coffee.

For the Kellys their night really came to an end when 'Hope at

Midnight' won that race, even though there were still four races
to go. They left the restaurant and walked in the direction of the
car park. The Spanish horses from Campbelltown were doing
a stint of entertaining on the racing surface and they stopped
to watch for a couple of minutes. Marree said to Richie, 'Hey, if
you want to kiss a horse you might as well kiss the best, have a
look at them.'

'Gee aren't they something? It's like they're from another
world.'

Jet-black in colour with platted manes and tails, and manicured from head to hoof, they were dancing around like fairies
in a daisy paddock. What a spectacle they were. The Kellys continued on to the car park and after saying goodnight to their
friends, they drove away in the direction of the North Shore
and their home.

As for the 'Great Race' — well, they'd be happy to watch a
replay on the big screen in their home cinema, sometime in the
near future.

The next morning, Donny King arrived at the Kelly home to pick
up Ronnie Bottles and take him to the Homeless People's Centre.
Kate put on a cup of coffee for him but he said after looking at his
watch, 'Sorry Kate, I've got a couple of appointments to attend
this morning ... but I'll take a rain check if that's all right.'

Jimmy introduced Donny to Ronnie Bottles and they hit it
off almost straight away, with Ronnie agreeing to go with him.
They said goodbye to Kate and drove away — their destination,
the Homeless People's Centre. Once there Donny introduced
Ronnie to a couple of workers who would now take care of him.

Later, Donny sat down in his office with his head in his hands
thinking. He looked at his watch, stood up, grabbed a very big
white envelope and headed for his car.

It was only a short drive to Macquarie Street to visit his doctor. Dr Harry Mitchell took the negative out of the envelope and placed it in a frame on the wall, turning on the backlighting and explaining the image. He put the negative back in the envelope, gave it to Donny then shook his hand, saying goodbye.

From there it was a short walk to 'Williams and Johnstone, Practicing Solicitors.' Inside he was talking to Mr Williams who was working on a document. When he printed it out he asked Donny, 'Are you sure you want to leave all this money to the Homeless People's Centre?'

Donny replied, 'Yes.' He signed the document and said goodbye as they shook hands. He then returned to his office at the Homeless Peoples Centre.

THREE

Off to America

The new year was closing in fast with three weeks of the year left. Boxing Day on Sydney Harbour was home to the internationally famous yacht race, the Sydney to Hobart. Eighty-plus yachts would race from the starting line inside the harbour, through the Sydney Heads and out into the ocean where a southerly course would follow the coast until they reached Tasmania. Jack Kelly and John Steed have taken part in this race for the last eight years as part of the crew on the super-maxi yacht, *An Incredible Time*, but this year John would be going alone as Jack and Kate would be off to the mightiest nation on earth — the United States of America — for a small holiday and some business.

In the meantime, The Christmas tree looked a lonely figure in the corner of the lounge room in its bare state. As Kate began decorating the Christmas tree, she remembered her early childhood, growing up with her mum and dad along with her sibling sister. This was a time when she believed in Santa Claus. Ah, the magic and joy of Christmas looking through the eyes of a seven year old. She would help to decorate the tree, then on Christmas Day she'd wake up early to race into the lounge room and frantically search under the tree for the presents that Santa had left overnight. Then as she grew into a woman, Christmas became more important as a family get-together, sharing presents and gifts on that special day of the year.

After four hours of tedious work, Kate turned on the switch that gave life to the hundreds of lights that covered the Christmas tree. They twinkled like the heavenly stars in the Milky Way, giving her immense satisfaction.

On Christmas Eve, the Kellys and the Scanlons would attend the singing of Christmas carols at Sydney Harbour's open area called the Domain. They would be joined by one hundred thousand other people who came into the city each year to celebrate at this spectacular concert, which hosted the finest singers in the country. The following day the Kellys would have twenty guests over for Christmas Day lunch and at the end of the day, anyone still there would enjoy a ride around the harbour in the beautiful Powermaran.

Christmas Day celebrations finally came to an end at 11.00 pm. Jack and Kate planned a little sleep-in for the next morning so it was no surprise when they emerged from their slumber about midday on Boxing Day. The Sydney to Hobart Yacht Race was due to face the starter's gun at 1.00 pm — approximately one hour's time. This year Jack would be watching the start of the big race from the comfort of the lounge room; Jack's dad Jimmy already had it on when he came in, while Kate went to make some munchies.

The starter fired the gun right on time at 1.00 pm and the eighty yachts that had been milling around behind the invisible starting line for at least forty-five minutes, jockeying for positions that could be more advantageous, instantly left as one. The race to the ocean was now on in earnest and the first yacht that cleared the Heads would get the applause and the headlines on the evening's news bulletin. The super-maxi yacht *An Incredible Time* was the sixth yacht to reach the unshackled waters of the ocean. Deckhand John Steed was probably thinking that this was a nice position to be in as they made a sweeping starboard turn and plotted a course to Tasmania.

In three to four days' time the race would be over for the maxi yachts. Cher would fly down to meet John at Constitution Dock to take part in the celebrations and to have a week's holiday. John would then re-join the crew to sail *An Incredible Time* back to its home in Sydney Harbour.

The week between Christmas day and New Year's Eve seemed to disappear so quickly. The good news from Tasmania was that *An Incredible Time* was third over the line — a great result. John Steed was over the moon and rang Jack all excited as soon as the yacht docked. They talked for an hour before hanging up.

New Year's Eve celebrations were the same every year for the Kellys. Along with their close friends they would anchor the Powermaran near the Opera House. This way they could take in the music from the front of the Opera House as well as being in a good position to watch the fireworks display that came at midnight from the Harbour Bridge.

Well, it didn't take long to burn a million dollars' worth of fireworks — thirty minutes to be exact — but it was spectacular. As soon as it started people were shaking hands, others were kissing and cuddling, whistles were blowing and boat horns were tooting. When it all ended the silence was deafening. It was like it should have gone on for much longer, but that was it for another twelve months. Because it was over, another round of handshaking was underway along with, 'Happy New Year mate,' and, 'All the best'.

Jimmy drove the Powermaran back over to the north side of the harbour and moored the vessel at its private jetty, where Jack made a little speech.

'Thanks for coming, everybody — we've had a beautiful time together. As you all know, Kate and I are going to the USA in two days' time and we're looking forward to what will be a new experience for both of us, so we'll see you all again in a little over two weeks. Happy New Year!'

Jack and Kate spent New Year's Day just relaxing and going

over their travel plans one last time. Tomorrow Jimmy would drive them to the airport and they would be on their way. In the morning they loaded their luggage into the four wheel drive and set off across the bridge, through the city, then on to the International Airport in Mascot a further twenty minutes away.

Jimmy helped them with the luggage, and as they walked into the terminal the usual sea of humanity greeted them. So many nationalities. The choices of travelling clothes was certainly a sight to see: laughing faces, anxious faces — then there were the sad faces. Kate wondered what their stories were.

'See you soon Dad.'

With that Jack and Kate disappeared through the electronic surveillance scanners. Jimmy purchased the daily newspaper and sat in the observation deck. He wouldn't leave until that Qantas 747 thundered down the runaway and lifted off, heading for the deep blue yonder.

Jack and Kate's seats were centre isle adjoining, so that gave them room to move around more freely. The flight left on time, while Jimmy watched the plane until he couldn't see it anymore; then he drove back through the city to their home on the north side of the harbour.

The fourteen hour flight went to plan with plenty to do and movies to watch on the personal monitor, along with some magazine reading or listening to a selection of music through the headphones. The three-course meals were good, as were the nibbles and choices of drinks.

It was nice to get the call to fasten seatbelts — before long the Flying Kangaroo, after fourteen hours of flying, touched down without incident at Los Angeles International Airport. They had a two hour wait for a connecting flight that would take them from the west coast to the east coast, involving another six hours of flying.

After landing at JFK Airport, a taxi drove them to Manhattan where the hotel was situated near the south end of Central Park. It was now twenty-three hours since they'd left home, so they would sleep well.

In two days' time they had an appointment with America's top conception specialists. Jack and Kate wanted a baby to complete their family unit, but at the moment it wasn't happening. They'd been to all the experts in Australia, with the test results always coming back the same: 'There is no reason why you two people can't have a baby, everything is fine.' That's why they came to America; maybe this world leader in his field might be able to shed some light on it. He might know something that the others didn't.

Jack and Kate spent the next day visiting a couple of museums, and Jack wanted to see the site of the Twin Towers that was attacked by terrorists in 2001. When they arrived, they stood in awe as they tried to imagine the carnage that went on before them. A new trade centre called Freedom Tower and a memorial had taken shape there. Their day of sightseeing around New York was fulfilling to say the least. The sheer size of everything was unbelievable: the buildings, the roads, the wide footpaths crowded with people — everything was based on *big*.

At 10 am the next day, they caught the lift up to the tenth floor of the New York Medical Centre. Professor Marsden was waiting for them and when all the formalities were over, the medical team took them away separately and began the tests.

At 8 pm that night Jack was reunited with Kate and they were told that results wouldn't be known for at least eight days. They made their way back to the hotel and headed straight for the restaurant. Roast chicken, baked potatoes and gravy, all nice with a couple of bottles of wine. A three-piece band was playing nice music, so naturally Jack and Kate had a few dances along with another bottle of wine; by the time they made it to their room, they were well and truly under the weather.

Since arriving in the US, the weather had been bright and sunny with the air being cold. Not bad considering it was the middle of winter. The next day Jack and Kate took in a tour of the United Nations and followed that up with a live show on Broadway. An early night was in order, for in the morning they would be rising at dawn to catch a flight to Vancouver, Canada. They had seven or eight days to fill in so a bit more sightseeing was in order.

The flight from JFK Airport to Vancouver would take six hours. With seats against the windows, they both marvelled at the unfolding snowy scenery, finally touching down at 2.30 pm. A yellow and black cab took them to their hotel, not far from where the cruise ship departed. First thing in the morning they had a seaplane ride over the local mountains, followed by a coach ride into the snow-covered Rocky Mountains that could have gone on forever.

The coach stopped at Lake Emerald, which was completely frozen over. This piece of scenery was the most photographed in the whole of Canada — truly chocolate box stuff. The Victoria Glacier was so beautiful, as was the Columbia Icefield glacier that looked mysterious and fabulous as heavy snow was falling, being fanned by a blizzard strength wind. Luckily, Jack and Kate were dressed for the occasion.

Next on the list was a train ride into a historic goldmining town in the Yukon. Then it was another seaplane flight where they inspected the massive Mendenhall Glacier.

They joined the cruise ship that took them to Glacier Bay National Park. The glacier here was as tall as the Empire State Building. A piece of ice the size of a two-storey house broke away with the roar of a lion, crashing into the sea and making a wave that violently rocked the ship. This was no small ship, but a very large vessel with seven decks. It gives an idea of the violent forces of nature. The cruise ship returned to Vancouver, where it was time for Jack and Kate to board a plane for the six hour flight back to New York and the awaiting test results from Professor Marsden, in two days' time.

The old professor was waiting for them when they arrived and he was eager to talk to them. His assistant made coffee and they enjoyed that with a couple of doughnuts while they chatted — certainly unusual behaviour for a medical facility to say the least. Then the professor delivered the test results. He had a small folder of papers and he went through all the pages slowly, explaining it as he went.

When it was all over he said. 'Jack, Kate … you know, I can't find anything that is wrong with you. Your doctors in Australia just about got it right. There is no reason why conception shouldn't happen. I'm sorry that you've made this trip for nothing and that it's cost you a lot of money for nothing, but I will tell you this … it will happen when you least expect it.'

They shook hands with Professor Marsden and said goodbye. He gave them the folder of papers to take back to Australia. There was one more day of relaxing around New York, then back home to Australia.

They arrived at JFK Airport and boarded a plane that would take them back to Los Angeles on the west coast, and then it would be a five hour wait before they could board a Qantas plane for the fourteen hour flight back to Sydney.

Before the plane could take off from JFK, all the passengers were asked to leave the plane and go back to the terminal, as a massive storm had hit not far from Los Angeles. Until this storm passed, they would be staying here, even though Los Angeles was six hours flying time away. After three hours the call came to re-board the aircraft and the plane took off without incident. That reduced the waiting time at Los Angeles to two hours, if they arrived on time — and naturally, there was a backlog of planes all wanting to land at the same time. After circling around for what seemed an eternity, suddenly the reality of missing the Qantas flight to Australia began to creep into their thoughts.

Finally the delayed flight came down, but at the domestic terminal. When they finally found their way to the international terminal, they were being paged at the Qantas counter; they had made it just in time. For the seventh time, Jack and Kate passed through customs and security, where they were cleared to take their seats in the Qantas 747 flight bound for Australia.

The return flight to Australia was a carbon copy of the flight from Australia to America, except in reverse. Jack and Kate held hands as the Spirit of Australia taxied down the runaway and lifted off. They had window seats for the long flight home and it wasn't long before the only thing that they could see was the clouds beneath them.

The fourteen hour flight seemed like it would never end. They watched all the movies again, ate and drank everything that the hostesses brought around, and snoozed and chatted as they reflected on all the highlights of their trip. The snow-covered Rockies, the seaplane flights, the cruise ship voyage to the Bay of Glaciers National Park — and of course, New York City itself. They talked about Professor Marsden's diagnoses and agreed that they wouldn't dwell on it; what else could they do except let nature take its course? In the meantime, they'd had a fabulous time in the USA and Canada.

Kate was sound asleep against the window of the Qantas 747 when the call came to fasten their seatbelts over the plane's audio system. That was followed by another announcement. 'Good morning ladies and gentlemen, this is Captain Ron Lucas speaking, I hope you have all had an enjoyable flight. We will be landing at Sydney's Mascot Airport in around twenty minutes and I look forward to seeing you all again in the near future.'

The hostesses were walking around the aisles of the plane, making sure everyone had their seatbelts on. The aircraft made a sweeping left hand turn and lined up in the direction of Sydney's north-south runaway, which was only a blip on the global positioning screen.

Kate was well and truly awake now, watching out the window as the plane travelled down the last piece of the Queensland coast. The view of the coastline and the ocean spotted with islands, reefs and boats was truly an amazing sight to see. The Byron Bay Lighthouse was the first landmark she noticed with some familiarity. It didn't take long before the mouth of the Hawkesbury River flowing around the gigantic Lion Island was visible and everything on the ground was getting bigger. The sight of the Sydney Harbour Heads was a magnificent sight, as was the harbour itself and all its wonders. Back in their own backyard, this scenery gave both Jack and Kate an attack of spinal goose bumps and an uncontrolled hug and kiss.

The aircraft was now skimming the tops of the city's tallest buildings. With the landing wheels locked in place and after a small correction, the runway was dead ahead and coming up fast. The squealing of brakes and a small bump was evident of a successful landing. The monster aircraft with the red kangaroo painted on its tail came to a halt beside the water in Botany Bay, where it made a u-turn and slowly made its way towards the passenger terminal.

Bill and Marree were watching from the observation deck as the plane came in; they knew it was Jack and Kate's plane. An airliner towing machine delivered the 747 to its precise resting place, where disembarking began straight away. Walking into the terminal area holding hands, Bill and Marree were looking and feeling glum.

Back inside the customs section, screening of the passengers was well underway. Jack turned his mobile phone on and called Jimmy's mobile. The dial tone ran out with the option for a message. Jack cancelled and then he said to Kate, 'That's funny, Dad didn't answer his mobile.'

'Maybe he's still in traffic somewhere,' replied Kate.

'That's a possibility,' answered Jack. The all-clear was given after a luggage search and paying the tax on a case of goods and presents they had purchased in the USA.

Plenty of people were now exiting the customs area into the main terminal lounge. Just as many were flooding through the scanners as they were about to leave Australia.

Jack and Kate, with their luggage in tow surrounded by a big crowd of people from the plane, were making their way into the airport lounge space. Kate spotted Bill and pulled on Jack's arm. 'There's Bill and Marree coming this way.'

Jack stopped to face them.

'What a nice surprise,' said Kate to Marree as they had a little embrace.

'Welcome home mate,' Bill said to Jack as they shook hands.

'Thanks Bill,' replied Jack, then he looked around, wearing his infectious smile. 'Where's the old fella?'

Bill seemed lost for words, they just wouldn't come out. The best he could do was, 'ahh … ahh … ahh.'

Jack could see something was wrong. 'What's happened?'

Bill replied, 'Let's go over there, away from all of these people, and I might be able to tell you.'

The four of them walked away from the main crowd, and then they huddled together. 'Jack, this morning at 3.30 we got a call from Jimmy … he had severe chest pains. An ambulance took him to the

Royal North Shore Hospital. Marree and I went there straight away. The doctors and the hospital staff did all that they could, but Jimmy passed away peacefully at 5.15 am. I'm sorry mate.'

Kate embraced Jack and they stood there holding each other for at least five minutes; they looked like a couple of statues in the middle of Rome. Tears were running down Kate's cheeks; Bill began to sob; Marree was ashen-faced with the smallest river of liquid spilling out of the corner of her eyes.

Jack gently broke away from Kate's embrace. He grabbed Bill by the arm and said, 'Give us a hand with this luggage mate.' Then it was down the lift to the car park level where Bill was parked in the police bay.

It was a quiet drive from the airport, through the city and across the harbour bridge to North Sydney, then on to the Kelly home beside the harbour.

The atmosphere in the three-level mansion was solemn to say the least. Bill and Marree left after a cup of coffee to give Jack some space, so that he could come to terms with the sudden passing of his father.

The next day Jack and Kate went to the funeral parlour and had a private viewing. Jack had to have one last look at his father. Before they left, Jack placed his hand on Jimmy's forehead and said, 'Sleep on, Dad ... Mum's waiting for you.'

This brought some sort of reality to the fact that the partnership between himself and his father was over. After signing all the paperwork and finalising the arrangements, Jack and Kate left the funeral parlour and returned home.

Jimmy would be buried in the Sydney Cove Colonial Cemetery beside the other members of the family. On the Friday at 10 am, Jack and Kate — along with Bill, Marree, John Steed and Cher, plus two hundred mourners — were asked to stand and say the Lord's Prayer.

The service had begun. Many people made speeches regarding the life of James B Kelly, but none more compelling than the one that Jack made. Tears flowed down his cheeks and his voice quivered with emotion, but he toughed it out and finished off with the words, 'I love you Dad. Goodbye.'

The curtains closed around the coffin as Jimmy's favourite piece of music played over the chapel's sound system. Kate ran to Jack and took him by the arm as a show of support; they then walked to the front of the chapel.

There were three times as many people outside as there were inside. Those outside watched the service on a monster TV screen that Jack had organised. He shook hands with as many mourners as humanly possible before the next part of the service, the burial, began. It was conducted by the City of Sydney's Salvation Army Chaplin, who had plenty of kind things to say. Jimmy was lowered into the ground to join his beloved wife Lucy. The flowers were dropped into the grave, bringing the service to a conclusion. There would be no wake today, but tomorrow one hundred invited guests would come to the Kelly home for a barbecue beside the harbour as a last show of respect for the person who touched the hearts of everybody that he met. Jack and Kate with their inseparable friends the Scanlons were the last to leave, and in due course they made their way back to the harbour-side mansion.

Kate made the coffee and they had a snack with it, while nice music was playing softly in the background. Jack excused himself for a minute and when he was out of earshot, Kate said to Bill and Marree, 'You know, I'm getting a bit worried about him. It's been five days, and he's been carrying on as if nothing's happened. The only time he's showed any emotion was while he was making that speech three hours ago.'

'The three of us have shown more grief than he has,' Bill

replied. 'Kate, try not to worry about it too much, everybody handles it their own special way. Jack's one hell of a tough man mentally, just wait and see what happens. In my job I see death all the time and there are no rules when it comes to things like this.'

'Yes,' replied Kate, 'I know you're right, but I would have just liked him to show a bit more emotion.'

Twenty minutes later Kate said, 'I wonder where he's gone. I wouldn't be surprised if he's taken the boat out for a ride.'

Bill had a nice clear view of the jetty through the large amounts of glass and said to Kate, 'No, the boat is still there, safely tied up.'

With that, she decided to go and find him. She checked all the usual places and then as she walked down the hallway she noticed the bedroom door was shut. That door was never shut. She silently turned the knob on the door and quietly opened it. Jack was lying on the bed in the foetal position, crying and sobbing his eyes out. Kate gently closed the door without disturbing him.

As she approached Bill and Marree sitting at the table, tears were running down her face. She dried her eyes and said, 'He's lying on the bed crying his heart out.'

Marree said, 'Don't disturb him. Let him do it by himself for as long as it takes.'

Bill said to Kate, 'It's funny isn't it, you were worried about him and then it suddenly happened.'

'Yes, I was worried but now I feel much better,' Kate answered.

The Scanlons stayed for dinner and left about 8 pm. An hour later Kate prepared herself for an early night. Jack was still lying in the same position, but was now sound asleep. She threw a spare blanket over him then climbed under it too. She wrapped herself around her man. Jack felt for her hand and clasped it tightly. That little act of acknowledgement was all that she needed.

At 7 am, Kate woke up to the sound of running water. Jack was having the first shower; she never even heard him get up.

Twenty minutes later, Jack emerged from the shower looking like a new man. He gave Kate that infectious smile with, 'Morning honey, it's your turn.'

'Did you leave me any water?'

Jack replied, 'Yes, all the water you'll ever need, a Warragamba Dam full.'

She laughed at that.

The barbecue was on at twelve-thirty. Everything was organised by a professional catering company. They brought everything that was required. Enough steaks, snags, beer, sparkling for the ladies and heaps more. The caterers set up the tables that the Kellys had in their storeroom. They did all the cooking and carried the drinks. Six young ladies dressed in red suits looked after everybody's wishes. But of course, they'd done this many times before.

Friends started arriving at midday with the last few stragglers showing up at 1.30 pm. All available parking was taken up, including every spare spot on both sides of the street. Mrs MacMillan from across the street came over with her husband Frank, as well as a number of other neighbours that lived in close proximity. The Harmon twins came with their extended family and nine grandchildren of varying ages. There were plenty of Salvation Army uniforms walking around, and of course one of the captains, Donny King — who Jack described as a pain in the neck sometimes. Cher and John Steed arrived by boat. Somehow they managed to scunge a ride across the harbour with somebody they knew. Walking up Lighthouse Lane arm in arm, they looked a picture of togetherness. The differences they'd had with each other prior to that night at the trotting races have now been resolved. No more silent treatment and no more late nights for John after attending committee meetings at the cruising yacht club. They walked through the open security gate and headed down to the barbecue area. Marree arrived by herself as Bill was part of a team searching for a bloke who killed two people at Darling Harbour overnight, but he would arrive when he could.

The afternoon went terrific and at 4 pm, people began to drift away. At 5 pm there were fifteen people left. Kate ushered those people up into the big lounge room while the caterers began to clean up and put everything back to normality in the harbourside backyard. Coffee, biscuits and ice cream were being served in the upstairs lounge room, where plenty of conversation seemed be the norm.

Jack slid open four sliding doors, revealing a shallow room. 'This is our home office. Kate runs the administration side of GD Constructions. She's the accountant; she knows what moneys are coming in and what moneys are going out. This duplicates her office at work. If she doesn't feel like going to work for some particular reason, she can run the company from here.'

The home office looked more like the cockpit of a spaceship with its computers, screens, printers and electronic gadgetry. Everybody found this interesting, but the real interest would be in the next four doors that Jack slid aside. This room was like a miniature museum. Jimmy had set it up and it showed the history of the family from the late 1800s. There were lots of old photos, family memorabilia and artefacts, with quite a lot of antique value.

Some photos of Jack's grandfather working on the construction of the Sydney Harbour Bridge seemed to attract a lot of attention. There was a photo of him shearing a sheep somewhere near Goulburn City in 1936, and another on a farm at Mildura, picking fruit. The prized photo seemed to be of Jack's grandfather being lowered from the arch of the bridge in a big cage with ten other guys. The rectangular cage wasn't big enough to hold them all so they were hanging off it everywhere. The construction workers showed no fear of the dangerous conditions that they were working in. A large launch was waiting to receive them before delivering its cargo of human beings back to the building site on the north-west side of the foreshore. Eventually a fun park was built on that site and given the name Luna Park.

Another photo was a clipping out of a newspaper, with Jack's grandfather kissing his wife goodbye at Circular Quay before he took to the road in search of work. A little girl was holding his hand, and a knife could be seen in his belt. There was a bag hanging off his shoulder and a bedroll was hanging off his back. This photo was taken sometime during the Great Depression. Unemployment reached a high of thirty per cent at this period in time.

There wasn't a person inattentive while Jack gave this interesting commentary about the history of the Kelly family. He removed a DVD out of a packet, placed it in the machine then pressed the button. The curtains opened on the home theatre screen as the production started. It was called 'The Building of The Sydney Harbour Bridge': a collection of old film spliced together to show the whole story from 1920 to 1936.

Bill came in while all this was happening. Marree soon had a beer and a steak in front of him, and he polished it off quickly. 'That was good,' he said, 'how about another one?'

He certainly was hungry and the first three Crown Lagers didn't even touch the sides. Jack came and joined him while the rest of the people were glued to the story on the Harbour Bridge.

Jack asked Bill, 'How'd you go mate, did the police get their man?'

'Yeah, after twelve hours we cornered him in the Chinese Gardens. One of the police dogs sniffed him out. Our orders were to take him dead or alive. Just before dawn a police sniper using the latest infrared scope shot him through the head. It's taken up until now to tidy things up and do the paperwork.'

Jack patted Bill on the back and said, 'Good on you mate.'

The caterers were still handling out the food and drinks and this would continue until there was nobody left. In the meantime they would have a feed and a drink of their own. They sat around the last table that was left beside the harbour shore, taking in the scenery of the finest harbour in the world, but one of the red-suited ladies was always on hand looking after the Kellys and their guests.

The DVD on the Harbour Bridge in the home theatre ended, with all those that had been watching it returning to the long table. Jack put another DVD on, one that would keep the two young girls that were still here occupied for at least forty minutes, then he went and joined everybody else at the banquet table — that is, except for Donny King, who was glued to the home museum.

After about twenty minutes Donny approached the table and said, 'Well, you know Jack, after looking at the history of your family, it would appear that your grandfather was the courageous one. I mean, he must have gone through hell. He had wife and a three year old daughter, no job and no money. Now, from what I've seen and know about you, you have cruised through life as if there was a golden path built especially for you. You wouldn't know what it was like to be suddenly in a city like Sydney without any money, like what happened to your grandfather in the 30s. I suppose being born with the silver spoon in your mouth, you take everything for granted.'

Now Donny had the attention of everybody — except the two young girls, who were happily watching a kangaroo movie on the big screen.

Jack responded. 'What about you? You never did a day's work in your life. You were a mummy's boy, a sissy.'

Everybody at the table was laughing at Jack's description of Donny King.

Jack continued. 'Then one day, a solicitor walked up to you and said, "Congratulations, you've just inherited a business worth one million dollars".'

Donny replied with a big smile on his face. 'I can't deny it, because that's exactly how it happened. But I'm not talking about me, I'm talking about you. If I was in your grandfather's situation, I would have probably gone to the Gap and jumped into the ocean.'

'Look Donny, you know I don't take things for granted. Everybody the world over went through that situation at that time, so you adapt to it. If I was around in the 30s I would have handled that situation just as my grandfather did. Sure, because of my father and my grandfather, today we have plenty of money, but don't forget I've contributed too. I was a carpenter, I went to university — that's where I met Kate — and we've been running this business for five years now. I rebuilt this house and turned it into what it is today, the envy of the shoreline.'

'Jack I'm not saying you can't build and do things like this; you could probably build the stairway to heaven. What I am saying is, if all of a sudden you were to find yourself in the middle of the Great Depression, you would go to water. Now, take Cher over there — there's no way that John Steed would take her to the Katoomba Mountains and spend the night in the bush with snakes and spiders. Why, she might break a fingernail or get a hair out of place.'

Model-looking Cher stood up and put her hands on her hips in her defiant stance. 'You're right about that, you psalm-singing freak, and if you don't look out I'll come over there and give you a black eye.'

Everybody laughed. Cher sat down.

Undeterred, Donny King continued. 'See what I mean, Jack? Your grandfather would have faced all sorts of dangers on his journeys into the outback looking for work. Snakes, spiders, wild animals — including the human variety — sleeping under bridges, facing unknown dangers at any time. If he hadn't succeeded, then you wouldn't be sitting here today. You wouldn't even be on the planet. Now, what I'm proposing is that in four weeks' time I'll give you five hundred dollars, a tent and swag, no phone or credit card, and you follow the footsteps of your grandfather from Circular Quay to Mildura, getting work as you go. You send the money you make back here just as your grandfather did and then you make your way back home in time for Christmas. What do you say?'

'I say, why would I want to go and do a silly thing like that?'

'To make one hundred thousand dollars for homeless people. I'm willing to donate that amount if you go and tramp in the footsteps of your grandfather from now until Christmas.'

All of a sudden everyone realised that psalm-singing Salvation Army Captain Donny King was quite serious about this.

'All right Donny, I'll go if you come with me. I'll be the cook, and when you ask me what's for dinner I'll probably say wild thistle and grass soup, followed by Murrumbidgee River mud pies.'

Everybody at the table had a good laugh at that one. Kate ran up to Jack and wrapped her arms around him. 'You're not going anywhere, are you darling?'

One of the Harmon twins said, 'We want you at the pacing and trotting track on Friday nights Jack, so don't take any notice of this silly fat man.'

Donny said, 'Think about it and let me know what you decide.'

'Hey Donny, don't call me, I'll call you, okay?'

Donny didn't answer. He leaned over the table and shook Jack's hand, again offering his condolences for the sudden loss of Jack's father. Donny said goodbye to all those at the table before disappearing with his band of Salvo people out the front door.

The Harmon twins decided to call it a day and called out to the two young granddaughters that were engrossed in the story on the big home theatre screen. When they didn't come Jack said, 'I'll go and get them,' and he returned with one in each hand. The two girls wanted to watch the end of the kangaroo movie so Jack gave them the DVD to take home. A taxi arrived and with that they departed.

Richie from the pilot boat was sitting at the end of the table with John Steed and Cher. Richie had bought his new girlfriend with him, one that he'd picked up at the Cruising Yacht Club last Friday night. They both enjoyed themselves immensely, but the heavy drinking was finally taking its toll on them as they were both paralytic-drunk. Richie slumped in the chair and he eventually fell onto the floor. The new girlfriend tried to help him and she finished up on the floor too.

Bill said, 'There's no doubt about that bloke, whenever he does something he goes all the way.'

To all those who were left, this was an entertaining time, laughing at the antics of Richie and his new girlfriend. It was considered the icing on the cake.

Mrs MacMillan and her husband Frank decided to go, but before leaving Mrs Mac said to Jack in that broad Scottish accent she'd brought to Australia with her, thirty years ago, 'Jack, I can see that you like kids and when you fetched the two girls in from the TV, it looked so natural for you. So when is it going to happen?'

'When is what going to happen?'

'You know what I'm talking about. When are the babies are going to start arriving?'

'Yes, Kate and I plan to have a couple in the future. And you know what, you'll be the first to know.'

Mrs and Mr Mac reached the front door; Mr Mac went

through but Mrs Mac turned and said, 'Hey Jack, for what it's worth, I'll send Frank over one night — he knows how to do it.'

'Do what?'

'You know, how to make the babies. Frank had no trouble making four with me. We had four, one after the other. Bang, bang, bang, bang.'

By now the three ladies, Kate, Marree and Cher were hysterical with laughter, while the other female was still lying on the floor with the also-unconscious Richie from the pilot boat.

Jack gave Mrs MacMillan a considered answer: 'I'll keep it in mind, but you've got to understand that Kate's pretty fussy who gets into her cot.'

When they finally left Jack said, 'Bloody old bat, I don't know why we invite them over here.'

Kate took up Mrs MacMillan's defence. 'Because they're our neighbours. They're a lovely old couple, I find her funny and entertaining.'

'Well, next time we go fishing outside the Heads I'm going to invite her along and use her for shark bait.'

Now it was time for the men to laugh.

The caterers had moved in unnoticed and were also enjoying the show. They poured everybody a custom coffee and talked freely with those who were left for quite a while. Jack wrote a cheque out and paid the caterers, who in due course packed up and left.

Jack said, 'Well Cher, you came by boat but now you might have to swim home.'

'You know, that harbour to me is like those spiders in Katoomba, so no thanks.'

Bill and Marree were staying the night, while John and Cher would catch a cab back to Bondi Beach. In the meantime the ladies would polish off another bottle of pink champagne. Jack and Bill picked up Richie, carried him to the Motel at the back of the house and placed him fully clothed on the double bed. Then they went and collected his girlfriend and placed her beside him, clothes and all except for her high heels. They were so drunk they didn't even wake up. As Jack threw a light blanket over them Bill said, 'I wonder if this is their first time in bed together.'

Jack replied with a grin. 'Might be an interesting night, especially when one of them wakes up. But one thing's for sure, there'll be no physical activity tonight.'

At midnight it was lights out. The day of mourning and respect was over, but one thing stood out: Jimmy's spirit would live on and no doubt hover over them, watching everything they do for some time to come, and Jack would probably be thinking, 'There's no hurry to go Dad, stay as long as you like.'

The following morning, Marree left at 8 am to go to work. Bill was rostered off after the big manhunt at Darling Harbour and he would be going home after lunch. Richie and the new girlfriend surfaced at 4.00 pm, both looking like death warmed up. Jack intervened when he saw them about to get into their car.

'Richie, you're in no condition to drive. Leave your car here and pick it up tomorrow when you're alcohol-free, catch a taxi or let me drive you home, but one thing's for sure — you can't drive this car.'

Richie was difficult to negotiate with. 'Yeah, who said I can't drive?'

Jack replied, 'I said you can't drive.'

'I'll be right Jack, don't you worry about it.'

Richie continued on and proceeded to put the key in the door lock. At that stage, Jack moved in and snatched the key out of the car door, putting it into his pocket.

Richie was instantly angry. 'Come on Jack, stop mucking around and give me those keys.'

'I'm not mucking around, and you're not driving this car for twenty-four hours. Now, you do one of those things that I suggested, or go back to the Motel for the night — take your pick.'

Richie had the look of aggression in his eyes, but he knew Jack would have him for breakfast if a scuffle broke out.

'Okay, we'll go back to the Motel — I'm sorry about that Jack.'

As Richie and his new girlfriend walked away Jack said, 'Come into the house at six for dinner, we've still got plenty of food left from yesterday to clean up.'

'Okay Jack.'

When John Steed rang Jack to find out Richie's condition, Jack was frank. 'Sick as a dog mate, I took his car keys of him so he couldn't drive away and he won't be getting them back until tomorrow afternoon.'

'Okay, I'll put him on a sickie — we've got a cruise ship coming in at midday, so I'll use somebody else. Thanks Jack.'

'Bye John.'

Eight pm that night, a message came in on the fax machine. *Increased prize money to 200 thousand, how about it Jack?*

Donny King was becoming active. Jack faxed back. *You wouldn't have enough money.*

At 10 am the next day, another fax came in. *Three hundred thousand dollars, silver spooner. You wouldn't know what it's like to do it tough, but your grandfather did didn't he?*

Jack showed it to Kate and said, 'Here's the latest one, and I've got to say that the pain in the neck is starting to get to me, especially when he compares me to my grandfather.'

'Kate asked, 'You're not thinking about it are you?'

'No, but he's right, I've never done it tough. I was born into all of this. I was lucky: a great mum and dad who brought me up to know right from wrong, to respect everybody and everything. They taught me to show compassion for people who were down on their luck and those less fortunate than ourselves, and most of all they showed me the way to respect women. The only thing I've got that's natural is my ability to fight. If I see somebody taking advantage of a weaker person then I'll help the weaker one, providing the weaker one's in the right.'

Donny King was starting to test Jack with his constant bombardment of fax messages and cash inducements. Another one came in: *Three hundred and fifty thousand for your favourite charity.*

Kate's advice was swift and simple. 'Throw it in the bin.'

That night at midnight the bedside phone rang, waking them up. Jack picked it up. 'Hello?'

'Hello Jack, this is Don King.'

'What do you want, you bloody idiot?'

'I want a starting date. When are you going to begin walking in the footsteps of your grandfather? The homeless could use the money.'

'You know what Donny?'

'No, what?'

Jack burped into the handpiece and hung up.

Kate said, 'The hide of that bastard ringing up at this time of night. He's more than a pain in the neck, he's a pain in the arse.'

Jack laughed at that.

The next night at 8.00 pm the front doorbell rang. Jack picked up a remote control and pressed a button. The big TV screen turned into a security screen, showing part of the front yard and patio door area.

'It's that silly Donny King, I wonder what he wants.'

'He wants you to go walkabout doesn't he,' said Kate.

Jack opened the front door. 'Come in Don, how are you?'

'I'm okay thanks, I was in the neighbourhood and thought I'd drop in and say hello.'

Jack took him into the lounge room where he made himself

comfortable in the plush lounge. Kate made some coffee and came back with some fruitcake as well. They sat there talking about things of common interest, such as the welfare of the city's homeless people. It wasn't unusual for Donny to drop in without notice and he was always welcome in the Kelly household, day or night — time didn't come into it.

When the coffee and fruit cake had been consumed, Donny began talking about Jack's grandfather and what he did in the 1930s. 'Three hundred and fifty thousand dollars Jack, are you going to have a go at it? You'll only be away about ten months.'

Kate interrupted in a stern voice. 'Listen Donny, Jack's not going anywhere. We've hardly been apart since we got married and suddenly you challenge him with this carrot, knowing that it would be hard for him not to accept. Of course the homeless could use that money. The business has been shut down for the Christmas break, we've got to get that going again and this whole thing you've dreamed up is out of the question.'

Donny just ignored what Kate was saying and carried on. 'Three hundred and fifty thousand dollars Jack, that's a nice incentive isn't it?'

Jack replied, 'Make it four hundred thousand.'

'Four hundred thousand it is. If that's what it takes I'll pay. When are you going?'

'When you sign a contract with my solicitor.'

Donny showed signs of displeasure. 'A contract! Don't you trust me?'

'Dad always said, beware of con-men and don't trust anybody when it comes to money. You'll not only sign a contract, you'll also have to lodge the money with an independent legal eagle and he will pay the money, not you.'

Donny was becoming nervous and angry at the same time. 'Nobody has ever questioned my integrity before. If I say I'll pay the money if you complete the journey, I'll pay the money. But I won't be signing a contract or lodging a bond.' He was almost yelling now as his big fat face was getting redder and redder.

Kate, who was normally a placid lady, suddenly got nasty. 'You know Don, you're not only a pain in the neck, you're also dumb and stupid — go and peddle your schemes somewhere else.' She could see her very settled and privileged lifestyle being thrown into disarray with this scheme that Donny had cooked up. She had to put a stop to it. But she also knew that sometimes, the more you didn't want something to happen, the more likely it would.

Jack looked him in the eye. 'So you're not going to sign a contract.'

'No!'

'Well Donny, it's time you were leaving.' With that Jack got to his feet and grabbed Donny by the front of his coat, viciously dragging him to his feet. 'Open the front door, Kate, while I throw him out. Go on quick, open the door.'

Jack had hold of him from behind now and marched him toward the front door, which was now open. He forced him onto the patio and when it looked like he was about to throw him off the two metre drop, Kate panicked. 'Don't hurt him Jack,' she yelled with urgency.

But Jack was only kidding. He pulled him back from the edge of the patio, balanced him up and then let him go. Donny had the look of fear in his face. He meekly said, 'I thought you were going to throw me off there, you know.'

'Now why would I want to do a thing like that?' replied Jack. 'But if you come here again and continue to talk about my grandfather, I'll drag you down Lighthouse Lane and throw you in the harbour. Now, have a good night.'

Donny was silent as he walked down the steps to his car. As

he reversed out of the driveway, Jack and Kate joyfully waved him goodbye. They were laughing as they walked inside and closed the front door. Kate was happy now, as it looked as though Donny's scheme had come to a halt, but Jack knew different and wondered what he'd do next to get it back on the agenda. One thing was for certain: he wouldn't be coming back here to talk about it.

The following Sunday night, Jack and Kate along with Bill and Marree attended the Salvation Army's service at the City of Sydney's Citadel. They did this once a month, and they enjoyed the company and the sing-along, along with some wonderful stories of the homeless people who had been rehabilitated over the years.

Donny King was there but he kept right away from Jack and his crowd; he didn't even say g'day. There were about one hundred people, mostly all Salvos dressed up in their uniforms, while one of the brass bands supplied the music with everybody really enjoying themselves. Jack sang a hymn and gave a talk on homelessness. Bill gave a talk on crime around Sydney. As Salvation Army Captain, Donny King was asked to close the service, which he did in his usual professional manner.

At the end of his calling he thanked everybody for coming, then before he finished he said, 'I'd like to apologise to Jack and Kate for invading their home the other night and trying to persuade Jack to take up the challenge to walk in the footsteps of his grandfather, who was one courageous man. Jack, if you don't want to accept the challenge, then that's your decision. But should you change your mind, I'm willing to donate five hundred thousand dollars to the homeless section of the Salvation Army's Sydney Fund. I'll sign a legal document and lodge the money with an independent solicitor, who will pay the money when you finish the journey. I was out of line the other night and I again apologise for that. Now I've met all of your conditions, so you can decide what to do in your own time. All right everybody, let's go into the hall and have a cup of tea and some cake.'

Kate now realised that this was a real challenge, with Donny King setting the scene in front of one hundred friends who were now patting Jack on the back as if he was some sort of superhero.

'Good on you Jack, if anybody can do it you can.'

'Good luck Jack.'

'Yeah Jack, the homeless could sure use that money.'

With every handshake and every pat on the back, Kate could see that the very thing she didn't want to see happen was now a real possibility. *Darn that Donny King, why did we have to come here tonight?* Her head was spinning with panic spasms, clogging up the workings of her brain.

She snapped out of it as Marree touched her on the shoulder and said, 'You all right Kate?'

'Not really, I don't like what's happened here tonight.'

'You're worried that Jack might take up the challenge.'

'Too right I am.'

'Kate, let's go and have a cup of tea, then we'll just have to see how it plays out.'

'All right, thanks for being so understanding.'

Kate, Bill and Marree had finished their tea and cake when Jack joined them — even then he had to drag himself away from the others, who were still treating him like a superhero. At 10 pm the hundred-plus congregation broke up to return to their homes.

Jack said nothing about Donny's speech on the drive home and general conversation was at an all-time drive home low, which gave Kate a bit more to be worried about.

That night Jack couldn't sleep properly. The pressure to take up the challenge was beginning to take its toll as he duelled with his inner self. He tossed and turned, then got up and walked around, eventually sitting on the back balcony looking out across the harbour towards the Opera House. Because Jack couldn't sleep, Kate couldn't sleep, so she joined him on the balcony.

Jack had one strange trait. Whenever he had a problem that he couldn't work out he would smoke a cigarette. The only other time Kate had seen him do it was when they had a union dispute on one of their building sites. They had a big concrete pour that would take twelve hours to complete. The union put in demands for outrageous payments and halfway through the pour they walked off the job. Jack and Jimmy were both union members but that didn't matter. They worked their guts out to finish that pour with seven other guys from other companies; they'd come through the picket lines to help out. They wouldn't give in to union blackmail and toughed it out. After eight weeks, half the guys came back to work while the rest were sacked, never to work for the Kellys again.

Kate sat down and they cuddled each other without talking about the obvious problem. First light was the beginning of dawn. They went back to bed and managed a couple of hours sleep.

In the morning the air was still contaminated with uncertainty. Jack went down to the Powermaran to do some maintenance, or so he said, but all he wanted to do was to stare into the water to receive some sort of solitude — another peculiar trait he had when problems arose. Kate looked to see what he was doing. He was washing the windows of the Powermaran. When she looked again he was leaning over the bow rail, looking into the water.

Kate went and opened up the museum. She had seen it many times before without having a proper look, but today she would have that proper look. She noted in her mind that something in here stoked Donny King's brain into action and the interest shown by the others that were here on Jimmy's day of remembrance was quite extraordinary. She had never seen it in that light. This time Kate studied all the photos carefully and began reading all the newspaper clippings. She also noticed three small rough-looking books that turned out to be Jack's grandfather's Great Depression diaries.

Jack came in for lunch at midday and found Kate in the museum. 'Enjoying your trip back to the past?'

'Yes I am. This afternoon I'm going to read your grandfather's diaries.' She had a newspaper clipping in her hand and said while she continued to look at it, 'Here's a photo on the front page of the *Daily Herald* that's more than interesting. It was taken ten years ago, and it looks like you.'

She smiled as she waited for an answer. Jack also smiled as he said without looking at it, 'It's me all right. It was taken in the centre of the bridge; I was leaning on the rail looking into the water. You'll see one of the harbour ferries heading towards the quay in the background.'

'But the headlines say, "Will this be the next one to jump?"'

Jack responded, 'That's all it is, headlines.'

'So what were you doing there?'

'I lived in the terrace house that we own behind the Rocks. I'd had a bad experience and a fight, so I walked up there before I mangled somebody else. I stayed there for about an hour then walked home.'

Kate never asked for the details. What's in the past is sometimes better left in the past.

After lunch Jack went back to the Powermaran and went to sleep in the deluxe cabin, while Kate settled in the most comfortable recliner lounge and began reading the diaries. After a couple of hours she couldn't believe the hardship that working people suffered during the Great Depression. With unemployment reaching thirty per cent it would have been a horror for those who had no job, no money and no food. How did these people live? The next page provided part of the answer:

Luckily for us the harbour is full of fish; I go out most nights and catch a dozen. The Government gives us two loaves of bread a week and the Salvation Army come along with handouts, but fish and bread won't pay the mortgage so I have to do something drastic like leaving home to find work. I'm not going to be thrown out of my own house that's half paid for.

A bit further on there appeared another interesting entry.

I said to Helen this morning that I'm taking to the road to look for work. The money I make I'll send back home so she can pay the mortgage. We have to keep this house at all costs. I know it will be hard but we have no choice.

Kate had another look at the photo from the newspaper clipping of Jack's grandfather saying goodbye to his wife and three year old daughter at Circular Quay, as he took to the road in search for work. They wouldn't see him again for another five years. Suddenly she felt privileged to be in the position that she found herself in, and all because she fell in love with and married Jack B Kelly.

The beginning of World War Two sounded the end of the Great Depression as governments around the world prepared for possible invasion. Kate thought to herself that Donny King was probably right; Jack wouldn't know what it was like if he found himself in the middle of nowhere, his only possessions he owned the clothes that he wore and the little bag of something that he carried in his hand. Donny wanted Jack to walk in the footsteps of his grandfather so he could feel a bit of pain and appreciate what he had.

Kate thought that maybe she understood it a little better, and her mind had opened up a bit. *If Jack wants to do it, why should I so selfishly try to stop him?* Jack was caught between the devil and the deep blue sea after Donny's successful ambush in front of that congregation, full of well-known friends and associates. He would be thinking that if he didn't do it, he'd be letting all these people down as well as the homeless people who could use that money. And he was a bloke who thrived on a challenge, as long as it was lawful and decent. With a diary in her hand she rested it on the arm of the recliner, breathed out heavily and relaxed her heavy eyelids.

Her fingers released the book and it fell onto the floor, making a noise that woke her up. She'd been asleep for one hour.

Then a voice that belonged to Jack said, 'A penny for your thoughts?'

Kate was like a drunken sailor, but she got her bearings, moved the recliner upright and said, 'Oh, I've just had a little doze after reading two of the diaries, they sure are interesting. I never knew that people did it so tough in those years.'

She picked up her mobile phone and pressed a number.

'Hi Marree, are you and Bill doing anything tonight? You're not, okay, what about dinner at the Cruising Yacht Club, say six? Okay, see you then.' She pressed another number. 'Hello John, it's Kate — I was wondering if you and Cher would like to join us for dinner at the club tonight … you would, you beauty, about 6 pm? Fine, we'll see you then, bye.'

Jack sat down in the recliner beside Kate and asked, 'What's this, dinner on a whim?'

'Yes, you could say that, I just feel like going out tonight.'

Hmmmm, thought Jack.

Kate had lifted the weight off her mind and at the moment she was feeling positive and happy as they approached the Cruising

Yacht Club, arriving a little bit early. After parking Kate suggested that a walk along the marina jetty would be nice, to have a look at the big yachts moored there. They stopped at the big maxi yacht, *An Incredible Time*, which had run third with deckhand John Steed on board in the Hobart Race while Jack and Kate were preparing to go to America. It looked so beautiful gently rising on the harbour swell, then stretching on the bow line then the stern line.

They walked the full length of the marina, talking about this yacht and that yacht before turning around and heading back towards the clubhouse, arriving right on time at the restaurant. A little while later the others showed up and after a bit of a chat and a couple of drinks, they ordered their meals and then it was business as usual for this select group. They were all talking at once except Jack, who was unusually quiet. A church mouse at midnight on a Sunday night would be making more noise than he was.

When everything had been consumed and the table cleaned up, Kate rose, and just stood there. This was unusual behaviour for Kate and all eyes were on her.

Jack broke his silence before she could say anything. 'Kate wants to sing a song.'

A bit of laughter followed but Kate was undeterred. She started by saying, 'I've asked you all to come and have dinner with us tonight as there's something I want to share with you.'

Jack cracked another joke. 'She wants to divorce me.'

A bit more laughter followed and then Kate continued. 'Since Donny King made that speech the other night at the Citadel, Jack's been carrying a heavy burden on his shoulders that I don't think he should be carrying. Jack has never complained about it, because he never complains about anything. My first thoughts about the challenge that Donny put up was a selfish one on my part. It was a straight out *no, he's not going, I'll be here by myself,* that sort of thing. I never thought of Jack at all. Can you all understand the pressure he's under to take up that challenge, when all those people that were there the other night expect him to do it and secure that money for the homeless people?'

Jack's eyes were saying, 'What are you up to?'

The other four people were curiously watching and listening intently. Kate continued. 'Jack hasn't said anything about the challenge because he doesn't want to upset me, he would never do that, but I know he could never walk into that Citadel and look those people in the eye again unless he goes through with it. We've been together eight years now and we could be together another forty or fifty years. So what's eleven months out of fifty years? Nothing.'

Jack was sitting down while Kate was standing. She now faced him squarely, looking down and directing her speech only to him.

'So, Jack B Kelly, when you go for that walk in the footsteps of your grandfather in two weeks' time, you make sure your back home in time for Christmas. When I look down Lighthouse Lane on Christmas Eve, I'll expect to see you walking back up and into my arms.'

She opened her arms in an inviting fashion. Jack stood up and accepted the invitation. He melted into her arms, which now closed around his back. They were stuck together for about a minute, then Jack gave himself a little space and while looking into her eyes intently said, 'Honey, when you look down Lighthouse Lane on Christmas Eve, I'll be running back up it and into your arms, no doubt about it.'

They embraced again. Then Kate, with tears flowing down her face, turned and directed her speech to the others, saying, 'And while he's gone I just need a bit of moral support from my friends, otherwise I mightn't be able to get through it.'

Marree stood up and gave her a hug. 'Of course we'll be there for you.' Cher followed and then Bill and John offered their support.

Kate dried her eyes then said, 'There's one more thing to do: ring the pain in the neck.'

Everybody had a bit of a laugh. Kate dialled the number. 'Hello Donny, its Kate Kelly.'

'Oh hello Kate, is anything wrong?'

'No. I wonder, can you come over to the Cruising Yacht Club right now?'

'Ahh yes, I suppose I can. Ohh! That husband of yours isn't going to throw me in the harbour, is he?'

'No, not tonight.'

'Okay, I'll see you soon.'

Donny King walked in fifteen minutes later. Jack had a non-alcoholic drink waiting for him and a plate of fish pieces. Donny sat down after saying g'day to everyone and began munching almost straight away.

Kate sat opposite him and began talking. 'You know Don, you very cleverly painted Jack into a corner the other night, so we'd like to inform you that Jack is going to accept the challenge that you put up. You get three people, we get three people. Those six will draw up a set of rules which you or Jack can veto. Our solicitor will draw up a contract between yourself and Jack. When you lodge the money with a third independent solicitor, Jack will be on his way, walking in the footsteps of his grandfather.'

Donny said nothing as he ate the last piece of fish. He picked up the paper serviette and wiped his mouth. Then a big victory smile appeared across his great big fat face. All he said was, 'Now *I've* been ambushed.'

Over the next couple of days, the six person committee was formed with an agreement being reached. Jack reserved the right to help other people just as he already did around Sydney, should the occasion arise. Certain steps were compulsory, based on the dairies that showed where Jack's grandfather got most of the work. No mobile phone was allowed, but it was agreed that if Jack picked up a job on a building site and he was supplied with a mobile phone as part of his employment, then that was all right.

The one thing that Donny King wouldn't budge on was that Jack couldn't see Kate during the journey — however, he could ring her on Sunday night from a public phone box, just as his grandfather did to his grandmother. Maybe this was the pain that Donny wanted Jack to go through.

Donny lodged the five hundred thousand dollars and after a week everything was finalised. Jack would leave after lunch on the first Thursday in February, which was next week. Bill organised security arrangements: a federal policeman and his wife (who was also an enforcer) would live in the east wing of the house, making Kate feel that much safer. The Salvation Army's Angels would monitor Jack wherever he went as best they could, taking photos and videos.

GD Constructions was back in action after the Christmas break, with Kate taking the reins. Jack's long-time leading hand and the company engineer would answer to Kate. They would be in charge of one hundred employees plus contractors. Jack would be a long range consultant on Sunday nights when he rang Kate. The media would be kept out of the journey until Jack reached the fruit-picking river town of Mildura, a little over 800 kilometres from Sydney. A reception had been planned at the Mildura Showground in December to mark the occasion. Hopefully the media would follow Jack home and create a lot of publicity, which could result in more money for the homeless people of Sydney. Jack and Bill went to Tent City and purchased the things that Jack needed to carry out the challenge.

Wednesday night would be Jack's last supper so as to speak, or at least for the next ten and a half months. Kate would be cooking a roast for dinner to mark the occasion. The next day after lunch, Jack would say goodbye and begin to walk in the footsteps of his grandfather — for him, a journey into the unknown.

FOUR

Leaving Sydney Harbour

Jack's grandfather left Sydney from Circular Quay on the southern side of the harbour, and this was where he would also leave. At 2 pm Jack and Kate walked down Lighthouse Lane to the jetty where John Steed would be waiting in the pilot boat. John would ferry Jack across the harbour to Circular Quay; Jack would then begin walking in the footsteps of his grandfather, who took up the swag when he couldn't get work in Sydney.

At the jetty, Jack kissed Kate goodbye and gave her a hug. Then the realisations of their separation for such an amount of time really hit them both as they confessed their love for each other, over and over again. Tears were running down their faces as Kate broke away and ran back up the lane to the house, sobbing her heart out. Jack wasn't much better as John Steed helped him onto the pilot boat. Richie gave it a bit of power and the pilot boat headed for the other side of the harbour.

'A bit rough, eh Jack?' said John Steed.

'Yeah,' replied Jack. 'Up till then we seemed to have it under control, then it just happened. You know, we've hardly ever been apart since we got married. Other than the Hobart Race every year, this is the first time.' He pulled his handkerchief out and dried his eyes.

John put his arm around Jack as a show of support and they sat down on the cockpit seat. Nothing was said on the fifteen minute trip until they pulled into the jetty at the quay. Jack climbed the ladder up to the walkway and John tossed him his backpack, then the swag tent combo. Jack leaned down, shook hands with John Steed then Richie and said goodbye.

Richie said, 'Good luck Jack, see you at the end of the year.'

'Righto,' replied Jack, and with that put his gear on and began walking.

Donny King was waiting a little bit further up the jetty with the official send-off squad, consisting of two Salvation Army ladies. Donny wished him well and they both signed a piece of paper that was witnessed by the two ladies, who were now video-ing the start of the journey.

Jack crossed the very busy road at the pedestrian lights and continued on. He turned the corner into one of Sydney's main roads, George Street; after about one hundred metres there was a twin cab courier van parked beside a parking meter, and the driver was standing in the middle of the footpath talking on his mobile phone. He smiled as Jack approached. Jack returned the smile and nodded back in reply, and the courier van driver said, 'Where are you off to mate?'

'South,' answered Jack.

'Well, I'm going south. Throw your gear in the back and hop into the front seat, I'll be with you in a minute.'

The back of the van had a roller door on it and it was in the raised position. He put his backpack and swag in the limited space that was there, as the van was full of parcels of all sizes. Jack was thinking that the look on the driver's face was so friendly, it was as if he was waiting for him. He got into the van's front passenger seat to wait for the driver.

Then a voice from the seat behind him said, 'Off on a holiday, Sir?'

Jack recognised that 'Sir'. It was Bill. Jack's face lit up with excitement. 'Hey matey, what the hell are you doing here?'

Bill replied, 'Oh I thought I'd give you a bit of a clean getaway.

I want you to take this. It's a police mobile phone with some special features. The sun will charge it and it's a silent number. If you call somebody no number will appear on their caller IDs. If you're in a bad reception area, you press this button and the signal goes to satellite. I know that under the conditions you're not allowed to have a mobile phone, but I want to know where you are, and I intend to make sure you have a safe and enjoyable experience until this thing is over. Now, that idiot Donny will be watching everything you do. He'll have his Salvo spies out all over the country, so this is what I'm doing here. Kate's not allowed to see you, but nobody said I couldn't.'

'Okay Bill, what he doesn't know won't hurt him eh? Thanks a lot mate.'

The courier van driver closed and locked the rear roller door and took his place behind the wheel. He introduced himself then started the motor and when the traffic was clear, moved off.

Ten minutes later they stopped at the Newtown Police Station, where Bill got out, and then they continued on driving south until they reached the coastal town of Cronulla, about a thirty minute drive from Circular Quay. This town had the ocean on the east side with the waters of Port Hacking on the southern side, which was a massive expanse of water like a big bay that worked its way inland for seven or eight kilometres before marrying up with a river.

'Well, there you are Jack. You catch the ferry to the other side, then it's fifteen minutes' drive to the highway, and a further one hour to the Gong. It doesn't look like accommodation will be a problem as you're carrying it on your back like a turtle.' They both had a laugh at that. 'Good luck on your journey Jack, I'm sure Bill will keep me informed on what you're doing ... in the meantime, I'll see you whenever.'

They shook hands and parted company. Jack walked over to

the ferry terminal and got a timetable. *Plenty of time*, he thought to himself, *Might as well have a look around while I'm here.*

He walked over to some shops and purchased a double choco-late ice cream before sitting in a nearby park and relaxing in the afternoon sun. He spared a thought for his grandfather, who spe-cifically said in his diary that he caught the ferry from Cronulla to the other side, and now he would be doing the same thing. A walk to the surf beach was an interesting experience as this was once the site of very serious race riots involving five thousand people. Jack relived the TV newsreel as he walked along the bou-levard. A lone policeman viciously swinging a baton, holding back a large crowd of rioters, stood out in his memory. This piece of TV footage travelled right around the world.

It was getting late when he arrived back at the ferry terminal. A large crowd was waiting to board the ferry; after buying a ticket he joined them. Soon they were given the all clear to board. A loudspeaker repeated a message several times. 'Last ferry for the day, last ferry for the day.'

The deckhand pulled the moveable gangway on board, the mooring lines were cast, and the ferry got underway. Twenty minutes later they were tied up at the wharf of the sleepy seaside village, Bundeena. Jack had a fair bit of gear to carry, so he waited until all the other passengers disembarked before he decided to leave. The deckhand left the scene with his workbag so he obvi-ously lived in the village. The bloke driving the ferry appeared from nowhere and said to Jack, 'Whereabouts are you off to? I see you're some sort of modern day swaggie.'

'Yeah,' answered Jack. 'I'm on a hitchhiking holiday, similar to what backpackers do. I'm going to spend the night here some-where, then move out onto the highway in the morning.'

'Oh,' said the ferryman. 'Look, for what it's worth, I'm sleeping here in the ferry tonight. There's room for you if you want it, and

I could sure use the company at the moment. I live on the other side of the bay. The wife and I are fighting at the moment … it's so bad we can't stand the sight of each other, so I'm staying here tonight, I've had enough.'

Jack said, 'I don't think you should ever go home. When love and respect go out the window, it's all over red rover, time to move on.' He extended his hand. 'Jack B Kelly.'

'Mal Hodge, Jack, nice to meet you. Throw your gear back inside the ferry and I'll lock her up while we go and have a beer.'

'Sure thing,' answered Jack.

A five minute walk and they arrived at the local RSL, the only club in the village. One beer turned into a lot of beers, and they enjoyed dinner in the Chinese restaurant. They played darts and snooker while engaging in some healthy conversation at the family friendly club.

A couple of the local ladies showed an interest, with Mal getting a phone number off one of them. The other one offered Jack her number; he offended her when he told her he was happily married, but thanks all the same. She swiftly got up out of her seat, snatching her handbag off the table and storming off without looking, knocking an aged lady rotten. Jack and Mal quickly rushed to her aid, getting her to her feet while the offending female disappeared out the front door.

It was 11 o'clock when they arrived back at the ferry and both were nice and tiddly. A light easterly breeze was blowing, making it ideal for sleeping; it was just a matter of getting comfortable before falling asleep.

The starting of the ferry engine woke Jack out of a deep sleep; it was well and truly daylight but very early. Mal came and apologised for being a nuisance but in fifteen minutes the ferry would begin its first run of the day. Jack had a quick wash in a bucket of water and said goodbye to Mal, and as he stepped onto the wharf the ferry's deckhand arrived for his day's work and already people were arriving for their trip across Port Hacking to the other side.

Jack made himself comfortable on the fixed seat that was built onto the wharf and took in the early morning activity. It wasn't long before the ferry, which was small compared to those on Sydney Harbour, had a full complement of passengers. Mal blew the little high-pitched whistle right on time, 6 am. The lines were cast and under the roar of the diesel engine, the ferry pulled away from the wharf and headed for the northern side of this massive expanse of water.

Jack watched the ferry diminish in size as it powered further into the distance. He put the backpack on, then the swag, and began to walk. He passed an arcade of shops, then it was around the corner past the RSL Club. Five minutes later he arrived at a small petrol servo. A mature-aged gentleman was filling his petrol tank up. He looked at Jack and said, 'G'day.'

Jack acknowledged with a nod and a g'day of his own.

The smell of fresh cooking dragged him through the self-opening doors, and when he emerged five minutes later he was carrying two bacon and egg rolls and a large strong coffee. *Fancy that*, Jack thought as he walked around the side of the servo and sat down on the grass, leaning against the wall. *To be able to get a feed like that at six-thirty in the morning is nothing short of amazing.*

A minute later the guy who was filling his car up came around the corner with a mug of coffee in his hand. 'Mind if I join you?'

'No, not at all, the more the merrier.'

'When I smelt that coffee you had I knew I had to have one. You can't tell I'm a coffee addict, can you?'

'Join the club,' replied Jack.

'So ... it looks like you're going walkabout.'

'Yes, I'm having a hitchhiking holiday. Last night I slept in the ferry with Mal Hodge and right now I'm on my way to the highway to get a lift to Lake Illawarra.'

'Well, I'm on my way to Sydney so I can drop you off at the highway.'

'Thanks a lot. I'm Jack Kelly.' They shook hands.

'Ron Taylor, I'm the local vet. I know everybody in this town and you're not one of them, but you've got a familiar face — where are you from?'

'Sydney Harbour.'

The breakfast was over for Jack; the coffees had been consumed and after putting his gear in the back of the station wagon they stepped into the vehicle. Ron Taylor started the motor, moving away from the petrol servo and onto the road. He proceeded in the direction of the highway, about a twenty minute drive through Australia's first declared national park. Pristine bushland full of kangaroos, wallabies, birdlife — in fact, every type of wildlife imaginable could be found here. Towards the end of the journey, there were beautifully developed picnic grounds with amenities situated beside a river, and should you wish to take your lady or your man for a row up the river, boats were available for hire from the historic boat shed on the water's edge. The river crossing was a causeway that kept water in the river in dry times, but after heavy rain the water flowed across the causeway, giving motorists a headache as it became impassable.

A little time later a railway station in mint condition was a reminder of what once was. This station proudly displayed its name: Royal National Park. These days it was just a museum station, a historical relic of the past, but there was a time when thousands of people would come here by train to spend some time in the bush; then the day of the motor car arrived, putting the train out of business.

Five minutes later Ron Taylor stopped at the highway to let Jack out; he then proceeded in the direction of Sydney. There was a large open area near a soccer field so Jack decided to stand there, hoping to hitch a lift south with any motorist that might be willing to help. Traffic was thick in the northbound lanes but nothing was coming southbound.

After fifteen minutes a car in the distance came into view. An aged husband and wife team were on their way to the sunny south coast for a holiday. The wife, who was sitting in the passenger seat, said to her husband, 'Look darling, it's a swagman, I've never seen one before.'

The husband replied, 'Well I have in the country, but it was a long time ago when I was a young man. I've never seen one on the east coast.'

'Slow down a bit while I take a photo of this East Coast Swaggie.' She put the window down and grabbed her camera, setting it on video.

Jack noticed the car slowing down; he took a couple of steps toward the road in anticipation of it stopping, only to be disappointed when he saw the female passenger with the camera out of the window. They gave a hoot on the car horn as they passed by, speeding up and disappearing into the distance.

Jack was thinking, *Ahh well, I didn't want a lift anyway.* He walked away from the roadway, continuing to wait.

Ten minutes later, a semi-trailer loaded with beer kegs pulled off the road into this very wide open space and began to slow down. For a minute Jack thought he might have to make a run for it, but the semi came to a halt a couple of metres away.

Jack looked up into the cabin at the driver, who was extricating himself from his very high position. The driver walked along the side of the semi-trailer, checking the gates and tie-down mechanisms. He continued on around the back then along the final side before walking to the front of the rig and leaning against the large and heavy bullbar. The driver made eye contact and said nothing. He pulled a cigarette out of a packet and placed it in his mouth, while the other hand produced a gas lighter for ignition. He took a big draw of air, and then slowly exhaled the smoke. Jack was watching this semi-trailer driver with interest. Up to now, Jack could have been the invisible man, and then he wondered if this driver was dumb and stupid or just plain ignorant, or a combination of them all.

Suddenly the driver said, 'How are ya?'

'Pretty good,' replied Jack, and then added, 'Nice day for it.'

'Yes,' said the driver. The ice between them had been broken and they seemed to hit it off. They introduced themselves and within five minutes they'd covered the weather, traffic and politics. 'Okay Jack, it's obvious you need a lift, so where are you off to?'

'I'm heading for Lake Illawarra.'

'Well, I'm going south but not that far … you can come with me and you'll be a lot closer than you are now.'

'Okay,' said Jack. 'That's the best offer I've had today.'

The two men climbed into the very high cabin of the semi-trailer and away they went.

Inside the cabin, Jack and truck driver Joe were getting on like a house on fire as they shared experiences and things in common. Joe was about sixty years of age and had spent his whole working life driving trucks.

'Yeah, being on the road is a different day every day. Now take today for instance — there's plenty of vehicles going north but nothing going south, but it's still early days and just like the lotto, anything can happen — but you never know when.'

The beer keg laden semi-trailer entered the freeway section of the highway. Joe lifted the speed from eighty to one hundred. Next minute an old GMH Torana that had been restored to mint condition sped by, giving the impression that the semi was standing still.

'See what I mean Jack? He must be doing 150 ks.'

'Yeah, he's certainly blowing the cobwebs out of it,' replied Jack.

The Torana disappeared out of sight on a curve, while at the same time a police car that had been hiding amongst some trees came out onto the freeway and set sail after the racing car driver. A short time later, Joe and Jack passed the police car and the Torana, which were both now parked on the side of the road.

'Well, it looks like the police car was faster eh?' Joe laughed. Then he glanced at the very large rear view mirrors that were attached to the cabin. 'Here's another one. I've seen this one a hundred times before in all parts of Australia.'

The car slowly went by; the occupants were four young men, all out to have a bit of fun. One of them had removed his trousers and was sitting on the back windowsill with his bare arse hanging out of the window. Jack started to laugh while Joe said, 'I wish I had a long stick I'd give it a bit of a whack.'

The car sped up and left the semi behind. The bare arse disappeared back into the confines of the car, at least for now, until they come upon another motorist to intimidate.

A couple of kilometres behind the semi-trailer, a white soft-top sports car with the number plate INLOVE99 came up in the fast lane. What sort of a person would have number plates like that? A silver-spooned twenty-one year old named Jan Halvorson. The car was a present from her mum and dad who owned a fibreglass fabrication business up on the Hawkesbury River. They loved their only daughter, and in return she was devoted to them. So it was decided that when she turned twenty-one they would give her a special reward in appreciation.

Jan was a beautiful lady who wouldn't look out of place in the fashion industry or as a hostess on a Qantas jet. She had long flowing brown hair and was dressed in a sleeveless tan-coloured miniskirt with criss-cross straps over the shoulders, tying off behind her neck to keep it all in place.

In the passenger seat was her boyfriend of twelve months, a fellow who could best be described as 'Deadly Handsome'. He was sitting low in the luxury seat with his eyes watching the road through a pair of wraparound sunglasses. The road wasn't the only thing that he was watching. Now and again he would sneak a peek at the beautiful shaved legs of his girlfriend, and today he was receiving a bonus due to Jan wearing a miniskirt, as more of the fleshy section at the top of her leg was exposed.

Wow, he thought to himself, *if there's a better sight than that anywhere in the world I've never seen it.*

Jan Halvorson and Deadly Handsome were just enjoying a drive together with no set destination. Eventually they would stop for lunch, possibly overlooking the ocean or a mountain lookout; *Who knows, who cares*, they thought, *we're together and that's all that matters.*

Jan gave Deadly Handsome a dig in the ribs to brighten things up a little, but there was no reaction. He was like a dead whale on a Gold Coast beach. She turned the radio up then pulled a lever on the dashboard. The soft top of the convertible began to fold back. Now Jan had the wind in her hair. The wind was also moving the miniskirt about, giving Deadly Handsome a bit more to get excited about.

As they came around the slightest curve, Joe's beer keg laden semi-trailer came into view and they began to overtake it.

Back in the cabin of the semi, Joe said to Jack, 'Gee, there's a beautiful white convertible about to overtake us and there's something in it that looks a bit of all righty.'

Jan Halvorson gave Deadly Handsome another dig in the ribs. This time he was waiting for her. He dropped his seatbelt and at a speed that completely took her by surprise, he threw his arm around her, got up onto his knees and began kissing her on the other side of the neck. This blocked her view and she began driving a little bit erratic. The convertible sped up and was in front of the semi-trailer but still in the fast lane.

Joe began talking quite excitedly. 'Jack, Jack, did you see that, did you see that?'

'Yeah, yeah, but I don't believe it.'

Deadly Handsome ran his hand under Jan's miniskirt, found the elastic in the leg of her pants and sprang it, stinging the side of her leg. As a consequence the convertible skewed across the road, finishing in front of the semi-trailer, and appeared to slow somewhat.

In the twinkling of an eye, Joe's attitude changed from happy to angry. 'What the bloody hell do they think they're doing?' He slammed on the brakes and gave a blast on the twin air horns.

Alerted by the screaming of the brakes and the ear piercing sounds of the horns, Deadly Handsome stopped kissing and started looking. He and Jan turned as one with fear in their wide open eyes as they saw the big bullbar and radiator of the semi-trailer almost in their boot.

Deadly Handsome yelled at Jan, 'Flatten the accelerator *now!*'

She responded straight away. The sporty convertible lived up to its superior acceleration hype and in a few seconds put a large gap on the semi-trailer, then drew right away and began to disappear into the distance.

'*Whew,*' said Joe. 'Well Jack, what did you think of that episode?'

'You know Joe, I think your experience behind the wheel saved their lives. I hope there's another copper along here that catches up with them.'

A big green sign that read 'Coastal Exit' came up and Joe eased the semi-trailer off the freeway, following the single road to begin his deliveries to the pubs and clubs. Thirty minutes later Joe dropped Jack off at the Australian Hang Gliders Club, a large paddock on the edge of a cliff overlooking the ocean. A camping ground had been set up there; this is where he would be spending the night in his tiny one-man tent.

Jack's stop-off here would be short lived, for in the morning he was hoping to get a lift to his destination, the coastal township of Lake Illawarra. There was plenty of activity happening here with a large crowd watching a hang glider being prepared for take-off. When all was ready and the pilot securely strapped up, a helper on each side to assist, the three of them ran at the cliff edge. The two helpers dropped off while the pilot virtually threw himself off the cliff, only to soar high in the air to join the other gliders there.

Lunch time was a couple of toasted sandwiches and a coffee from a food van. Jack sat down on one of the logs that acted as a boundary and watched as these daredevil aviators did their stuff, which was pretty exciting at times — especially when they come in to land. At 4 o'clock Jack paid for a site and erected the one man tent. It was a simple task and he stood back to look at it, but it looked a poor cousin compared to the other luxurious tents and camper vans that occupied the area.

While he was standing there surveying a job accomplished, a voice from behind said, 'You're not gonna sleep in that thing are you?'

Jack turned around, sporting that charismatic smile, and answered the pleasant looking gentleman standing there. 'Yep, this is home sweet home tonight. I'm going to lock myself in there and let the rest of the world go by.'

They both had a good laugh together.

'Look mate, we're having a sausage sizzle at six thirty if you're interested, ten bucks and all you can eat.'

'Sounds good to me,' replied Jack.

The gentleman took his name and said, 'See you then.'

There were thirty people at the sausage sizzle and Jack was the only one there that never had an interest in hang gliding, but he soon made friends and a lot of wholesome conversation followed. The fellow who'd invited Jack to join them for the sausage sizzle interrupted proceedings with a couple of announcements.

'Well fellow gliders, it's congratulations to Colin and Carol who have just announced that they're going to have a baby in the second half of the year, and we look forward to seeing this new member of the Australian Hang Gliders Club when he or she arrives.' A round of applause followed.

Somebody asked Colin, 'Have you got morning sickness?'

All Colin could do was laugh, along with everybody else.

'Okay fellow members, another important announcement. Congratulations to Steven and Faith who have just announced their engagement. Must be something in the wind here today. They tell me that they're going to get married here ... I mean, up there.' He pointed to the sky and continued. 'Where else would a couple of hang glider pilots get married?'

A lot of applause followed by plenty of laughter. Jack was thinking, *Gee these people are having a good time; it's so good to see.*

There were many more announcements and to finish off he said, 'I'd also like to welcome Jack Kelly as an honorary member tonight. We don't know anything about him but this morning I saw him getting out of a truck with a swag on his back. We've never had the pleasure of a swagman at our club before, so we look forward to seeing the first hang gliding swagman — think of the publicity we'll get! I've only seen pictures of swagmen and you don't look anything like the ones in the book.'

Jack responded, 'That's because I'm a modern day swaggie.' Jack could see that he had centre stage and these people were eager to hear his story, but of course he couldn't tell them.

'Where are you from Jack?'

'Sydney Harbour.' He was asked many questions and answered them all with the skill of a politician.

The night moved on with more eating and drinking, with the final hour a hang gliding sing-along. They asked Jack would he like to sing a song — he obliged with a rendition of 'Up, up and away', and all these people joined in too. They'd had a great time, but now it was time to say goodnight. He already had a lift lined up with one of the guys that was going near Lake Illawarra and they would be leaving at about nine in the morning.

At 8 am Jack was packed up and ready to go. His first sleep in the tiny tent was indeed an experience, and he agreed with himself that it wasn't his cup of tea after the life of luxury that he was accustomed to. He purchased a large coffee from the coffee truck, went to the edge of the cliff overlooking the ocean and leaned on the safety rail that had been installed there. The view from this position was nothing short of magnificent. The rich blue ocean stretched as far as the eye could see in a panoramic view. A couple of early morning aviators had already taken to the air with a few more buckling up.

The guy that Jack was getting a lift with was a contractor for Aussie Post. Instead of delivering parcels on Friday, he decided to go hang gliding because the weather was perfect — a lot of other people were there with the same idea. So now he would do the job today, hoping Aussie Post wouldn't find out.

Jack and the contractor left the Hang Gliders Club at 9 am — travelling south, following the coast for about thirty minutes. A right hand turn was executed and now they were heading towards the mountains, skirting the south coast capital of Wollongong — locally called the Gong.

A left hand turn took them in a southerly direction, eventually arriving at a large industrial complex. The Aussie Post van pulled off onto the side of the road and came to a halt. Jack thanked the driver for the lift, opened the door and got out. The driver told Jack to walk to the next intersection, and then turn left and he would be going in the right direction. Jack put the backpack on, then the swag, and set off along the footpath beside the busy four lane road.

As he neared the intersection, the traffic lights changed to red and stopped the approaching traffic. A twin cab ute passed by Jack with its left blinker on, stopping at the lights. As he levelled up with the ute a voice said, 'Where are you off to mate?'

Jack looked towards the occupants of the vehicle. Three young men with scarves around their heads. 'Lake Illawarra,' answered Jack.

The young fellow in the front passenger seat said, 'Throw your gear in the back and get in, we're going by the lake.'

'Thanks a lot,' said Jack with a smile.

The traffic lights turned green just as Jack finished putting his gear in the back tray, and then he had to get into the cabin. The drivers of the two cars behind the twin cab were now showing a bit of impatience as Jack slowed their getaway on the green light. One of them was revving his motor while the other one was honking his horn. Jack finally got seated and closed the door; the red-scarfed driver accelerated away and turned left, followed by the other two drivers. Red Scarf then moved his vehicle across three lanes to be beside the centre island. One car followed while the other one sped up and passed on the left. Jack had a casual look around the vehicle; obviously some sort of gang culture with the scarves and that, otherwise they seemed all right, but sometimes looks could be deceiving.

The car that was travelling behind Red Scarf seemed to be getting just a little bit too close for comfort. Inside that car there were three occupants: the male driver Scott, his girlfriend Mary, and on the back seat in a restrained capsule their three month old baby, Emma.

Mary said to Scott in a worried voice, 'Don't drive so close Scott, back it off a bit.'

Scott replied, 'I'm sick and tired of these people that think they own the road, they've got no respect for other drivers at all.'

Mary said, 'I don't know what you're on about, they haven't done anything wrong. You saw them give that guy a lift; they held us up twenty or thirty seconds, hardly anything to get upset about. Now back it off a bit.'

Scott ignored her.

Back in the twin cab, Red Scarf and his two mates were becoming a bit agitated by this ignorant tailgater. There were no other cars in the rear vision mirror, so after indicating, Red Scarf moved his vehicle into the centre lane so that the other driver could have that lane to himself and go away. Scott continued his aggressive driving tactics and followed the twin cab into the centre lane. Red Scarf moved his vehicle back to be beside the centre island. Scott also followed.

Now Red Scarf knew that the driver behind was hell bent on causing some sort of trouble. He said to his two mates, 'Get ready for a bit of action boys.'

Jack had a bad feeling come over him. *Whoever is driving that car behind isn't showing a lot of sense.* He also knew that gang culture thrived on what was happening here, as a bit of spice got injected into what becomes a challenge. Jack didn't know what they were going to do but he mentally braced himself for some sort of violence.

Mary's voice was reaching concert pitch as she pleaded with Scott to give up this dangerous campaign of tailgating before somebody got hurt. She screamed, 'We've got our baby in the back!'

Exactly at that time Red Scarf put his foot on the accelerator and quickly sped up, putting a fifty metre gap on the car behind, and then he suddenly put his foot on the brakes, bringing the twin cab ute to a stop.

Scott in his car said, 'What the hell!'

Mary interrupted in a frantic voice. '*Brake, brake* you idiot!'

Scott put the brakes on in panic mode and the car skidded to a halt just behind the ute. Scott yelled to Mary, 'Did you see that? Did you see what they did?'

He opened the door and stepped out with the intention to confront the red scarfed driver, but Red Scarf had a surprise of his own. Scott made two angry steps toward the ute, but the sight of two youths with half-size baseball bats coming out of the confines of the ute, homing in fast towards him, brought a quick reaction from his marble size brain.

'*Holy shit!*' he yelled as he turned and ran to get back inside his car. He slammed the door shut and locked it, attempting to get the car into reverse gear. He was all hands and fingers as he fumbled for the gear lever. Mary screamed as the first baseball bat struck its mark beside Scott's head, shattering the window. The other bat-wielding youth lined up the back seat window behind Mary, but hesitated when he saw the baby. The wheels of Scott's car were now burning rubber as it took off in reverse with both youths getting a final shot in the centre of the bonnet before running back to the ute. Red Scarf slowly drove away as if nothing had happened.

Scott didn't know it but he'd had a bit of luck with his aggressive tailgating incident, although you wouldn't have thought it with the smashed window and the dints in the bonnet. His luck was that there were no other cars on this stretch of the road. But now the traffic lights had released a full quota. Three lanes of traffic flooding his way at 80 kilometres per hour and he was still going in reverse.

'*Oh no!*' he yelled as he spotted them coming. He switched from reverse to forward and had thirty seconds before they would swamp him. Reluctant to follow the ute, he took a chance while there were no cars in the opposite lanes and drove across the centre island with urgency. In the process he ripped the muffler and muffler pipe off, leaving it on the road behind him.

Mary was screaming at him, 'Now look what you've done, you idiot!'

Scott could hear Mary berating him over the now muffle-less engine, and as baby Emma started to cry he could see the foolishness in the situation that he'd placed his girlfriend and baby daughter in. One would think that it would be a long time before Scott would practice a bit of road rage again.

'Sorry about that,' Red Scarf said to Jack.

'No worries,' was Jack's reply. He wasn't going to get into the politics of it — after all, they didn't start it but they certainly finished it. They were armed with those little baseball bats and they carried knives in their belts — not the time to be brave.

The big buildings of the Port Kembla Steelworks were on the left as they made a right hand turn into a very big estate of industrial buildings, past the city crematorium and up a very long hill. On the left there was a much higher hill with a water reservoir sitting on the top. As they reached the crest of the hill, there it was: Jack's destination. Lake Illawarra, sixteen kilometres long and eight kilometres wide.

The blue waters of the lake looked magnificent from this elevated position and to take it all in you had to scan your eyes 180 degrees. There were some smaller islands in the foreground, with a couple of large islands on the other side where the tidal channel began its three mile journey to the sea. Further out the ocean could be seen, and in the far distance towards the south there was the famous Bass Point, where an American oil freighter ran aground during World War Two. On the southern end, farmlands ran for over thirty kilometres before gradually sloping into the base of the Great Dividing Range. There were a few sailing boats out and about, their colourful sails contrasted against the beautiful blue waters.

Leaving the crest of the hill, the road continued down until it became a gentle slope, then it levelled out. A four lane highway was approaching with a roundabout directly in front. Those blue waters of the lake were now only one hundred metres away. Red Scarf drove around the roundabout and came to a stop on the side of the road. He said to Jack, 'There's Lake Illawarra.'

'Thanks a lot fellas, I'll get my gear out of the back.'

FIVE

Lake Illawarra

Jack stood on the side of the road with his backpack and swag and waved the three young gangsters goodbye. Despite the excitement, he was grateful for the lift.

Jack had a look around; he was between the mountains and the sea. This was the north-western side of the lake. Several man-made harbours and channels, and a boat ramp to launch several boats at a time, were all part of the scene here. Seafood marketplaces and shops along with plenty of parking, and to the north of that the popular Port Kembla Sailing Club. Some thirty odd people were preparing their boats for the day's racing. Outboard motor boats along with mechanical jet skis added to the marine activity. Jack cast his eyes across to the eastern side of the lake. This was where he was headed: the channel where the lake entered the sea, along with the township of Lake Illawarra.

He looked at his watch; it was 10.15 am. A cup of coffee would go all right, and then he would hitch a ride around to the lake entrance. There were half a dozen cars parked outside the fish market with a number of people inside buying freshly caught fish and prawns. They were also cooking fish and chips. *Christ it smells good*, he thought, so he ordered a large coffee and a box of fish and chips. It took a while and when he received it, he made his way around to the back of the building towards the protected channel. There were some seats along with a couple of large landscape boulders and a small car park. Jack placed the backpack and swag on the ground before sitting on the seat and removing the lid off the box. All of a sudden he was joined by a small flock of seagulls looking for a free feed.

A rock wall was the dividing section of the protected channel and it was situated about thirty metres away; it was also home to about forty or so pelicans. In the channel itself several birds of the black shag variety were spending more time under the water than on top of it, searching for fish. Some pelicans were doing a bit of paddling around, hoping to pick up the odd surface fish while the rest were catching some morning sun while resting on the rocks.

Jack started on the coffee, then he had a few chips. He broke the hot fillet of fish in half and began eating it. Jack noticed some pelicans leave the rock wall and slide into the water ever so gently, but never believed for one minute that they would be dropping in to say g'day. The pelicans slowly paddled the distance of the channel then waddled out of the water and up a nice sloping bank to be on the same level as Jack. Five large pelicans were only three metres away when he realised, *Hey! They're coming to get my fish. Well, they're not going to get it.*

The closer they got to their objective, the faster they waddled. Four or five more pelicans joined in with an aerial assault. They'd taken to the air and glided to a synchronised two feet landing. Jack was almost surrounded, their big beaks getting closer. He could see the excitement in their eyes as they began to home in on the second half of that fish that he had in his hand. When it came to food, birds lost their sense of security and only focused on the task at hand.

Jack got up from the seat and walked back towards the road with the half eaten box of fish and chips. The pelicans, all nine of them, were now in tow. The faster Jack walked the faster the pelicans waddled behind him. Their great big wings came out to help with a bit of extra propulsion as their excitement grew.

A beautiful six metre half-cabin motor launch was travelling in the channel beside Jack on its way to the boat ramp. One of those on the boat had a video camera recording this spectacle of nine very large birds chasing a guy with a box of fish and chips.

One person on board called out, 'You all right mate?'

Jack turned to them and answered, 'Yes,' then laughed.

Some people came out of the fish market and gathered to watch. A car came off the main road and down the entry driveway quite fast, spooking the pelicans who automatically sensed that they were well and truly out of their safety zone — it was time to get the hell out of there. They took to the air with urgency, flying back to the safety of the rock wall on the other side of the channel.

The young video cameraman on the half cabin launch called out again. 'Thanks a lot mate.'

'You're welcome, I do this all the time,' replied Jack.

The small group that had gathered outside the fish market gave Jack a big clap for giving them some unusual entertainment. He acknowledged them with a bow and a smile before returning to the seat beside the channel; he still had the chips and coffee to finish, and he knew he wouldn't be bothered by those pelicans anymore, as they knew that the piece of cooked fish was gone.

After throwing the remaining handful of chips to the few seagulls that were patiently waiting for leftovers, he finished the coffee, picked up the backpack and swag then walked up to the road, crossing over the four lanes in order to hitch a ride to the township of Lake Illawarra.

It wasn't all that long before a young lady pulled up in a restored green metallic Volkswagen Beetle. Jack thanked her for the lift and there was just enough room to place everything in the rear of the vehicle. The road went east, following the northern perimeter of the lake. They passed by another yacht club with a beautiful clubhouse overlooking the lake, with a million dollar view right down the centre. The yachts there were much larger, being of the trailer sailer class. A race was underway with full sails and colourful spinnakers in use. The residential section was coming to an end with a large commercial environment coming into view. A right hand turn changed the direction to south but still following the edge of the lake.

It was a very interesting conversation inside the Beetle as they travelled along, talking about this and that and everything else. A holiday park passed them by, then the twin towers of a radio station. A little further down the road she moved the car onto the side of the road and came to a halt. The young lady pointed towards the lake and said, 'I'm going in there.' The nice looking sign said 'Jetties By The Lake Retirement Village'. 'My grandfather lives in there, I'm going for a visit. The Big Lake Hotel is five minutes' walk in that direction.' She pointed south.

Jack again thanked her for the lift, removed the backpack and swag from the limited space, closed the door of the Beetle and waved her goodbye. She waited until the traffic was clear then drove the vehicle across four lanes of traffic and into the picturesque village.

Jack had been here before. As a fourteen year old and again as a seventeen year old, when the family came on summer holidays. His grandfather worked on building the original wooden bridge during the Great Depression. But that wasn't the only reason Jack had come here. Jack's one time girlfriend, Chantal, lived here somewhere, and as he was in the area he thought it would be nice to look her up. There was a lot of hurt involved in their emotional breakup at the time, but after plenty of years down the track, the brain begins a healing process that eases the hate and disappointment, until it doesn't become an issue any more. They'd had plenty of good times together, so it would be nice to see her again.

Jack's mother Lucy remained good friends with Chantal after her breakup with Jack, so he knew that Chantal had left Sydney five years ago and bought a house overlooking the Lake Illawarra channel. A check of the family's phone diary revealed her mobile number, the same number she's always had, and the street address. A Google map supplied the location.

Walking towards the Big Lake Hotel, Jack noticed that things had changed so much he could hardly recognise anything. The service station on the west side of the road looked like a brand new one, while the one on the east side wasn't even there any more, having been replaced with an automatic car wash. Jack remembered this site very well, and he stopped to have a look. Friday nights on the big open spaces of concrete was home to the local marching girls team; they would train here for at least a couple of hours. The thirty-odd young ladies looked good in their formations, doing circles to the left, then to the right, while the trainer would be calling time and singing out instructions. And of course, where you've got young ladies you've also got young gentleman, and at the end of the training session this contingent of young gentleman would attempt to get to know these young ladies a little bit better — some did, some didn't.

Jack's brain went into meltdown as the past became so real. Superimposed over the brand new automatic car wash, he could see it all happening so clearly, with the old tape deck machine playing the big band marching music. The girls were in their uniforms, all marching in complete unison.

A driver made a mistake in the traffic; tyres were screeching and horns were blowing. This noisy intervention instantly brought Jack back to reality. He turned to see what was happening, but it was all over — the cars were slowly moving again. In the end nothing came of it, but it was close.

Enough excitement for one day thanks, thought Jack. He

continued walking on toward his destination, and at midday booked a unit in the Big Lake Hotel for three days. After spending the first night sleeping in the Cronulla to Bundeena ferry and last night in his tent at the Australian Hang Gliders Club, it was nice to see the inside of a room with modern conveniences. There was no hot shower in the tent, but there was certainly one here, and a shave would go well too — but later. Right now it was a walk over to the lake entrance.

Jack emptied out his backpack and hung the few clothes that he had in the tiny wardrobe. He put his big-brim sunhat on and placed the mobile phone that Bill gave him in his top pocket, along with a little black book. A tan coloured cattle coat finalised the ensemble. This coat had a big collar and finished down between the ankles and the knees, while the buttons were of the big fabric type. A wide matching belt completed it. A pair of small binoculars went into the coat pocket, and now it was time to go.

On leaving the Big Lake Hotel and walking towards the bridge, Jack passed through the shopping centre, which was about one hundred metres long and comprised a mixed variety of businesses that would cater for almost anything that one might need.

On the right, in an open paddock beside the King Prawn Bowling Club, was the local Surf Club Carnival. It had all the usual amusements that would suit people of all ages, including a ghost train and the air-hissing hurricane that would scare the living daylights out of any young lady or man. The road began a gradual rise to meet up with the four hundred metre long bridge that crossed a series of channels and waterways. After a fork in the road it went left, dropping down quite steeply before levelling out to meet with the water at the base of the bridge pylons. The road made a left hand turn at this point and followed the lake channel.

The concrete bridge carried four lanes of traffic with a walk-way on each side. Jack walked onto the bridge on the eastern side walkway and stopped when he reached the middle of the channel, which was one hundred metres wide. He looked into the beautiful clear aqua-green waters of the fast moving current that produced a swirling pattern on the surface. He also noticed the difference in water colour here compared to the other side of the lake, which was blue. From his aerial position he could see a school of fish quite clearly.

His eyes followed the channel for about six hundred metres where it and the road parted company as the waterway changed course. The boat ramp was here along with a dozen or so permanently moored boats. Behind the boat ramp was the local holiday park with its row of Norfolk Island pines that ran the full length of the boundary fence. On the south side of the channel was a very large sandbank, then a second channel about fifty metres wide followed by a small island covered in trees with sandy flats extending into the water. Behind the island was another channel that had a beautifully mowed grass foreshore, and fifty metres behind that, a food kiosk. There was plenty of activity happening on the bridge where several fishermen were trying their luck, while in the channel itself half a dozen runabouts were anchored with the occupants, all happily fishing.

Jack pulled the little black book out of his pocket and found Chantal's phone number. She lived opposite the boat ramp on a corner, in a two-storey townhouse that she owned. He punched the numbers into the mobile, and then put the binoculars up to his eyes.

Yes there's the boat ramp, and opposite should be the townhouse … ahh yeah, there it is. There doesn't appear to be anybody around, at least on the outside anyway … hang on, there's somebody on the second-storey balcony sitting in a lazy chair with a cup of coffee. Yes, I think that's her.

He pressed the green button on the mobile; the dial tone was ringing. The female on the balcony picked up her mobile phone and answered. 'Hello, Chantal speaking.'

'Hi, this is Jack Kelly, how are you?'

'Jack! Oh, what a pleasant surprise.'

Yes, I'm in the area and I thought I might drop in and have a bit of a chat while I'm here. I was thinking about 10 am tomorrow.'

'Yes that would be fine, I'll look forward to it. Where are you now?'

'I'm in the Gong.'

'Gee you sound so close, it's almost as if you're at the front door.'

'Yes, you know telephone technology is getting better all the time.'

Chantal was on her feet now and looking around, scanning the bridge with her eyes. Half a dozen fishermen there, one with a big sun hat that was leaning on the rail. Jack hastily put the binoculars away in case she saw the glare.

A pedestrian said to Jack, 'What are you perving on?'

Jack ignored him and said to Chantal, 'Okay I'll see you tomorrow at 10 am. Bye.' Call ended.

The pedestrian was still there waiting for an answer. Jack looked him straight in the eye and said, 'You know what mate? Curiosity killed the cat, and I think it's time you had a swim, so I'm going to throw you over the rail.' He kiddingly moved to grab the pedestrian, who was shocked at Jack advancing toward him.

'Get away from me, whatever you are, you misfit.' And with that he was off. He wouldn't have broken any records but he was certainly exiting the area with plenty of urgency. Jack laughed to himself as he watched him scamper away.

Jack moved on to continue the walk across the bridge to the south side. A fisherman pulled up a fish and landed it on the walkway in front of him. Jack said, 'Okay mate, give it a kiss and throw it back.'

The fisherman looked at Jack and replied, 'Like bloody hell, this is my tea tonight.' He took the hook out, placed the fish in the box and closed the lid, then threw the line back out. Jack continued walking on, and then the fisherman called out, 'I got another one.'

Jack turned to face him, saying, 'Good on ya, get as many as you can.' He waved and carried on.

He passed by the large sandbank then over the second channel, which was only half the size of the main one. The small island was next, with heaps of birds congregating in their various groups. A small hill that jutted out from the sandbar was the high ground for the pelicans, where it was standing room only. Not far away were the common seagulls just standing there, waiting and watching. A large group of small birds with long beaks like drinking straws were busy worming. The worms lived in little silos that they make in the sand flats, and as the tide went out it left the hole exposed. The drink-straw birds simply insert their beak and suck the worm into its mouth. A very simple way to get an exclusive feed for this species.

Half a dozen black and white shags were standing in their own group, holding out their wings in order to collect the slight breeze that was blowing, to assist in drying their wings. There were a few large white cranes equipped with long legs, enabling them to wade into the deeper water. With a long curved beak they were having a pick at something, possibly shrimps that lived in the seaweed.

Approaching the end of the bridge, a set of steps invited Jack down to the foreshore ground level. The walking track was busy with mostly young scantily-clad ladies, walking in pairs and carrying their bottled water. Following the channel that went behind the small island was an interesting one indeed. Along this beautiful manmade hilly landscape were at least one hundred people of all ages. There was fishing, picnics and kite flying. Some were kicking a football around, while further away a team of six youths were having a game of cricket.

Jack passed by what was probably the perfect family unit: Mum, Dad and two girls about fifteen and sixteen, all dressed in karate uniforms. They were kicking their legs and punching the air in the usual karate practice regime.

Ahh, wouldn't that be nice, he thought. *If I could be so lucky as to have a couple of kids like that one day.*

The food kiosk was coming up and a food sign caught his eye: 'Hot meat pie and sauce $3.50'. Of course he would have to have one and a can of Coke.

Now it wasn't any wonder that the pedestrian on the bridge called Jack a misfit and people here were staring at him. Here he was, unshaven with a big sun hat on and a long coat that would be more suitable for a cold rainy day in the middle of winter rather than a hot summer's day. This fashion just seemed way out of place.

To those that over-stared, Jack would nod and say, 'How ya going?' Then they would look away.

From the water to the kiosk would have been fifty or sixty metres. Bench seats were placed randomly all over the place with plenty of people taking advantage of them. The kiosk was quite crowded with three people serving the usual popular takeaway food and drinks.

After purchasing a meat pie and a coke, Jack sat down on the seat that was closest to the kiosk. He leaned back and relaxed in order to take in this beautiful scene. Earlier he had seen a gentleman with a kelpie playing fetch. These dogs could run all day. Next minute, that dog appeared right in front of him with the stick in its mouth. The dog dropped the stick on the ground, looked Jack in the eye and breathed quite excitedly.

Jack thought, *Ahh well, I won't disappoint you.* He picked up the stick and threw it as far as he could. The kelpie took off after the stick like a rocket, picked it up, delivered it back to Jack's feet and looked him in the eye again.

Jack continued throwing the stick and each time the dog excitedly brought it back. The owner showed up. Jack said, 'I hope you don't mind.'

'No, not at all mate, I get a sore arm throwing that stick all day, but the dog just loves it. I'll take him for a walk over the beach.' With that the beautiful red kelpie and his master set off along the walking track towards the beach.

Some seagulls had landed near Jack as soon as the dog was gone, hopefully to pick up a free feed. Suddenly the birds were in emergency mode, scattering and taking to the air. *Hmmm, that's strange*, thought Jack. But then quite a large black magpie landed right where the seagulls had been. Normally not the sort of bird you'd see on the foreshore of the lake channel. It kept looking at Jack and everywhere else at the same time. Shyness wasn't part of its make-up, as it was only two metres away.

Jack noticed five pelicans flying in a V-formation high in the sky, travelling in a southerly direction but directly over the bridge. The magpie, ever on the alert, spotted the pelican bomber squadron and launched itself in their direction.

The lead pelican, a Captain Big Beak, with plenty of aerial missions behind him, noticed on his radar a flying black missile approaching at high speed from the ground, and immediately ordered evasive action.

'Every pelican for itself!' he squawked.

The first four pelicans changed their course to the west and climbed higher. The fifth pelican that was on the east flank and a little behind the others turned east, heading towards the island that sat in the ocean beside the mouth of the channel entrance. The magpie decided to tackle this lone pelican, who by now knew that this evil bird was on its tail. For a couple of hundred metres the magpie appeared to be catching up and closed to within a metre or so. By now the magpie had been travelling at full speed for at least eight hundred metres; the stamina it showed to sustain that was very surprising indeed, but it seemed intent on wanting to viciously pick the eyes out of the larger bird no matter what.

But that would be as close as it would get. The pelican, with its Boeing 747 wings and supercharged with fear, started to draw away and soon put a gap on his smaller rival. The magpie, obviously disappointed at the outcome, decided to call off the mission and returned right back where it started, two metres in front of Jack — who couldn't believe what he'd just witnessed. He'd seen many wonderful things around Sydney Harbour and the ocean, but this was different: a real education on estuary wildlife. Two small boys of around five or six were kicking a soccer ball along and scared the magpie, who took to the air and landed in a tree a couple of hundred metres away.

The conversation at the kiosk, which was just behind Jack and within hearing distance, was of a happy nature. Customers and the kiosk staff were enjoying idle chatter as they shared experiences on the run. One of the ladies was heard to say, 'Hey Len, there's those bloody kids that were here yesterday … it looks like they're coming this way.'

Jack's head turned left and right until he spotted the so-called bloody kids. There were four of them, dressed in identical clothing. Worn-out jeans, imitation joggers, and denim shirts with the sleeves ripped out at the shoulders. They were sporting stick-on tattoos that represented the violent insignias of criminals and the darker side of society. They also wore bright coloured bands around their heads that was probably the gang signature. Over the years Jack had seen all or most of the gang cultures around Sydney but this lot were dressed a little bit differently, not unlike the three young guys that gave him a lift earlier this morning. A new type of gang had spawned on the beautiful South Coast.

They were heading for the kiosk all right, and as they got closer, Jack could see that they would barely have been out of high school. The one leading was a very tall lad with blood-coloured hair, two more were a bit smaller, while the fourth was a little on the short side but had the most pleasant face.

Jack heard the owner say, 'I gave them a free drink yesterday but they won't be getting one today.'

The four approached the counter full of confidence, and Jack noticed the concerned look on the face of the owner, as he was not a young man.

'Four Cokes,' said Mr Blood Nut.

The owner answered, 'That'll be twelve dollars, thank you.'

'We haven't got any money,' answered Blood Nut. 'You gave us a free drink yesterday and if you know what's good for you, you'll give us a free drink today.'

Jack, sensing trouble, ambled up to the counter and stood beside Blood Nut. The owner and Blood Nut were exchanging nasties. Jack stuck his bib in and said, 'You heard the man — no money, no cans. There's a water tap around the corner for deadbeats like you.'

Blood Nut turned to face Jack and said, 'Who's talking to you, eh?' he looked Jack up and down then they levelled their eyes again.

The number two in the chain of command said, 'Go on Gildo, smack him in the mouth.'

He then moved in closer to support his leader. Gildo clenched his fist and moved it into the ready-to-throw position.

Jack responded by saying, 'Now before you throw that punch, there's something you ought to know.'

'Yeah, and what's that Queero?'

'If you do throw that punch, and I hope you do, that will give me the excuse to bash that big ugly nose right down level with your face.'

Jack ditched the hat, took a step back and moved into a defence position. The smallest gang member turned and walked away, followed by the number three in the chain of command. Gildo looked around and saw them walking away.

Jack seized the opportunity. 'Well come on, you gutless wonder — what are you waiting for?'

The number two said to Gildo, 'I think we'd better go.'

Gildo dropped his fist and they both painfully walked away.

When they were out of earshot, the owner of the kiosk said, 'Thanks a lot mate. Here, have a drink on the house.'

Jack replied, 'Thanks, I don't mind if I do. Oh, could you make it one of those large white coffees?'

'Yeah sure.'

One of the ladies asked Jack, 'Gee, were you going to do what you said you were going to do?'

'Too right I was. There's one thing we don't need and that's people his age running around doing an apprenticeship on urban violence. To show him a bit of real violence right now at his stage of life might just turn him towards the peaceful fork in the road instead of the violent one. Somehow I don't think we've seen the last of him, so I'll hang around for a while.'

Jack collected his free coffee and returned to the garden seat. Before long the counter at the kiosk was again full of customers, all happily talking again. It was as if the interruption by Blood Nut and his gang had never happened. The after-midday sun beamed down as more people swelled into the area; they had come to enjoy this imitation garden of Eden.

A woman of about thirty years of age walked past Jack, then she turned and looked at him. 'Look, I'm sorry to bother you but my car's got a flat tyre. Do you know how to change a wheel?'

Jack smiled at her and said, 'Yes, where's your car?'

She pointed to the car park behind the kiosk. 'Over there, it's that white station wagon.'

'All right, let's go and have a look.'

They walked away in the direction of the car with the flat tyre.

Beneath the bridge where the walking track goes, the blood-headed Gildo was stirring up his troops. 'Were not gonna cop that are we? He's only one, we're four … if we attack together, it's all over.'

The number two in command said, 'Yeah, but that guy looked pretty tough, I wouldn't like to take him on.'

All right, we'll keep away from the kiosk, but we'll have us some fun along the shore, okay?'

'Okay,' said the others as they punched the air with their fists. The smallest one said, 'I can't see that guy, the seat's empty.'

'Maybe the arsehole's gone,' answered Gildo.

There were a lot of people lining the sandy shores of the channel with most people fishing. Some were swimming where there were no fishing lines, and further away a couple of canoeists paddled by, accompanied with a lone sailboard rider. There were two distinct age groups: the very young and the very old, with only a sprinkling of men and women in the thirty and forty year age bracket.

This suited the young gang as they approached their first victim, a pensioner couple sitting on their fold-up chairs. They both had fishing rods and were enjoying their carefree day, even though the fish weren't biting. Beside them was a fishing basket and a picnic box.

'How are they biting?' asked Blood Nut on his best behaviour.

'Oh, we haven't had a bite yet,' answered the elderly gentleman. 'What have you got to eat?'

'Oh just some plain old sandwiches,' he answered.

'Yeah, well I like plain old sandwiches,' said Blood Nut, and with that he grabbed the picnic box and began going through it. The elderly man jumped up and protested, but the two bigger boys took hold of him and held him while the short one looked on.

The man's wife said, 'Go on, you can have the food, we're not hungry anyway,' trying to diffuse the situation. Blood Nut took two cans of soft drink out of the picnic box, and then he threw the box out into the channel. The two gang members then pushed the pensioner over. He fell onto the soft sand without hurting himself. They all laughed at him lying there.

Now Blood Nut and his followers were feeling all-powerful as they began their crusade along the shore, harassing people as they went. The fish had started biting up in front of the kiosk area and the main concentration of people was there. Blood Nut had a good look around to see if he could spot Jack. The seat where Jack was sitting is empty, so he was gone.

In the car park, things were going well. Jack had changed the wheel, tightened the nuts and put the hubcap back on. He removed the jack and packed it back in its place inside the station wagon. 'There you are, all done.'

'Thanks very much, I didn't know what to do,' the lady replied.

'No worries, glad to help. See you later,' replied Jack.

The job finished, he headed back to the comfort of the garden seat. As he came around the side of the kiosk he heard shouting and couldn't believe his eyes. The Blood Nut, Gildo, was back with his gang. Two of them grabbed a young boy who was fishing, while Gildo seized his fishing rod and threw it out into the channel as far as he could whilst laughing with glee. Then they threw the boy into the water just for the fun of it.

Jack put his head into the kiosk and said, 'Call the police and the ambulance.' He took off the long coat and the sunhat, put his wallet into the coat pocket and folded it up, asking the ladies to mind the items before heading down to the channel for an appointment with the local gang.

There was a fair crowd well back, watching this gang creating havoc. He could see some people who wanted to help, including the karate family. They were hanging back, waiting for a leader. Now they had one. Jack was three metres away and closing in fast when the four of them grabbed another old fisherman and dragged him into the water. This old guy was putting up one hell of a struggle and it took the four of them to get him in, and even then he grabbed one of them by the hair and dragged him along as he went under. The man's wife picked up the nipper pump and wacked the smallest one over the top of his head, just about ending his fighting career.

Jack waded straight into the water. He grabbed Blood Nut by the back of his shirt collar and pulled him over backwards so that his head was just out of the water. 'Come on, get up, you miserable excuse for a human being,' yelled Jack as he stood over him.

Blood Nut had fear on his face as he looked up at Jack. Jack grabbed him by two handfuls of hair and dragged him to his feet. Blood Nut was swinging wildly without connecting to the intended target. Jack was hoping he'd do that — now he could throw one himself. And what a vicious punch it was, right on his belly button, taking all of his precious air.

Then Jack said, 'I told you what I was going to do, didn't I?'

Blood Nut couldn't answer, he was half bent over and gasping for air. Jack lined up his nose and connected with a beautiful punch. As Blood Nut tumbled backwards into the shallow part of the water, blood was already pouring out of his nose.

The karate family were now in a position to help. The two

girls cleaned up the smallest one, who was already wounded due to that blow on the head, so he'd had enough. The father was fighting the other two, although he needed a hand — but first Jack would help the old fisherman, who was spluttering his way to the surface. He dragged him into the shallows then headed towards the other two gang members and the father, who were fighting in waist deep water.

Jack approached one of them from the back and punched him on the right side of the body. This gang member, who had probably never felt real pain before, got a real taste of it. He screamed as the blow hit him and half turned around only to cop a punch on the nose too. He crashed backwards into the water.

There was only one left standing and he was no match for the father when it became one on one. The martial artist gave him a chop on the neck and that was the end of him. Jack dragged his conquest to the bank, then he helped Blood Nut to the shore. The father dropped his opponent onto the bank, face down in the sand. The two girls took their eyes off the short one for a few seconds; he decided to make a run for it. The father called out to the two girls, 'Don't let him get away!'

He had a three metre start on them when the chase began. The magpie that attacked the pelicans dropped out of the sky and attacked the short gang member. He stopped to ward off the bird that was flapping its wings above his head as the girls approached. They grabbed him by the arms and the magpie flew away. One of the girls counted — *one, two, three*. They let him go and spun around only to kick him in the head at the same time; he fell to the ground in an instant. A large crowd had assembled, watching all the action. They applauded the two young karate ladies for a good job well done. The girls took their prisoner back down to the shoreline and made him sit down with the others.

The police paddy wagon arrived and drove onto the channel shoreline. 'Is this them?' asked the policeman.

'Yes,' answered the old lady who had used the nipper pump on the head of the short one.

'Okay, we'll take it from here. Would anybody like to make a statement?' asked the policeman.

Ten people came forward as the ambulance pulled up. The ambulance officers checked out the gang members one by one. Gildo had a broken nose and the smallest gang member would need to be monitored for signs of concussion. The police then escorted them one by one and virtually threw them into the caged section of the paddy wagon. One officer was heard to say, 'No good being nice to them.'

Jack was having a conversation with the karate man. 'Thanks for the hand, mate.'

'You're welcome. I wasn't game to have a go by myself, but you were. When I saw you run into the water I knew I had to help you.'

They chatted for ten minutes then Jack said goodbye. He retrieved his hat and coat from the kiosk and thanked the owner for the entertainment, then began the two mile walk that followed the channel to the lake entrance.

The walk was an enjoyable experience for Jack. It was a complete change from Sydney Harbour and all its wonders, but this area had its own type of wonders. A manmade billabong beside the channel provided a safe area for swimming. Beside the billabong on the continuing grassy reserve were barbecues and children's playground equipment. The sand hills that Jack remembered as a young man were no longer there, having been removed by the vandalism of man before the conservation movement began. The hills had been replaced with manmade dunes covered in a green marine growth to keep the thin layer of sand in place. These dunes provided a buffer between the ocean and the lake.

The lake entrance consisted of two parallel rock walls one hundred metres apart that jutted out into the ocean, and of course a lot of fisherman were attracted to fish there. It was a very deep and wide channel, with the water swirling and the current strong as it merged with the ocean on the run-out tide. On the beach the lifesavers had the flags out and were keeping an eye on a large crowd of surfers that were catching waves, while a contingent of board riders were out the back behind the line of breakers waiting for their perfect wave. A number of surf kites were in action, dragging their board riders through the waves at considerable speed, while further along some men were fishing. Others were beach worming; the worms made the best bait, but it took a bit of skill to catch them. The majority of beach goers were just sunbaking with their various boyfriends or girlfriends.

Jack made his way along the beach before taking a track through the manmade dunes that delivered him onto the grassy reserve beside the billabong and the kid's playground area. The little ones were busy trying to wear out the swings and slippery dips with enormous amounts of energy while their mums and dads looked on anxiously. These kids would sleep well tonight.

Walking back towards the kiosk, Jack stopped to look at the biggest building in the street. It was a white double-storey of colonial design and it was called the California. Jack knew its history very well. It was built during the Great Depression as a destination for Sydney holiday-makers. Jack's grandfather worked on the original wooden bridge over the various channels and waterways in the 30s and the California Guest House, as it was known as then, was where he stayed some of the time. In his diary he described his time here as a very happy one.

Jack walked on and as he passed by the kiosk he gave the

owner and the workers a wave. It was all peaceful again after the invasion of Blood Nut and his gang. He reached the steps that went up to the bridge but he decided to go underneath and take the steps on the other side to use the western walkway. Looking to the west as he walked north across the bridge, there were two large islands standing one hundred metres apart, signifying the beginning of the lake channel.

On the other side of the big lake were level plains mixed with hilly areas, and in the distance the Great Dividing Range. He passed over the small channel, then the large sandbank before coming to the main channel, where a large number of people were fishing.

A speedboat was coming from the big lake toward the bridge in the main channel, and he leaned on the rail to watch it with interest. It slowed down and glided toward the sandy shore beside the 1930s-built boat hire shed, which was situated just beside the base of the bridge.

As the speedboat came to a rest people were clapping, blowing whistles and carrying on in a happy fashion. It was some sort of party all right, because there were lots of kids, parents and grandparents, along with some friends best described as possible hangers-on.

From his aerial view Jack noticed that the speedboat was a relic of the past. It was about five metres long and made of plywood, with a front and rear cockpit with the motor situated in the middle. The deck was of beautiful African mahogany with the grain clearly visible.

He walked past all the people who were fishing; some men had their girlfriends with them, making a day of it.

Jack decided to descend the stairs for a closer look. He made his way through the large crowd where all the kids with party hats on were having a ball, blowing whistles and running around with balloons on strings. The total group must have numbered sixty or seventy with half a dozen dogs thrown in.

The speedboat must have been at least sixty years old but in perfect condition. It had probably been locked away in a garage and only recently been discovered by a family member.

As passengers disembarked, new passengers would replace them. The boat was then pushed out bow-first into the channel, where the driver simply hit the start button and put his foot on the gas. It soon hit a very fast speed as it made its way up the channel and into the basin of the big lake. The channel speed marker said ten knots and Jack was thinking, *Cripes, that's a bit of a concern, that boat must be doing at least fifty knots.*

Ten minutes later the speedboat re-appeared. The driver knew just when to cut the motor and a perfect glide was executed into the sandy shore, where all the passengers exited and another five would get in — and so the process would repeat itself, over and over.

There was a young lady amongst the partygoers who looked about eighteen or nineteen years old and she had her dog with her. It was a red cattle dog, on a leash that she kept a firm grip on. It wasn't hard to work out the name of the dog because as the speedboat returned from its trip to the big lake, he would bark like hell and try to get into the front cockpit, and she would sing out, 'Nebo stop it ... stop it Nebo, you naughty dog.' Nebo was a very strong animal and it took the female handler all her strength to control him.

The speedboat returned, gliding to a halt on the sandy shore. A bunch of kids got out, leaving it empty for another complement of passengers. This time Nebo caught her handler by surprise as he pulled the leash out of her hand and got his front legs up onto the boat, trying to get himself into the front cockpit.

She picked up the leash and said, 'Come here you naughty boy.'

Nebo turned to look at her with his tail wagging at the same time.

The speedboat driver was laughing as he watched the dog's antics. He thought it funny to come across a dog that actually wanted a ride in his boat. He said to his mate, who was standing there, 'Help the dog in Nat.'

Nat grabbed Nebo around his belly and lifted him over the gunwale and into the front cockpit, where he sat beside the driver. 'You'd better come too Hazel.'

With that Hazel got into the front cockpit and sat beside Nebo, who was sitting up and looking out over the front through the windscreen. She put her arm around him. Nebo quickly responded with his own form of affection. His big red sploshy tongue came out and licked her around the face. She turned her head away and said, 'Ahhhhh,' as the back of her hand came up to wipe away the moisture.

The back cockpit had a new bunch of kids. Nat pushed the bow out, the driver hit the starter button and the Holden 179 engine roared into life and propelled the boat towards the centre of the channel.

A pelican that was swimming nearby decided to get the hell out of there and took to the air. Nebo hurried it along with a couple of good barks.

Hazel said, 'Stop it Nebo, that bird's not hurting you.' She patted and stroked his head until he settled down as the speedboat disappeared into the big lake.

Behind the open park area was the King Prawn Bowling Club. The lady bowlers looked fabulous in their all-white uniforms, contrasted to the perfect green lawns. They underarmed their bowls with the grace of Great Britain's historical pirate and champion bowler, Sir Francis Drake. One end of the green began clapping and cheering with a lot of hoorays — an obvious winner no doubt. Some serious guzzling would now follow inside the clubhouse.

Next to the King Prawn Bowling Club was the Surf Life Saving Summer Carnival, and today a matinee was being conducted. Looking at the amount of people roaming around, it was certainly being well received — and that's probably why this area was chosen for a birthday party.

Somebody said, 'They're coming back.'

The mob all moved to the shoreline to watch the arrival of the speedboat. At the back of the crowd, two fox terrier dogs were eyeing each other off; the two of them were almost out of the puppy stage and on their way to their first bit of maturity. Both dogs, a male and a female, had leashes on their collars but they were loose and dragging along the ground.

The male dog was standing there with his chest pulled in and his front legs as straight as a gun barrel, while his wiggling stubby tail was pointing to the heavens, as if it were an antenna waiting for a signal from a satellite deep in outer space.

As he continued studying the female foxy he was thinking to himself, *Hello there, why haven't I seen this bitch before today? There's something different about you, I think I'd like to get to know you a little bit better.*

The female foxy continued to stare back at the male foxy and she was thinking to herself, *Gee, he's a nice type with that black patch around his eye. Mum said to be very careful of dogs that look like this.* They stood there, continuing to eye each other off. Then just like any male at a Saturday night dance, the male foxy with the black patch around his eye strode over to meet his attraction. She stood there while he licked her around the face; at the same time she was thinking, *Gee that's nice, that really feels good.*

Enjoying this new type of affection, she never moved — that is, until the male foxy worked his way around behind her and put his two front legs up on her back in piggyback fashion. Both the dogs were too young for any hanky-panky as nature hadn't turned their switches on yet.

The speedboat motored away for another run to the big lake.

Someone in the crowd called out, 'Hey, look at those dogs.' It was instant laughter at the antics of the two young fox terriers, until one of the partygoers scooped a bucket of cold seawater out of the channel and dumped it on them. The female foxy, surprised by the cold water and all of the sudden attention, took off and headed for the road and the carnival on the other side.

The male foxy was on the move too, but someone grabbed his leash and restrained him before he had time to get into full stride.

A short little plump but pleasant-faced lady came running out of the birthday crowd, chasing after the female foxy and calling out, 'Dolly, Dolly, come on Dolly, come to Mummy.'

Dolly had reached the road at panic speed. A teenage girl riding a bike down the centre of the road saw the runaway dog with the owner in hot pursuit. She dropped her bike quickly and gathered in the leash, stopping Dolly in her tracks.

A car was approaching but the driver figured out what was happening and pulled the car up.

Dolly's mummy came onto the scene huffing and puffing; she knelt down on the road to cuddle her darling Dolly, reassuring her that everything was all right. She thanked the girl on the bike and then led Dolly away back in the direction of the party crowd. The teenage girl picked up her bike and peddled away, while the car that had stopped continued on its way.

Two young policemen walked through the birthday party crowd to the edge of the channel, where they looked up and down. One asked, 'Where's the speedboat?'

Nobody answered, and then one of the senior men said, 'Yes, there was a speedboat here but it's gone now.'

'Oh?' said the young copper. 'Where did it go?'

The gentleman replied, 'I think it went back to the yacht club.'

'Okay, we'll go for a drive and check it out, fast boats are not allowed in the channel.'

Jack watched as the policemen drove away and headed north in the direction of the yacht club, about a twenty minute drive away.

The senior partygoer pulled his mobile phone out and pressed a pre-selected number. 'Plan B, Wally — the police are here looking for you. Take the boat to the southern ramp and I'll meet you there in fifteen minutes.'

He shook his head as he acknowledged the answer before putting his mobile phone away. He was next seen walking under the bridge towards the boat ramp, where his four wheel drive and trailer were parked.

For Jack the excitement was over, but there was plenty going on over at the carnival with heaps of squeals coming from the ghost train and the Hurricane. It was time to head back to the Big Lake Hotel to indulge in a favourite pastime: a nice cold beer in a relaxing atmosphere.

Back in his motel unit, Jack changed out of his damp clothes and had a thirty minute catnap. Now for that beer!

It was 4 pm when he arrived in the main bar and gee whiz, he'd never seen anything quite like it — the place was absolutely crowded. Ten percent were females, all happy to be there with their men, drinking and watching the horse racing on Sky Channel from Royal Randwick.

Some big shouts were heard, followed by, 'You little beauty,' as a groups horse saluted.

The poker machines were all occupied and all the tables were taken. The outside section that catered for smokers was quite large, and still chock-a-block with human beings all talking at once. Their voices resembled the hum of the interior of a bee hive. The dartboards were flat out, and in the lounge there were carpet bowlers along with a two-piece guitar band entertaining those relaxing away from the hustle and bustle of the main bar, where it was six-deep standing room only.

Jack worked his way through the standing drinkers toward the bar. A short fellow, who had just paid for two schooners, picked them up and spun around quickly, taking one step with purpose — and crashed into Jack. Neither was expecting the other and so it wasn't surprising when he dropped one of the beers. He turned back to the bar and placed the beer that was in his hand back on the bar.

Jack said, 'Sorry mate, I'll buy you another one.'

It was as if the scene had happened many times before, because suddenly there was open room around them as all the patrons moved away to give them space. The short guy turned back to face Jack and angrily shouted, 'Why don't you look where you're going, ya fuckin arsehole!'

A voice nearby said, 'Get into him Shorty.'

That was all the encouragement Shorty needed. He charged at Jack with an attempted king-hit on the way. Now, Shorty was as pissed as a parrot, and Jack towered over him, so the punch was easy to evade. At the same time Jack managed to get behind him and get a grip on his shoulders.

Jack said again, 'Look, I'm sorry; I'll buy you another beer.'

Shorty was difficult to negotiate with; he began to kick backwards and throw his head about.

The bouncer who was pouring beer said to the publican, 'I'm going to throw that little bastard down the steps; all he ever does is cause trouble.'

The publican responded, 'Hang on a minute, let's see what this bloke does, he seems to have it under control. Just watch that Shorty's mates don't come and give him a hand.'

'Right.' The bouncer joined the crowd watching Jack man-handle Shorty.

Jack forced him onto the ground and straddled him with a knee in the middle of his back; Shorty's arms were all twisted up behind his back, completely paralysing him, but even then he continued to struggle. One of Shorty's mates came to give him a hand. He came up behind Jack for an ambush, but before he could do anything the bouncer grabbed him by the hair and said, 'Don't even think about it, now get.'

Shorty's mate walked away, rubbing his head.

Jack had Shorty all trussed up and hadn't even hurt him yet. Jack said to him, 'Now I've got all day or what's left of it, so it's up to you. I offered to buy you a fresh drink, that's the decent thing to do — so now we just wait here like this until you accept my offer. I don't care how long it takes.'

The bouncer knelt down to talk to Shorty. 'Come on, short arse, wake up to yourself … you're going to get yourself another beer, what more do you want? This guy could have bashed your head in by now but he hasn't.'

'All right, all right, you win. I'll accept the free beer.'

Jack slowly let him go and stood up, moving out of the way in case he took another swing, but it was out of the question as Shorty was having circulation problems; he had to be helped to his feet.

The publican poured Shorty another beer, which Jack paid for. Then Shorty's mates came and helped him back to his table.

'Thanks for that mate,' said the publican as he handed Jack his beer.

'No worries,' answered Jack as he picked up the beer, took it into the lounge and relaxed in the comfortable chair, listening to the two-piece band.

At 5.00 pm Jack went and had a shower and a shave and

generally freshened himself up a little before going to the restaurant at 5.30. A lone guitarist provided some nice soft background music, entertaining the twenty-odd people as they ate their meals. Before long the waitress brought the Chinese meal over with a bottle of Jack's favourite lager, Crown. On the other side of the room there was a woman having dinner by herself and Jack couldn't help but notice that she was giving him the eye. He acknowledged with a nod and a smile.

With dinner over, Jack went into the main bar looking for a game of darts. Holding a beer in his hand, he stood near the dartboards watching the action and it wasn't long before one of the guys came over and offered him a game, adding, 'You're the guy that had a fight with Shorty this afternoon, aren't you?'

'Yes,' answered Jack. 'But I wouldn't exactly call it a fight; it was more like stopping a fight.'

'Yeah, when Shorty gets pissed he always wants to thump somebody. They tolerate him and his mates because they spend all of their money here. That table over there is *his* table ... he's been sitting there for ten years, and woe to anybody else who sits in it.'

'You know.' said Jack, 'I've never seen such a wholesome place on a Saturday afternoon anywhere.'

'Yeah, she certainly comes alive doesn't it?' answered the dart player.

'It sure does, looking at it now it just doesn't seem like the same place eh?'

At 9 o'clock after wrapping up the game of darts Jack said, 'Ah well, I'll be heading off now, thanks for the game and I'll see you later.'

'All right, you were too good for me tonight,' answered the dart player. Jack walked away in the direction of his unit.

The woman who was in the restaurant actually had the unit

beside his, and as he walked up the hallway he couldn't help but notice, as her door was open, that she was sitting in a two seater lounge watching TV and smoking a cigarette. He passed her doorway, then he heard a voice say, 'Excuse me.' Jack turned to acknowledge her presence. She came to the door, put her hand out and said, 'Hi, I'm Kelly Marsden, I saw you at dinner tonight.'

When Jack heard the name 'Marsden' his mind flashed back to the American professor whom he and Kate visited on their recent trip to New York. 'Yes, I couldn't help but notice you too.' He took her hand and said, 'I'm Jack Kelly. Isn't that funny, your first name and my last name.'

They both laughed. Then she said, 'Look Jack, I was wondering if you'd like to come in for a cup of coffee.'

'Sure,' answered Jack. She led the way with Jack following; when they were both inside she closed the door. Kelly Marsden appeared to be about thirty years old; reasonably tall, she carried a nice figure topped off with short hair and was dressed in modest clothes that complemented her cute face. Jack sat down on the lounge while Kelly made the coffee and put some biscuits on a plate. Kelly asked, 'So Jack, what brings you to this area?'

'Oh, I'm on a hitchhiking holiday along the coast. I'm booked in until Tuesday … if I don't pick up a bit of casual work by then I'll be moving on. What about you?'

'My sister lives at Shellharbour and is getting married in three weeks, so I thought I'd come a little early to have a look around this beautiful area.'

Jack asked, 'Where do you come from?'

'Newcastle.'

'You're a long way from home.'

They chatted for an hour on life in general then Jack closed the evening down by saying, 'Well Kelly, it's been nice to meet you, maybe I'll see you at dinner tomorrow night.' He stood up to go.

Kelly took him by the hand. 'You don't have to go, you know … you can stay the night.'

Jack replied, 'Kelly, I'm happily married but I want you to know that I appreciate the offer.' He said goodnight and went to his own unit.

Jack lay down on top of his bed with only his boxer shorts on. The small wall fan was blowing just the perfect amount of air across his near-naked body to provide some relief from the coastal humidity. As he lay there in the dark just prior to sleep, his thoughts were with his one-time girlfriend Chantal, and for the first time he was beginning to feel a bit anxious and nervous about their meeting tomorrow. *Oh well, I'll worry about that at 10 o'clock in the morning.* That was the last thing he remembered thinking before falling asleep.

As the big deep breaths of sleep got into a nice rhythm, the cinema of his brain was about to screen a replay of a time when he was living with Chantal over twelve years ago.

The projectors started whirling; the dream had begun.

SIX

Chantal

Jack found himself on a building site at Sydney's Rushcutters Bay, where a new house was under construction. Jack was a young builder working for his father, who owned the company. He had a couple of roof beams to nail in place, then it would be lunch time.

The team of six sat down on the grass and leaned against the site shed. They were no different to any other bunch of guys having lunch together. There was a bit of debating, a bit of arguing, some food swapping and of course some sleeping. They were all compatible young men who enjoyed each other's company, both on and off the job.

Bazza, one of the carpenters, asked Jack, 'What are we doing Friday night?'

Jack replied, 'Ah, I've got a special night this Friday so you'll have to go without me.'

'Geez,' answered Bazza, 'it must be a pretty special occasion for you not to be coming.'

Terry butted in. 'So what's this function Jack, or is it a secret?'

'No, it's a special occasion for Chantal and myself. We've been going out for three years and living together for the last eighteen months, so I've organised dinner at the Rocks Restaurant… and I'm going to give her an engagement ring, she doesn't know about the ring yet.'

Mike the brickie, who was in a full stretched sleep but obviously had his ears open, propped himself up onto one elbow and said, 'Don't do it this Friday. Here, take my mobile phone, ring up and cancel it.'

Jack replied, a little bit puzzled, 'What the bloody hell's wrong with you?'

'This Friday is Friday the 13th, a real sign of bad luck if ever I've seen it.'

'Don't be stupid! I don't believe in hocus pocus, star signs, black cats or that crap about walking under ladders.'

Mike came back. 'Okay Jack, have it your own way ... I'm not a church-going man, but I'm going to pray that everything goes well for you.'

'What could possibly go wrong?' answered Jack. 'For years now all of us have been hanging out together doing everything that people our age do, and there's never been any real problems. I can't see what you're on about.'

'But now you're about to break that cycle, and you don't do that on Friday the 13th.'

Jack answered with a bit of laughter. 'I'll bet you take a bucket of tea leaves with you when you go and visit Madame Fifi to have your palms read at the Royal Easter Show.'

'Have it you own way, but don't say I didn't warn you,' answered Mike. He lay back down, re-closed his eyes and continued to soak up the sun for the rest of lunchtime.

Thursday's lunch break was similar to Wednesdays. The topics changed, the disagreements came and went and at times they were all talking at once, trying to get their points across. As was usual, when brickie Mike finished his Big Mac and French fries (washed down with a bottle of Coca-Cola) he would place himself horizontal with his rolled up shirt as a pillow. Under the heat of the midday sun, he would gently close his eyes and go to sleep, snoring loudly.

Jack remarked, 'I'll bet that bastard could go to sleep on a barbed wire fence in the middle of a snowstorm, eh? What do you reckon, fellas?'

Louie replied, 'There's no doubt about that Jack.' They all had a good laugh at Mike the brickie's expense. One of the other bricklayers, a guy called Rick, decided that this was a good opportunity to have a bit of fun. He gently untied Mike's shoelaces without alerting him, then he tied both shoes together.

A bird was seen hovering near a pallet of bricks. The electrician asked, 'What's that bird up to?'

Terry the apprentice plumber had the answer. 'There's a spider there somewhere.'

And with that Terry was on his feet and walking towards the pallet of bricks, rolling up the newspaper that he'd been reading. The bird flew off as Terry walked around the side of the pallet, and there it was: a rather large huntsman. He gave it one hit with the newspaper and it fell to the ground stunned. Terry picked it up by one of its eight legs and took it to where Mike was comfortably sleeping, placing it on his chest. Now anybody could see what was going to happen here.

'Oh no,' exclaimed Jack.

Terry grabbed an empty drum and a piece of timber, and then gave it one big hit close to Mike's head. Mike's eyes opened instantly, and straight away spotted the spider with its wiggling legs as it began to recover from being hit with the newspaper. In panic mode Mike sat up and brushed the spider off his chest with the back of his hand, screaming, 'Oooohhh I hate them things!' He instinctively stood but he couldn't spread his feet and it looked as though he was in for a heavy stumble, but before he hit the ground Jack had hold of him.

Everybody was laughing their heads off, except Mike. He was no stranger to horseplay, and he was usually the one who handed it out; that's probably why Jack let it go on for as long as it did. Mike looked around and spotted the apprentice plumber with the drum and piece of wood in his hand, still laughing quite hysterically. *Ahh there's the culprit, I'll fix him up real good shortly.*

Jack sat Mike down against the site shed and untied his shoelaces to give him back his freedom.

Louie yelled out, 'Hey, that spider's still alive.'

The spider was scurrying across the ground in the direction of the bricks.

'I'll get it,' said Louie as he picked up a brick and took aim, but all of a sudden the bird that had been eyeing off the spider swooped down, picked it up and carried it away.

'Bloody hell,' said Louie. 'That bird beat me to it.'

All eyes were watching the episode with the spider except for Mike, who seized the opportunity to extract some revenge. He picked up a drum of water that was used to wash and clean the trowels and tipped it all over the young apprentice plumber. Soaking wet with mortar and cement running through his hair and down his face, Terry the apprentice plumber turned and yelled at Mike, 'You dirty bastard.'

Now it was Mike's turn to laugh.

Building site war was declared and for the next two minutes, chaos reigned. It was simple hard fun, throwing buckets of water and handfuls of mortar, but nobody could beat the accuracy of Mike the brickie when it came to throwing mortar off his trowel. He certainly was the Deadeye Dick of that competition and he rarely missed a human target with his sploshy mix. It all ended with everybody laughing like a bunch of schoolkids.

Lunch was over; the building site returned to normal. Jack continued working on nailing the roof battens while working on top of a ladder that was leaning on the facia board. He noticed Mike pointing his trowel toward the bottom of the ladder.

Thinking something was wrong, he looked down. A black cat was grooming itself between the wall and the ladder. Jack looked at Mike, who was standing on his scaffold with a big smile on his face, obviously expecting some sort of an answer.

'So what?' said Jack. 'That cat roams around here all the time.'

Mike carried on laying bricks while shaking his head from side to side. Jack came down from the ladder and slowly but surely befriended the cat. The cat responded and trusted him. Gently he put his hands around the cat, then he picked it up and stroked its head before looking it in the eye. 'You're not going to hurt me are you?'

The cat started purring. He placed the cat back from where he picked it up, and continued working on the roof battens.

Thursday night was a standard night out for Chantal and Jack: they would meet Jack's mum and dad at the Cruising Yacht Club for dinner, and then they would participate in club activities. Midway through the evening the club would hand out plates of cheese, salted crackers and little frankfurters, so Jack pigged out on his own and anybody else's that he could get his hands on — he just loved the things. They finished the night in the cappuccino lounge and left the club at 10 pm to go to their respective homes.

That night Jack had a restless sleep. The frankfurters at the Cruising Yacht Club had a habit of disagreeing with him, but never as bad as this. Constant belching, belching and heartburn had him vowing to never to eat the darn things again.

Arriving at work the next morning, Jack was noticeably under sufferance as he worked on the roof timbers. Chantal rang up at 11 o'clock to find out how he was. They talked for five minutes and he assured her he was fine, but he was lying — he was as sick as a dog.

At lunchtime Jack sat down with his gang of building mates. One of the apprentices returned from the fast food shop and began handing out their orders. He threw Jack a hamburger, which he unwrapped and began to eat. Halfway through the hamburger Jack began to heave; everything was coming up. He ran to the back of the site shed and vomited up everything that was in his stomach and more. He was down on his hands and knees when his leading hand Bruce came around. 'You okay mate?' he asked.

Jack replied, 'Ahh, I don't think I'll die today, probably tomorrow. Listen Bruce, I'm going home for the afternoon so you take over, okay?'

'Yeah sure,' answered Bruce. 'But we're going to need that hardware straight away.'

'Oh shit! I forgot about that … look, you drive me home and keep the ute, then go and pick that stuff up. It's all organised, the order's on the board in the ute.'

'Yeah sure.' answered Bruce, who then drove Jack home to a terrace house situated just behind the Rocks area. The historic dwelling was owned by the Kelly family as part of their business assets. There was no front yard, hardly any backyard and no off-street parking, but it was worth a lot of money. The main bedroom was where Jack and Chantal slept. A second bedroom was turned into an office storeroom, with a single bed in it. The third bedroom was a spare, and it was used when they had visitors that came to stay. For no apparent reason Jack opened the door to the office, entered, then closed the door and lay down on the single bed, going to sleep almost straight away.

Some time had passed — maybe half an hour or a couple of hours, who knows — but Jack's subconscious was picking up a female voice, then a male voice, then laughter, then nothing — then the female's voice talking and laughing. Jack's mind was receiving a signal that this was a familiar voice.

He opened his lifeless eyelids and listened — nothing. The eyelids gently closed again, his imagination obviously working overtime. Then more laughter, male and female, quite loud this time. His eyes opened. This time he was alert. That voice was Chantal's.

Jack picked up his thoughts and his bearings, looked at his watch — it was 1.15 pm. He'd been asleep for one hour. He stood up and opened the door. The talking and laughter was coming from the spare bedroom. The door was shut. Jack looked in the main bedroom; it was as it always was. *Maybe there's a simple explanation here*, he thought, despite imaginary alarm bells ringing.

Chantal's shoulder bag was on the dining room table. Jack quietly moved to the front of the house, pulled the curtains aside and looked out. The car that was parked out the front belonged to Chantal's boss, Ross Peace. He owned the 'fashionable' hairdressing 'salon' in George Street where Chantal was an apprentice hairdresser. Jack's heartbeat was about to hit top speed as controlled rage started to creep in.

He turned and walked towards the closed bedroom door, while at the same time a little voice inside his head was giving free advice. 'Go on Jack, get in there and bash him to death.'

He'd reached the door and stood there; they were still laughing and talking. He knocked on the door and opened it at the same time, saying, 'Do you mind if I join you?' Ross was lying on top of her, kissing her around the neck. They were still in their underwear. Act three hadn't started yet, but curtain rise wasn't far away.

Shocked by the sudden intrusion, Ross rolled onto the spare piece of bed beside Chantal, who was instantly screaming. Jack grabbed Ross by the foot, screwed it one hundred and eighty degrees and dragged him over the end of the bed where he landed on the floor. Jack seized him by his long perfumed movie-style haircut and pulled him to his feet, where he got behind him and forced one of his arms up behind his back in a hammer lock. With one arm up behind his back and a good grip on that hair, Jack frogmarched him out of the bedroom and towards the front door.

Everything happened so quickly that hairdresser Ross never really got his bearings, so he was at a complete disadvantage when it came to defending himself, but as the front door was coming up he started to put up a struggle. It was all in vain, because Jack rammed him into the door face first and let him go. Ross fell to the ground in a screaming heap. Jack showed him no mercy as he dragged him out of the way to open the door, then he man-handled Ross outside and dragged him down the steps by his feet, leaving him on the footpath lying in his underpants.

Jack went back inside to the spare bedroom where Chantal was in severe distress, lying on the bed in the foetal position. He picked up Ross's belongings: a beautiful white shirt, maroon vest, top class tailor-made coat, pleated trousers and the finest pair of shoes you could ever find. The car keys were in the trouser pocket. Jack took all the articles out to Ross's car, threw every-thing inside and put the keys in the ignition.

Opposite Jack's place, Mr and Mrs Smith, who were in their eighties, had just stepped outside to have a cup of coffee on their front patio. They saw Jack throw the clothes into Ross's car. They looked at each other, then looked back to see what Jack was doing.

Jack still had his steel capped work boots on and as he walked around the car, he kicked all the door panels in on this 300 000 dollar BMW. He opened the driver's side door, and then walked back to the wounded Ross Peace, who was half sitting up. Jack stood over him; the hairdresser's nose was bleeding and there was skin off him all over his body.

From the ground Ross looked up and said, 'I'll be calling the police you know.'

Jack bent over, took a big grip of that hair again and pulled his head back as far as it would go. 'You started this, you *arsehole*, so if you go to the police I will hunt you down like the snake that you are. I will find you and turn you into a paraplegic so you can wheel yourself around in a chair the rest of your life, then you won't be cheating on your beautiful wife any more, you great big bag of smelly cow shit.' Jack raised his voice. 'Do you understand?'

He dragged Ross to his feet by the hair and was going to throw him over the bonnet of the BMW. Ross, fearful of losing great tufts of hair out of his scalp or having his teeth smashed on the bonnet, began screaming, 'Yes, yes, okay, okay.'

Jack manhandled him around to the open car door and viciously shoved him inside head first. He landed face down across the two front seats with his legs still outside the car. Then Jack walked away.

Mr Smith called out from across the road. 'Everything all right Jack?'

'Everything's fine Smithy, my guest is just leaving.'

'Ahh … okay Jack.'

Jack disappeared into the house.

Mr Smith said to his wife, 'You wouldn't want to get on the wrong side of that bloke, eh?'

'No,' said his wife. They laughed as Ross began getting dressed in the street.

Inside, Jack could hear Chantal crying inside the spare bedroom. He went to the kitchen and filled up a saucepan with cold water, taking it into the bedroom. 'Shut up!' he yelled to Chantal. 'We'll talk tomorrow.' And he threw the cold water all over her.

Back inside the Big Lake Hotel, as the cold water from the saucepan hit Chantal, Jack was instantly awake and sat up in the darkened motel room. His heart was pounding along with fast and deep breathing. He realised it was a nightmare.

He thought to himself, *Thank heavens for that. Boy, that was too real … but that's exactly how it was.* Jack's brain was sending him a message: *You don't need to go anywhere near that Chantal tomorrow.*

He lay back down and attempted to go back to sleep, but it wasn't going to happen. After tossing and turning he'd had enough. He put his jeans back on and then knocked on the door of Kelly's motel room. She answered the door and upon seeing Jack was quick to say, 'I was hoping you might come back.' Her face was a loving big smile.

Jack answered, 'Sorry to bother you, but I wonder if I could bludge a cigarette off you. I've been asleep but a very bad nightmare woke me up.'

'Gee it must have been real, your face has a look of fear all over it and you're covered in perspiration. Come in and I'll have one with you.'

Jack sat down. Kelly offered Jack the cigarette, which he took and placed in his mouth while Kelly had the flame of a gas lighter under it. Jack took a big inhalation of air that piped its way through the tobacco. The end of the cigarette glowed red like the fire in an old steam train; he removed the cigarette and exhaled in slow motion, then remarked, 'Ahhhh, beautiful.'

Before long the two of them were inhaling and exhaling, filling the room with smoke in a short space of time.

Kelly said, 'I didn't think you smoked.'

'I've probably had two dozen in my whole life, but when I toss and turn and can't get back to sleep, the only way it will happen is if I have a cigarette.'

'That's funny isn't it?' Kelly said, and then she laughed.

She went and got a towel and wiped the perspiration off him — and at the same time she had a good feisty look at those nice shoulders and muscular upper body. It was just what her lusty eyes were looking for. She sprayed Jack with a bit of perfume saying, 'Now that's better isn't it?'

Kelly then sat down beside Jack. It was approaching midnight, and there was something on the TV that interested Jack. It was an old cowboy movie and it was halfway through. The character in the movie was played by iconic actor Glenn Ford, who looked fantastic on a horse with two six guns strapped to his waist and tied down at the thighs.

In the scene he was surrounded by five evil gunfighters, and against all the odds he said to them, 'Don't force me to fight, because you won't like my way of fighting.'

Jack jumped off the lounge and with his back to the TV repeated those words with his imaginary guns at the ready while looking Kelly in the eye from two meters away. 'Don't force me to fight because you won't like my way of fighting.' He drew those imaginary guns. 'Bang bang!'

By now Kelly was hysterical with laughter. Jack blew the smoke off the end of those imaginary barrels, and then he put those imaginary guns back into the imaginary holsters, and sat back down beside Kelly. There certainly was a bit of chemistry between them. Kelly's eyes were sparkling like diamonds as she threw her arms around Jack's neck, poked her tongue in his ear and whispered, 'You can stay the night, you know.'

She had that skimpy night attire on with plenty of exposed flesh, and that made it harder for Jack to say no — but there was no way he could agree to her request. But how in hell could he tell her without upsetting her? He'd give it a go anyway.

'Kelly, we've known each other only a short time ... I'm talking just a couple of hours, really ... and in normal times I'd say we wouldn't be sitting here holding hands like we are now, would we? I can tell that you'd be a lot of fun to be with and I'm sure you could be sincere in a relationship. You know, I've been married for eight years to the most wonderful female that God ever placed on the earth. All I can offer you tonight is to hold your hand until this movie is over, but I'm not rejecting you … I'm just doing the right thing by my wife and the rest of my immediate family. To quote an old saying, lots of people rush in where the angels fear to tread, and the consequences can destroy lives and spread hate all over the place. Now, are we still friends?'

'Of course,' she replied. 'It's not every day I get the offer to watch a cowboy movie in the middle of the night.' They both had a good laugh together, while still holding hands.

The old western movie came to an end, and as is usual, good will always defeat evil. Jack pecked Kelly on the cheek then said goodnight.

He returned to his room and continued on with his sleep. That saucepan of cold water that he threw on Chantal was still fresh on his mind. The command centre of his brain wouldn't let it go. The projectors were turned back on — the dream continued.

As he walked out of the spare bedroom, he slammed the door in the process.

He took a cold beer out of the fridge, sat on the lounge and tried to relax, but he couldn't. He had to get out of there, but he would drink this beer first.

Outside the terrace house he thought, as he walked down the front steps and onto the footpath, *I'm glad that hairdressing scumbag and his car are gone, otherwise I might have gone over and smashed all the windows.*

The Sydney Harbour Bridge was a fifteen minute walk away. He reached the massive sandstone blocks of the main southern pylon, which had a lift and a set of stairs. He decided to take the stairs to the eastern side walkway, then continued walking north until he reached the centre of the bridge and leaned on the rail, looking into the water below. Jack rang his leading hand Bruce and they arranged a time to hand over the ute, then he rang his Dad.

'Hi Dad.'

'G'day Jack, how are you feeling?'

'Better now that the frankfurters are gone but I've got ... I mean, I've had a bigger problem.'

'Oh yeah?' said Jimmy. 'The building's going all right isn't it?'

'Sure, nothing wrong there but, there was a problem when I got home.'

Jack filled his dad in on what happened.

'Oh gee Jack, I'm sorry. Both your mother and I love that lady, you can never tell, can you? What are you going to do?'

'I'm going to tell her to vacate the place when she finds somewhere else to live. I might come home for a while, even if I have to live on the boat.'

'Yeah sure.'

'There's something else, Dad. I might do that uni course, Bachelor of Building and Business.'

'You little beauty, I've been wanting you to do that for a while now.'

'Yeah I know, so now's the time, right? I'll see you over the weekend. Bye Dad.'

'Bye Jack.'

Oblivious to the peak hour traffic, trains and pedestrians, Jack continued to take in all the harbour's glory and beauty. Pleasure craft were in abundance; some were parked, and others were under power. The harbour ferries were busy moving the city's population at the end of the workday. The Luna Park speedboat was operating and did a beautiful wavy turn right in front of Jack, then disappeared under the bridge as it headed back to base wharf for another batch of thrill seekers. In the distance seven or eight sailing boats could be seen practising for the weekend's competition; further afield the Rose Bay seaplane was about to lift out of the water. A Qantas 747 passed overhead on its way to the International Airport, while beneath the bridge the western RiverCat with one hundred passengers on board was heading to unload at Circular Quay, near the Opera House.

The low western sun cast a shadow of the bridge on the water. The moving shadows of the bridge climbers could be seen quite clearly as they made their way over the top of the arch. The atmosphere had a soothing effect on Jack as the tension, hate and aggression, fuelled by today's events, began to filter out of his body. A major chapter in his life was about to end, but surely another was about to begin. He stayed on the bridge looking into the water until it turned dark, and then he made his way back to the terrace house.

The lounge room was the place for Jack; he would stay the night in front of the television with a few bottles of beer for company while Chantal uncomfortably stayed where she was, in the spare bedroom.

In the morning Jack made his usual strong cup of coffee and took it outside onto the front patio, sitting down on one of the chairs and looking into space. The approaching footsteps were Chantal's; she stepped onto the patio and asked, 'Can I sit with you for a while?'

'Sure, go make a cup of coffee and come back.'

When she returned she said, 'Jack, I suppose I owe you an apology. Look, I'm sorry for what's happened.'

Jack replied. 'An apology's not necessary ... it can't change anything. If I hadn't have come home early I wouldn't have known, would I? After three years together things were beginning to look a bit permanent, and I can honestly say that they've been the best years of my life so far ... but you know yourself, all it takes is something like this to bring all those years to an end.'

He placed his arm around her and they continued talking.

'Jack, I can't believe I've been so stupid, you mean everything to me, so why would I do such a thing?'

'You know it's part of human makeup. An opportunity comes up for a quick thrill and some people take it knowing only too well they shouldn't. The only one you can hurt is the one you love.'

'In your job you get around here there and everywhere, you go out with your mates a couple of nights a week, so you can't tell me that you've never cheated on me. I see the way women look at you; I was one of them three years ago.'

'You know what? I can tell you exactly that. I've never cheated on you; I'm strictly a one-woman man.'

Chantal squeezed Jack's hand and asked, 'So where do we go from here?'

'Next weekend I'm moving out. You can stay here until you find yourself somewhere else to live, there's no hurry. I'm going home to live with Mum and Dad for a while, but I want you to promise me something.'

'What's that?'

'Promise me you'll finish your hairdressing apprenticeship. You're going to need this for your own independence and financial viability.'

She thought about it for a while and said, 'Yes.' Then she stood up and walked away, sobbing uncontrollably.

During the afternoon Bruce showed up with the work truck so Jack drove him home via the Cruising Yacht Club to have a beer.

'How'd it go last night?' Bruce asked with a smile on his face.

'Oh, it turned out to be a bit of a fizzer. I took Mike's advice and cancelled out. Lunch time Monday I'll tell you all about it, and don't laugh.'

'Sorry to hear it,' replied Bruce. 'You know Jack, you're looking a bit rough around the edges today. I've never seen you without a fresh shave and all spruced up, even when you've got your work gear on.'

'You're right, I drank myself to sleep last night and I haven't even had a wash today.'

They were interrupted by the commodore of the club. 'Hi fellas. One of the guys in the eighteen footers needs a crewman for tomorrow's racing, anybody interested?'

'Yes,' replied Jack. 'Me. Which one is it?'

'That skinny guy with the cap on that says Sydney Harbour.'

'I'll go and see him,' answered Jack as he walked away and over to where the skinny guy was. He interrupted him while he was talking to two other fellows. 'I hear you're looking for a crewman tomorrow.'

The skinny guy turned and looked at Jack and said, 'Yeah, you signing on?'

'Yes.'

'All right, see you in the morning at 8 am. Oh, by the way, my name's John Steed.'

'Jack Kelly.'

They shook hands, with John Steed saying, 'Nice to meet you Jack, see you in the morning.'

After that he continued talking to his friends. That was the beginning of a friendship that would last and last. They would spend premium time sailing, fishing and boozing, but the ultimate bonding experience would be the classic yacht race, the Sydney to Hobart, where they would serve as part of the crew on the million dollar yachts every Boxing Day.

When Jack arrived back at the terrace house, his mum and dad were walking up the front steps; they'd come to see Chantal. Dad gave Chantal a hug then Mum did the same, then Mum said, 'You pair go and sit on the porch; I want to talk to Chantal by myself.'

They did, and after a while Lucy was crying when she came out; it was as if she was losing the daughter she never had. Lucy and Jimmy drove off in the direction of their place on the other side of the harbour.

Jack made a fresh cup of coffee, returned to the front porch and continued to stare into space.

The dream expired as memory lane came to an end in the Big Lake Hotel. It was 8 am when Jack woke up. After having a shower he decided not to wear the big brim hat or the long cattle coat. A blue shirt and jeans with a black baseball cap would do.

He made himself a nice strong cup of coffee and two slices of well buttered toast. *Ahhh, beautiful,* he thought as he sipped the coffee in a relaxing position on the lounge with his feet up on a stool. At 9.45 he was beginning to feel a bit anxious as he took a big breath and walked out onto the street, beginning the walk to Chantal's house about ten minutes away.

The direction was the same as yesterdays, but instead of going onto the bridge he would take the fork in the road and follow it down until it reached the water. The road turned left and now he was walking beside the channel. This wasn't Sydney Harbour but there was a lot to like about it. Nothing had changed overnight with plenty of boats and bank fishing going on; birds were still in abundance in the same areas, while the boat ramp was even busier than it was yesterday.

Chantal's house, 10 Channel Drive, was coming up on the next corner; there was one car parked out the front. Jack walked through the front gate, up the path to a set of steps, onto a patio and walked the four paces to the front door. He pushed the little button beside a tag that said 'Welcome'. He could hear

Corinthian bells sounding in the interior of the house. Jack's heart was pounding as the door opened up — and there she was.

'Hi Jack, come in.' She stepped aside and Jack walked in.

At exactly that same time a souped up purple utility with chrome carry bars attached was driving by. The occupant of the vehicle, a male, had a good look and noticed a tall man going through the door, then the door closing. *She didn't tell me she was having visitors today, especially a male one*, he thought. This gentleman was Chantal's boyfriend, and a guy who was more than extremely jealous. As he looked for somewhere to turn around, his blood began to boil.

Back inside the townhouse Jack and Chantal had a nice hug, then she invited him to sit down at the dining table. Chantal turned on the jug and asked. 'Coffee?'

'Absolutely,' replied Jack. 'I can't believe so many years have gone by since we last saw each other.'

'No, neither can I. You're looking pretty good Jack, but then again you always looked good.'

'Yeah, you too mate, you haven't changed a bit.'

Chantal placed a plate of cakes and biscuits on the table along with two mugs of coffee, she then sat down opposite Jack. 'So what brings you down this way?' she asked. 'I never thought you could ever drag yourself away from your precious Sydney Harbour.'

'Believe it or not, I'm having a hitchhiking holiday of sorts.'

'I know you,' responded Chantal. 'You don't go on holidays by yourself — you go with your woman. So what are you really up to? Look don't get me wrong, I'm so glad you're here just to have a talk and a cup of coffee with me again.'

Out in the driveway, Chantal's boyfriend got out of his super ute and was about to put his key in the front door. A little alarm went *beep, beep, beep*.

Chantal said, 'There's somebody coming.'

The front door opened and in walked the boyfriend. He left the door open and walked into the dining room. Chantal said, 'Hi Bozz, I didn't think you were coming until late this afternoon.'

Bozz answered in a sarcastic voice. 'Well it's a good thing I did come, isn't it? You didn't tell me you were entertaining this morning.'

Chantal answered in a nice voice. 'I don't know what you're inferring, but as you're here, go and close the door and come and have a cup of coffee, the cakes are beautiful.'

'The door stays open until this creep leaves.'

'Don't be silly Bozz, this is an old friend of mine and we're having a cup of coffee and a bit of a chat. Besides that, you don't tell me who I can or can't see in my own house.'

Jack's brain was checking Bozz out. Fairly tall, nice and solid, nice face, short cropped hair, nicely dressed with a bit of fat around the belly. He certainly wouldn't go the full ten rounds, was Jack's assessment.

Chantal raised her voice up a notch. 'Go and close the door.'

'No,' was Bozz's answer.

Jack had a gutful of this bloke. He stood up and said, 'I'll close the door for you mate.' Then he walked past Bozz towards the front door.

Bozz followed hot on his heels. He grabbed Jack from behind and said, 'Now keep going and don't come back.'

Jack was ready for something, but he didn't know what. Bozz had a tight grip on his arms between the shoulders and the elbows, pulling them towards the centre of his back, and the open doorway was looming.

'All right, all right, I'll go,' said Jack.

'Too right you're going, head first,' answered Bozz. At that instant, Jack swung his head back in a reverse head butt and collected Bozz's forehead and nose area. So surprised was Bozz that he weakened his grip on Jack slightly, only to receive a second reverse head butt. That did it. Bozz weakened at the knees as his grip became undone. Jack spun around and punched him in the stomach. Bozz was instantly gasping as he bent over before sitting on the floor, waiting for his breath to come back. Jack closed the door and sat back down at the table opposite Chantal, who had more than a concerned look on her face.

Jack said, 'Geez, a man can't have a cup of coffee these days without getting into trouble. Look, I'm sorry for what just happened and it's not my intention to hurt your boyfriend, so I think I'd better go.' He stood up to leave.

Chantal said. 'You sit back down, you're not going anywhere. Lately he's been looking for that. He's that jealous of anybody who even looks at me I'm considering dumping him. You take away the jealous streak and you're left with one beautiful person, but he didn't even want to know who you were. You could have been my brother or my cousin or my medical practitioner — now that's not normal, is it?'

'No it's not,' replied Jack. 'That would be the worst case of jealously that I've ever seen ... yes, he certainly needs a bit of help all right.'

Chantal said, 'The other night at the King Prawn Club there was a young fellow on the other side of the table minding his own business, but his crime was he had a couple of sustained looks at me. Bozz lent over the table, grabbed him by the throat and said, "Stick your eyes back in your head or I'll punch them back in." That young fellow got up and left, but when we went to go home he was outside with three friends waiting for us. The club security kept them away until we drove out of the car park. You know, anything could have happened. This is a beautiful community and I want to lead a peaceful existence.'

Bozz was back on his feet; Chantal went out to talk to him. 'Bozz, come and meet Jack and have a cup of coffee, please.'

She took him by the arm in a gracious manner; he sharply pulled away as if she had the black plague. 'Like hell! I'm going and I won't be back, so there.' He disappeared out the front door, slamming it behind him.

As Bozz walked down the front steps he was full of hate and revenge. 'Harrr, the creep's car.' His unrealistic mind had taken over as he walked up to the passenger side door of a car parked on the street and kicked the door panel in.

Chantal, upon hearing the loud bang, raced to the front window to see what was happening, and then she sang out to Jack, 'Is that your car out there?'

'No,' answered Jack. He joined her just as Bozz lined up the driver's side door with his boot and kicked that in too.

Across the road on the lake channel bank, a fisherman and his two adult sons were cleaning their catch of fish. 'Hey Dad,' said one of the sons, 'Look what that bloke's doing to your car! Come on Rod, let's get him.'

The two ran across the road and attacked poor old Bozz from behind; he didn't know what hit him. They soon had him down on the road, lying on his stomach with his arms twisted up behind his back.

A car stopped as the struggle finished up in the centre of the road. The driver was seen talking on his mobile phone, possibly ringing the police; he stayed in the car. The fisherman couldn't leave the fish on the bank as he was surrounded by some five pelicans and a small flock of seagulls eager to help themselves to a free feed — but as soon as the fish were secured in a lidded box, he grabbed a rope that still had an anchor attached on one end. While his two sons continued to hold Bozz down, he tied Bozz's legs together, then they dragged him onto the footpath so the traffic could flow again.

The local busybody, Mrs Hobbs, was walking by at the height of the trouble with her redheaded ten year old son asking, 'Mum, what are all these people doing?'

She answered, 'I don't know, there's always something happening at this house, nothing would surprise me. Come on, come on, mind your own business.'

The son said in reply, 'You mean like you do, Mum.'

'Don't give me any cheek Sonny Jim or I'll pull your ear.' With that she grabbed his ear and twisted it, inflicting a bit of soft pain. He screamed blue murder and bunged on a bit of a sob.

One of the men in the growing crowd called out to Mrs Hobbs, 'I'll come over there and pull your ear and see how you like it, you little fat mother from hell.'

She quickly let him go; her little legs soon hit top gear as all of a sudden she was on a mission to get away from there as soon as possible.

Chantal and Jack watched from the townhouse window as the police paddy wagon pulled up and started interviewing people. Chantal said, 'I feel as though I should be out there trying to help him, but what could I do?'

Jack replied, 'At the moment you can't do anything. They'll take him to the station and frighten him into paying for the damages; if he refuses they'll charge him with malicious damage. In a few days' time when he settles down, then you might be able to help him.'

Bozz was placed in the paddy wagon and taken away; the fisherman and his two sons were happy with the result and so they returned to finish scaling and cleaning their catch of fish. The pelicans that had patiently waited during the fracas were now getting excited, knowing that the fish scraps would be coming their way.

Chantal had lunch organised. A van pulled up and delivered

a charcoal chicken, plus all the things that go with it. A couple of Crown Lagers went Jack's way while Chantal enjoyed some cold sparkling. They shared a lot of precious memories, but never touched on the events of that Friday the 13th.

'Jack, Wednesday night there's some entertainment on at the King Prawn Club. Maybe we could go there for dinner and have a dance? Later on in the night we could walk through the carnival and stick a ball in the clown's mouth, maybe win a useless prize.'

They laughed at the thought of that. Jack responded, 'All right, if I'm still here, I'll call you Tuesday night to let you know.'

'I'll wait to hear from you.'

With that Jack departed 10 Channel Drive, and walked back to the Big Lake Hotel. On arriving back at the hotel Jack went into the main bar and ordered a schooner of beer. The publican brewed a nice head on it and handed it over. Jack took a sip as the publican asked, 'Where you from mate?'

'Sydney,' answered Jack.

'How long will you be hanging around here?'

'I'm booked in until Tuesday. I'll be leaving Wednesday unless I can pick up a bit of casual work, then I'll probably stay a month or two.'

The publican responded, 'The reason I ask is, I liked the way you handled yourself yesterday afternoon. I mean, you handled that situation like a real professional. Most bouncers would have flogged that bloke but you didn't, and you got a peaceful resolution. You know we're always concerned about litigation, it can cost us a lot of money. What do you normally do for a living?'

'I'm a builder,' answered Jack.

The publican looked surprised. 'What? You mean you're a licensed builder able to do extensions, or build houses or a garage?'

'Yes, no job over fifty million.'

The publican laughed but he noticed Jack wasn't laughing. 'Okay, I could use a bloke like you as a bouncer on Fridays, Saturdays and Sundays. If you have a building license I can give you that two months' work you want, providing the price is right, but I need to see your license.'

Jack pulled out his wallet and handed over the credit card sized license and a business card.

'Wow,' said the publican. 'Can you come and see me in the morning?'

And with that, Jack picked up his beer and headed off towards the dartboards with the thought of getting a game before dinner. Over in the corner, half a dozen men who were obviously Big Lake sponsored footballers were wrestling with a large banner. The banner was about eight metres long and one metre wide. Working off ladders, the banner was being attached to the exposed steel trusses that supported the ceiling. On the white background, the big letters read:

Summer Grudge Match
Shellharbour V Shoalhaven River
Cossie Oval. 10 am Sunday 25th February

Jack thought, *Cripes! Summer grudge match ... sounds interesting.*

There were six dartboards, with only three being used. The guy that Jack had a game with last night came over and invited him for a contest. After a while, in between sipping beers and throwing darts, Jack asked, 'What's this grudge match?'

Dart player Ernie said, 'Obviously you don't live around here or otherwise you wouldn't be asking that question. Where do you come from?'

'Sydney.'

'What are you doing down here?'

'I'm doing a job for the publican, probably take a couple of months.'

'Oh,' said Ernie. 'The Summer Grudge Match is a game of rugby league between two teams that've been brawling with each other for forty years. A team from the Shoalhaven River, which comprises Indigenous players, and a team from Shellharbour Rugby League Club. It's a battle of the fittest and sometimes rules don't apply. This is Shellharbour's biggest day. Business gets right behind it. There'll be forty thousand people down there on the day. Bands, beauty competitions, marching girls and more, all in a carnival atmosphere. You can even bet on it. We've got four guys in the team so far, and because it's a hard game, it's tough to get players for as it's usually pretty hot.'

Ernie threw a double six, finishing the game with 301; Jack had lost.

'Thanks mate,' said Jack. 'I'll catch you later.'

At 6 o'clock Jack went to the restaurant and ordered dinner. Kelly joined him, where they shared some wholesome conversation and good food. A three-piece band was playing all the old favourites, so Jack and Kelly joined the other six couples on the dance floor and enjoyed themselves immensely.

They went back to Kelly's unit where she made coffee and they watched a DVD of *Spiderman*. When it ended Jack said goodnight and returned to his unit. This time she didn't ask him to stay. Jack rang Kate to let her know where he was and gave her a report on the things that have happened so far. An hour later he rang Bill and filled him in.

Down at the office the publican and his wife were working late. They had a look at the GD Constructions website and they both agreed it was super impressive, and they wondered why this Jack B Kelly fellow was interested in doing a small job for them; they put it down to marital problems.

In the morning Jack went to the office, where the publican was waiting for him.

'Hi Jack, I'm Harry Bush.' They shook hands then got down to business. Two hours later they'd agreed on a working relationship for the next six to eight weeks. The publican had a second ute that Jack could use as a work truck; his office would be a table in the corner with a screen around it. It took two days to work out a programme for the renovations with work beginning on Wednesday.

Bill arrived at lunchtime Tuesday with some gear and tools that Jack required, plus his trusty laptop. They had a good talk over a cup of coffee and a sandwich, and then Jack showed him around the Big Lake Hotel and pointed out the alterations that he would be doing. In due course Bill said goodbye, but he would be back next week.

That night Jack rang Chantal to let her know that he was staying on for a while — and yes, they could go to the King Prawn Bowling Club tomorrow night and do those things that they talked about.

Wednesday night Jack met Chantal in the club foyer at 5.30 pm, where they made their way to the restaurant. Dinner was a buffet, so they selected their food and sat down. After dinner Jack asked Chantal, 'Have you seen Bozz since the other day?'

'No, when I got home from work yesterday the ute was gone. Other than that I know as much as you do.'

Jack said, 'Don't forget to give him a call just to let him know he's not alone. You know, I've been thinking about the other day, and I remembered one of our carpenters who was the perfect tradesman. But over a period of time he turned into a cranky, abusive, lazy person that nobody wanted to work with. One day he called me a nasty name, so I took him into the site shed and shut the door. He said, "What are we doing in here?"

'I said, "I'm getting a bit tired of your attitude. There's something wrong with you and I want to know what it is."

'He answered, "There's nothing wrong with me, I'm going."

'I grabbed him by the shirt and shook him, then slammed him up against the wall and said, "You're not leaving here until I find out what is wrong with you, now what is it?"

'Judging by the terrified look on his face, I think he must have thought that I was going to kill him. He broke down and began to sob; I let him go, stood back and waited. He gathered himself back together and said, "I don't know what's wrong with me, I can't concentrate, and everything and everybody annoys me."

'"All right then, you'll have to see our doctor." I took him to our medical people a couple of days later, then he had to see a specialist. Guess what they found? A brain tumour. He had the operation to remove it and returned to work three months later as the beautiful person that he once was, and he's still working for us.'

'All right, I'll talk to him,' replied Chantal.

It was time to go into the dance hall section and after finding a table and sitting down, a waiter came, took their order and returned with the drinks. Thirty minutes later all the seats were occupied. A couple of beats on a drum, then a spotlight shone on the stage curtains as the lights dimmed to quarter power. The curtains began to open. The compere's voice was dominant: 'Ladies and gentlemen, please welcome the Jens Black Showband.'

The four musicians dressed in identical clothing sprang into action with an instrumental called 'The Phantom of the Opera' — their version. They went on to play all the latest material. Jack and Chantal had a couple of dances then the band announced that somebody from the audience could sing a song. There didn't appear to be any takers, and then the leader of the band noticed Chantal pointing at Jack.

'Yes what about you Sir? They tell me you can sing a pretty good song — yes, you.'

'All right,' answered Jack as he left his seat and walked up to the stage. He talked to the musicians for a couple of minutes before he took the microphone. The song that he sang was one of the latest on the Coastal Hit Parade. It was a nice slow ballad that he sang beautifully with the backing of the three guitars and a set of drums. Behind him they were working in unison, lifting their guitars as one. Stepping to the left, then to the right. One step back, two steps forward, all in the rhythm of the music.

When it was all over, Jack received a standing ovation. He sat back down and Chantal said, 'Gee that was nice Jack, but I hope that song wasn't about me.'

'Of course not,' he replied.

She put her hand on top of his hand and said while studying his eyes, 'You know Jack, I've never been able to get you out of my mind. I hoped that one day you might be able to forgive me and maybe we could get together again. I even went to church for a time, but that didn't work, and now you show up here and I get my hopes up again.'

'Chantal, I haven't given you any false hopes; my marriage to Kate is as strong now as it ever was. Me being here with you tonight says that whatever differences we had have long gone. We can still enjoy a feed, a dance and have a good laugh together. Now, if we're going to the carnival we'd better get going.'

Walking through the Surf Club Carnival was a real experience. A nice crowd was on hand to enjoy this atmosphere on a beautiful summer's night. The physical rides were doing good business, and the merry go round was loaded chock-a-block with young ones. An old fashioned horse-a-plane was doing well along with a miniature steam train that had a full complement of future train drivers. The feared Octopus was producing plenty of squeals while the dreaded Hurricane was the main attraction for a certain brand of thrill seeker. The main crowd was at the fixed stalls along one side.

Oops! There's Madam Fifi's palm reading crap, thought Jack. *I won't be going anywhere near there. Cripes, I hope it's not the 13th.*

Madam was doing great business with a long line of teenagers willing to pay five dollars to see their futures. Little did they know what was in store for them later on as they travelled through the book of life, without the protection of their mums and dads.

Jack had two games of darts and won a prize after mastering the lopsided weighted darts, while Chantal was the champion of the Clown's Head and got herself a large Bugs Bunny. They worked their way along the stalls without any further success.

Jack said, 'Let's go and have a ride in the ghost train.'

'I don't know about that,' replied Chantal.

Jack was persistent. 'C'mon, c'mon, you don't know what you're missing out on.'

Chantal relented. 'Ahh okay, let's go.'

After purchasing tickets they got into the little black carriage. When the other carriages were all occupied, the train slowly moved away and disappeared into the darkness of the unknown. All the kids were screaming as plenty of spooky things happened and it was all in good fun. In the final section just prior to coming out, a skeleton jumped out of nowhere. The skeleton made a lunge and got a bit too close to the carriage. Jack grabbed it in a headlock and dragged it into the carriage.

When they came out of the darkened chamber the skeleton was sitting on Chantal's knee. It was a guy in a black body suit with a luminous skeleton painted on it. Jack was laughing his head off as this guy jumped off Chantal's knee and confronted Jack. He angrily shouted, 'Come on you dirty bastard, I'm going to thump the living daylights out of you!'

Jack was still laughing as he said, 'Look Skello, I'm having a good night, now you can't blame me for having a good night, can you? Here's $50 for your troubles, okay?'

The sight of that $50 note settled the skeleton down straight away. 'Oh yeah, right-o mate, okay.' He grabbed that note and ran back inside the darkened chamber.

Chantal said, 'You bought him off, that's not like you.'

'No,' said Jack. 'But I was in the wrong, I shouldn't have done it. He's trying to make a living doing carnival work; they only make a pittance, now tonight he made a little extra.'

'Hmm, I never thought of it like that,' replied Chantal.

They went and had a ride on the Hurricane, which was terrifying and exhilarating at the same time, especially when the arms dropped down only to fling back up again. The hissing sounds of the air hydraulics added a mystery to the drama, like it was a massive serpent about to gobble you up. Chantal was hanging onto Jack with all her might and screaming like a teenager until the ride came to an end with a slow and gradual stop.

As soon as Chantal stepped onto the ground she said, 'Thank heavens for that, I was absolutely terrified, I'm so glad it's over.' She got down on her hands and knees and kissed the ground she walked on.

Jack laughed at this little ceremony, as did a few other people that got off the ride, but a few other people also kissed the ground, declaring, 'That's the last time I'll ever get on that bloody thing.'

They went over to the food caravan and ordered two old fashioned banana splits and a couple of cappuccinos, sitting down at one of the tables. The dodgem cars were located nearby with a full complement of young drivers hell-bent on destroying each other. The attendants were working flat out trying to untangle them and sort out the traffic jams. For Jack and Chantal, this was very entertaining to watch as they enjoyed those banana splits.

'So how long are you staying?' asked Chantal.

Jack replied, 'Six to eight weeks. I'm doing some renovations at the hotel; apparently he's having trouble getting licensed trades-people at the moment, so I'm helping out.'

'Well, it looks like we'll be neighbours then.'

'Yes,' replied Jack.

At 11 o'clock the carnival began to shut down for the night. Jack walked Chantal back to the car park and said goodnight, then he headed back to the Big Lake Hotel.

In the morning Jack was doing some brickwork, and at 10 o'clock he decided to have a smoko. He went to his unit and made a couple of toasted sandwiches and a cup of coffee. Ernie the dart player appeared in the doorway.

'Sorry to bother you Jack.'

'Come on in and have a toasted sandwich and a coffee.'

'Ah gee thanks.' During the course of conversation Ernie said. 'Jack, we're short of players for the grudge match and I was wondering if you'd like a game. Just looking at you I can see that you're physically fit. Have you ever played rugby league?'

'I played for the North Sydney Bears as a young bloke, so I know all about it.'

'We need twenty players all up, and yesterday a couple of the Shellharbour boys dropped out so I'm on a recruitment drive. The squad's been training for over four weeks but as we've only got a couple of weeks left to the game we need to step it up a bit. Normal rules, except that the changeover rules don't apply. Because the match is played in the middle of summer it's stinking hot, so we can change players at random. If you feel you've had enough, off you go. What do you say?'

Jack replied, 'You can pencil my name in; if I beat you at darts tonight you can ink it in.' He smiled at Ernie. 'Now there's something I need to know about you. You seem to hang around here all the time like you live here.'

Ernie said, 'Well, sort of. You know, I never made much out of my life as a young bloke, even though I was given every chance. I passed all my school exams so I had a good foundation to become anything that I wanted to be. But I fell in love with surfing and football, so I became the perfect dole bludger. Oh, I had a few bit jobs here and there just to satisfy the dole office, who was always chasing me to do job interviews. I never appreciated Mum and Dad; they were so patient with me. My life was divided between the surf beach and the pub, and I would stay at the pub until closing time every night. My girlfriends were whatever I could pick up either around here or over at the surf beach.

'One day the publican asked me to run the raffles for the football and fishing clubs, and he paid me a bit of hush money … being the ideal dole bludger, that suited me fine. Then out of the blue he announced that he was giving his daughter a twenty-first birthday party out in the lounge on the next Saturday night. Cripes, we didn't even know he had a daughter, let alone two. The publican asked me to give him a hand to set the lounge up for the party on the Saturday morning of the party. Then he wanted me to work as a roustabout while the party was going on that night — you know, to pick up the glasses, keep the tables clean, that sort of thing. Naturally I said yes.

'I arrived at the hotel at 8.00 am to help prepare the lounge for that night. For the first time in my life I worked my guts out. I wouldn't even help my old man mow the grass. I paid no rent and ate all their food, and still they were nice to me, but this Saturday morning I was inspired for some unknown reason. I felt like a flower about to get its first ray of sunshine. We finished the job at 11.30 am, and the publican gave me two meat pies and a schooner of beer as a thank you gift. He said, "Ernie, you surprised me today, that was a good effort, thank you."

'I said, "No worries boss."

'Now don't ask me why but I walked home, which was only three streets away. The only thing Mum and Dad wouldn't do was lend me money, and when I walked into the house they were having lunch at the dining table.

'I said. "G'day, ahhh ... Dad, I was wondering if you could lend me $100 and I'll pay you back as soon as I can."

'Dad replied, "You know Ernie, that's the first time you've ever said you'll pay me back as soon as you can." Then he started laughing, and then Mum joined him in hysterical laughter. It must have been the joke of the year for them, and then there was silence after they laughed themselves empty. I was about to turn away and leave when Dad said, "And what are you going to do with this $100?"

'I replied, "I want to go up to the Shellharbour Square and buy a new pair of jeans, a shirt and shoes. If I've got anything left I'll get a haircut."

'Dad looked at Mum and said, "You know, that sounds like a fair proposition to me." And with that he pulled out his wallet and gave me the note.

'I said. "Thanks Dad, I'd better get going."

'I walked away, and then I heard him say, "I'll run you up there if you like."

'We went into the stores together and he helped me buy the things I needed. That was the first time in five years we'd done anything together other than what went on inside the house.

'Anyway, I arrived at the party all dressed up for the first time in my adult life, and began doing the things that they told me to do. There were three hundred people in that lounge. I carried out drinks, plates of food, I was everybody's slave.

'When everybody had a plate of food Harry came in with his daughter on his arm like he was giving her away at a wedding. The volume of the band went up a notch, playing a special song as they walked this pathway towards the stage where he introduced his daughter to the guests. I took one look at her and was immediately smitten. I couldn't take my eyes off her, it was a feeling I'd never experienced before. I was walking on air and on cloud nine at the same time. Then I thought, she wouldn't have anything to do with me. A bloke without a job who bludges off anybody and everybody who's occupation is drinking, playing darts, pub football, surfing and chasing women? Nah. But there's nothing wrong with dreaming, eh?

'I had a tray in my hand with empty glasses on it and my binocular eyes were indecently checking the publican's daughter out when a partygoer called out, "Hey waiter, stop daydreaming and get me two schooners of new beer, you gotta earn your money so come on."

'Heck, I didn't even know if I was getting paid or not, so to cut a long story short, during the evening she had a couple of decent looks at me, which gave me a bit of encouragement … and I thought, well, stranger things have happened. She danced with every Tom, Dick and Harry but never the same guy twice. She asked me to get her some pink champagne. I brought it back, de-corked it and poured it out like I'd seen on the Benny Hill Show. Harry said to his wife, "Geez Ernie would make a good waiter; I never knew he had these skills."

'The daughter — her name was Beth — was starting to get more than a little bit tiddly, and at 10 pm they cut the cake and made all the speeches. They sang "Auld Lang Syne" — I thought it was New Year's Eve, and that was followed by "For she's a jolly good fellow" and more dancing. I must have walked a hundred miles, back and forth to the kitchen and the bar, then Beth came over to me and asked, "What's your name?"

'"Ernie."

'"Well Ernie Dingo, I'm Beth." She grabbed me, gave me a very long kiss and then she went back to her seat. Wow ... I couldn't believe it.

'We became an item and we've been together ever since. Harry gave me a job and I do all the things that need doing around here, I've learnt the bar and the TAB, and I mow the grass and do all the gardening. I bought a unit not far from here and to top that off we've got two beautiful kids, a boy and a girl ... and next week I come off holidays so you'll see me here all the time.'

Jack said, 'Gee that was a wonderful story mate, and you'd have to think that there might have been some sort of divine intervention involved here.'

On leaving the unit Ernie said, 'We're having a run along the beach on Friday afternoon as part of our training, at 5.00 pm sharp.'

'I'll be there,' answered Jack.

'Also, Sunday morning at the Cossie Oval Shellharbour, 7.00 am where we'll work on a few moves, how will that one go?'

'No worries, I'll see you at the dartboards tonight.'

At 5 o'clock Kelly and Jack went to the restaurant and ordered dinner. Patrons spilled out into the lounge due to an extra-large crowd showing up. A young lady was playing music on a keyboard, and she could sing too.

After dinner Jack said to Kelly, 'Come and have a game of darts.'

Kelly answered, 'Do you think it would be all right?'

'Sure, I'll protect you from the ruffians of the public bar.'

Ernie was at the dartboards when they walked into the main public bar, where there was a fair crowd on hand. Jack noticed that the guys who were hanging up the grudge match banner last night were all sitting around a couple of tables enjoying a drink and a conversation. As Jack and Kelly walked past them, one was heard to say to another, 'Wow, that's the best thing that I've seen today.'

Kelly turned and gave them a lovely smile for the compliment. Jack introduced Kelly to Ernie and they began to play a threesome. Jack won the game — there was no way Ernie was going to win, because he wanted Jack on that football team.

Kelly and Ernie played for second place, with Ernie winning that one, but it could have gone either way as Kelly could throw a real mean dart. One of the footballers had a sheet in his hand and called out to Ernie, 'Who's this other footballer called Kelly, do we know him?'

Before anybody could answer Kelly said, 'My name's Kelly.' She walked over to them. The six of them looked at each other in disbelief then they began to laugh one by one.

Jack said to Ernie, 'Don't tell them, I'll tell them tomorrow at training. In the meantime we'll have some fun.'

Kelly began to flirt with the footballers. One of them had very long hair and fuzz all over his face — he could have been a cross between Vlad Dracula and the Wolf Man. He said to Kelly, 'Why don't you come home with me tonight Kelly? I'll show you the finer points of a game.'

Kelly replied, 'And what game is that?'

'Ahh, you'll have to trust me on that one.'

Another footballer asked, 'Can I come too?'

Footballers have been getting a lot of bad publicity of late and Kelly was thinking of this while she was leading these pub footballers on — or was she? It all ended when two people walked up to the table and she introduced them. 'This is my sister Veronica, and my future brother-in-law Clive. We're on our way to the WIN Entertainment Centre to watch the country and western show, so I'll see you all later.'

Vlad Wolf said, 'Oh Kelly, we could have had so much good fun.'

Kelly laughed and said, 'That's why I'm going.'

The half back sitting at the end of the table said, 'You know Kelly, you can put your slippers under my bed anytime you want.'

She replied with a full smile on her face, pointing at him at the same time. 'You know what, little fella? I might just take you up on that offer one day. Goodbye.' It was good harmless fun and for those in close proximity a bit of good entertainment, but in the end she was only having them on.

The next day was Friday, and at the end of the day all the footballers of the local grudge match team met at the mouth of the lake entrance. The squad numbered twenty, and was made up of Big Lake Pub members, Shellharbour Rugby League Club and a couple of independents like Jack. Ernie was the captain and all those who didn't know each other were introduced. Training lasted a couple of hours and was full-on with Ernie calling the shots. A two-mile run to begin with, then one hundred metre sprints, push ups, then finally a thirty minute game of touch football in the soft sand.

At the end of training Ernie had a few things to say. 'Okay boys, we'll meet at the Shellharbour Oval at seven in the morning for some real work. Now Mick, I want you to put in plenty of goal kicking practice over the next week, you've got to be spot on. See you all tomorrow.'

At 7 am the footballers congregated at the Cossie Oval in Shellharbour, a standard football paddock with the perimeter fence in the shape of an oval, hence its name. Cossie was Shellharbour's favourite son. The young champion footballer went on to play rugby league for Australia and did his hometown proud. The training started with the usual run along the beach and back to where they started from, then it was on the grass proper where they did a lot of work with the ball as if they were in a real game, then finished with thirty minutes of touch football.

After football training, Jack went back to the hotel and did four hours work on the renovations before having a late lunch and going into the main public bar. Part of his deal with the publican was to give the bouncer a hand on Friday nights and Saturday afternoons as well as being on call.

The hotel wall clock said 2.00 pm and the atmosphere was a replay of last Saturday. The beehive hum of voices, the standing room only around the bar and the yelling of the punters watching the horse racing live on Sky Channel from Royal Randwick.

Jack noticed the bouncer running into the far corner so he decided to go that way in case he might be needed. Three young pub boys had a bloke bailed up against the wall just inside the rear entrance; he was defending himself with a chair. Bouncer Fred arrived and told the three young ones to find something else to do or face the consequences.

They turned on him. The bravest one said, 'You're a bit outnumbered mate, there's only one of you.'

Jack silently came up behind them. Fred had something to say. 'Sorry to disappoint you but there's two of me.'

They looked around and saw Jack, a lean man with a rugged look about him. Jack had a badge on that said 'Hotel Security'; that changed the climate. They decided to go away and ambush this guy another day.

Fred said to the bloke holding the chair, 'Now listen mate, I'm getting a bit sick of you. Every time you come in here there's trouble.' He viciously snatched the chair off him. Fred's fist automatically came back to launch a haymaker.

Jack called out frantically, 'Don't hit him Fred, he's sick.'

'All right Jack, you put him out.'

Fred walked away. Jack said to this fellow, 'How are you Bozz?'

'I was good until I saw you.' He seemed quite passive compared to last Sunday.

'Would you like a beer?'

'Sure.'

Jack asked one of the footballers to go and get two schooners of beer while they went and sat on the steps.

'What do you do for a living, Bozz?'

'I'm a fitter and turner.'

'How's that going?'

'Not good, I almost told him to shove it the other day. He won't stop picking on me, I can't stand it.'

Jack said to Bozz, 'You know, I'd like to help you if you'll let me. I'm the owner of a very big company in Sydney. I'd like you to see one of our doctors. It won't cost you anything and maybe we can find the problem, what do you say?'

Bozz replied, 'Okay, it can't do any harm can it?'

'All right, I'll arrange it. Give me your mobile phone number so I can contact you.'

'You don't even know me,' said Bozz. 'And I've been nasty to you, yet you still want to help me. I don't understand.' He was looking at his feet and shaking his head.

Jack answered. 'Sometimes in life things don't work out, but in the end if we let people help us we can get results for the better. You've still got a girlfriend, you know.'

'Yeah, I've been nasty to her too. She rang me up but I hung the phone up on her.'

They finished their beers, shook hands then Jack watched as Bozz got into his super ute and drove away. The three young drinkers that wanted to bash Bozz were still close by and had been watching Jack talk to him.

Jack walked over to them and said, 'Now listen fellas, if that guy comes in here and you bash him up, you could quite easily kill him because he's sick. If you happen to do that, then you go to jail for twenty-five years. That's twenty-five years without alcohol, racehorses and kissing women. Remember that.'

They looked at each other before walking away and sitting down at one of the tables. Jack walked past Shorty's table, shook his hand, then walked back to the bar.

Harry said to Jack, 'What did you do to them, hypnotise them?'

'Something like that.'

Harry said, 'Even Shorty's behaving himself and I haven't seen that in a long time. He's the biggest pest we've got, but I like the colour of his money.' They both had a good laugh at that one.

On Monday morning, Jack rang Marree at St Vincent's Hospital in Sydney and explained Bozz's problem. She rang back an hour later with an appointment for him at 8.00 am Wednesday morning. Bill would drive down Tuesday afternoon and take him back to Sydney, then bring him back Wednesday night.

This week everything went to plan, things just fell into place: progress was made on the renovations and football training was coming along good, while Bozz had been diagnosed with inflammation of the brain. A date was set for the beginning of specialised treatment in a private hospital and Chantal was supporting him after he apologised for his erratic behaviour.

SEVEN

Summer grudge match

The whole of the community was awaiting the entertainment extravaganza called the 'Summer Grudge Match'. For the footballers, all the training and preparation was over and now that Sunday had come, the battle was about to begin. The football teams from both sides arrived at the marshalling area at 10.00 am, where the road had been closed to allow the procession participants plenty of time and room to assemble prior to the start.

The main street of Shellharbour is built on the side of a hill. It's one long sloping road about five kilometres in length. The procession would start at the top of the hill where it's level, and then it was a gradual slope down to the historic steamboat harbour where a one hundred year old restored cargo steamboat was moored, open for inspection at five dollars a head. The CB *Blackbutt*, as it was named, looked similar to the paddle wheelers that work on the Murray River today. These steamboats took over from the sailing ships that serviced the coastal town with supplies. Eventually the railways came through and put the boats out of business.

At the steamboat harbour the road split. Turning right followed the rocky foreshore in a south-easterly direction where there were plenty of picnic tables and covered areas, along with coin operated barbecues scattered around on the well-manicured green grass. A wader pool for children and a set of tidal baths complemented this beautiful area beside the ocean. The Cossie

Football Oval was a further three kilometres away. This was the route that the 'Shellharbour Summer Grudge Match Procession' would take.

The main street was commercial on either side and very modern. Shellharbour Primary School was home to Sunday markets, but today there were market stalls spread out along the procession route as well. The footpaths on both sides of the street were home to the spectators, patiently waiting for the procession to begin. These people were packed together like tinned sardines without the tins.

At the count of one, two and three the Southern Highlands Scotch Marching Band sounded the first notes of music. The procession had begun. Two young Koori ladies led the way, carrying a large banner with the words 'The Shoalhaven River'. Those two ladies were dressed beautifully, making their men feel proud.

The Shoalhaven River Football Team was next, dressed in their all-orange uniforms, with black football boots and long white socks sporting three black rings at the top. Black baseball caps around the wrong way finished off their dressage. They marched in perfect stride, with purpose. Every four or five strides they would punch their fists into the air and yell, '*Hey!*' It looked impressive, giving clear defiant intent that they'd come here to win this game. A lot of time and practise had gone into this part already, giving them that all-important physiological advantage.

Behind the Shoalhaven boys were the Scotch marching band from the Southern Highlands. The only thing that anybody could say about these fellows dressed in their tartan skirts would be 'fabulous'.

The Shellharbour footy side was next, casually walking along without any type of window dressing as compared to the Shoalhaven boys. Maybe their motto was, 'We'll save our energy for the game.' But it didn't matter to the biased spectators; they clapped and cheered them anyway.

Following the local footballers were the girls from the Shellharbour City Marching Team. All the teenage males had to push their eyes back in after they went by.

Next was a series of floats that created a lot of interest due to their local content. A six metre replica of a steam driven paddle wheel cargo boat of yesteryear, similar to the one on display in the harbour, attracted a lot of attention as it went by.

The following float contained the beauty contestants: ten attractive young ladies vying for the title, 'Queen of the Grudge Match'. It was only natural that the next float contained ten young men parading their muscle-toned bodies searching for the title, 'Hunk of the Grudge Match'.

The next float was car-sized and in the shape and colour of a white swan. Sitting in the double seat was last year's Queen and Hunk, and with them their two month old baby. Two young people had found themselves, and now they had a little family.

A variety of commercial floats followed, along with a group of clowns entertaining along the way. Two more clowns followed but this time they were on stilts. Six vintage cars followed and they looked better than brand new.

A float from Main Street Dive Shop was next, then the contestants for the best decorated bike — nobody older than sixteen. One kid was riding a penny-farthing, a bike that was over one hundred years old. It would be hard to beat on looks alone. Next came the contestants for the best decorated character — again, nobody older than sixteen years. All these superheroes looked so good. It would be easier to pick the winner of the Melbourne Cup.

The procession was now the length of the main street, with the two banner-carrying Koori girls about to make the right hand turn that followed the rocky foreshore. Then, out of nowhere came a red twin-wing Tiger Moth aeroplane of 1940s vintage. It swooped down at the top of the hill and made a rooftop run at high speed over the main street, frightening the daylights out of everybody before disappearing over the steamboat harbour and out across the sea. The pilot wasn't the famous 'Red Baron' — there would only be ever one like him — but a good description of this fellow would be the 'Mad Baron'. It was a dangerous thing to do and it certainly provided a buzz while it lasted.

A truck with half a dozen monkeys chained on the back was next, then a four wheel drive towing a cage with two male lions inside — must be a circus in town somewhere. A large gap followed, then the final item. It was the Royal Australian Navy Band, marching with purpose and playing 'Waltzing Matilda'. Looking magnificent in their uniforms, the procession spectators gave them a thunderous reception, clapping and cheering as they made their way down Main Street. It was a case of saving the best for last, although the Mad Baron in the red twin-wing Tiger Moth may have stolen their thunder. Still, the Navy Band appeared to be the favourite with plenty of females giving these fellows more than a passing glance. There was no doubting the professionalism of Australia's Defence Forces.

As the tail of the procession worked its way down Main Street, the spectators spilled onto the road behind it, giving a breather to the sardine-can conditions that existed on the footpaths. The Grudge Match Procession made its way along the rocky foreshore, but it would be another fifteen minutes before it reached its destination: the Cossie Oval. Both sides of the route were packed with people wanting to get a glimpse of this rare type of entertainment.

The procession entered the competition arena, and for the footballers this was the 'holy grail'; there was just no other sight like it. The waiting fans stood as one, clapping and cheering until the entire procession was on the oval. How the two clowns on stilts made it all the way was anybody's guess. A platform had been built on the back of a truck so they could get on and off and it was waiting for them when they arrived. When they did get off they both laid down, exhausted. A paddock beside the oval had a large television screen erected to show the game to those who couldn't get on the oval. The monkeys and the lions were on display and they complemented a carnival with a couple of bigger rides a bit further away. There were a variety of food vans, along with all types of stalls selling a variety of goods and souvenirs.

Back inside the oval after everything had been sorted out, the local marching girls were giving a fine display of their skills to the sounds of the Scotch band. After that the Queen and Hunk of the Grudge Match were decided by a panel of experts, and what a fine couple they were too. It would be interesting to see if these two make a baby like last year's winners; time would tell. The best decorated bike went to the oldest bike, the penny-farthing, by a country mile, while the best character competition went to a young Spiderman enthusiast. All those who took part were given one hundred dollars while the winners were given two thousand dollars each.

At 1.15 pm the oval was cleared in readiness for the start of the Summer Grudge Match.

For security reasons based on forty years of experience, the Shoalhaven supporters were all ushered to the southern side of the oval while the Shellharbour supporters were on the northern side. Team Shellharbour marched onto the centre, then the visitors joined them in one long line. A mobile stage was in place in front of the footballers. The Navy Band assembled themselves behind the stage. One of Australia's finest singers, dressed in a white suit, walked up to the microphone. This gentleman lived local and was best known for his singing role as the Phantom in the stage hit, *The Phantom of the Opera*. But today, as the Royal Australian Navy Band started the musical introduction, he would be singing 'Advance Australia Fair'. Halfway through the anthem there wouldn't have been one person who wasn't standing and singing their hearts out as they joined in with this beautiful singing sensation.

Silence reigned. The mobile stage was rolled off. The linesman took their places. The ref came on and tossed the coin high in the air. Shellharbour won, with Captain Ernie deciding to run with the north-easterly breeze. The ref looked at his watch and right on 1.30 pm he blew his whistle. The Summer Grudge Match had begun with the approval of the spectators, who let out one big cheer.

From the kick-off the ball went deep into Shoalhaven's territory. No sooner had the fullback received the ball than a bee-like swarm of Shellharbour players had hold of him and crashed him to the ground quite viciously. He hit the ground that hard he spilled the ball. The fullback took offence and came up swinging. The first of many on-field fights had begun. Within a few seconds just about all the players were pushing and shoving; some were trying to stop it. The ref was blowing his whistle to no avail. Then as quickly as it started, it ended. The ref put the scrum down with Shellharbour winning the ball, then spreading it quickly along the back line with a cut out pass to the winger, who scored the first try. The goal kicker from the Big Lake Hotel converted the try. Shellharbour now led by six points to nil in the first six minutes.

The restart was a carbon copy of the kick off, only this time Shellharbour was on the receiving end. The Shellharbour fullback caught the ball and passed it cleanly after getting out of the quarter zone. The receiver of the ball was tackled by five players from Shoalhaven. They picked him up off the ground and dumped him heavily on his side — then they jumped on him to add to his misery.

The Shellharbour players started the fight this time. Law and order was restored with the game continuing like a quality game of football with some very entertaining moves. The Shoalhaven side grafted their way down into Shellharbour's quarter.

On the fifth tackle, one of them kicked the ball high into the air hoping for a bit of luck. Shellharbour was waiting for the ball to come down; it seemed like an eternity. Finally, Shellharbour's fullback jumped up to claim the prize, but Shoalhaven's Louis Longbottom had different ideas as he came onto the scene with speed, gusto and perfect timing. He leaped high into the air, snatching the ball and knocking the Shellharbour fullback rotten. Louis landed in goal and all he had to do was place the ball down for four points. The Shoalhaven's goal kicker converted from right in front. Now the score was six all.

The game continued like a normal game of rugby league, but ten minutes before half time with the score line locked at six points each, the massive crowd on the oval and paddock were becoming restless; they weren't enjoying this stalemate at all. As a matter of fact they were yelling for action, anything but a slug fest.

The Shoalhaven side got their back line working brilliantly and quickly worked their way down into Shellharbour's danger zone, and it looked like it was only a matter of time before they crossed the line. The Shoalhaven River boys spread the ball from one side to the other, but there was a long gap on the final pass to the winger.

Jack B Kelly sensed an opportunity. He timed his intercepting run perfectly to latch onto the ball as he burst through the opening and continued running as if his life depended on it. So far it was plain sailing and the fullback wasn't at home either, with the only problem being whether these old legs could carry him the full length of the football paddock at full speed. He'd only been training for three weeks!

Shellharbour's supporters were on their feet yelling encouragement. 'Come on Kelly, come on Kelly, go go!' The football commentator, a Roy Warren sound alike, was describing what was happening. 'Ohh, a sensation at the Summer Grudge Match on the Cossie oval as Shellharbour has intercepted the ball. Jack B Kelly came down from Sydney Harbour to give his mates a hand to win this match and only bad luck can prevent him scoring a try as he's racing away with the ball.'

Two teams were chasing: Jack's own in case he needed a hand, and the Shoalhaven River team who were out to get him — they didn't care how they did it, as long as they got him. Jack was clear by six metres and it looked like it might stay that way as the chasers weren't making any impression on him for the moment. One side of the ground was screaming. 'Get him, *get him*,' while the other side were yelling. 'C'mon Jack!' Chantal and Bozz were in the crowd with Chantal yelling herself hoarse, while Kelly and her sister were adding their voices to the noisy encouragement.

With half a dozen strides to go, Jack's legs were beginning to go up and down in the one place. A well-known South Coast speedster specialist left the chasing pack and set sail after Jack. Jonathon Blacklock nearly had him now. Jack tried the old swerve trick and it worked for a couple of strides, then he could feel Jonathon's fingers trying to get a grip on the collar of his football jersey. He threw his head forward and dived over the line, crashing onto the ground with the ball underneath him — he had made it. The northern side of the oval went wild with excitement, while the southern side went into disappointment overdrive.

The referee was caught flat-footed when Jack sprinted away with the ball, and it took him a while to catch up. When he did, he conferred with the in-goal linesman who confirmed Jack had scored a legitimate try. He walked to the spot, pointed at the ground and blew his whistle. Shellharbour's goal kicker converted the try and now Shellharbour led, twelve points to six. Jack was lying between the goalposts, trying to get his breath back, and was joined by half a dozen teammates also out of breath after the big chase. They rallied and made their way to their own half in time to receive the ball from the restart.

With five minutes till half time the Shoalhavenites were getting a bit anxious. After receiving the ball from the restart, Shellharbour worked their way to the middle of the pad. A vicious tackle by three Shoalhaven footballers saw Shellharbour spill the ball forward, with the ref putting down a scrum. Captain Ernie moved Jack to the front row while the hooker went off for a rest. They packed down and waited for the ball to be fed in.

A sudden impact and burst of pain just below Jack's right eye saw him drop his arm and scream, 'Ooh, that hurt!' He rubbed the area with his hand to try to soothe the pain. He looked across to his opposite number, who had a sly smile on his face with the look of accomplishment written all over it. Jack thought to himself, *Yeah, you'll keep, you ambushing bastard.*

The scrum with all the pushing and shoving skewered around a half circle. The ref blew the whistle and made them form up for a second time. As they packed down, Jack was on the lookout — he wasn't about to happily receive another punch to his face. It was time for payback. An eye for an eye. He let fly with a decent punch of his own and got the bloke that punched him, fair and square on the nose. The ball was fed in and raked out. Shellharbour's number seven, Rodney Wishart, quickly sent the ball out to the back line. The scrum broke up with Jack's victim collapsing onto the ground backwards with blood running over his face. The half time whistle sounded as the ball went dead. Two ambulance officers were on the scene instantly to attend the wounded Shoalhaven player. They placed him on a stretcher and carried him off the field to the makeshift medical tent.

A well-fed Indigenous lady, who was well and truly pissed, angrily ran across the field carrying an empty Tooheys longneck and confronted Jack. She screamed at him, 'Go on you dirty Aussie bastard, look what you did to my man you rotten bastard, I'm gonna bash your ugly fucken head in.' She raised the bottle.

Jack's first thought was to run very fast, because this lady meant business. But he didn't have to as two security guards came up behind her and seized the bottle, and then advised her to go back to her own area. She continued yelling abuse at Jack as she was escorted back to the southern side.

Rest time was thirty minutes. Half a dozen volunteer doctors were checking pulses and blood pressure along with recovery rates, as the furious pace of the game on a hot summer's day would be taking its toll on the players, even though a nice easterly sea breeze was blowing across the oval.

During the break one of the local bands, The Tornadoes, provided some rocking entertainment. Someone yelled out, 'Here comes that plane again.' The Mad Baron was back, approaching low from the ocean at full speed. As he neared the oval he released a trail of red smoke and speared his red twin-wing aeroplane straight up until it looked like it was going out of sight, then he performed a couple of loops before cutting the motor back to idle. The plane plummeted down in a spiral. At a given point the Mad Baron put his foot on the accelerator and pulled out of the dive before disappearing out over the ocean — much to the delight of the grudge match crowd, who gave this daredevil plenty of applause.

After the break the two teams assembled back on the oval for the second forty minutes, with Shellharbour leading the match — twelve points to six. After the kick-off the second half was no different to the first: survival of the toughest. With twenty minutes to full time, Shoalhaven's captain Louis Longbottom burst away for his second converted try, making the score line twelve-all.

The slug fest continued and with five minutes to go, desperate measures were now the norm. These human gladiators had nothing to lose as both sides tried every dirty trick in the book to break the deadlock. Changes on the bench were now one per minute — it was like a relay team. Big Lake Hotel player Vlad Wolf got involved in a nasty tackle. The Shoalhaven River boys played stacks on the mill and wouldn't get off him, so he bit one of them on the neck and a fight got underway. They settled down after the ref inspected the bite marks on the neck in question and sent Vlad Wolf off for biting, but he wouldn't go.

The ref completely lost control of the head high tackles, fighting in the scrums and the heavy dumping — then in an operation the ref himself was put out of action. The ambulance boys carried him off on a stretcher — much to the delight of the replacement referee, who'd patiently waited to have his day in the sun at the Summer Grudge Match. He'd no sooner got there than he realised that it would be safer to walk along the middle of a freeway on a holiday weekend.

Jack lined up a Shoalhavenite who was a pain in Shellharbour's neck and put him out of action with a ripper of a shoulder charge. Jack then went and retired to the bench forever. One minute to full time, and extra time was looking a real possibility.

Shellharbour were trapped in their quarter and trying to graft their way out of the danger zone, when Ben Hall from the Big Lake Hotel spilled the ball after taking a simple pass. Chica Ferguson, a young Shoalhaven cadet from the Jervis Bay Naval Academy, swooped on the ball like a hungry lion. Then he borrowed his grandfather's legs, and showing scintillating speed he burst through a narrow gap and put the ball right down between the posts. The Shoalhaven supporters realised they'd won the game and went totally ballistic. They'd come prepared for this with whistles and horns; they released balloons and started dancing up and down, and most of all they were yelling and screaming. They'd won the Summer Grudge Match for the third year in a row.

Both teams fell onto the ground and just lay there. The ref ordered the Shoalhaven captain to convert the try. Louis Longbottom said, 'Go and kick it yourself ref, the game's over! Go and have a beer and come back next year.'

The ref put his hands on his hips and was about to say something when he looked around and saw the playing field disappearing in front of his eyes in a sea of spectators. There was only one side of the field left with any open space. He decided to get the hell out of there and ran towards that section, as spectators didn't usually like referees.

The full time hooter sounded; the Summer Grudge Match was over for another year.

In due course the Mayor of Shellharbour, Cec Glenholms, made a speech on the fine traditions of the Summer Grudge Match. A champion boxer in his younger days, he remarked that the game today was the best game of football that he'd ever seen. Ron Cossie, Shellharbour's favourite son, presented the trophy to the winning side and offered his condolences to the losing side.

After a shower and fresh clothes the two teams caught a bus to the hotel that overlooked the old Steamboat Harbour, where some refreshments and booze would take place in a friendly atmosphere. Even the guy who thumped Jack came over and apologised, then Jack said he was sorry for retaliating. They had a bit of a laugh and a beer together and shared some good wholesome conversation.

It was dark when they came out of the hotel, and shortly there-after the Shoalhaven River team departed in their bus while the Big Lake Hotel footballers were ferried back to their hotel. Jack was under sufferance and he decided to lick his wounds listen-ing to the three-piece band entertaining in the lounge. Kelly and her sister came over and joined him, talking about the Grudge Match Festival and agreeing it was the best they'd ever seen. They invited Jack to the wedding next Saturday and of course he accepted. At 10.00 pm Jack called time-out; he would sleep well tonight. But first he would call Kate to let her know what he was doing.

Kate said, 'That football match you said you were taking part in was on one of the digital channels. Gee, what a day you must have had.'

'Yeah, it was one hell of a game, but we lost.'

'Oh well, you can't always win you know. That try you scored looked fantastic, and they kept replaying it but I didn't mind because it give me a chance to have a look at you.'

They talked for another half hour before signing off. Then he rang Bill for a chat. Bill confirmed he would be coming down Wednesday for lunch. After that it was time for sleep, and it was 11 o'clock when he turned the light out.

In the morning Jack had a long hot shower, and then it was time for a post mortem. He was sick, sore and sorry; there was skin off everywhere and a bruise was coming out around that eye and cheekbone. His muscles were sore from head to toe, and he said to himself, 'Well, I just had my last game of footy.'

There would be no work until the pains of the grudge match began to subside. On Tuesday, Jack and Kelly went for a day of sightseeing. They bought fish and chips where the pelicans chased Jack on his first day in the area. They drove a little further south to Australia's best speedboat course.

Jack wanted to relive a moment in time when his father had taken him here on two separate occasions as a young fourteen year old. At that time the family had come on a camping holiday and stayed at the lake entrance. But looking at the course today, he couldn't believe the changes that have taken place. All the open spaces had all but disappeared under the weight of urban expansion. As for the speedboat course itself, it looked like it was all over red rover. The wharf and handicap clock tower were still there but you could tell that nothing had happened here for a long time. As an area's population grows it squeezes out the noisy sports, and that's obviously what had happened at this site.

What a pity, he thought as they drove away to their next destination, a thirty minute drive to the Minnamurra Falls. Nestled amongst one of the few remaining rainforests, it certainly was a beautiful look, as was the popular Mount Keira Lookout.

They ended up having dinner at the local airport. Jack said to Kelly, 'Hey! There's that red aeroplane that frightened the daylights out of us on Sunday ... gee, that pilot's mad!'

They both agreed and had a good laugh about it.

On Wednesday Bill came down from Sydney and joined Jack for lunch in the hotel dining room, where the Chinese cuisine was pretty good. They left the hotel and went down to the old boat shed to hire a runabout for the afternoon, exploring the lake along with the channel and the entrance.

Before Bill left to go back to Sydney he said to Jack, 'Tomorrow I'm going to see Ronnie Bottles. Donny King reckons we might be able to completely rehabilitate him, so I'll let you know what happens.'

'Okay Bill, I'll look forward to it, see you next Wednesday,' replied Jack.

On Saturday Jack went to the wedding with Kelly and thoroughly enjoyed himself. It brought back memories of his own wedding to Kate. A beautiful ceremony it was too, and witnessed by eighty guests dressed to the nines. At 10.00 pm the bride and groom drove away in their car, towing a couple of dozen jam and fruit tins, much to the delight of the wedding guests and those that put them there.

On Monday morning Kelly packed her bags in readiness for her trip back to Newcastle, a major city some three and a half hours to the north. She had morning tea with Jack, and then he carried her bags out to the car. They had a bit of a hug, then he opened the car door for her. They both had some things to say to each other. 'Jack, you know I wish we could have met somewhere in the past before you met your wife. I think we could have made a good life together.'

'Yes, there's no doubt about that. Look Kelly, I'm sorry if I wrecked your holiday ... you came here three weeks before your sister's wedding day to have a look around and to have a bit of fun, and I feel I robbed you of that fun.'

'Jack, I still had fun, but a different kind of fun. When I couldn't get you I didn't want anybody else. So I leave here a better human being, just because I met a very special person. You've got my phone number and my address, so if ever you're in Newcastle don't forget to look me up.'

Jack answered, 'We might pick up one of those old western movies eh?' He pulled out those imaginary guns and said the lines out of the Glenn Ford movie. 'Don't force me to fight because you won't like my way of fighting. *Bang bang.*'

A bit of raw emotion came into the goodbye, as they had a decent hug this time. Kelly had a tear in her eye as she got into her car. They were waving to each other as she drove away. Kelly turned north at the traffic lights and they both wondered if they'd ever see each other again.

EIGHT

Christine Bottles Bennett

Back in Sydney, Bill Scanlon was having four days off work due to an accumulation of roster days. He arrived at the homeless shelter at downtown Sydney and walked into the old converted factory that housed four hundred down-and-outs. He soon found the bloke he was looking for: Ronnie Bottles.

According to Salvo Captain Donny King, Ronnie had good prospects for complete rehabilitation and that would take another twelve months. Ronnie was washing the kitchen floor when Bill approached; he was so engrossed in what he was doing he never noticed Bill standing there.

'Hello Ronnie, how are you doing?' asked Bill.

Ronnie stopped mopping and looked up. He smiled as he said, 'It's Bill isn't it? Where's that Jack Kelly?'

'Jack's gone for a walkabout down the coast,' said Bill.

'I'm sure glad he was on my side that day in the lane. Ever since then I think I can see a future for myself.'

'Come and have a cup of coffee, Ron. I want to have a talk to you.'

All these homeless people were the same; they wouldn't divulge their pasts. Smooth-talking Bill, who could sell ice to an Eskimo, didn't get a lot of information — but Ronnie let slip that he was a fitter and turner and worked for 'Precision Engineering' at Alexandria. After the coffee and a couple of biscuits along with a thirty minute conversation, Bill said goodbye and headed for his next stop — Precision Engineering, about a twenty minute drive southward.

He introduced himself with his police badge to the manager and owner, a gentleman called Harry Whittaker. Bill explained the Ronnie Bottles situation and wanted to know if Ronnie had any family or friends that he could talk to so that he could better understand Ronnie and what might be able to bring him back into the world. First of all, Harry wouldn't help — but then again, he'd never met a guy like Bill and after a while he did start to talk. The office girl found Ronnie's old file and an earnest conversation got underway.

'You know Bill, Ronnie Bottles was my best turner. He served his apprenticeship here and stayed on. He gave me one hundred per cent and it was so sad to see what happened to him.'

Now Bill was all ears.

'This guy was everybody's friend; he didn't know how to get angry. There was another fitter and turner here called Doug Cameron. Doug became Ronnie's best friend and together with their wives it became a terrific friendship. They'd go on holidays together, camping, trips to the snow and God knows what else … it was one of those friendships you read about, but one that never happens to you.

'Then something happened. Doug Cameron began having an affair with a woman who lived next door to his place. Doug's wife found out about it by chance one day and all hell broke loose. During one of their heated arguments Doug viciously bashed his wife. The police were brought into it and they carted Doug off to jail. When they let him out he was never allowed to go back to the house or go anywhere near his wife. With nowhere to go he went and saw Ronnie. He allowed Doug to use his spare room until he sorted out his life. Doug started taking days off work under the guise of being emotionally sick and things like that. But in reality he was having an affair with Ronnie's wife.

'What do you think Bill? Here's a bloke who wears his heart

on his sleeve, opens his house to his best friend and then the mongrel takes advantage of it. When Ronnie found out about it he went to pieces. He divorced his wife; they sold the house and divided the money. Their sixteen year old daughter wouldn't talk to him because she thought her father had walked out on them … and the mother wasn't about to volunteer the truth. Ronnie never came back to work, he was too embarrassed. I've still got his tools and his locker is just the way he left it. I wouldn't have it any other way because one day he might walk back in here and I'll say, how're you going mate.

'At the time when Ron and his wife split up we didn't see Doug for six weeks, then one day he bowled up like nothing had ever happened … but the union delegate had already said if Doug shows up here for work and I let him start, then they're all going out the front to put a picket on the place. So when Doug arrived I gave him his pay packet. He couldn't believe he'd been given the sack. He had to go into the workshop to get his tools and naturally the boys gave it to him — when he came back here it looked as if he'd been in World War Three. He was covered in oil and grease, his clothes were torn and he had one shoe missing. He didn't even say goodbye, how ungrateful!'

Bill laughed. Harry continued.

'Ronnie's wife and Doug moved to a flat in Sutherland. He helped her spend her money and when it was all gone he shot through.'

Bill said, 'What a nightmare of a bloke, must have been a real conman.'

'Yeah,' said Harry. 'The daughter got married about ten years ago — she had her picture in the paper, that's how I know that. Now if you want to go out into the workshop and talk to the boys, it's all right by me.'

'All right, thanks a lot Harry … I might just do that.'

Bill spent thirty minutes talking to Ronnie's old workmates with a couple of them saying that they would go to the shelter and visit him.

Bill occupied most of the next day trying to find out the name of Ronnie Bottles' daughter, and then he had to find her married name. The police computer finally coughed up two names: Christine Bottles and Christine Bennett. He followed a trail of Christine Bottles' past driving licences and found one where she changed her name to Bennett. Her current license was issued just four weeks ago with an address at Sutherland.

Bill left North Sydney at 9.00 am the following day and arrived at Christine's modest townhouse in the southern suburb of Sutherland at 10.00 am. He pressed the welcome button and waited. The door opened and a voice said, 'Yes?' The solid security door on the outside stayed locked, so Bill was looking through the grill.

'Ahh, hello, I'm Detective Bill Scanlon from Sydney CIU.' He held up his ID so she could see it through the bars. Bill was looking at a woman twenty-eight years of age, with a slim figure and long black hair — and a few features of her father. 'Are you Christine Bottles?'

'Yes, but my married name's Bennett.'

'I'd like to talk to you about your father,' said Bill.

'My father!' She was shocked and said, 'I don't have a father. He walked out on my mother and she suffered enormously because of him. I don't care if he's dead. I never want to see him again.'

'You would remember a friend of your father's — a fellow called Doug Cameron.'

'Of course. When Dad left he stayed to help Mum.'

'Your father gave Doug a room when he needed a roof over his head, when he had nowhere else to go.'

'Yes, that's right.' Christine was becoming annoyed by all this type of questioning but Bill continued on.

'Did you know that when Doug Cameron moved into your house, he began having an affair with your mother? When your father found out he suffered a mental breakdown and went to pieces. When you wouldn't talk to him he thought, "What's the use of it all?" His life sunk to an all-time low as he squandered the money that he got from the sale of the house as part of the divorce settlement, then he went to live on the streets of Sydney without even collecting unemployment benefits.'

Christine replied quite nastily, 'Well, that was his choice, and that story you just told me is all bullshit. He's just trying to justify why he left Mum.'

'Your father didn't tell me that. I couldn't get a word out of him, but I found out where he used to work and spoke to his old workmates at Precision Engineering.'

Christine said with venom, 'I didn't know that the police investigate this type of thing.'

'They don't. The police couldn't care less. I belong to a group of people who try to help others. If we can help get unfortunate people back into society and repair the threads of their families, then we've done our duty as human beings. This is my day off and I thought I'd see if I could help patch things up between you and your father. It's never too late, you know. Where's your mother now?'

'She lives in Campbelltown in public housing. When the relationship between Mum and Doug ended there was no money left. I see her every Sunday. She's only a shadow of her former self. She's lost weight, her hair's turned white and I don't think she's long for this world.'

'So Doug Cameron not only destroyed your father's marriage, but when your mother had no money left he ran away. What an arsehole, and this was your father's best friend.' Bill bent down shaking his head and slid a card under the security door. When he stood back up there was one last thing to say to Christine. 'If you need a hand with anything you can call me on that number. Thanks for listening to me. Goodbye.'

'Yes, goodbye.'

Christine closed the door as Bill walked back to his car; she picked the card up, glancing at it, and then threw it in the kitchen tidy.

Bill had done this journey hundreds of times in the past and had a fair idea of what was going to happen here; he was thinking of this as he drove through the city toward his home in North Sydney. Christine Bottles Bennett would be having a restless night tonight, as her brain tried to digest the conversation that she'd just had with Bill Scanlon.

Just as Bill had predicted, Christine Bennett began wrestling with herself after he left.

She spent the rest of the day doing household duties, but that conversation just wouldn't go away; it kept on repeating itself over and over. She picked her daughter up when school was over and after her husband came home from work they went to the local supermarket to do some shopping. Things seemed to go smoothly for her within her family unit, and a couple of sparkling wines after dinner did wonders. Up to this point she hadn't told her husband about Bill's visit — after all, this was her personal problem and she'd already dismissed it as garbage.

Getting to sleep after bedtime didn't seem a problem, but once asleep her dreams turned into nightmares. Images of long ago when her mother and father were breaking up kept swirling around in her head — and then Bill Scanlon's echoing voice: 'It's never too late you know, It's never too late you know!'

Then, an ugly head coming out of a dead calm lake, screaming, 'Your mother cheated on your father, your mother cheated on your father. Ha ha ha ha haaa!'

This was the pattern for the rest of the night. She woke at 3 am and wasn't game to go back to sleep — the torture was too much for her. Then, as the dark of night turned into the light of day, the machinery of her brain bought reason to bare.

Over breakfast Christine told her husband about Bill's visit and it was decided that she would have to confront her mother on her weekend visit to Campbelltown in an attempt to discover the truth. There was something else she didn't want to do, and that was to fish Bill's card out of the kitchen tidy — but come Monday morning, she was hoping she would be able to throw it back in, this time ripping it up.

On Sunday morning, Christine Bottles Bennett set off for Campbelltown, just as she did every week to visit her mother. They had a cup of coffee and a bit of a chat and then Christine said, 'Mum, I've heard a story about you and Doug and I want you to tell me the truth about it. When did you and Doug become an item?'

Christine noticed the black look that came over her mother's face and she knew that she struck a nerve. The mother answered. 'Look, I'm not going into that. That part of my life is behind me now and after going to hell and back I'm not about to talk about it. So, end of story.'

'Mum, I've talked to somebody who worked with Dad and he told me … I need to know what happened. Did you and Doug begin having an affair while he was living with us, before Dad walked out?'

Christine was firm in her speech. Her mother was frail and bent over and it was obvious that she was a sick woman. This was the last thing that she needed, as all the pain of the past came back to haunt her. She began to cry.

Christine remained firm. 'Well Mum, I'm not leaving here until I get some answers. I need to know for my wellbeing. We can't change what's happened and no matter what, I will always be here for you.'

After a period of silence Christine's mother said, 'Your father was such a caring person, a good provider. I knew I was doing the wrong thing but I couldn't help it. Doug was such an irresistible, handsome man and I fell in love with him. There's a passage in the Bible that says, "Your sin will find you out," and well, your father found out that his wife and best friend had betrayed him — so he filed for divorce. We talked through solicitors after that and here I am today with nothing, after having everything. The only thing I live for is you.'

Christine said, 'You told me Dad just up and left us, and I've hated him ever since when all the time I should have been hating you.'

'Yes, you're right, but I didn't want you to find out that I'd been a bad person, so I'm sorry, I'm sorry. I can see that I made two mistakes: falling for Doug's charm and not telling you the truth. I didn't want to lose you. I wish I was dead.'

Mrs Bottles started crying again. This time Christine went and comforted her; she had the truth now, that's all that mattered. And of course, she would have to ring that policeman and talk to him.

It looked as though it was going to be a tough week for Christine Bennett as she pondered over the events of the last few days. Three times during the week, she picked up the phone to dial the number that was printed on Bill's card, each time deciding not to go on with it. She was nervous but she knew she had to do it. On the fourth occasion she let the dial tone ring on.

A voice on the other end of the line said, 'Bill Scanlon.'

'Hello Bill, this is Christine Bennett.'

'Hi Christine, how is everything?'

'Okay. Look … I'm ringing to tell you that you were right about my father, as much as I didn't want to believe it. But you can't escape the truth can you? So I'd like you to make arrangements for myself, my husband and our daughter to see my father. I owe him that much and I want to tell him I'm sorry. Any Saturday will do.'

'Okay Christine, I'll be in touch. Goodbye for now and thanks for calling.'

And so it was arranged that the following Saturday at 1.00 pm the meeting between Ronnie Bottles and his daughter would take place. They decided it would be a surprise, therefore eliminating any anxiety that could cause Ronnie to scuttle the meeting.

At 1.00 pm, Ronnie Bottles went into Donny King's office, which was more like a large lounge room with an office in one end of it. Donny asked him to sit down in the lounge and they would discuss aspects of his rehabilitation. Donny looked quite dapper in his new clothes, bought for this special occasion. A haircut along with some fine grooming and a precise shave earlier in the morning must have surely alerted Ronnie's brain that something was in the wind — but if that was the case, he wasn't showing it.

Timing was all-important here. The lounge that Ronnie Bottles was sitting on faced the doorway. After a prearranged signal, Bill Scanlon ushered the Bennett family to position themselves just outside that door. Christine appeared in the doorway and stood there. Ronnie looked up, his puzzled mind analysing the person standing there.

Then Christine said, 'Hello Dad.'

Ronnie just stared at her. His face changed shape as he lost control of his emotions; tears began to flood out of his eyes as his hand came up to cover his face. Christine walked quickly over to the lounge and sat down beside him; she placed her arm around him as comfort. There was no talking; they just held each other as all those long years of absence caught up with them, taking control of father and daughter in magnetic emotion. They broke away from each other and dried their eyes.

Ronnie said, 'You know, I dreamed a couple of times over the years that one day we would run into each other. I'm sure glad it wasn't two months ago, otherwise you wouldn't have recognised me.'

Christine replied, 'I recognise you all right, and I've got to say that you look pretty good. Dad,' she said, holding his hand, 'I'm sorry for the past twelve years. I had no idea what happened, but I know now. Please forgive me.'

Ronnie replied, 'Of course, forgiveness is an automatic reaction when you love someone ... and wow, look at you, you're all grown up.'

'Yes, and there's somebody I want you to meet.' She walked over to the door and came back with her husband and daughter. Ronnie stood up out of the lounge as they approached him. 'This is my husband James.'

James stepped forward and shook Ronnie's hand, then he put his arm around him saying, 'Nice to meet you, Mr Bottles.'

Christine continued. 'And this is Carol, our daughter. Carol, this is my father and your grandfather.'

Nine year old Carol walked up to Ronnie, who was now down on his knees. They held hands as tears ran down his face. He gave her a nice soft hug, trying not to frighten her; after all, they were complete strangers.

'Thank you Carol,' said Ronnie as Carol walked back to her mother.

With the formalities over Christine said to her father, 'Dad, we're going down to the harbour foreshore around Circular Quay and the Opera House. Maybe you'd like to come?'

'If Donny says I can go, sure — what do you think Donny?'

'Of course you can go, I think it would be just the sort of medicine you need. I'll see you when you get back.'

The four of them caught a yellow cab down to the waterfront. They soaked up this beautiful area of wonders, enjoying a simple ice cream and watching the harbour ferries power on by. They stood and watched the kerbside buskers and the didgeridoo players. They took in one of the thirty minute concerts from the Opera House Theatrette and had afternoon tea on the boulevard.

For Ronnie Bottles, his time of living to hell and back was just about as good as over. He'd found his family and they would go on to enjoy many good fulfilling times together. No doubt Ronnie Bottles would now find his way back to Precision Engineering until retirement.

For the likes of Bill and Marree Scanlon, and Jack and Kate Kelly — along with Donny King and the Salvation Army — they would celebrate what happened here today. It was Ronnie Bottles' day in the sun; tomorrow it would be another down and out who, after some sort of catastrophic life event, would choose to live on the streets of Sydney in a twist of fate difficult to understand.

Bill had one more thing to do: ring up Jack and tell him about the successful meeting with Ronnie Bottles and his daughter, almost bringing to an end this particular chapter.

Jack agreed. 'What a sensational outcome. I can't wait to see him, and I look forward to inviting him to a barbecue and a drive around the harbour when I get home at Christmas time.' They talked for another ten minutes before signing off.

NINE

Leaving the Big Lake Hotel

The next eight weeks went smoothly for Jack, without any problems. After his operation, Bozz would need a few months of rehab, but already the signs were good. The renovations that Jack had to do were now complete, and next Saturday he would be leaving and heading to the nearest highway to continue walking in the footsteps of his grandfather.

On Friday night the publican organised a goodbye party for him. Chantal came around and at the end of the night Jack said goodbye to her. All his football mates formed a guard of honour that Jack had to walk through while they sang 'For he's a jolly good fella'. Tears swelled in his eyes but the dams of emotion held up well. He spent thirty minutes shaking hands with everybody before calling it a night.

In the morning, Jack rose early, packing his backpack and readying the swag. He put the big coat and hat on then the tent swag combo, before closing the door of his unit for the last time. He spared a thought for Kelly Marsden as he walked past the doorway of the unit that she'd stayed in when she came to her sister's wedding.

Harry the publican and his wife were waiting for him when he reached the office. Mrs Bush gave Jack a hug and a kiss. 'Good luck Jack, wherever you go,' she said.

Harry shook Jack's hand saying, 'Goodbye Jack. I don't know what you're up to mate, but I suppose in time it might be become apparent, eh?'

'Probably,' answered Jack, and with the goodbyes over, he walked out onto the footpath and headed south, in the direction of the bridge. A car was parked outside the hotel and as he approached it he noticed two mature ladies in the front seat. They both had Salvation Army uniforms and hats on. Jack half-stopped, looked at them, lifted his hat and said, 'Ladies.' He put the hat back down and continued on. It wasn't the first time he'd noticed this car and it didn't take long to work out that it was Donny King's spies keeping an eye on him.

The two Salvo ladies in the car looked at each other, with one of them saying, 'Well, I wonder where he goes now.'

The other one replied, 'God only knows that but wherever it is, we'll know. I'll give Donny a ring so he can mark the map.' While she opened her handbag to retrieve her mobile phone, the first lady picked up a digital camera and took a photo of Jack as he walked on.

A short time later Jack was walking through the commercial centre for possibly the last time. He noticed the vacant land where the carnival was. The personality was gone; it was empty and bare as only the ghosts from the ghost train were there now. But the lawn bowlers at the King Prawn Club were at it early today, enjoying the competition — might be a long day today. Walking onto the bridge walkway, he couldn't help but think of his grandfather, who was here a long time ago working on the building of the old wooden bridge during the Great Depression. It was time to move on.

Several fishermen had their lines out trying their luck, and just as he did on that first day that he came to this area he stopped in the middle of the first channel, leaned on the rail and looked into the water. The tide was coming in and the water was crystal clear. A small school of fish were frolicking around the bridge pylons. Bill's mobile phone came out of his coat pocket along with the binoculars. He dialled Chantal's number and put the binoculars up to his eyes.

There was no sign of life — then she appeared on the balcony, picked up the phone from the table and sat down in the recliner. 'Hello.'

'Hi, this is Jack.'

'I thought you were leaving today,' said Chantal.

Jack replied, 'Yes I'm on my way now, I thought I'd have one last look at you before I went … you know, something to remember you by, something to think of while I'm on the road. How's that coffee?'

'Beautiful.'

'Gee, look at that beautiful boat going past your place now.'

'Where are you?' Chantal was on her feet looking over the road, then the footpath.

'No no, I'll wave.'

Chantal saw the human figure waving. 'Is that you on the bridge?'

'Yes.'

'So that was you on the bridge the first day you came here.'

'I thought I'd have a bit of fun with you that day.'

'Yeah you had a bit of fun all right, and now you want something to remember me by eh? Well, how about this?'

She put the phone down on the table and pulled her t-shirt off, standing there in her red lace bra.

Jack was surprised. 'Wow, more than I could have hoped for … nobody's got a better set than you. See you!' He had one last goodbye wave and walked on.

In front of Chantal's house, walking on the footpath were Mrs Hobbs and her son Malcolm. They saw Chantal pull her t-shirt off and stand there.

The son asked. 'Mum, what's that lady doing?'

Mrs Hobbs looked up at Chantal then looked back at Malcolm and said quite snappily, 'It's that disgusting woman again, now shut your eyes and stop looking at her, you dirty little boy.' She followed that up with a good slap across the back of his head.

Malcolm took off and ran a couple of metres, then turned to face her. He put a finger in each side of his mouth, stretching it as wide as he could, then he poked his tongue out at her. She ran at him with her hand up to hit him a second time, but he turned and ran away from her.

She knew she couldn't catch him but she called out to him, 'I'll fix you when we get home, Sonny Jim!' Mrs Hobbs turned and looked up at Chantal and spoke very loudly at her, 'You disgusting woman, why don't you go and live somewhere else?'

Chantal looked down at her and said, 'Why don't you mind your own business, you bloody old bat?'

Chantal looked back to the bridge. Jack was walking south; she looked at the phone. *Call ended.* She put her t-shirt back on, sat back down in the recliner and watched Jack until he disappeared on the southern side of the bridge.

Jack had passed a couple of fisherman, and then the second channel. He noticed the pelicans still had the high ground on the small island. As he reached the other side of the water, a bloke about twenty-five years of age with a backpack on came up the steps from the base of the bridge and almost ran into Jack. Jack stopped to let him onto the footpath and they started talking.

'So how are the fish biting down there?' asked Jack.

The backpacker replied in a beautiful English voice, 'I don't know, I was only having a cup of coffee at the kiosk.'

'Right,' said Jack. 'Where are you off to?'

The backpacker answered, 'About fifty kilometres down the coast. I've got some friends there and they've got a job for me that will last a month.' He stopped walking and said, 'My name's Roy

Charles, I'm a backpacker from South Hampton in England and I'm exploring Australia.' He put his hand out.

Jack accepted the friendship and shook his hand, offering his own resume. 'Jack B Kelly from Sydney Harbour. I'm walking in the footsteps of my grandfather — and that could take me anywhere but I have to be in Goulburn City in two weeks' time. I started a couple of months ago with another eight or nine left.'

They hit it off straight away with Roy saying, 'Why don't you come with me for a couple of weeks? There's a bit of work where I'm going and you never know where that will lead.'

'Yeah, you're pretty right about that — okay, you lead the way. How do we get there?'

'We catch the train from Oak Flats.'

'Oak Flats! Christ, it sounds like the end of the line.'

'No, it's the end of the line where we're going, the Shoalhaven River.'

When Roy said those words a buzz went up Jack's backbone as thoughts of the Shoalhaven footballers from the grudge match flashed into his mind.

Roy remarked, 'We need to get a lift.'

And it didn't take this Pommy backpacker from South Hampton long to catch the attention of a motorist willing to help. Ten minutes later they were standing in front of what looked like a brand new railway station called Oak Flats: the beginning of a thirty minute train ride to the end of the line.

TEN

That train ride to the end of the line

After purchasing tickets, Jack and Roy joined the other ten or so commuters on the platform that were awaiting the arrival of the train. One person was heard to say, 'Here it comes.'

The new-looking six car silver double decker electric train glided to a halt, with all those waiting stepping on board to claim seats. The train was virtually full but the swaggie backpacker team of Jack and Roy found seats opposite one another in the front of the second-last car. The journey to the Shoalhaven River would take about thirty to forty minutes, with the train stopping at five stations along the way. It passed through lush green hills and at times beside the ocean.

The young man and lady sitting across the aisle were obviously very much in love, as they were all over each other. They didn't seem to know or care that they were in a crowded train with people all around and that it would be most uncomfortable for those in close proximity. Their thoughts must have been of two people in a carriage all by themselves. The young lady with her tight shorts and skimpy top was half-straddled over her boyfriend with her eyes closed, kissing him around the neck. He also had his eyes closed, enjoying this moment of togetherness. Roy was trying to look anywhere else but with this sort of distraction, he wasn't having much luck.

Three stations came and went with some people getting off and others getting on. They passed through a tunnel, emerging beside the ocean and the picturesque harbour belonging to the fascinating village of Kiama. The train travelled across the main street on a trestle bridge before coming to a halt at the biggest station so far. Jack noticed seven or eight commuters waiting on the platform. Four of them were young men with green bands around their heads.

Bloody gang culture, I hope they don't get in this car as they usually start causing trouble, were Jack's immediate thoughts. His fears were realised when one of the gang members came into the car to take up the only seat that was available. As he walked down the aisle he gave the two backpacks belonging to Jack and Roy a good sideways kick, even though there was plenty of room to pass on by. He sat down in the four-seat layout opposite the two young lovers, who had come up for air and were now holding hands and watching out the window to get their bearings. The guard's whistle sounded, the doors closed along with a sudden jerk and the train moved off to continue the journey.

The young lovers began to embrace again; she draped her leg over his and passionately kissed her boyfriend on the lips. Roy Charles had a big grin on his face, as did Jack. A minute or two went by and finally the green-banded gang member couldn't stand it any longer. 'Heeey, how about inviting me to the party? I'm getting a bit lonely over here.'

She turned to him, giving him a black look, then continued on undeterred — but it took the gloss off her boyfriend's concentration. Green Band was all mouth now as he raised the level of smutty harassment. Jack could see trouble brewing so he pulled Bill's phone out of his pocket and texted a message to the police. *Green head band gang causing trouble on train south of Kiama.*

A minute later an acknowledgement came back. He then put the phone on video, and from his leg he inconspicuously aimed it at the proceedings across the aisle.

'Hey sexy, come over here and sit on my knee and I'll show you what it's like to be kissed by a real man.'

She just ignored him but her boyfriend was becoming agitated.

Green Band stood up and grabbed her by the arm, saying, 'Well come on, sit on my knee for a while.'

The young lady was shocked and said loudly, 'Get away from me,' dragging her arm away from his hand.

'Don't you go touching my girlfriend mate,' said her boyfriend.

Green Band looked at him. 'Well, who's going to stop me? It won't be you.'

The rest of the passengers in the car were closely watching this escalating incident, some with worried looks in their eyes. The boyfriend stood up to face Green Band, who had by then spotted the phone. Jack had lifted it up to the normal videoing position, hoping to stir him up. It worked.

'Heeey you, what do you think you're doing with that phone?'

'Oh, I'm just making a video,' replied Jack.

The gang member wasn't happy with that. 'Like hell you are! And I don't like the look of you so you'll be getting off the train at the next station — now give me that phone.' He moved toward Jack, who quickly put the phone away. Green Band grabbed Jack by the front of the big coat and tried to drag him to his feet.

Jack said, 'All right, all right, give me a chance to get up.'

Jack reached full height and found he was much taller than the gang member, who didn't know what hit him as Jack's powerful head butt caught him by total surprise. Green Band was stumbling backward as Jack's next punch struck him in the stomach, followed up with a punch to the left ear that rendered him useless. Jack grabbed him by the scruff of the neck and said, 'Now we'll see who gets off the train.'

He forced him to the centre of the car and only waited a minute or so before the train slowed down to stop at the next station. As soon as the doors opened Jack manhandled the half-limp body onto the platform and sat him on one of the seats. Roy

Charles followed behind, carrying the backpack that belonged to the troublemaking gang member and placing it on the seat beside him, then they both got back on the train.

The guard at the rear of the train saw Jack sit the gang member down on one of the station's seats and thought, *Yeah that bloke looks pretty sick all right.* He made a note of it in the train log then carried on with his duties.

Some of the passengers gave Jack a clap as he walked back through the car to his seat. The young lady's boyfriend said, 'Thanks very much for getting rid of that arsehole, here's my name and address if you need a witness.'

'Thanks,' said Jack as he looked at the piece of paper, then folded it up and put it in his top pocket.

The rest of the journey was a peaceful ride through rural countryside and the two young lovers were now innocently holding hands as if they were at a Sunday night church service. The train began slowing down and a short time later it pulled into the final station and the end of the line, Shoalhaven River. There were taxis and buses waiting; all those who were on the train disembarked to go to their various places. The other three gang members were on the platform waiting for the fourth member to get off the train.

Jack said, 'I think they might have a long wait Roy, what do you reckon?'

Roy laughed as he said, 'Yes, it could be all day and up into the night.'

They were both laughing as they continued on towards their destination, which was a ten minute walk to the other side of the very wide river. Once across it was then a right hand turn and a couple of hundred metres to the Shoalhaven Backpackers Hostel. After booking into their simple accommodation it was almost time for lunch. A couple of Aussie meat pies and

Coca-Cola would do the trick and across the road, the grassy southern bank of the mighty Shoalhaven River would be their lunch room. And what a lunch room it was, watching the busy river traffic. Opposite on the northern bank was a wildlife park and zoo, which also operated river cruises and speedboat rides.

Jack intended to stay here only a week as this area wasn't in his grandfather's diary. He didn't care if he worked or not but if there was something to do, then he would do it. After lunch he ditched the swaggie uniform and came back into the real world. Roy's two backpacker mates arrived home and in the morning he would be going with them to work on one of the bigger fishing trawlers, working out of a place further down the river called Greenwell Point.

Late in the afternoon the owner of the wildlife park came in looking for somebody who could drive a commercial tour boat that travelled up the river one day and down the river to the ocean the next. The fifteen people on board would stop for lunch along the way then return to the wharf in a total of four hours. Six backpackers put their hands up, but to be a skipper in charge of paying customers some certification was required. The owner of the park was disappointed he couldn't find anybody and said, 'Ahh well thanks a lot fellas.' He began to walk away.

Jack called out to him, 'Maybe I can help you out.'

He turned to face Jack, who had his boat licence in his hand. After looking at it he said, 'You're hired for four days. Come over to the park in the morning at 9 o'clock and I'll give you an induction. The boat has to leave at 10 o'clock. Thank you, Mr …' He looked at the license. 'Mr Kelly.'

He gave Jack back his documentation and said, 'See you in the morning.'

'Right,' said Jack.

After dinner all the backpackers plus one swagman went

down to the Shoalhaven RSL, a fifteen minute walk away. It was a good night of casual drinking, playing darts and snooker. A big poster dominated the club notice board; it was advertising the Berry Agricultural Show. Jack was studying it when Roy Charles came up and said, 'Hey Jack, what do you say we go to the show on Saturday? We might be able to pick up something with a skirt on.'

Jack had a laugh at that one before saying, 'Yes, I like the shows and I'd love to go. How do we get there?'

Roy replied, 'We catch the train, it's one station back.'

'You beauty. It's Saturday Show time.'

The next four days driving the tour boat up and down the river was just what the doctor ordered. Jack's love of boats and water was testament to that. On Wednesday afternoon the park manager gave him a cheque for four days' pay, and they shook hands and said goodbye. He would bank the cheque into the swagman account, where the money would eventually find its way to the homeless peoples centre in Sydney. As he walked away from the wharf and fun park his thoughts were a couple of days ahead of him — to Saturday, in fact. He was looking forward to the Country Show in the nearby town of Berry.

On Saturday morning the ten backpackers and Jack arrived at the Berry Showground right on 10.00 am after travelling by train from the Shoalhaven River, a journey of some fifteen minutes. All shows are typical of each other, but with different personalities, and you could be sure everybody's taste will be catered for somewhere on the day.

It was early but already the sideshow alley was doing good business — and yes, Madam Fifi was there with her palm reading and as usual, there was quite a lot of giggling girlies there enjoying the aura of the future that surrounded this particular type of entertainment. Next were all the carnival rides, which were pretty quiet, but one would imagine that as the day rolled on this place would be swamped by young teenagers looking for a quick thrill.

Walking on, there was a very large tent. The big sign said 'Vince O'Sullivan's Boxing Tent — first fight 11.00 am'.

Jack said to himself, 'This is one place that I must visit today.'

By midday all of the exhibition pavilions had been inspected, and now it was time for lunch, and relaxing in the grandstand with a box of fish and chips while taking in the equestrian events was the only way to go.

Leaving the horse jumping behind them, they came onto the Miss Berry Beauty Contest. A large stage and catwalk was host to these ambitious young ladies. As they were introduced one by one, they would strut their stuff under the watchful eyes of the judges, along with a large audience of young males whose eyes were well and truly hanging out of their heads. For a few of these young teenage ladies it was quite intimidating, as some of the sexist remarks from the young males left a lot to be desired.

The sound of the big bass drum was loud and clear and it seemed to have a magnetic effect on Jack and his newfound backpacker friends. They left the beauty contest to go and watch the boxing.

At Vince O'Sullivan's Boxing Tent it was fifteen minutes until the next round of one on one combat. Up on a narrow platform were six boxers. They had their gloves, boots, shorts and colourful robes on and all looking athletically impressive. One of them had control of the bass drum and was thumping it in a one-two rhythm. A large crowd of mostly men had assembled to watch this last-of-his-kind entrepreneur. One time, there were half a dozen boxing tents that roamed the countryside bringing boxing to the people — but due to government red tape, do-gooders and insurance companies, the era of boxing tents would be over when Vince decided to hang up his gloves — or should it be said, his tent.

He picked up the microphone and said, 'Holder, holder.' The bass drum went silent.

Vince, who had been a boxer in his younger days, introduced the members of his boxing team one at a time and simultaneously tried to entice members of the public to come forward and have a fight. Over the last forty years Vince had perfected the art of showmanship and was the ultimate professional. He was often mean, insulting and crude but sometimes it got results.

'Come on you guys, what are you waiting for? I've got six blokes looking for opponents and all you lot can do is to stand there looking all googly-eyed like a bunch of dummies.'

A young overweight teenager was standing in the front row.

'What about you Fatso, are you thinking about having a bit of a go, eh? Well, what about it?'

'Yeah I'd like to have a go at you, you old bastard,' answered Fatso in a nasty voice.

Vince kept it alive by saying, 'Now now Fatso, there's no need to get nasty. Just get yourself up here and meet boxer number one. He's only half your size and even if you lose you still get a hundred dollars, so what do you say?'

Fatso answered with the two finger salute. Vince moved on; he was thinking to himself, *Enough time spent on this idiot.* He continued stoking up an audience that had now swelled to about eighty or so people — and slowly but surely, he began getting opponents for his boxers.

'Come on fellas, show a bit of guts, stay four three-minute rounds and get five hundred dollars for your trouble — win the fight and get two thousand dollars! What could be fairer than that? It's money for nothing!'

Now Vince turned his attention to Jack's new friends. 'Well

what about you bunch of Pommy bastards — oops, I mean you gentlemen backpackers from England. Surely there must be one amongst you that's got the red badge of courage. Don't be shy, come up and show us what you're made of. The old British Empire was made up of people that could and would fight, but Pommys today are just a bunch of sissies! Your ancestors are rolling in their graves! You disgust me, get out of my sight, take yourselves back to the White Cliffs of Dover and see if I care.'

Vince had five of his six boxers accommodated with challengers, but he was having trouble getting a match for the sixth: an Indigenous lad six feet tall, and he looked like a real mean fighting machine too — and that's probably why opposing contenders were scarce. This boxer had the X factor written all over him.

Vince continued trying to sell him. 'Fellas, this gentleman has been with me for the last three years and has won most of his fights. He's come all the way from Alice Springs, now is there anybody from you bunch that will have a bit of a go and take him on?' He was getting desperate. 'Okay, let's make it *one thousand* dollars if you stay the four rounds and *three thousand* dollars if you can beat my boxer from the Red Centre.'

Jack was thinking, *Now he's making it hard.* He put his hand up and said, 'Yeah, I'll have a go at him mate.'

Vince looked at Jack. 'You little beauty, the last great white hope eh? Come up here fella.'

As Jack started to walk away Roy Charles said, 'Gee you're a gutsy bastard Jack.'

Jack replied, 'I need the practice.' He made his way up the stairs to join the others.

Vince put his arm around him and shoved the microphone in front of his face. 'What's your name, son?'

'Jack Kelly.'

'Where do you come from Jack?'

'Sydney Harbour.'

'Well you know what Jack? My boxer's going to send you back to Sydney Harbour, what do you think about that?'

'Not if I send him back to the Alice first.'

'*Wow*, they're fighting words Jack! So there it is customers, buy your tickets, the boxing starts in ten minutes.'

The bass drum started up again and the large crowd surged to the ticket box to buy their entry. The tent boxers and the public challengers made their way down the steps from the platform and entered the tent. By the time the 'house full' sign went up the first fight was ready to begin. It was a grudge match between two high school kids who hated each other's guts, but at least they were mature enough to settle it here.

The bell sounded for the start of the first of four three-minute rounds. The two fifteen year olds couldn't wait to get to the centre of the mat and start swinging punches. Their intentions were obvious: knock the other person's head off. It was a ripper of a fight and for the full four rounds they never let up, but in the end Vince declared it a draw. They'd have to live to fight another day. Both lads received $50 for their troubles. They would both sleep well tonight.

Now the first of the adult fights got underway — and after one minute it was all over with the tent winning that one easily. The second fight went three rounds but the challenger surrendered after a heavy onslaught by the tent boxer. The third fight went the full four three-minute rounds. Although the challenger acquitted himself well he came a good second and picked up five hundred dollars for twelve minutes' work. The tent won the next two fights and now it was time for Jack to step up to the plate.

The Indigenous boxer from the Red Centre was about the same height and weight, so neither had an advantage in that area. The real difference between the two were their ages; Jack was ten years older and the tent boxer was a professional fighter.

The bell sounded and round one got underway and both fighters circled each other, with the odd punch and counter punch being thrown. There was an obvious mutual respect going for both of them as they continued the cautious approach, neither landing a serious blow. The second round was better, with some pretty good exhibition boxing delivered by both fighters, and when the bell sounded at the end they still rated even. Two rounds to go.

In the third round the bout went up a notch, with some pretty hard thumping. At times it was intense, with the paying customers getting their money's worth in that round, but still no clear mandate at this stage for either boxer.

During the one-minute break before the final round, Jack heard Vince say to his Alice Springs fighter, 'Now stop mucking around and put this arsehole from Sydney Harbour into Ga Ga Land, understand what I'm saying boy?'

'Yes Boss.'

This infuriated Jack and for the first time a bit of nastiness came into his character.

The fourth and final round got underway with the fight now on in earnest. It was vicious and brutal. On the sideline Roy Charles had the Pommy backpackers rallied and they began to chant: 'Come on Jack, come on Jack, come on Jack.'

Vince wasn't stupid; he could see that Jack could box and now he had a cheer squad. He muttered to himself, 'Jesus Christ, I don't need a bloody cheer squad for him.'

Jack hadn't used all of his punches, while his opponent from Alice Springs had thrown everything but the kitchen sink. For Jack time was running out; he knew in his own mind that he was behind on points and there was only half a minute to go. Vince's words were still ringing in his ears: *Put the arsehole from Sydney harbour into Ga Ga Land.*

He could hear the backpacker cheer squad yelling their heads off and then the rest of the audience joined in. The volume went up. 'Come on Jack, come on Jack.' It gave him encouragement. *It's now or never,* he thought as he raised an all or nothing effort.

Jack swiftly moved up close to his opponent, swinging wildly and viciously. A flurry of punches rammed into the tent boxer's head and for the first time, the lad from the Alice took a backward step and automatically put his gloves up to protect his head from this sudden and unexpected onslaught. Jack seized the moment and sunk a massive punch into his unprotected stomach, taking all of his precious air. The fight was almost over as Jack lined up the tent boxer's head; a left and then a right found their mark with the force of a sledgehammer.

The Alice champ was severely wounded and he began to wobble; again Jack lined up his head for a final punch but before he delivered the blow that would have finished him off, Vince rushed in and got between them. He gave his boxer support so that he wouldn't fall over. Two assistants came and helped him back to his corner where they sat him down on a chair. The tent audience, realising the fight was over, let out a big *hurrah*.

Vince walked over to Jack, took hold of his wrist and raised it into the air. 'And the winner is Jack Kelly from Sydney Harbour.'

It was spontaneous applause from all those inside the boxing tent and they were glad Jack had won — and in doing so had provided them with twelve minutes of terrific entertainment. In due course Vince paid Jack the three thousand dollars in hundred dollar notes. It was then time to say goodbye to the Berry Agricultural Show, and what a good time Jack and his backpacker friends had.

That night they all went down to the RSL for dinner in the club restaurant and Jack paid for their meals — after all, they helped him win that fight when they started chanting that slogan,

'Come on Jack'. It was a lifting experience that made him produce that little bit extra.

Tomorrow was Sunday and for Jack that meant relaxation day. Time to lick his wounds and the best way to do that was to go fishing. He borrowed a fishing line and bought some live beach worms. He selected a spot on the riverbank beside the bridge pylons and settled down there on the sunny side. He caught four decent size bream and two blackfish. They would go well for Sunday night dinner, Jack's last meal at the Shoalhaven Backpackers Hostel, as in the morning he would be leaving to continue walking in the footsteps of his grandfather. His next destination would be south of Goulburn City.

Jack had left a note on the notice board indicating he required a lift to the Southern Highlands. A bikey answered his call and after inspecting Jack's luggage, gave his approval. The bikey's name was Derek Dunn and his Harley motorbike had a sidecar attached, otherwise Jack wouldn't have accepted the lift. Derek asked Jack not to have breakfast in the morning as he was meeting a few friends at a place on top of the mountain and it would be nice to have breakfast together. Jack said goodbye to Pommy backpacker Roy Charles from South Hampton just in case he missed him in the morning.

At 7 am Jack walked out to Derek's motorbike. The backpack went into a compartment in front of the sidecar, then Derek tied the swag onto a rail that was on the outside. Jack got into the comfortable seat, inserted a pair of ear plugs then put on his helmet. Derek started the bike's motor and it was goodbye to the Shoalhaven River.

They travelled north for ten minutes, then turned left and began travelling in a westerly direction. The ride from this point on was up; they had to reach the top of the Great Dividing Range. But before that happened a massive valley appeared in front of them with a river running through it. The road went down to the floor of the valley and passed through a village aptly named Kangaroo Valley, and then it was across the river on a beautiful sandstone bridge at least one hundred and fifty years old.

The road continued to ascend for the next twenty minutes and at times it was quite steep, but it eventually levelled off at the top of the mountain where it led into a major intersection; they turned right and ten minutes later they arrived at the Robertson Pie Shop for breakfast. There were some other people having pies for breakfast, about one hundred to be exact. The paddock beside the pie shop was full of Harley motorbikes.

Jack was thinking, *It must be Harley day, an organised meet no doubt.* Then he noticed their leather jackets had the insignia of the Hell's Angels. *Cripes, consorting with this bunch of outlaws isn't my cup of tea, but it looks like I might have to grin and bear it.*

Derek had a plain leather jacket on but not for long. As soon as he parked and switched the bike off, he changed his jacket to a Hell's Angel style. Jack said nothing and carried on as if this was the norm. They made their way into the Pie Shop and ten minutes later came out with their picnic-type breakfast and sat down amongst the Hell's Angels members. Several outlaws came over and had a talk to Derek; after a forty-five minute stopover, it was time to go. Jack placed himself back into the sidecar while Derek went to talk to the bosses for a couple of minutes. When he came back he swapped jackets, putting the plain one back on. Jack said nothing and Derek didn't offer an explanation.

The chopper sound of the Harley motor roared into life and they continued on, doubling back the way they'd come and continuing west until they reached the beautiful highlands town of Moss Vale some twenty minutes later. Derek steered off the road and came to a stop just short of the main street. Jack put his swaggie coat and hat on, then the backpack and swag followed.

Derek said, 'You know what Jack? You look like the last swaggie.'

They had a good laugh at that while shaking hands and both hoped that they'd see each other again someday. Derek started the Harley and cycled off; he made a right hand turn at a round-about while Jack made a left hand turn on the footpath and into the main street.

At the same time, forty kilometres to the west, a rather large motorhome van was travelling south along the Hume Highway, the east coast link between Sydney and Melbourne. The van was also towing a covered box trailer. The beautifully decorated signage on the sides of both vehicles said it all.

MacGregor's Dog Circus
Starring
Prince the Wonder Dog

A large painted picture of Prince was in the middle, with five other smaller painted pictures of the other dogs in the show randomly spread around. Inside the van were the owners of the dog show, Mr and Mrs MacGregor. Mr MacGregor was driving and sitting in the passenger seat was his wife.

The MacGregors were in their early sixties and they were driving to the Goulburn City Agricultural Show, where the dogs would perform their circus to the paying public. They'd been doing this for forty years and had made a very handsome living along the way. Their dogs had taken them all over Australia, enabling them to enjoy the whole of this wonderful country. They'd also been married forty odd years and had three grown up children and five grandchildren. Because they had everything that they needed in life — and the fact that they weren't getting any younger — they'd scaled back the circus performances and at the moment a couple of dozen shows a year was all they were looking for.

The interior of the van has been converted into triple star rating dog accommodation and was separated from the driving section. As far as the dogs were concerned it couldn't get any better than this.

It was 10 am on a beautiful autumn day, with the sun shining brightly through a clear blue sky — except for some dark black clouds in the far south east that were possibly issuing an ominous warning. A big green highway sign pointing to an off ramp said 'Moss Vale' — the sign passed by.

Mr MacGregor said to his wife, 'Those couple of shows we did there one time were well received.'

'Yes, I loved that little place, we'll have to go back there one day, what do you think?' was her reply.

He answered, 'Yes, we might fit it in next year eh?' Mr Mac-Gregor was in a happy mood. He placed his hand high on her thigh and gave it a little rub, then said, 'Well Lassie, is tonight the night?'

'Why Mr MacGregor, what on earth are you talking about?' answered Mrs MacGregor.

'You know what I'm talking about, is tonight the night?'

She put her hand on top of his hand and graciously said, 'I don't think you can handle it any more. It took you a week to get over the last one, and now we've got three shows in the next couple of days. Let's get them out of the way, then we'll see what happens.'

Mr MacGregor took the one hand that he had on the steering wheel and triumphantly punched the air with his fist, excitedly saying, 'You little beauty, I might have bought me a ticket.' At the same time he continued to squeeze her leg.

Mrs MacGregor had the last say. 'Now you ought to know by now that you don't count your chickens before they're hatched.'

They both had a bit of a laugh before she kissed him on the ear. Driving returned to normal and the dog van continued on along the highway. They passed a big truck stop, then a short time later, another.

Fifteen minutes further on they came to an area where a lot of road resurfacing had been undertaken. Mr MacGregor slowed down when he saw an area off the highway that had been levelled off, accessible by a road leading up a small slope. He drove the van up this slope and onto the level area.

'We'll give the dogs a bit of exercise here Lassie, then we'll have a cup of tea and a bun,' said Mr MacGregor as he turned the motor off.

The level area was manmade, about the size of a country park, and was basically a road base dump. Big piles of blue metal and mixed road base along with all the machinery required to build and repair the highway were all parked here. Large trucks, graders, bitumen machines, road rollers and a couple of lunch rooms on wheels were all located at the southern end. At the moment the place appeared to be deserted, but you could see that a lot of activity had been going on.

Mr and Mrs MacGregor took three dogs each on leashes and proceeded to walk the outer extremities of the level area, which was surrounded on three sides by heavy bush and trees. The star of the dog show was the wonder dog Prince. One look at this large blue cattle dog and you were immediately impressed; he looked like a champ and he was a champ. The other five dogs were three French poodles and two fox terriers and were only half the size. After exercising the dogs, the MacGregors tied their leashes to the side of the van on a purpose-built rail, and then they were given a bowl of food and a bowl of water each.

While the dogs were enjoying the hospitality, Mr and Mrs MacGregor had a cup of tea and a bun. They'd set up a portable table and two chairs on grass in front of the van, while a small digital radio added to the relaxing scene, beaming in some nice music from Goulburn City.

Prince the Wonder Dog licked his bowl absolutely clean and in his own mind he felt like having a look around, but he was tied to the side of the van. Standing up on his back legs he could reach the knot quite easily. It was a simple one-bow knot and it didn't take the wonder dog too long to work it out and undo it — now he was free.

Prince had a bit of a run with the leash dragging along the ground. He went to the trees and sniffed his way along the northern perimeter, inspecting everything as he went. The five remaining dogs had now finished their meals and were watching Prince; they started to get a bit jealous of Prince roaming around by himself and decided that they'd like some of that freedom too. They strained on their leashes and started to bark.

Mrs MacGregor, enjoying her cup of English tea, said, 'I wonder what those dogs are barking at.'

Mr MacGregor placed his cup on the portable table. 'I'll go and have a look. Hope it's not a snake.'

He walked around the side of the van and the first thing he noticed was that Prince was gone. Mr MacGregor followed the dogs' gaze and there he was, sniffing along the ground about thirty metres away and coming toward him. Mr MacGregor grabbed a spare leash and angrily walked towards Prince shouting, 'Come here, you bastard of a dog.'

Prince stopped instantly and watched Mr MacGregor aggressively approaching. He put his tail between his legs and began to cower.

Mrs MacGregor was running, trying to catch up. She called out, 'Don't frighten him, don't frighten him.'

Mr MacGregor had his dumb and stupid suit on today and ignored his wife, charging on to terrorise his star dog. As he neared Prince he raised the doubled-up dog leash into a striking position. Prince knew what that meant and a piece of steel came into his backbone. The cowering stopped, the tail came back out to the normal position and he began to back away sideways like a crab.

'Don't you run away from me, you arsehole of a dumb animal!' yelled Mr MacGregor, who was now in full flight.

Prince, terrified of that raised dog leash, decided to put the foot on the accelerator and get the hell out of there; he lengthened his stride. Mr MacGregor, sixty years of age and now out of breath, lunged at Prince. His legs overreached, tangling his feet together, and he crashed to the blue metal and grass surface. Prince was off and heading toward the bush and trees on the other side.

Mr MacGregor just lay there. His wife arrived and helped him sit up. He had skin off his hands and a hurt Scotch pride but other than that he seemed okay. Mrs MacGregor said, 'Come on love, let's go and finish our cup of tea. Prince will come back, he always does.'

Mr MacGregor, still in a sitting position, said, 'You know what Lassie, I don't care if he doesn't come back ... I've had it up to here with that dog.' He put the stiff palm of his hand in the middle of his forehead to illustrate. 'If he's not here when it's time to go, then he can stay in the bush and live on rabbits, I don't care anymore. The other day he bailed me up, I thought he was going to eat me.'

Mrs MacGregor never argued with him; he was the boss of the family and had guided their lives since the day they married. Their lives together had been exciting and fulfilling and they wanted for nothing, so she wasn't about to change the recipe that had been so good for so long. She also knew that when he got in this contemptuous mood, hell and high water wouldn't make him change his mind. He dusted himself off and they walked back to the table, arm in arm. Mrs MacGregor had noticed a change in her husband's temperament lately when it came to dealing with Prince, and she was pondering this as they continued on with their morning tea, albeit in silence, except for the digital music coming from the radio.

Later, Mrs MacGregor went for a walk around the bush line of the road base dump, calling out, 'Prince, Prince, come on pretty boy.' She repeated this over and over again for the next thirty minutes to no avail. Prince the Wonder Dog was nowhere to be seen or heard.

When she arrived back at the van, everything was all packed up, the other five dogs had been placed back into their luxurious accommodation, and Mr MacGregor was ready to go.

'What about Prince?' she asked.

'Like I said Lassie, he can stay here. I've made up my mind. I'm going to get a six week old blue cattle pup and train him up from scratch. Even without Prince we've still got one hell of a dog show, so let's go.'

Tears began to run down her face. She loved her favourite dog and didn't like the idea at all. She had visions of the highway — just metres away, really. Prince wouldn't last a couple of minutes out there. She could see him being run over by a monster truck, being attacked by a snake or a dingo and being shot or wounded by shooters only to die an agonising death.

Mr MacGregor said, 'Come on Lassie, let's go.' He was becoming impatient.

Mrs MacGregor replied, 'Well, if you won't wait for Prince to come back then I want to leave a bowl of meat and some water for him.'

He angrily said, 'The dog doesn't deserve anything, I've had it with him and I'm not feeding the birds.'

She answered back with a bit of grit this time and raised her voice in emotion that was just short of screaming. 'I'm not leaving here unless there's food and water left here for him to find.'

Mr MacGregor was taken aback by this unusual show of rebellion from his wife and angrily replied, 'Suit yourself then.' He then went and climbed into the van to sit in front of the steering wheel and have a good sulk.

Mrs MacGregor filled two empty ice cream containers — one with canned meat, and the other with water — and left them under the shade of a small bush. She knew that this was only a token thing to do and she silently preyed in her mind that a miracle might happen to save her dog from a disastrous end. Mr MacGregor started the motor of the van, turned it around, then it was down the ramp and back onto the six-lane highway to continue driving to the next major centre, Goulburn City — without their star attraction, Prince the Wonder Dog. Continuance of their journey would be icy indeed.

The two big eyes of Prince the Wonder Dog never missed a thing as he peered through the blades of thick long grass. Prince watched as the van drove down the ramp, turned left and disappeared on the highway. Only then did he come out of his hiding place with his wagging tail and began to explore the complete area. He soon found the food and water but at the moment wasn't hungry; he would save this for later.

It was mid-morning as Jack trudged his way through the main street of the beautiful self-contained town of Moss Vale, nestled on top of the Great Dividing Range — a prettier town you'll never see. He was receiving the usual stares people reserved for one who looked like a homeless individual — and Jack looked that picture. Big long coat, large and rough looking summer hat, backpack and swag.

A little girl with her mother were walking toward Jack on the footpath. The little girl gave Jack a sustained look, while the mother (who looked about twenty-five) looked towards the other side of the road, avoiding eye contact. Jack heard the little girl say, 'What's wrong with that man, Mummy?'

The mother said, 'Oh, that man hasn't got a home to live in; he just lives in the street somewhere.'

The little girl was looking back and said, 'He could come and live at our place.'

The mother replied quite crossly, 'No he can't, you don't talk to people like that. Okay?'

'Yes Mum.'

Jack smiled as he thought, *Good advice — that's the advice I'd give if I had a daughter like that.*

It was another thirty minutes before he reached the end of the town limits; now he needed a lift. Jack stood on the side of the road, taking in this beautiful rural setting. On the other side of the road were picturesque pastures that looked like spelling paddocks for race horses. Lush, rich and green, all the fences were painted white, giving that perfect contrast, while the horses added the final touch. The place was a picture, as was everything in this area. A dozen vehicles passed by with nobody interested in helping out (who could blame them?), and then a rather big station wagon slowed down and stopped on the side of the road, just in front of Jack. The driver stepped out and waited until Jack approached the vehicle.

'Need a lift mate?' asked the driver.

Jack replied, 'Yeah, if you don't mind.'

'Where are you off to?'

'South.'

'Well I'm going south so you're in luck put your gear in the back and hop in.' Before the driver started the motor, he introduced himself. 'I'm Kyle Walker.'

Jack shook hands with him and at the same time said, 'Jack Kelly.'

'Nice to meet you Jack.'

The station wagon slowly found its way onto the road to join the other cars. Some good conversation followed for about ten to fifteen minutes, and then a big green highway sign came up, along with an onramp:

Hume Highway

Goulburn City — Canberra

Melbourne

A sweeping left hand turn took them down the onramp and onto the southbound lanes of the Hume Highway. Conversation carried on with Kyle now slanting the conversation towards Jack. 'So how long have you been on the road?'

'About three and a half months.'

Kyle Walker continued the conversation and it centred on homelessness. He seemed to know what he was talking about, as the statistics he was coming up with were the state statistics found on the government's website. He would be assuming that Jack was homeless, and Jack's attire had it written all over him. Of course Jack couldn't tell him why he was on foot.

The second truck stop came and went with the conversation continuing. Jack was thinking that Kyle Walker seemed to be talking and putting things together as if he was some sort of trained counsellor or religious man. Kyle's mobile phone rang. Jack got the feeling by Kyle's answers that something had happened and it needed his immediate attention. The phone call ended with, 'Okay, I'll turn around and come back.' He put the phone away and said to Jack, 'I have to go back to Moss Vale. My wife's been involved in a car accident and is on her way to hospital, so as soon as I can find somewhere to turn around we'll be going back.'

Jack said to him, 'I'm sorry about your wife mate, but when you do find somewhere to turn around, you can let me out and I'll do a bit of walking.'

Kyle Walker replied, 'I thought you might come back with me, there's room in our hostel for you.'

'Hostel?'

'Yes, I run a hostel for disadvantaged people. If you come back with me, we can settle down all the fears and troubles that you're running away from. We can find you a job on one of our farms that we've got in the area. You might even find yourself a good woman, so you can settle down to a normal life. What do you say?'

Jack replied, 'Thanks for the offer Kyle, but I have to get to Goulburn City. There's a sheep farm waiting for me.'

'Ohhhh, okay,' answered Kyle in a somewhat of a disappointed voice, and it wasn't too long before Kyle could safely switch onto the northbound lanes of the Hume Highway that would take him back to Moss Vale. The station wagon came to a halt on the side of the freeway. Jack retrieved his gear from the rear of the vehicle then shook hands with Kyle.

'Jack, are you sure you won't come back with me? I really don't like leaving you out here in the middle of nowhere.' He was virtually pleading to Jack. 'If you come back with me, I can restart your life for you.'

Jack answered. 'Kyle, you're a good bloke all right, I can see it in your eyes. If the world was full of people like you, wars would be a thing of the past, there'd be no more fights in bars and clubs, and nobody would steal another man's woman. Now off you go, your wife needs you now.'

'Okay, I'll go, but take this card. You can always ring me if you're in strife.' He handed Jack a business card that said:

Moss Vale Uniting Church
Agent of the Wayside Chapel
K. Walker.

Kyle's last words were, 'If you're ever back this way in the future, please drop in and have a talk.'

The traffic thinned out a bit and the Ford station wagon motored across the lanes of the southbound freeway to the lanes of the northbound. There was one last wave as they continued on in opposite directions. Jack looked at the card again then put it in his wallet; he now knew why Kyle Walker was interested in him. Kyle was a full time do-gooder from the Southern Highlands, whereas Jack and his few friends were part timers. It was time to move on.

His thoughts were with his grandfather, who made his way along this route some eighty-odd years ago. Those days this road was little more than a goat track compared to the amazing freeway that now prevailed, and walking on the side was extremely dangerous in itself. The only thing like a footpath here was covered in thick high grass, shrubs, stinging bushes and small trees and it made the going tough, so it was easier to walk along the road on the breakdown lane. But sometimes idiot drivers used this narrow section to illegally overtake.

Cars and trucks whooshed by like bullets, just a couple of metres away. Sometimes the air displacement could hand out quite a bit of buffeting. So far Jack had picked up lifts without too much trouble — probably too easy — and after about twenty minutes his feet and ankles began to ache on the bitumen surface. He would have to stop and rest somewhere and have a drink and a biscuit. He looked at his watch; the sun was at its highest point, midday. A little further on Jack came onto where the freeway had been re-surfaced — he thought to himself, *Gee, there's been a bit of work going on here all right.*

Then he spotted the level area and the sloping road that led up to it; now he would get off the roadway for a while.

A couple of kilometres behind Jack and travelling in the slow lane was a restored 1964 Holden coupe. This vehicle looked fabulous in its bright red colours. The occupants were four twenty year old youths. The windows were down and the radio up. These three young gentlemen were just enjoying their day, driving and singing along with the music. The driver was the owner while the other three were his best mates. The one in the front seat was eating a banana just like any monkey would.

Jack walked off the side of the freeway and began the walk up the sloping road to the road base dump. Back in the restored Holden, the front seat passenger took his last bite of the banana, then Jack came into view. He said to his mates in the car, 'Heeey, look what we got up ahead, a hermit carrying a swag. Slow down a bit and I'll get him with this.'

Some light hearted banter followed.

'Bet you can't.'

'Bet I can.'

'Betcha can't.'

'Yeah, well watch this!'

The red restored Holden slowed down to about a third the speed as it approached Jack. The front seat passenger yelled out, 'Why don't you get a job, ya bludger!'

Jack turned to look and copped the banana skin fair and square in the face. *Whack!* It really stung.

The four men burst into hysterical laughter as the banana skin found its mark. The driver put his foot on the accelerator and the Holden coupe picked up speed again. Jack reacted quickly; he bent down and picked up a soft ball of clay a bit bigger than a golf ball, took aim and let it go. It struck the top of the car and skidded across the bonnet. He memorised the number plate, pulled his notebook out and wrote it down in his book. He continued walking up the sloping road, thinking to himself, *He who laughs last, laughs longest.*

The hysterical happy session inside the restored Holden came to an abrupt end as the piece of clay bounced across the roof then the bonnet. The driver cursed. 'Dirty rotten bastard, I'm going back to have a go at him,' he ranted as he brought the car to a halt.

One of the guys in the back said, 'Let it go, we started it. Now that it's backfired on us we have to wear it.'

The driver was angry and said, 'I didn't spend four thousand dollars on the best paint job just so a homeless dill could throw rocks at it.'

He put the car in reverse and began driving back to the sloping road of the road base dump.

Jack had reached the level area now and began surveying the area. From the wooded area, the two eyes of Prince the Wonder Dog were also doing a bit of surveying as he peered through the long thick blades of grass from his hidden position, watching the approaching stranger with interest.

Jack heard the noisy exhaust of that car and looked back down the sloping road. The four youths in the red restored Holden coupe would be up there in twenty seconds; they'd obviously taken offence at the piece of clay skidding across the roof of their car. Jack quickly put a battle plan together: keep close to the wooded area where he was now walking. Some big trees here to jump behind should he need a shield from the approaching car.

There was plenty of ammunition laying around here — large rocks and boulders along with steel pegs and small tree branches that could make good whacking sticks. But the big weapon here was the element of surprise. They would probably be thinking he was a homeless bum that would cower at the thought of a bit of violence.

Back on the freeway the Holden coupe was about to start the ascent to the road base dump. The guy in back again said to the driver, 'I can't see what you're trying to achieve. All that's going to happen here is some sort of violence, and I'm telling you now, I won't be having any part of it. This guy could be carrying some sort of horrible weapon.'

The front seat passenger said, 'Ah shut up you whingeing bastard, if you don't like it get out and walk.'

'You know what? Right now that doesn't sound like a bad idea,' replied the youth in the back seat.

As Jack walked close to the wooded area, he half-turned to watch the approaching car, ready to sidestep behind a tree if it got dangerous, but the car came to a halt just behind him. The banana peel thrower was out of the car moving swiftly and aggressively toward him.

'Hey, you!' he yelled out. 'What's the idea of throwing rocks at us?' He had his fist cocked back and ready to let it go.

Jack didn't have long to wait until he was in range; one more step exactly. They both let go at the same time, but Jack's fighting experience won the day and stopped the aggressor in his tracks. A straight left to the nose, followed by a savage right punch to his left ear that knocked his balance haywire. He fell to the ground on the soft grass with blood running down his face.

Jack quickly discarded the backpack and swag combo along with the hat and coat. The driver armed himself with a shifting spanner from the front of the car. He had no intentions of a fair fight here. The driver yelled at his two reluctant mates sitting in the back of the car. 'Come and give me a hand, you pair of gutless wonders!'

Neither of them moved or said anything. Jack looked the driver in the eyes as he left the car and surged toward him, the shiny shifting spanner high above his head. The driver screamed, 'Now you're going to get it, you homeless freak.'

His mission was cut short as Prince the Wonder Dog charged out of the trees, ran past Jack and savagely bit the driver just below the knee, in a sudden and strange twist of fate. Taken by complete surprise, as was Jack, the driver turned his attention toward the dog. 'Bloody mongrel,' he loudly cursed. 'I'm going to bash your dog's head in.'

He lined up the dog's head and viciously brought the spanner down, but in his haste and a bit of evasion by Prince he missed. Prince instantly grabbed him on the wrist and sunk those big front teeth in hard.

'Ohhhh,' he yelled as he dropped the spanner.

Prince let go and ran back into the bush. Jack couldn't believe what he'd witnessed here. That blue cattle dog was like a wild animal, but somebody owned it — there was a leash attached. Perhaps the owners were around here somewhere too.

The driver was seriously hurt with that bite to the wrist, which was showing a fair amount of blood. He picked up the spanner that was lying on the ground and headed back to the car. The banana peel thrower also got back into the car and sat there rubbing the side of his head while the driver wrapped his wrist with a handkerchief, started the motor and moved off. The red Holden made a big circle and appeared to be heading in the direction of the freeway, and then it turned around and began travelling in Jack's direction. Jack moved close to the trees and armed himself with two large rocks the size of house bricks.

The driver screamed, 'I'm going to kill him,' as he aimed the car at Jack and sped up. His mate sitting behind him in the back dropped his seatbelt and leaned over the front before grabbing the steering wheel and forcing it to turn the car away from the tree line. At the speed and direction that the car was travelling in, they would have crashed into the tree that Jack was now standing behind — at least for now they were heading away from it.

The driver's mate, while still holding the steering wheel, said, 'Stop this, take your foot off the accelerator and let's go home!' He grabbed him by the neck. 'Or I'll break your neck.'

That brought a bit of reality to the scene, as the driver slowed the car down, turned it around and disappeared down the sloping road of the road base dump and onto the southbound lanes of the Hume Highway — and possibly to the nearest medical facility for treatment of those two serious dog bites. A simple bit of fun escalated into what could have been attempted murder or murder. One would have to think that these four people remaining close friends in the future after this incident would be highly unlikely.

With all the dramas seemingly over, at least for the time being, Jack breathed a sigh of relief. His brain was bringing up scenarios. Would they come back with reinforcements? Would they notify the police? Would the police come? If they did, they would certainly shoot that dog. Jack had a good look around. He noticed the cans of food and water and said to himself, 'There could be a number of answers here and the obvious one is that the person who owns that dog is coming back.'

He settled on a plan should he need it and planted weapons in different areas; after thinking about it he decided to stay the night as he would be an open target on the highway should they return. He picked a strategic area behind the piles of blue metal, with the heavy timber at his back, and erected the one-man tent where it couldn't be easily seen, hoping it would be a case of out of sight, out of mind.

The tiny gas stove boiled some water and a cup of coffee followed. That would go well with the Anzac biscuits from the backpack. A little note fell out of the packet on opening.

Hope you're having a good time, love Kate. xxx.

Jack answered in his mind: *No I'm not; it's the worst day I've had since I left home.* He felt lonely and slightly vulnerable and felt like having a bit of a cry, but that's as close as it got — he would tough it out.

Sitting on a log, Jack began reading the newspaper that he'd purchased in Moss Vale. He switched on the tiny radio and it provided a nice musical background.

Looking through the blades of grass on the fringes of the heavy timber were the eyes belonging to Prince the Wonder Dog, watching Jack's every move. Meanwhile, dark clouds were gathering in the southeast and every now and then a bolt of lightning would shoot out. In complete contrast the western horizon was as clear as a church bell on a Sunday morning.

Jack noticed the weather activity in the southeast and thought, *Looks like a storm brewing; we might get some rain tonight. In the meantime, it's going to be a long afternoon and a longer night.*

Dinner was more Anzac biscuits and coffee, plus a couple of apples. A block of chocolate provided a luxurious dessert. The sun disappeared over the western horizon, leaving behind a beautiful crimson sunset that seemed to stretch on forever. Jack was thinking, *If there is a god, then his office would have to be in there somewhere.*

At 6.00 pm Jack zippered up the tent, which was completely sealed except for a couple of waterproof vents. It was so dark he couldn't see his hand in front of his face. He lay down on the air mattress fully clothed and covered himself with a blanket.

His thoughts were again with his grandfather, who would have stopped in places like this. *But at least I've got a tent ... he only had a bedroll.*

Jack's mind moved on and he began to feel slightly vulnerable again, as this little tent was no protection against a pack of wild dingoes or a rampaging bull, and it was at this point that he discovered what going to bed early meant. It was going to be a long night, and he could smell rain in the air, but eventually he did go to sleep.

A massive clap of thunder had Jack instantly awake; it frightened the daylights out of him. Light rain was falling accompanied by a gusty wind. A lightning bolt lit up the inside of the tent like a house globe; a silhouette of that dog appeared, sitting just outside the tent.

Jack said softly, 'I'd like to bring you in mate but I'm afraid you might eat me.'

The lightning and thunder turned into a full on storm with heavy rain. Another bolt of lightning; no dog shadow this time. His watch said 3.30 am.

The gates of heaven were well and truly open now as the rain become torrential. The wind tried its utmost to rip the little tent apart but it held up well. Jack just lay there waiting for it to subside and within forty-five minutes the storm's fury had passed over with the wind dropping to an acceptable level. The lightning was still sparking but the thunder could hardly be heard, indicating the storm had moved a long way away.

He didn't think he'd be able to sleep now but was pleasantly surprised when he realised it was daylight. The watch said 7.00 am. 'Gee, I dozed off all right.'

A look outside the tent revealed one beautiful day coming up. The wind was gone. The sky was clear and the air refreshed. Everything was dripping wet; vegetation, twigs and leafs were plentiful and completely covered the ground like a new carpet. Breakfast was two strong cups of coffee and more Anzac biscuits. *Getting a bit sick of these biscuits but I'll bet the soldiers at Anzac Cove never got sick of them ... yeah, stop your whingeing Jack, and be thankful you've got a feed.*

It was time to pack up and hit the road; he would dry the tent out at his next stop. Now dressed in his swaggie uniform, Jack walked up to the dog food as a matter of curiosity. Both containers were full of water due to the torrential rain but it looked like the dog had eaten the food.

From the now wet wooded area, the eyes of Prince the Wonder Dog were watching everything that Jack did as he left the road base dump. He watched as Jack walked down the sloping road, only to see him disappear as he began walking south along the Hume Highway. The dog made a decision based purely on instinct — he didn't think about it, it just happened. He would follow Jack.

Every now and then Jack would turn around to attract the attention of a driver that might be willing to offer a lift to his next destination, a little place thirty minutes south of Goulburn City. The highway wasn't all that busy but it was still early morning. A quick peek behind him, nothing coming — then he spotted Prince walking strongly and with purpose.

Holy mackerel, it looks like the mongrel's following me. That's one thing I don't need, a baby to look after.

Jack faced Prince squarely. Prince stopped. Jack waved in a shooing motion and yelled angrily at him at the same time, 'Go on, get.' He walked towards Prince continuing to yell. 'Go on, get.'

Prince turned and ran back towards the road base dump. Jack continued on. A couple of looks behind, Prince was still walking away from him.

'Yeah, that's it you flea bag, keep going,' yelled Jack, giving Prince a bit of a hurry up.

Half a minute later Prince was back in Jack's slipstream and about ten metres away. Jack was getting a bit sick of this; his patience was beginning to wear out. It was time to get fair dinkum.

'Go on, get! You blue bastard.'

He bent down to pick up a rock that wasn't there and kidded to throw it. Prince turned and ran again. Jack continued on. When he looked back, there he was.

'Oooh no, here he comes again. There's never a dog catcher around when you need one,' muttered Jack. He walked on; he'd had enough of this game. *Oh well, if I get a lift he'll have to find his own way. I don't wish the animal any harm, but if he gets mangled on the road then I suppose that's what you call bad luck.*

Thirty seconds later Jack sensed that the dog was right behind him. He shaped his hand like a revolver and quickly spun around, thrusting it at him and yelling, 'Bang bang!'

Prince rolled onto his back and put his legs straight up in the air.

That made Jack laugh. 'Ha ha, he knows one trick anyway.' Jack continued on, readied his hand again in the shape of a revolver, quickly spun around and pretended to shoot him. 'Bang Bang!'

Prince again rolled onto his back and put his legs straight up in the air.

'Wow,' said Jack. 'What sort of a dog have we got here?'

He slowly walked up to Prince and sat on his haunches about a metre away, at the same time feeling into his pocket for the Anzac biscuit that he'd put in there to munch on later. When he offered it to the dog, Prince got to his feet and accepted the gift from Jack's outstretched hand. As he chewed it up Prince was looking Jack in the eye, his tail wagging slightly.

'Now yesterday I saw you nearly eat a bloke and I hope you're not thinking of doing that to me.' Jack began to stroke Prince's head. 'It's against my better judgement but okay, we'll give it a go.' He picked up the leash and said, 'Come on … because of you, my chances of picking up a lift have just nosedived to zilch.'

A Double-B semi was coming. Jack tried the technique that Pommy backpacker Roy Charles from South Hampton had used. The semi began to slow down, coming to a halt a bit further down the highway.

'Ahhh you little beauty, maybe the dog brought me a bit of unexpected luck, you'd never know.'

The driver of the truck was out of the cabin when Jack caught up. 'Hi,' said the truckie. 'Need a lift obviously.'

'Yes, thanks for stopping. I thought with the dog it would be a bit of a handicap,' answered Jack.

'Not really, it's because you had a dog that I stopped. He's a fine looking one isn't he? How long have you had him?'

'About fifteen minutes.'

'Fifteen minutes?' exclaimed the truckie. 'Now you're not making any sense.'

'I got as far as the road base dump by midday and I stayed there overnight. I saw the dog there for one minute but he ran into the bush. Since I left there he's been following me, I tried to discourage him but he wouldn't have it. There was a bowl of food and water there, so I think he's been dumped.'

The truckie interrupted. 'I doubt he's been dumped, it looks like he's run away. Nobody would dump a dog that looks like that.' He patted Prince then rubbed him along the spine, then he patted the ground. Prince lay down and rolled over. 'He's a beautiful animal and smart too, about six or seven years old, been well looked after — look at that coat, magnificent. What are you going to call him?'

Jack replied, 'I don't know, probably Dog.'

'Look, can I give you a suggestion?'

'Sure.'

'That's the best looking cattle dog I've ever seen so the answer is obvious — Bluey.'

Jack punched his fist into the air saying, 'Bluey it is.' They shook hands and introduced themselves — Jack the swaggie and Stan the truckie.

'So Jack, where are you off to?'

'I'm going to the Bushranger Hotel.'

'Yeah? I used to know the bloke who owned it ten years ago. He had a collection of Ned Kelly memorabilia. One night thieves broke in and stole the lot — gee he was disappointed. Are you any relation to the Kelly gang Jack?'

'No, my father went into it but they couldn't find a link.'

'All right, we'd better get going. I'll stop on the highway then you've got a five minute walk. That'll be one hour from now.'

Jack's gear went into the accommodation compartment behind the driving cabin. Bluey jumped up into the cabin with a minimum of assistance, and Jack sat on the seat beside him. Stan took his place behind the wheel and the very long Double-B joined the other traffic on their southward journey. Bluey settled down quickly and began to doze.

The kilometres went by and the changing landscape appeared to be endless; the vastness of Australia had to be seen to be believed. Jack and Stan were enjoying each other's company with some good healthy conversation as they motored on their way to this one-time historical outpost called Collector. The population one hundred years ago numbered fifty. The population at present was a couple of thousand, with some modern housing on newly-released land. A big green exit sign came up that said 'Goulburn City', but Jack's destination was a little bit further south.

Before long they came to a fork in the highway. Stan eased

the Double-B rig left and in doing so departed the Hume Highway and entered the Federal Highway. Twenty minutes later the landscape began to dramatically change as the bush came to an end and to the west a mountain range seemed to pop out of vast level planes. Stan slowed down the Double-B and moved onto the side of the highway. A squeal of the air brakes and a couple of jerks brought the vehicle to a halt.

A large sign read 'Collector', while a smaller sign with an arrow pointing west indicated 'The Bushranger Hotel'.

'There you go Jack — the hotel's over there. You've got a five minute walk, then you can have a beer, and while you're at it you can have one for me. It's been nice to meet you mate, and I hope we run into each other again someday.'

'Likewise Stan, see you whenever,' answered Jack as they had a farewell handshake. Jack exited the cabin, retrieved his gear from the second compartment and placed it on the side of the road. He took hold of Bluey's leash and helped the dog down, then closed the door of the cabin.

Stan Dent slipped the gear lever of the large automatic gearbox into drive. One last wave and the Double-B trailer began to move away. Jack watched as it picked up speed and when the time was right, Stan drove onto the left lane of the Federal Highway and continued driving south.

To get to the hotel, Jack and Bluey had to cross the six-lane highway with a grassy section splitting the three southbound lanes from the three northbound lanes. Bluey strained on the leash and started to whine. Jack turned to look at what was going on. Where they were standing was a strand wire fence. The land was level for about twenty metres, and then it sloped up gradually for what looked like a hundred metres before going up quite steeply. It was like the horizon: you couldn't see the top of it as it curved over. Just inside the fence about seven metres away was a very healthy looking brown bunny rabbit, quietly munching on some beautiful moist green grass. The rabbit didn't seem at all worried about their presence but Bluey was now starting to get real excited. Rabbits' eyes are on the sides of their head, so they can see both sides at once, and even though it didn't appeared to be worried, rabbits are like cats, ready for instant action.

Jack had a good grip on Bluey's leash and quickly assessed the situation. The dog wanted to chase the rabbit, no doubt about that. How could it matter? He wouldn't be able to catch it and it might be fun. He removed the leash but kept hold of the collar. Bluey stopped making noises as they moved right up to the fence; he knew he would get his chance. The rabbit stopped eating as his alert gauge went into red. Jack lifted the bottom strand of wire up and let Bluey go. The rabbit took off like a rocket, with Bluey in hot pursuit.

There were fresh diggings right where the hill went up sharply; obviously that part of the hill was full of burrows. The rabbit was about six metres in front of Bluey, who was chasing with the keenness of a champion greyhound but the rabbit was always in charge. They headed up to the burrows but the rabbit surprised Jack when it did a u-turn and headed back down toward the fence for about fifty metres before making another turn. This time when it reached the burrows it shot into the safety of the family home at full speed. Bluey pulled up at the burrows and had a look inside the hole, and then he barked and pawed at the loose dirt outside.

Jack was beside him now and patted him on the head saying, 'Okay mate, that's it. Come on, we'll go and have a feed. That bunny rabbit was too fast for you eh?'

They both walked down toward the highway and at the fence, Jack put the leash back on Bluey's collar and then it was only a matter of getting through the fence. Jack put the backpack and swag on, waited for a clearance in the highway traffic and crossed without any dramas, now a five minute walk away from the 'Bushranger Hotel'.

ELEVEN

The Bushranger Hotel

On arrival at the hotel office, Jack booked a room for the night and a kennel for Bluey. That was the one thing about country accommodation houses: they usually had dog kennels and horse stables, a tradition left over from yesteryear. The publican couldn't help enough to ensure that both man and dog were comfortable in their respective accommodations.

Jack ditched the swaggie uniform, the big sun hat replaced by a common baseball cap. A service station wasn't far away, so a walk to the shop section and the purchase of a couple of tins of dog food was number one on Jack's mind. He had to feed the dog before he fed himself.

There were six kennels at the rear of the hotel and not far away were the horse stables, which looked very ancient indeed, possibly one hundred and fifty years old — and were still being used today by visiting equine enthusiasts. Bluey was patiently waiting when Jack poured the contents of the tin of Pal into the plastic container, and soon a hungry Bluey took to it like he'd been told it was his last feed.

Jack then took the opportunity to go into the hotel dining room and ordered a t-bone steak along with a Crown lager or two. After lunch it was time for a one hour catnap; before falling asleep he had a good think about the wild weather last night and his short stay at the road base dump. He was the only person in the ten-room hotel at the moment, so obviously a quiet time at present, but just the same everything was up to scratch and it was a delight to be here.

Jack's grandfather came to this area and stayed in this hotel for a time while working on the roads. When the job came to an end he went over the mountain and got a job on a sheep property called Laredo about thirty kilometres to the west. That was one of Jack's targets; he had to go to that property if it was still there and shear one sheep. A photo would provide proof that he'd been there, as per the rules.

At 3.00 pm Jack took Bluey for a walk with the intention to do a bit of urban exploring. Lots of old housing, all in good condition with well-kept lawns and gardens. Not far from the Bushranger Hotel was what looked like an old community hall or picture theatre. A wrought iron sign confirmed it as the Claremont Guest House — but gee, what a dump. It was in a dreadful state of repair and needed a complete makeover. The front gates were hanging off their hinges, while the lawns and flower beds were completely out of control and overgrown with weeds, thistles and anything else obnoxious. But he did see something that interested him: a sign hanging crooked on the front fence that said 'Handyman Wanted'.

'Well Bluey, what do you reckon mate? Tomorrow we'll come back here and apply for that job.'

Jack leaned over Bluey and patted his belly. Bluey's big red tongue, loaded with dripping wet saliva, came out and tried to wrap itself around Jack's face but Jack pulled his head out of the way just in time.

Seven hot rod cars were parked higgledy-piggledy in the main driveway of the Claremont Guest House, blocking any access. The young drivers were all down at the far end, laughing and carrying on. *Must be hoon weekend*, Jack thought as he passed on by.

It took about an hour to see most of the sights in this tiny historical town. The difference in housing between the old estate and the new estate was like black and white. Jack sat down on the bench seat in the very spacious park and removed the leash from Bluey's collar, who immediately began enjoying his freedom checking out all the nooks and crannies, sniffing everything as he went over the well-mowed lawn like a vacuum cleaner. After about ten minutes Bluey came back, lay at Jack's feet and just relaxed there.

Jack was again thinking to himself as he watched Bluey lying there as if he hadn't a care in the world. *Why me, dog? Why am I the chosen one? And what's your story, dog? You've had your chance to run away but you haven't, so it looks like you're stuck with me, for better or for worse … at least for the time being anyway.*

The sun was losing its heat and the afternoon was all but gone when they made their way back to the Bushranger Hotel, where Jack put Bluey back in his kennel. He then went and relaxed in the residential lounge, turned on the TV and made a cup of coffee, enjoying it with a couple of Anzac biscuits.

That night Jack took Bluey into the hotel bar and he was well received by the locals. Some wives were there with their husbands, just enjoying the company and a beer. The snooker table was busy and the dartboards had a full complement, while the one TAB machine was taking the farmers' hard earned cash but they loved their night-time trots.

One of the ladies took a liking to Bluey and before long she had him doing things that dogs don't normally do, like walking on his back legs and rolling over — before doing what we'd call in human terms a handstand, then he'd chase his tail around and around. The dartboards and the snooker table stopped; everybody was watching the talented Bluey performing a series of tricks. Nobody in this area had ever seen a dog like this before and that included Jack, who said, 'He's got one more trick.'

'Oh yeah, and what's that?' asked a patron.

Jack began to walk away. Bluey knew what that meant — he

was ready. Jack suddenly spun around and with his hand shaped like a revolver, thrust it toward him and loudly said, 'Bang bang!' Bluey dropped down and rolled over onto his back with his four legs straight up in the air.

Well, that brought the house down with laughter and clapping. One by one everybody in the bar went to Bluey and patted and touched him, saying nice things like *good boy*, *nice fella* and *you bewdy*.

The publican went to the kitchen and came back with a big bone. 'Do you think Bluey would like this Jack?' He held the bone up in the air.

Bluey immediately sat on his rump in a begging position.

Jack answered, 'I'm sure he would. Look at him, he can hardly wait for it.'

The publican put the bone in Bluey's mouth and then Bluey looked at Jack as if to say, 'Can I eat it now?'

Jack gave him a big smile; Bluey went and sat under the television to begin eating what could only be described as every dog's favourite dish. Jack had a couple of beers and a game of darts, then he was invited to have a game of snooker, which he won. He was thinking that this would be the happiest crowd in a pub that he'd ever seen; there just wasn't a bad word at all. Who would have thought that it was in a one horse town called Collector? This was once an outpost of Goulburn City that once had a population of fifty — amazing.

Bluey never moved from eating that bone and they stayed until closing time. The publican gave Jack a padlock for the dog kennel, as this was no ordinary dog; he would have attracted more than his fair share of attention, so better to be on the safe side from a would-be dog thief. Jack went to get Bluey from under the TV. The dog was happily chewing that bone and Jack knew that it might be awkward to interrupt him at this time, as most dogs would protect the bone at all cost. He saw him bite that bloke's leg and wrist, so if he was going to show any aggressive action it would be now. Jack thought he'd try the ultra-cautious approach. About two metres away he went down on one knee and said as he patted the other knee, 'Come on boy.'

And to his surprise Bluey dropped the bone and walked up to him.

'Good boy,' said Jack as he patted Bluey's head and picked up the end of the leash. Then he intimated to Bluey to pick up the bone, which he did, and carried it in his mouth until they reached the kennels. Jack locked him in for the night then he went to his own room, and as he turned on the beautiful hot shower he said to himself, 'Gee, it's nice to have civilisation again … yeah, nothing quite like it.'

He finished the night watching TV until midnight then turned off the light.

In the morning he remembered having a dream: guns and horses, Cobb and Co coaches, outlaws on horseback. Ned Kelly, one of the namesakes of the Bushranger Hotel, was there — and so was Jack's grandfather. He couldn't remember what part he played but he was pointing a revolver at somebody. Staying in the Bushranger Hotel, you'd have to think it was going to happen.

After feeding Bluey then himself, he washed his clothes in the coin operated washing machine and dried them in the also coin operated dryer. He got dressed in his swaggie uniform and closed the door of the hotel room, collected Bluey who was patiently waiting, and then it was down to the office to pay his bill and sign out.

The publican said, 'You know Jack, It's been nice to meet you and your beautiful dog and I kinda wish you were staying around here a bit longer. When you're not wandering the countryside what do you normally do for a living, or is that an awkward question?'

'No, it isn't. I'm a builder — you know, a carpenter and joiner,' replied Jack.

The publican said, 'Look, you could get plenty of work around here.'

'I'm going around to the old boarding house to see what's happening there.'

The publican responded, 'The owner's been looking for somebody for a while now, but she's got no money. Her husband couldn't stand the strain and ran away, but to her credit she's battled on and scraped a living out of the few people that stay there. She's got a mongrel of a kid, a seventeen year old with a chip on his shoulder. When his dad shot through he blamed his mother for it and he's the biggest lout in the area. He's got four mates and they terrorise the local community at night.'

'Sounds interesting,' said Jack.

The publican was astonished. 'Interesting! Jesus Christ, if I was you I'd walk on by.'

'Tell you what, if I'm still here in the morning I'll drop in and tell you what happened. Or you never know, I might need that room again.'

'Make sure you bring that dog with you, I've got another bone for him,' said the publican.

'Okay, we'll see what happens — but no matter what happens Bluey's coming back to get that bone.'

The publican gave Bluey a pat and watched as Jack and Bluey walked out the door and down the road.

The old boarding house wasn't far away, around the corner and a ten minute walk. One of the cars that was parked on the footpath yesterday was now parked in the driveway. Boy, the old place certainly needed some work done to it.

I don't know how she'd get one person to stay here, looking at it, let alone make a living out of it, thought Jack. He made his way through the front gate, which was hanging on one hinge but open. *Geez, some welcome to a prospective customer looking for a bed for the night. Only the broke and the needy would stay here.*

The front of the building had a nice style about it and after walking up half a dozen steps, then onto what you could call an outside foyer. A sign said 'Reception' but the door was closed. Beside the reception door was a little button and a small printed sign that said 'Press for Service'. Jack's finger came out to press the button but was interrupted by some yelling and screaming coming from the driveway side of the guest house. He dropped the backpack and swag off and put Bluey's leash on one of the pickets belonging to the front fence, then headed off to investigate.

As he came around the corner, there was a middle aged woman arguing with a young man. She was screaming at the top of her voice. 'All I want is a bit of a hand.'

His reply was in the same pitch. 'I'm sick to death of you, you silly old fat bitch, do it yourself.'

They were so intoxicated with themselves that they never saw Jack coming. He grabbed the young man from behind and put him in a vice-like headlock. The woman jumped back in fear at the sight of the tall rugged-looking stranger in the long coat and big hat.

'There's no need to be frightened, I'm not going to hurt anyone. It's just that I don't like to see a young man abuse a lady.'

The shocked look faded a little off the woman's face. The young man was held in a complete grip and couldn't move.

Jack said, 'Now mate, I want you to apologise to this lady and then I'll let you go. If you don't then we're going to be here a long time.' Jack increased the pressure on his head a little bit more.

The young man under sufferance said, 'I'm sorry Mum.'

Jack let him go and said to him, 'This is your mother? You speak to your mother like that? That's disgusting.'

The young man jumped away from Jack, rubbing his neck, and ran to the car parked in the driveway. He drove away, burning rubber as he went.

Jack looked at the lady and said, 'Look, I should have minded my own business but I can't stand disrespect, I'm sorry.'

She replied, 'It's okay. As you can see the place is a shambles and all I wanted him to do was to mow the lawn.'

'I'm Jack Kelly and I'm passing through town. I saw the sign on your front fence — I was wondering if that job is still available.'

'Yes but I imagine you'll be like all the others. I can only pay $200 a week and you can have free accommodation, but you have to pay for your food.'

'I'll take it. I've got a dog, is that a worry?' asked Jack.

'No, there's kennels out back, as long as you keep it under control and it doesn't bark all night. Where is it?'

'I put his leash on the front fence.'

They walked around to the front where Bluey was lying down on the long grass. He jumped up with a wagging tail as they approached. Jack took the leash off the picket and said, 'Bluey, I'd like you to meet ... ahhh ...'

'Lynn Cowdery, Bluey.' She kiddingly put her hand out as if to shake and was completely surprised at what happened next — so was Jack. Bluey sat on his rump and put his paw out so Lynn could shake it. 'Well I never,' she said. 'What a marvellous dog you have.'

'Yeah he's full of surprises,' said Jack. 'Come in and have a cup of coffee. Bring the dog with you, he won't hurt.'

Before they'd reached the front steps she turned quite rapidly and pointed at Jack as she said, 'Were you and your dog at the pub last night?'

'Yes,' answered Jack.

'One of my neighbours, Mr Wheelan, passed by this morning

and said a bloke at the pub last night had a dog that was doing circus tricks. The same bloke could play snooker too. Was that you?'

'Yeah, that was me all right,' answered Jack.

She asked, 'Is that your stuff?' while pointing to the backpack and swag on the ground.

'Yes.'

'What, are you backpacking around or something?'

'Both,' answered Jack and laughed.

They walked into what appeared to be an old dance floor. It had built-in wooden seating along both sides and this told Jack that the building was designed around the early 1920s. The kitchen was at the far end and in front of that was the dining section — its look was actually quite classy.

Jack sat down at one of the tables while Lynn disappeared into the kitchen. He noticed that the interior of the building was in good condition; it just needed a new paint job. A little while later Lynn appeared with a pot of coffee and some biscuits. She sat down opposite Jack after giving Bluey a couple of dry dog biscuits and a bowl of water.

'Looks like you've had a dog or two,' said Jack.

'Yes I love dogs, I've always had a dog but I don't have one at the moment. Every Thursday night I go into Goulburn City to pick up supplies and have a break from here, it's the only outing I have. When I go out I lock the dog in my bedroom, that's where she sleeps. A couple of months ago I came home I went to let her out — she was asleep on her bed. I couldn't wake her up. My darling little Tootsie had passed away. She was fourteen years old. We buried her near the rose bushes around the back. At the moment I'm happy to be living in the shadow of the memories ... I may get a new dog sometime in the future. I still keep a supply of dog food to sell to customers.'

Lynn sighed as she continued. 'The state of the books at the moment says that I'm just making ends meet. I'm not getting behind but I'm not getting in front either, I'm just staying stagnant. I own the property so no one can take it away from me, but it has to pass license every year as a guest house and that happens in eight weeks' time. If I can just tidy it up a bit I might have a chance. Last year they warned me that if I didn't make certain improvements by this year I wouldn't get the license renewed. If that happens I'll have to sell … I don't want to do that, this place means everything to me.'

'Nobody ever volunteered to do some odd jobs for you, knowing your predicament?' asked Jack.

She replied, 'Yes, but there's always a catch. One bloke wants a sleepover once a week to keep the lawns in order and he's a married man. I've got too much pride for that sort of thing. There are thirty rooms in this place and at the moment occupancy rate is six — that allows me to break even. My son is going through a bad patch and it's obvious he needs someone to control him, but I can't do it. He's got some bad friends that he hangs around with and they frighten good customers away too. The way he's going, he'll finish up at the police station.'

'His car looks all right,' said Jack.

'Yes, that was his father's car. When his time came up to get a license I paid to have it restored, but now I wished I hadn't. You saw the way he drove away. How long do you think he'll last before the police catch him?'

'Won't be long.'

'You haven't asked me about his father.'

'None of my business,' replied Jack.

'Well, I'll tell you anyway. I grew up in this place. When my father died he left the guest house to me. My husband wanted to sell it and move away but I wouldn't do it. He said he felt like a second class citizen and was always jealous that I had something and he didn't. One day three years ago I went into Goulburn City to do some shopping, when I came home there was a note on the kitchen table that read, "Goodbye, give my car to our son when he turns seventeen". I've never seen or heard of him since.' After coffee Lynn said, 'Come and have a look around, you can pick your own room.'

Jack and Bluey followed her around while she pointed out things that needed fixing. At the back there was a big shed filled with plenty of tools and equipment, timber, paint and a great range of gardening equipment.

Jack asked Lynn if she'd like him to encourage her son to at least do a bit of work, even if he didn't want to.

She answered, 'Well, I can't do anything with him … if you want to try, go right ahead. I'll back you in anything you want to do.'

'Okay, tomorrow we'll mow the grass and do the edges.'

'Good luck with that one, but by 10 o'clock he'll be gone.'

'Not tomorrow he won't. Might be a bit of skin and hair flying around eh?' said Jack with a smile.

The dog kennels were terrific, large and spacious; Bluey should have no complaints about his accommodation. Jack picked a room overlooking the dog kennels and the big shed at the back of the large block of land, where there was parking for twenty cars.

That night Jack took Bluey to the Bushranger Hotel and while Bluey sat under the television eating a fresh bone that the publican gave him, Jack had dinner in the restaurant. It was a similar night to last night, staying until closing time before making their way back to the guest house.

Inside, Lynn's son Tom was watching television in the main area. Jack sat nearby and tried to engage him in conversation.

'Look, I'm Jack Kelly, this morning we got off on the wrong

foot. I'm going to be hanging around here doing all the odd jobs for a while and I was hoping you might be able to give me a hand.'

Tom replied in a raised and nasty voice, 'You're getting paid so I'm not helping. As a matter of fact, you shit me to tears.' With that he stormed off.

Jack took Bluey out to his kennel with his well-chewed bone and locked him in for the night, before going to his own room to hit the sack.

In the morning Jack went for breakfast and was pleasantly surprised when there were two more people there. A couple of backpackers had dropped in overnight. They shared a small amount of conversation whilst having the first meal of the day. With breakfast over Jack attended to Bluey's needs, then it was down to the big shed where he found a pair of pliers and an old coat hanger. Now to spoil Tom's day.

It took him two minutes to get the driver's door open on Tom's car; next was the engine bonnet. Jack removed the rotor from the distributor, then closed it all up again. He fuelled up the mower and the whipper snipper and brought them out of the shed. Tom was right on time, 10 o'clock. He opened the car door in anticipation of driving away.

Jack called out, 'Hey Tom, what about giving me a bit of a hand to mow the lawn?'

Tom responded with the two-fingered salute, putting in an extra good effort in the upward motion. This made Jack see red but he kept his cool as he knew he wouldn't be going anywhere any time soon. Tom turned the key to start the motor and was puzzled when it wouldn't start.

Jack walked up to the car and said to Tom, 'Looks like you've got a problem, so you might as well give me a hand.'

Tom screamed like a maniac. 'I told you I'm not helping.'

Jack pulled the rotor out of his pocket and said, 'Your car

won't start because I took this out of the distributor. Now you put in three hours work on the lawn and I'll put it back, so you can decide your car's fate.' He turned and walked away.

Tom leapt out of the car and screamed, 'Who do you think you are? You filthy swagman! Put it back or I'll –'

Jack turned to face him. 'Or what?' They were looking each other in the eye now. 'Go on, I'll give you one free shot, then I'm going to level you down with the grass, you ignorant arsehole of a human being. Look at the place you live in, you can't even give your mother a hand to mow the lawn while she gives you a free roof over your head. Don't you care? You lazy good for nothing.'

Tom grabbed Jack by the shirt with both hands and began to shake him. He yelled, 'No, I don't care.'

At that point Jack gave him a head butt that almost knocked him over backwards. As well as being a surprise, it hurt. His hand came up to rub his forehead. Tom decided to attack; he charged at Jack with the intention of kicking him in the tenderest of places. Jack was ready and as the foot came up he grabbed it and pulled it skywards. Tom fell to the ground on his back.

'Come on Tom, you gutless mongrel — get up so I can knock you down again.'

Tom replied, 'I'm going to call the police.'

Jack responded, 'Whenever a coward can't get his own way they want the police. Well, go on you heap of slime, ring the police. You're not man enough to work it out, you're like a little kid who's lost its dummy. Now I don't care who you ring but you're not getting that rotor until you start snipping those edges.'

Jack had called his bluff and it worked. Tom was showing signs of conciliating. 'Three hours you say.'

'Yes. That will be 1 o'clock, and then you can go,' replied Jack.

'All right, I'll do it,' said Tom.

He got himself off the ground, put the goggles on, started the whipper snipper and began doing the edges. Jack noticed that he was quite the professional too, so obviously he'd had some training — possibly in happier times when his dad was around.

At 1 o'clock they knocked off for lunch. Tom's job was done but Jack's mowing would take the rest of the day, plus tomorrow as well. Jack replaced the rotor in the car then went to have lunch. Tom was whingeing to his mother when Jack came in, but he shut up as Jack approached the table. Lunch was sandwiches and coffee. Tom got up to walk away; it was time for him to disappear for the rest of his day.

'Oh Tom.' Tom turned to look as Jack said, 'Don't forget: three hours — Monday, Wednesday and Friday. And don't park in the driveway.'

The answer was two fingers in the air and the words, 'You don't tell me what to do.' Obviously the lesson today had taught him nothing.

That night at 11 o'clock the noisy sound of automobile burnouts out the front of the guest house was heard. Lynn said, 'That's Tom and his mates making all that noise. There'll be four or five cars out there.'

'Sounds like World War Three. I think I'll go out and have a look,' said Jack.

Lynn followed, and then Bluey thought he'd get into the act as well. They walked into the front foyer but Jack closed the door on Bluey, who was disappointed that he had to stay inside.

There were four cars engaged in burning rubber, and if it was on a race track these four young men would be an attraction. Not only were they doing doughnuts, they were zigzagging in front of each other. Watching it was quite spectacular, but on a narrow residential road it was too dangerous — besides, the noise at 11 pm was quite intimidating. Two neighbours from across the road came out and began yelling at them but it only spurred them on. After five minutes the cars headed towards the Bushranger Hotel and turned left.

Lynn said, 'They'll do a circuit of the outpost now before disappearing.'

Sure enough you could hear them coming up past the park at high speed, around the corner and back into the street, where they gave their horns full blast until they past the guest house. One car drove into the driveway of the guest house while the other three kept going. Tom parked his car where Jack told him not to, and approached the foyer as happy as Larry. He enjoyed being a hoon and was smiling as he walked up the steps. Jack's heart began to thump a little faster; he knew an altercation was possibly about to happen.

Lynn said, 'Having a good night Son?'

He was more than surprised to see his mother there and answered, 'Yeah.' But then he saw Jack. 'What are *you* doing here?' he growled.

Jack replied, 'I thought I'd wait up for you to see where you parked your car.'

Tom got nastier. 'That's where I park my car and that's where it's staying.' He went to step around Jack to open the door.

Jack moved in front of him and said, 'Move that car out of the driveway now!'

Lynn chimed in. 'Please Tom, move your car. The guests in number three are leaving at six thirty in the morning.'

He never got a chance to answer as Jack snatched the keys out of his hand. 'Don't worry about it Tom, I'll do it for you.'

'Give me back those keys, you rotten bastard!'

Jack was off so quickly that Tom had to run to catch up. When he felt Tom's hand grab the back of his shirt, he drove his elbow back and caught Tom on his chest. Tom stopped as if suspended in time.

Jack turned and faced him squarely and said. 'Are you going to move it? Because if you're not, I'm going to do it. I'll drive it into the bushes opposite the park and throw the keys away. Now make up your mind.'

There was no answer as they continued to look at each other in silence. Jack turned with purpose and headed towards Tom's car. Tom with a panicked voice said, 'Okay I'll move it.'

Jack gave him back his keys and walked back to the foyer.

A little while later Tom moved the car. As he walked past the foyer to enter the guest house Lynn said, 'Thank you son.' And of course that only added insult to injury.

Tom walked down to the dining section and sat down watching television; he was rubbing his chest, so it was obvious that Jack's elbow had found its mark. Jack sat down one table away while Lynn sat opposite Tom.

After a while Tom said, 'Got anything to eat?'

Lynn replied, 'Dinner's between five and seven. If you want something to munch on, go and make it yourself.'

Tom sat there sulking for a while but eventually he went and made himself a sandwich. He came back and said to Lynn, 'You know Mum, just as you drove Dad out, you're driving me out.'

Lynn replied, 'I never drove your father out, he wanted me to sell this place and I wouldn't. I went out shopping one day, when I came home he'd left me a note that said, "Goodbye, give my car to our son when he turns seventeen".'

Tom replied, 'That's a likely story; you could tell me any old bullshit.'

Lynn got up and went into the family section of the guest house. After a couple of minutes she came back with a piece of paper. 'Here's the note just as I found it.' She gave it to him.

He read it then asked, 'Can I keep it?'

'No, I have to keep it as a record of the incident at that time.

If ever it comes down to a court case to do with divorce I have to have the evidence. But I will get you a copy tomorrow, so give it back to me for now.'

Tom got nasty. 'No, I want it.'

They began arguing over it. Tom must have forgotten that Jack was sitting one table away as he began to exit with the note that his father had written. Jack moved in front of him, blocking his way. 'Now give it back to your mother,' ordered Jack.

Tom tried to evade but Jack grabbed him by a handful of hair and the collar of his shirt and forced him back to his mother.

Tom threw it on the table. 'There you are, stick it up your arse. Listen Mum, if you don't get rid of this bum I'm leaving here and you won't see me again.'

'You know Tom, that's the best news that I've had in the last twelve months. You've turned into a horrible and obnoxious person and I won't miss you at all. As a matter of fact I'll help you pack your bags, and you can do me a favour.'

'What's that?'

'Please don't come back.'

Jack let him go and stepped aside just in case he took a swing but he left in the direction of his room. Jack thought he'd have the last word. 'Don't forget Tom, three hours work Friday morning or you won't have a car.'

Tom turned and delivered the two fingered salute again.

TWELVE

Staying at the guest house

At 7 am, Jack clipped the dog leash onto Bluey's collar to take him for a walk. He stopped in the middle of the road to inspect the doughnuts that the hoon vandals left last night.

The neighbour across the street walked to where Jack was standing. 'G'day mate, I'm Col Lucas, I've noticed you doing a bit of work.'

'Yes, I'm Jack Kelly and I'm the Claremont Guest House handyman for a while. She seems to think that if we tidy it up a bit, a few more customers might be attracted.'

'Ahh well, good luck to her but it won't happen while that kid of hers is there.'

'I'm taking my dog for a walk and I see you've got a dog, why don't you put a rope on it and join me?'

'Okay, I'll go and get her.'

Col's dog was a golden labrador and Bluey took an instant shine to her. Why wouldn't he? She was a beautiful looking animal. They walked around to the park and gave them their freedom, and what a good time they had together. Jack and Col had a good talk, with Jack learning that Lynn's husband was a roving womaniser. He came to the outpost looking for work. 'A good-looking, handsome man full of charisma' was how Col described him. Lynn fell in love with him and they got married, with Tom coming along twelve months later. He was a lazy man without any real skills except the eye for a woman — and he could pick them up just like that (Col flicked his fingers).

'Behind her back he was chasing everything that had a dress on. He got bashed up a few times because of it. One day a couple of city ladies came to stay at the Bushranger Hotel and he struck up a friendship with one of them. Christ, she was beautiful. They had an affair and one day he ran off with her. I was glad when he went because he was persistently chasing my wife too. My wife would have to be at least fifteen years older than him but he didn't worry about that. He used to walk to the Bushranger Hotel every night and walk home after closing time. One night I stepped out from behind one of those bushes beside the guest house and shoved my shotgun in his face, threatening to blow his head off if he ever came near her again. The sight of those two barrels frightened the crap out of him.' Col laughed. 'I can still see the look on his face as he begged me not to pull the trigger. He never bothered me again. Lynn's had to bring that kid up for the last three or so years by herself.'

'She must have been aware of what was going on behind her back, wouldn't you think?'

'As far as I know she never found out, we didn't want to hurt her. She was an only child, a naive country girl. That guest house and the block of land on each side belong to her and that's all she's ever known. What about you Jack? I saw you at the pub the other night with that dog — gee he's a beauty — then the next day you walk into Lynn's place with a swag on your back and take a job that pays hardly anything. So what's your story, the missus throw you out or something?'

'No, not at all. I'm having a hitchhiking holiday — stopping here for a while, then stopping there for a while.'

'Where do you come from?'

'Sydney Harbour.'

'How far will you be hitchhiking?'

'I'm due in Mildura about the end of November, then I'll make my way back home in time for Christmas.'

'Cripes Jack, you're a braver man than me to travel all over the countryside by yourself.'

'Yeah, I've had a couple of hair-raising experiences so far.' Jack pulled out his notebook and pen and said, 'What was the name of the husband, Col?'

'Lucas Cowdery.'

'And the one he ran away with?'

'Her name was Elizabeth Symonds. You're not going to go looking for them are you?'

'No, but you never know what can happen, maybe I can get some information on them one way or another.'

Bluey and the labrador had been in the far end of the park. Jack gave a whistle and the two dogs came running at full speed back to where Jack and Col were seated on the park bench. As they slowed to a halt Jack pulled out his two finger guns and said, 'Bang bang.' Bluey dropped down onto his back and stuck his legs straight up.

'How do you get him to do that?'

'You've got to teach them young Col, that's all I know.'

Jack walked over and gave Bluey a pat on the belly while he was laying there. Bluey took Jack by surprise as he jumped up quickly and licked him around the neck and face with his sploshy tongue.

'Ahhh yuck,' said Jack. 'The bastard got me that time.'

Col laughed and said, 'I know how you feel. Goldun gets me the same way sometimes.'

They put the dogs back on their leashes and began walking back towards the guest house.

Col said to Jack, 'You'll find most Thursday nights interesting in the old guest house.'

'Oh yeah?' replied Jack.

Col continued. 'Yeah … Lynn goes late night shopping into Goulburn City. Tom's supposed to look after the place but he invites his mates around and they take their skateboards into the old dance floor and make a lot of noise. When Lynn comes home she chases them out. Then they get in their cars and race up and down the street, burning rubber as they go.'

'How long's it been going on?'

'About twelve months.'

'Cripes,' said Jack.

'Yeah,' said Col. 'I feel like getting the shotgun out.'

'Don't even think about it mate.'

Col went into his place while Jack went into the guest house. At 8.00 am Jack decided to do a bit of work in the entry area; it needed a lot of work to bring it back to its best. There was still plenty of lawn mowing to do and he would get back to that this afternoon or tomorrow. Jack was working up on a ladder with a can of paint, putting an undercoat on the ceiling when he saw one of the hot rod cars pull up in the driveway. Tom's car was where he parked it last night and Jack was thinking that maybe he'd slept in. The young driver walked up the steps and into the entry area but couldn't get through the door, as that's where the ladder was.

'I want to get in,' he barked in an aggressive voice, shaking the ladder at the same time. 'Hey you — deaf, dumb and stupid, I'm talking to you.'

Jack lathered the brush in the paint bucket that was hanging on a hook on the side of the ladder, and then he began to descend the ladder.

'Come on come on, I haven't got all day you old bastard.'

Jack reached the bottom rung of the ladder; the young hoon shook the ladder again and as he went to say something he copped the paintbrush full of paint in his mouth. Then Jack painted his eyes and face. The hoon was shocked but couldn't do anything about it, as he couldn't see what was going on. Jack grabbed him by the hair and spun him around. Holding him by the back of his shirt and the hair, Jack forced him down the steps then launched him into the lawn face first.

The hoon spluttered and snorted as he rolled onto his back, his face covered in fine grass clippings. He pulled his handkerchief out and wiped his eyes so he could see a little.

Jack stood over him and said in a firm voice, 'Now you get going before I kick your head in.'

The now terrified young driver crawled across the lawn like a crab until he found the hose. The paint was water based and the fresh water soon cleaned up his eyes and face.

Jack wasn't finished yet; he walked over to him and said, 'When you come around here you show some manners and be nice. If you park in the driveway again I'll let your tyres down.'

Jack took a photo of the car and number plate with his tiny Nikon camera, then walked back to the entry and continued painting. A little while later Tom's mate drove away without finishing the business that he'd obviously come to do.

After lunch Jack continued painting the entry ceiling. He noticed Tom's car was gone and a short time later a very expensive Jag stopped on the side of the road in front of the guest house with a tall, fit, good-looking gentleman getting out. Then he saw the same rubber-burning misfit that he painted before lunch get out of the passenger side door.

Here's trouble if ever I've seen it, thought Jack. *It looks like he's gone home crying to his father. The suit on this guy's at least a thousand dollars' worth, cripes! He looks good enough to be the local funeral director.*

The gentleman boldly walked straight up to Jack and said, 'You punched my son and put paint in his eyes. That has made me very angry.'

Jack kept painting and ignored him.

The gentleman started shaking the ladder while yelling, 'Get down here, I want to talk to you.'

Jack had a full brush of paint and meekly said, 'Okay, okay I'm coming, don't you push me off.'

The gentleman turned to look at his son; Jack seized the opportunity and shoved the paintbrush in his face. Jack jumped off the ladder and stood out of the way. The painted gentleman couldn't see but he was having a go all right, swinging wildly where he thought Jack might be. When he could, Jack got behind him and with a handful of hair and a good grip on the coat collar he marched him down the steps and launched him onto the same piece of lawn where his son landed before lunch. He hit the ground like a plane without wheels.

His boy was in shock horror, watching a replay of himself only a couple of hours ago. He decided to help his dad when it was all over and came at Jack. As soon as he was in range Jack slapped him across the face with two open handers and said, 'Now get over there before I knock your teeth out.'

He'd had enough already and walked away. Jack got the paint tin off the ladder and poured about a milk carton's worth of paint over the most fashionable of suits around the stomach area. The father was ropeable but he couldn't see. Jack grabbed the hose and gently sprayed the water on his face and eyes, washing away the paint. The father could see now but he was like an angry lion.

'Look what you've done to me, I'm on my way to an important meeting,' he yelled. 'You've wrecked my suit and you're going to pay for that.'

Jack answered, 'You'll need a dentist if you don't get going. And I'll tell you something else. I won't be paying for anything — and I didn't punch your son. I did to him what I did to you. When you come around here, you be nice. When people are nice they usually get what they want.'

The father got to his feet as Lynn came out the door to check on the commotion. On spotting the gentleman she said, 'Why Mr Dittman, what on earth's happened to you?'

Jack answered for him. 'Oh, he fell in the paint tin.'

Lynn thought it was funny and started laughing hysterically, as a little ray of sunshine beamed out of the big smile on her face.

Mr Dittman said, 'If you've got any sense Mrs Cowdery, you'll get rid of this madman.'

She didn't even answer but kept on smiling. Mr Dittman and his son decided to leave and went to their car. Lynn couldn't stop laughing at Mr Dittman's condition. He was soaking wet from the hose, there was white paint all over the front of his clothes, and water was dripping off the bottom of his trouser cuffs, while fine grass clippings left over from the mowing were stuck all over him.

As the Dittmans made a u-turn and drove away Jack added insult to injury and happily waved them goodbye. Then he said to Lynn, 'You know him eh?'

'Yes, he manages the biggest sheep farm in the district. It's a massive spread five kilometres out of town. I've always found him very nice; he's even offered to buy the place if I couldn't manage it.'

Jack said. 'But you don't want to sell it do you Lynn?'

'No, but every now and then I get fed up with the struggle and I do feel that way. This time last year I went through a bad patch and I decided to sell it to the Goulburn City Police Sergeant, but I pulled out at the last moment. It's a funny thing, every now and then he reminds me that he's still willing to continue on with the sale — whenever you decide, he says. Oh, there's one other person interested, the owner of the Royal Hotel in Goulburn City.'

'No shortage of buyers in this part of the world. You still got the dog in there?'

'Yes, he's no trouble. He follows me around, and right now he's sitting under the TV chewing one of those dry dog biscuits. And today you made my day, giving me some free entertainment.'

Lynn was still laughing as she went back inside while Jack went over to Col's place and asked him if he saw what happened.

'Too right I did Jack.'

Jack then filled him in on how it happened before saying, 'I think he'll ring the police, so we can expect them out here shortly.'

'If the police come out here, it'll be the first time that they've come out here to investigate anything. You see what those car hoons do, but the cops won't investigate. The odd occasion when they have come out, the hoons have long gone. We give them the number plate numbers, they do nothing. Listen Jack, that young Dittman is the worst lout in the area and you'd think his father would pull him into line, but he spends his time defending the boy — and as far as a police investigation is concerned, I didn't see anything, so you've got nothing to worry about mate.'

'And you reckon these hoons have been annoying everybody around here for twelve months?'

'Yes.'

Jack went back to his painting in deep thought; he might have a talk to Bill. Then he noticed Col paying the houses in close proximity a little visit.

At exactly 4 o'clock Jack noticed the police car pull up on the street. The young policeman put his cap on as he approached the entry. Jack said to himself, 'I'd better not paint this one.'

In typical police-manual approach the constable said, 'Good afternoon Sir.'

'Afternoon,' answered Jack.

The young copper pulled out his notebook, opened the page and spoke. 'I'm investigating a complaint from a Mr Michael Dittman and his son Anthony.'

Jack interrupted. 'What's the name of the person you're investigating?'

'I don't have a name at the moment, but I'm led to believe it's the bloke that's painting in the front of the guest house. Are you that person?'

'I can't tell a lie, I am that person.'

'What's so funny?' asked the policeman.

'I'll tell you what's funny,' said Jack. 'There's a bunch of young car hoons that terrorise these streets late at night, three or four times a week. His kid is one of them. But you do nothing about it. Have a look at the burnout marks if you don't believe me. But when the manager of a sheep farm in his best suit comes out here to thump me and comes off second best, he goes crying to the police like a sooky baby and a policeman is despatched urgently to investigate. It doesn't seem quite right does it?'

The young copper said, 'Look Mr … ahhh …'

'Kelly, Jack Kelly.'

'Mr Kelly, I'm only out of the academy a couple of weeks and the job I've been given is to investigate a complaint about you. I've specific instructions to only do this and not worry about anything else, so the complaint is, you assaulted Anthony Dittman and threw paint over him. Sometime later, you assaulted Anthony Dittman's father, Mr Michael Dittman, and threw paint over him, destroying his suit worth fifteen hundred dollars. Anthony Dittman witnessed the assault on his father, then you threatened the two of them with violence.'

'All I did was to threaten them with the paintbrush if they didn't get going.'

The young copper laughed. Jack explained how a simple visit by a car hoon to visit his car hoon mate developed into World War Three.

'So,' said the young copper, 'Mr Dittman was shaking the ladder that you were working on.'

'Yes, with both hands.'

The young copper wrote everything down meticulously then said, 'Thank you Sir, I'll be in touch when the investigation is complete.' He tipped his hat with a g'day, and then he left.

Jack watched him as he walked to the centre of the road and inspected the burnout marks before going into the houses opposite the guest house. Col seemed the most vocal and was waving his hands in the air as they walked to the centre of the road, where the waving and pointing continued.

Finally the young copper shook his hand and left in the police car to return to his base in Goulburn City, a thirty minute drive away. Once back at his base he completed the necessary paperwork, signed off on the incident and filed the report in the police computer.

The next morning at the Goulburn City Police Station, Sergeant O'Leary was keen to find out from his newest and youngest recruit how the incident at Collector's Claremont Guest House went. The sergeant put his head out of his office and called out, 'Constable Ron Gatten, could you come in here for a moment?'

The young constable left his desk and walked into Sergeant O'Leary's office, where he was invited to sit down, and at the same time said, 'Thank you Sir.'

'Now Constable, how did things go out there yesterday? Unfortunately I wasn't able to be here when you got back.' It was early and Sergeant O'Leary was in a happy mood, waiting in anticipation for the answer.

'Ahhh yes Sergeant, after investigating a Mr Jack Kelly and taking statements from witnesses, the assaults couldn't be substantiated.'

'What about the threats of violence?' asked the sergeant in a somewhat disappointed voice.

'Mr Kelly threatened them with a paintbrush full of paint. Mr Dittman almost pulled Mr Kelly off the ladder that he was working on and that's when he painted Mr Dittman's suit.'

'So what did you do?' asked the sergeant.

The constable replied, 'There wasn't enough evidence against him so I signed off that way.'

'You mean you've already signed off and filed a report?'

'Yes.'

Sargent O'Leary was about to show his nasty side. He raised his voice to another level. 'Look young one, I told you to go out there to investigate, then charge that son of a bitch. You don't decide whom to charge, I do that. Now you haven't done what I told you to do. If you want to get on here you'll do exactly as I say. You're in the real world now and it doesn't matter what they taught you in the academy, those idiots wouldn't know the time of day if you told them. Next time you do what I say and if you don't, you'll get no more recommendations and you'll finish back with your uncle Harry shovelling sheep shit for the rest of your life. Do I make myself clear?' Sergeant O'Leary smashed his fist down onto his desk and then he swept his arm from one end to the other in a fit of rage, sweeping everything that was on the desk onto the floor. 'Now get out.'

Constable Gatten stood up and walked away, his face red with embarrassment. He couldn't believe he'd screwed up his first job. He turned and said, 'The people I spoke to yesterday only wanted to talk about a gang of car hoons that disturb the peace with burnouts and street racing.'

Sergeant O'Leary replied very nastily, 'Now don't you worry about that! That's my baby to catch those bastards and I won't have it any other way, right?'

'Yes Sarge,' Constable Gatten said as he exited the door of the office.

Sergeant O'Leary slammed the door that hard behind him that the chief superintendent came out of his office to investigate and went into the sergeant's office. 'You all right Bruce?'

'Yeah, just giving the new recruit a bit of a bollocking. He didn't do as I told him yesterday, you know what it's like.'

'Yes I do. It seems like yesterday that I walked into this police station. I was nineteen years old and I wanted to clean up all the bad people in Goulburn City inside a week, ha ha … gee, that was fifty years ago. When I finally give all this away I'm recommending you for the job.'

He patted Sergeant O'Leary on the back, and then walked back to his own office, while the sergeant began cleaning up the mess he made.

Over the weekend things went really well for Jack, with a fair bit of work being done on the entry foyer and the mowing now completed. Monday morning breakfast was underway with eight guests plus Jack and Tom. Jack spoke to Tom. 'Well Tom, are you ready for a couple of hours work?'

Tom looked at Jack with daggers and said, 'You can sit on this and rotate.' He gestured with his thumb in the vertical position, and then walked away in the direction of his room.

Jack finished his coffee; now it was time to make sure that Tom and his car were not about to go anywhere. This time Jack removed the valve out of the front passenger side wheel. The air was soon expelled, with the tyre becoming as flat as a pancake. He knew that as Tom approached the car he would spot it straight away, and then the fireworks would begin.

Jack continued working around the front of the guest house. Earlier he had set up a sander around the back for Tom — now to get him there. He never had long to wait, as Tom came out as happy as a pig in a dam of mud. Then he spotted it.

'*No, no,*' he screamed. Then he looked at Jack with hate in those eyes.

Jack said, 'What?'

'You know what.'

'Well, you do your three hours work then you can be on your way.'

Tom was about to do his nut. He raced at Jack yelling, 'I've had a gutful of you, I'm going to punch your fucken head in.'

He was swinging wildly and Jack soon had him under control. Tom had no idea how to fight; he was brought up in a non-violent household by a peaceful mother. Jack had him on the ground, he never hit him, and he just held him.

He said to Tom, 'Let me know when you're ready to start and I'll let you go.'

Eventually Tom said, 'All right, tell me what I've gotta do.'

They both got off the ground and walked around to the back. Jack explained what it was all about. 'There's a dust mask and a set of goggles, make sure you wear them.'

Thirty minutes later Lynn came out the front and asked, 'Where is he?'

'Around the back sanding.'

'How'd you get him to do that?' she asked.

Jack pointed to the flat tyre. She was laughing as she walked back inside to continue with her work.

After two hours Jack pumped the tyre back up with a little compressor he found in the shed and then he went to Tom and told him to knock off, as he would need a shower and fresh clothes. Thirty minutes later Tom drove away, but not before doing a defiant burnout in the middle of the road and screaming away towards the Bushranger Hotel at high speed.

A clean-looking Toyota sedan pulled up across the road with two ladies inside. They were dressed in black suits with a small red stripe on their collars. Jack could spot a Salvo a mile away. *Donny King's spies*, he thought. *Well, I'll give them a bit of a surprise in a moment.*

Lynn called out. 'Lunch, Jack.'

'Okay, I'm coming,' replied Jack.

In the car the two Salvation Army ladies were talking between themselves. 'Well, it seems like he's settled in here for a while. I'll ring Donny tonight to let him know.'

'Fay! I think he's coming this way.'

Jack stopped at the edge of the road and did a Dick Whittington bow.

'Quick Fay, start the motor and drive away.'

It was too late; Jack ran across the road to the car and said, 'Hello ladies, having a good time spying on me? Tell Donny to go jump in the harbour, preferably in front of a hungry shark.'

The two ladies sat there expressionless.

Jack continued on. 'I know who you are, now come and I'll shout you lunch.' He opened the door. 'I won't take no for an answer, come on — there's no alcohol in there, it's just an old guest house full of old memories.'

The two Salvation Army spies looked at each other. 'Will we … why not?'

As they walked across the road to the guest house Jack said to them, 'Now nobody around here knows what I'm doing, so we'll keep it that way eh?'

'Of course,' was their reply.

'Two special ladies for lunch Lynn, and charge it to me,' said Jack as they walked in.

Lynn replied, 'No worries.'

'Yeah, they pulled up over the road and asked me where the best restaurant in town was, and I said you're looking at it.'

Lynn started to laugh and said, 'The only people that come here are those who don't have enough to go around, but you two ladies wouldn't fit into that category.'

There was no answer, they just smiled. There wasn't much on

the lunchtime menu, but toasted ham sandwiches seemed to be the favourite around here. While munching was underway, Jack had a good conversation with the two Salvation Army spies, who seemingly enjoyed their lunch — and confirmed that when they said they would come again soon. They finished off with mineral water while Jack had a nice cold can of Coca-Cola. He walked them out to their car and watched as they drove away, then he returned to his job working on the front of the guest house.

At 5.30 pm Jack took Bluey down to the Bushranger Hotel. Parked outside on the road was an old 1934 English Bedford truck loaded up with bales of hay. The spoked wheels caught Jack's attention.

'Wow, there's a trip back to the past if ever I've seen it.'

Inside the hotel, the two ladies were here that seemed to be here after work every day and today they were drinking schooners. As soon as they saw Bluey they went and collected him off Jack, and the dog didn't mind at all. Before long they had him doing his half a dozen tricks to the clapping of the hotel patrons.

Sheep farm manager Dittman, whom Jack painted the other day, came into the hotel and watched the wonder dog. He was with his hoon son Anthony and after ordering a schooner each, continued watching with interest until Bluey's routine was finished.

The publican said, 'This dog is costing me a fortune in bones,' as he passed the bone over the bar to one of the ladies to give to him. Bluey took it to his favourite spot under the television and began chewing.

Sheep farm manager Mr Dittman in his new suit said to one of the ladies, 'I'll give you $2000 for that dog.'

'I don't think he's for sale,' she replied.

The other one said, 'If he were mine I wouldn't be selling him.'

Dittman snapped in his usual manner. 'I'm not talking to you,

I'm talking to her.' He looked back at the other lady. 'I'll give you $4000 for that dog.'

Jack stepped out from behind a group of patrons with a snooker cue in his hand and said, 'The dog's not for sale.'

Mr Dittman, surprised at seeing Jack, asked, 'Is that your dog?'

'It sure is, and you'd be the last person on earth that I'd give him to.'

Mr Dittman placed his beer, or what was left of it, on the bar and said to the publican, 'I don't like the company you keep. Come on Anthony, we'll go somewhere else.'

But there was nowhere else in the outpost of Collector; the Bushranger Hotel was it. Next was a can or a bottle at home.

After Dittman and his son left, the publican said, 'I don't know why that bloke comes in here at all. He's so far up himself he just doesn't seem to fit in. Look at you people, all hands-on farmers and farm hands who come in here to enjoy a beer and a bit of mateship after a hard day's work. Then you've got Jack over there who's a swaggie jackaroo, doing anything to make a dollar — blokes like him haven't been around here for seventy years, and he fitted in with you fellas like he'd been here for that seventy years.'

As Mr Dittman drove away he said to his son, 'Gee I'd like to get my hands on that dog.'

'There is a way you know,' replied Anthony.

Mr Dittman answered with panic in his voice, 'No, no, don't even think about it. Everybody here would know that dog, you can't hide a dog like that. It's important I keep a clean reputation or I'll lose my job. The owner I'm working for is a religious freak and has got zero tolerance on bad behaving managers. I've got an appointment with the number one solicitor in Goulburn City on Tuesday morning to begin proceedings against that bastard.

Seeing as the police wouldn't charge him with assault we're going to get our revenge one way or the other — through the legal system.'

At the hotel, a large group of farmers up one end of the bar were enjoying some light-hearted banter, ribbing each other at the end of their day's work while washing down the dust with a beer. Amongst them was quietly spoken farmer Roy; he was the owner of the antique truck parked outside. Roy Bron was a third generation sheep farmer with everything being handed down from father to son. He was near retiring age, but nobody really knew how old he was. He was enjoying a nice cold glass of Tooth's Stout. The black-coloured drink was more a health drink to him, like a tonic with only a touch of alcohol in it — and people who drink stout don't fall into the category of a guzzler-drinker, so were often teased and joked at because of their choice. Nonetheless, Roy seemed to enjoy the banter and laughed and joked along with them.

The time had come to stir up farmer Roy. One of them looked at Roy and asked, 'Hey Roy, who's the oldest, you or the truck?'

Farmer Roy answered, 'Could be a couple of years either way, why don't you go and ask the truck you dickhead.'

Another guzzler-drinker chimed in. 'Roy, are you sixty going on eighty, or eighty going on sixty?'

'Take your pick, you peanut-brained imbecile.'

The young thirty year old farmer, who last year won the district's top farmers award, called out, 'Hey Roy, come up here mate and I'll shout you a real man's drink, a Tooheys Super.' He lifted his schooner up high above his head and waved it about.

Roy was quick to reply. 'Yeah? It hasn't done you much good has it? Your hair's already falling out and you haven't even fathered a baby yet. What a useless individual you are.'

The young farmer ran his hand through his thinning hair, or what was left of it, and said, 'Yeah, he's got me there all right.'

Everybody had a good laugh at that one.

Jack was enjoying this fun time amongst the farmers and he liked the way that Roy gave those humorous answers. There's no doubt, he won the last round. Jack was thinking, *Well, I've still got plenty of hair and I haven't made a baby either, but I've got a dog that I didn't want.*

Roy upended his glass of stout and placed the empty glass back on the bar. He said, 'Ah well, I suppose I'd better be getting on home, Mum'll have tea cooked by now.'

As he walked away another question came in. 'Hey Roy, what's for tea tonight?'

'Kangaroo tail soup and possum fritters. You see, I live on the land and I also live off the land, not like you blokes that buy your meat from the butcher's shop.'

'You know what Roy, I don't think the RSPCA would like you cooking up those possums, eh?'

'Probably not, but they don't live in the bush do they?' replied Roy.

The farmers that were in the corner drinking with Roy all walked out to the antique truck with him. One of the farmers called out, 'Hey Roy, do you reckon this thing will get you up and over the mountain?'

'My truck will drive up a gum tree,' replied Roy.

'Now about those koala bears in the gumtrees Roy, what happens to them?'

'Oh, they hop in the back for a free ride.'

Another smart-aleck farmer said, 'Do you stick them in the mincer too?'

'No, but if you like, you can hop in the mincer,' answered Roy.

The banter continued: 'Hey Roy, its 6.30 and it's a half hour drive to your place, but in this truck you'd be lucky to get home by midnight.'

Roy had the last word. 'It'll beat you lot home anyway.'

Farmer Roy started the motor; it gave a couple of coughs and after a bit of decent revving the engine settled down, then he crunched it into gear. The antique truck loaded with hay began to move off but not before doing a couple of hops and jumps — much to the delight of his farmer friends, who were now clapping and cheering as the truck set off towards the setting sun and the 'Collector Mountain' to the west of the outpost. All those outside went back inside the Bushranger Hotel laughing like a bunch of schoolboys.

On Tuesday morning, sheep station manager Michael Dittman drove into Goulburn City to keep an appointment with the leading legal firm. It was exactly 9 am as he walked through the front door and approached the reception desk. The receptionist ushered him into the office suite that belonged to the owner and practising lawyer, Brian Lamberton.

'Ahhh Mr Dittman, come in please and have a seat. Now, after our telephone conversation the other day I've prepared all the necessary paperwork and I've also had a look at the police report. They wouldn't lay charges because of conflicting and insufficient evidence. In other words, there were no independent witnesses and neither of you needed medical treatment. But you still want to sue Mr Jack Kelly for assault and the cost of a new suit. He has no ID or fixed address as such, so we're dealing with somebody that we know nothing about. Before we proceed we need to find out a bit more about him. We know he has one dependent, a blue cattle dog. This fellow certainly sounds like some sort of uneducated moron who roams around doing anything to scunge a feed for himself and that dog. So what do you think Mr Dittman, you still want to proceed?'

'Yes, I don't care how much it costs; as long as it teaches that type a lesson. We can't let him get away with it.'

'All right Mr Dittman, tomorrow I'll go out there and interview him. If he fails to co-operate we'll have to hire a private detective to find out about him.'

'Is that necessary?'

'If I register this complaint at the courthouse, it's going to be six months before we get into court. Now where will he be in six months? He could be in Central Australia sitting on top of the Olgas for all we know. Whichever way we do it it's going to cost you a lot of money — you know that, don't you?'

'Yes,' replied Mr Dittman.

'All right, I'll proceed.'

The following morning, Mr Lamberton and his assistant drove out to the old guest house. Lynn and Mr Lamberton had a cordial chat about Jack over a cup of coffee and a slice of toast. She showed him the guest register but there was nothing there that he didn't already know.

'Where is he now?' asked Mr Lamberton.

Lynn replied. 'He's taken the dog for a walk; you'll probably find him down at the park if you want to talk to him.'

'All right, we'll drive down there and see if can we find him — it's not like you can get lost in this place, right?'

'No,' replied Lynn.

'But it won't always be like this. The State Government's got a few big plans for this area in the not too distant future. Okay Mrs Cowdery, it's always a pleasure to talk to you, goodbye for now.'

'Yes goodbye.'

Down at the park, Jack was enjoying the bliss of the big open spaces while reading one of the free newspapers that come in from Goulburn City. Bluey was running around like a lunatic looking for something to chase, but at the moment there was nothing. So

Bluey then sat in front of Jack facing the road. A couple of woofs brought Jack's attention: two people walking toward him from the road. The one on the left was a tall suited elegant man carrying a slim document case, and the person on the right a woman.

There's no doubt that she was conceived at the right time of the year, thought Jack, *she's absolutely beautiful*. The sun was behind them and just at the right angle, spotlighting her moving legs. *Wow! Enough to send a bloke mad.*

His concentration was zapped when a voice said, 'Mr Kelly I presume.'

'Why Dr Livingston, I thought you'd never find me in the jungles of Collector,' was Jack's response.

The two lawyers looked at each other; she smiled, he didn't. Bluey started barking at them. Jack put the paper down and said to Bluey, 'It's okay mate, go and sit down over there, good boy.' He gave him a pat and pointed to the ground. The dog obeyed immediately, sitting down and watching with interest.

'Shouldn't that dog be on a lead?' said Mr Lamberton.

Jack replied, 'There's a lot of humans out there that should be tied up, but they're not, and I consider my dog better than them.' Another vision came into Jack's head. *Gee I wish I had that bucket of white paint with me, I'd paint the front of that suit in record time.* He smiled as he imagined lawyer Lamberton squawking like a chook about to have its feathers pulled out as the white paint made contact with him.

'What's so funny?' asked Mr Lamberton.

Jack replied, 'My mind's running ahead of myself, that's all — I thought of something funny.'

'Well, I'm Brian Lamberton and this is my assistant, Vicki Thistlewaite. We're representing Michael Dittman and his son Anthony. They both intend to sue you for damage to their clothes and common assault. I've come out here today just to have a talk to you; maybe we could come to an agreement whereby you could pay for a new set of clothes for each of them and I'll try to talk the Dittmans into dropping the assault charges. That sounds like a fair deal, doesn't it Mr Kelly?'

'You can call it whatever you like, Mr Lamberton, but I decline the offer. You go tell your client that I'll see him in court and I'll shake his hand while he's paying my bill as well as his own. So I suppose you'll be sending him a bill for this morning's recreational activities?'

'What do you mean, recreational activities?'

'Well, I'll bet you've already had coffee and I'm sure while you're here you'll drive around for a bit of sightseeing, then you'll finish up having lunch and buying the most expensive thing on the menu. When you finally arrive back at your office you'll probably say to your assistant here, "Well Vicki, what a good day we had".'

'Now Jack, your mind is running ahead of itself isn't it? So I'll write down here, "Client uncooperative, will see him in court".'

'Sounds good to me,' answered Jack.

As they began to walk away Jack said to Bluey, 'Say goodbye to the nice man and lady.'

Bluey sat straight up with his paw outstretched. Vickie said, 'Oh Brian, look at him, isn't he beautiful.' She gave that paw a little shake and a complimentary pat on the head.

Jack called out, 'Lunch at the Bushranger Hotel's pretty good, 11.30 to 2.00 pm.'

They just ignored him as they headed towards their car. The two lawyers sat in the car watching Jack throw a stick that Bluey chased, then picked it up and brought it back to Jack only to do it all over again.

'Well Vicki, what do you think?'

'He's funny and he was pretty sure of himself when he said he wouldn't be paying any bills.'

'Yes ... ah well, we'll go and have a look around while we're here.'

'He must be Nostradamus; he reckoned we'd have a look around and have lunch.'

'The Bushranger Hotel?'

'You bet, lunch at these old pubs is always good.'

They both had a good laugh as they continued on their sightseeing tour at the expense of sheep farm manager, Michael Dittman.

At 1 o'clock Jack left Bluey with Lynn and walked around to the Bushranger Hotel to see if the two lawyers were having lunch. Sure enough their car was parked there.

'You're a bit early Jack,' remarked the publican on seeing him.

Jack replied. 'There are a couple of people in the restaurant that I want to talk to, but you can sell me a bottle of Crown Lager.'

He entered the restaurant, walked straight up to their table and said, 'Do you mind if I join you?'

'Yes I do mind,' replied Brian Lamberton, but it was too late as Jack pulled out a chair and sat down.

'Now I'm going to tell you this whether you like it or not, then you'll understand what's going on here.' Jack explained it like it happened, except slapping the young Dittman or throwing them into the lawn. 'Now that might give you an idea of the people you're dealing with. They started it, I finished it.' Jack upended the bottle of Crown Lager, looked at his watch and said, 'I can recommend a good private detective if you want one.'

'Now why would we need a private detective?'

'To investigate me.' Jack pointed his finger at them as he walked away.

Brian said to Vicki, 'Yes, he certainly knows how the legal system works; I suppose you don't know what a bloke like him has done before he took up wandering around the countryside. There he is, working on a building that's about ready to fall down for hardly any money — but one thing I do know, the work he's done on the front of that old building is first class. He's no handyman, he's a professional.'

Thursday night began as Col said it would. Lynn's mate Molly from the Uniting Church arrived at 6 o'clock to pick her up and the two of them would drive into Goulburn City to do some late night shopping. Jack was here last Thursday night but according to Col it was one of the few Thursday nights of the year that she didn't go into the city.

At 7 pm, eight hot rod cars pulled up with the occupants all coming into what Col called the old dance floor with their skateboards under their arms. Some young hoons had their girlfriends with them. Jack had locked Bluey in the kennel early, as he didn't know how he'd handle the noise if it turned out that way. It wasn't Jack's problem, so he'd keep out of it and just be an observer. He'd made friends with three guys that were staying there and they sat at one end of a table playing cards while sharing some healthy conversation.

Tom was probably the noisiest one there, while a couple of them got into an argument over one of the girls and a bit of pushing and shoving went on. The skateboard noise was quite loud as it echoed around the interior of the old guest house. Tom gave them whatever food and drinks they wanted, which wouldn't be helping the bottom line of the guest house balance sheet. Young Dittman wasn't amongst the hoon skateboarding team and Jack wondered why he wasn't there; perhaps he didn't want another confrontation with the handyman.

Since his run-in with the Dittmans, Jack had been recording the number plates of the burnout vandals and right now there were eight cars out the front, so it made sense to go out there and get those numbers. He went out a normally locked side door with a key that Lynn gave him and it didn't take long to write them down; he was on the last one when one of the hoons and his girlfriend came out of the guest house. They were all over each other and never noticed Jack. The girlfriend leaned against the car and lay backwards over the bonnet while the boyfriend lay on top of her and began kissing her around the neck. She saw Jack's silhouette shape in the dark.

'Bob! There's somebody there.'

Bob stood up and walked aggressively toward Jack. 'And what do you think you're doing, pervert?'

'I'm collecting number plate numbers, it's a hobby of mine,' answered Jack.

The hoon said, 'Well I don't like your hobby; now give me that book so I can shove it down your face.'

He approached Jack like a wild pig and Jack took no chances. As soon as he was in range Jack punched him with a straight right to the nose that stopped him in his tracks, then a left to his jaw. The hoon wobbled and fell over onto the ground. His girlfriend was in shock.

Jack said to her, 'If I were you I'd take your boyfriend and get going now, before somebody gets hurt.'

'Well you started it, hiding in the dark,' said the hoon's girlfriend.

'You know young lady, this is a guest house. There are eight or nine people that come and go at their leisure through that front door — I was out here when you came out. Because I live in there I have every right to be where I am, but you don't.'

She helped her boyfriend to his feet and said, 'Come on, let's get out of here.'

They got in their car and drove off with the driver saying, 'I'm going to get that bastard.'

'Let it go,' she replied. 'You can't afford another conviction can you?'

'... No,' was his reply.

Jack went back into the guest house via the side door and re-joined the three people he'd been playing cards with.

A bit after 10 o'clock Lynn arrived back from her shopping expedition with her friend Molly. Lynn began shooing all the skateboarders out and before long they were driving away, only to reassemble on the street to begin doing burnouts and then to race up and down the street at high speed, much to the annoy-ance of the neighbours. Jack helped Lynn and Molly carry all the bags of supplies inside, then Molly said goodnight.

Jack noticed that Lynn was more than annoyed at the invasion of those car hoons, but Thursday night shopping was her only luxury of a change to her routine: a chance to have time out, to look at all the things that ladies like to look at — dresses, shoes and handbags — without actually buying any. He was thinking that what a useless mongrel of a son she had; he couldn't even mind the guest house for four hours a week to give her a bit of a hand.

The three card players decided to call it a night and left for their rooms, while Lynn made a pot of coffee and a couple of toasted sandwiches, which she shared with Jack along with some interesting conversation. During this conversation Jack said, 'You know Lynn, it's none of my business but I could tell you didn't like coming home to all those people in your dance hall.'

Lynn said, 'Well, if ever you owned a house and you came home to unwanted people invading your space, how would you feel?'

'I suppose if ever I was lucky enough to own a house and I came home to that, then that would be the last time it would happen — even if they were my son's best friends. Now if you want me to put a stop to it, I will ... it's up to you.'

'How would you do that Jack? There's nobody in this town

that will help me. Everybody's scared of those young blokes including my son ... but you're not scared, are you?'

'No. Now do you want me to put a stop to those skateboarders coming in here on Thursday nights?'

She closed her eyes and leaned her head into her hands, thinking about it. She took her hands away and said, 'Yes.'

On Friday Evening Jack rang Bill and they had a good chat about the old guest house's problems — mainly the car hoons, of which the owner's uncontrollable son was one of them. After an hour they came up with a couple of plans that might make a difference to the situation. They would work that way in secrecy. Bill had given Jack the phone number of a trusted security firm that worked out of Canberra; he would ring the firm of Covert Security first thing in the morning before continuing with his work out the front of the guest house.

A white restored Holden ute stopped on the street. An elderly policeman exited the vehicle without his cap on, so presumably it was a friendly visit. He disappeared into the guest house to have a chat with Lynn. Jack was thinking that this might be the copper that wanted to buy the place.

After thirty minutes he came out of the guest house and headed for Jack. As he approached he said, 'I'm Sergeant O'Leary from Goulburn City Police. Do you mind if we have a bit of a chat off the record ... it's Jack, isn't it?'

'Yes, I'm Jack Kelly.'

'So what brings you to Collector? You know, a stranger stands out in this ... ahhh ...'

Jack interrupted. '*Dump* is the word you're looking for.'

'Ah, you've noticed have you?'

'Sure have, but I won't be hanging around here much longer. Another couple of weeks and I'll be gone.'

'You've trod on a couple of toes since you've been here.'

'You're obviously talking about the Dittmans, a more arrogant pair I've never seen. They came here looking for trouble and found it.'

'Now Jack, if you're only hanging around here another two or three weeks, I won't be giving you any trouble. It'll be like you never came here.'

'Don't tell Lynn, she doesn't know. I'll tell her the morning when I'm about to leave.'

'So you're just travelling around doing handyman work to make a living, so to speak.'

'Yeah, that's about it,' replied Jack.

'Where do you go from here?'

'Up over the mountain. I want to get a job on a sheep farm, and then I'll head to the National Capital.'

'All right Jack, I'm glad we had this little talk, I'll see you later.'

'Okay,' said Jack as the sergeant put his hand out in a gesture of friendship. Jack shook it. Sergeant O'Leary walked back toward his vehicle but before he got there, young Tom in his car came to a halt behind the ute. Tom got out and struck up a conversation with him. Tom and the sergeant seemed to get on like father and son, and it wasn't long before they walked away down to the back of the guest house to talk in private.

Jack saw Col in the front yard and walked over for a bit of a chat. On his way he took a photo of the sergeant's vehicle, taking in the number plate.

Col asked, 'What's he doing here?'

'He came to talk to Lynn, then he wanted to know how long I'd be staying here. I told him a couple of weeks. That seemed to make him happy.'

Col said, 'And now he's happily talking to one of the burnout gang. It sort of stinks doesn't it?'

'It sure does mate, it sure does,' answered Jack, who turned to walk away.

Col had one last thing to say. 'Wouldn't it be nice if he did a bit of police work for a change?'

'Yes it would,' replied Jack.

Col wouldn't stop. 'What did you think of the noise on Thursday night?'

'Like you said, disgusting. Look, don't say anything to anybody but Lynn gave me permission to put an end to the hoons entering the guest house on Thursday nights when she goes shopping.'

'Geesus, how are you going to do that? The older ones are a nasty bunch.'

'Ahh I've got a few ideas Col, we'll have to see how we go. Catch you later.'

Thirty minutes passed by until Sergeant O'Leary drove away, his business seemingly over.

Lunchtime Monday, Jack would be having lunch in the Bushranger Hotel with the boss of a Canberra security firm, Covert Security. Jack would be using this firm to hopefully put an end to young Tom bringing his mates into the guest house on Thursday nights, when his mother went late night shopping in Goulburn City.

As was expected, both the lunch and the meeting went well. The plan would be put into action on Thursday evening. Jack had to sign papers taking responsibility on behalf of the owner, Lynn Cowdery — and he also had to pay in advance, which he did electronically on Bill's mobile phone. The money would be coming out of the GD Constructions account.

At 10 am on Thursday morning, a twin cab utility pulled up on the side of the road in front of the guest house. A big GD was painted in the centre of the door on both sides. Jack put down the welder that he was using and walked over to the driver, named

Marty, who was now out of the vehicle. They greeted each other gleefully and shook hands.

Jack asked, 'Have a good drive down mate?'

'Yes, I sure did, how's life back on the tools?'

'Yeah, yeah, I'm really enjoying it. How's things going in Sydney?'

'Everything's going like clockwork, Kate's doing a real good job.'

'Okay Marty, you know what we have to do. This guest house has to pass certification soon, so I'll walk around with you while you do your report. Did Kate give you my laptop?'

'She sure did, it's on the seat.' He pulled two laptops out of the cabin and gave Jack one.

Jack put his laptop in the now-renovated office in the front foyer. First of all they walked around the perimeter of the building. Marty was taking pictures and writing in a book. Then they went inside and did the same thing. Lynn was watching with more than a passing interest and wondered what they were doing.

Finally they went and sat down at a table where Marty went to work on his laptop, and after thirty minutes he pressed the print symbol and gave the four printed sheets to Jack, who said, 'I'll shout you lunch before you go, how does toasted corn beef and cheese sandwiches sound?'

'Sounds bloody beautiful,' answered Marty.

Jack called out to Lynn. 'Another one for dinner Lynn, and put it on my tab.'

'Okay,' was the distant answer.

After lunch Jack walked out to the work ute with Marty and said, 'So you're off to Canberra now?'

'Yes, we've got another dozen certifications to do there.'

All right, I'll see you when you come back to write out the certificate.'

'Okay Jack, goodbye for now.'

They shook hands and Marty drove away while Jack went back inside and made another cup of coffee. He'd picked up his laptop on the way in and it was sitting on the table beside him.

Lynn came over and asked, 'Jack, would you like to come into Goulburn City with us tonight? Molly suggested it. I don't even know if you like going shopping or not.'

Before she could finish what she was going to say Jack interrupted. 'I'd love to Lynn, I've forgotten what a decent shop looks like.'

Lynn then said with a puzzled look on her face, 'I've never seen a swagman with a computer before.'

Jack smiled and answered, 'That's because I'm a modern day swagman.'

She had a hearty laugh at that then asked, 'Who was that gentleman that you had lunch with, or is it a secret?'

'No, that gentleman is a certifier of public buildings. He gave me a list of things that will have to be done. I will do these things, then he will come back and issue a certificate — then some of your troubles will be over.'

She again looked at Jack with those puzzled eyes and asked, 'Who are you, Jack Kelly?'

He replied with that big charismatic smile right across his face. 'I'm Jack Kelly. Now I'd better get out the front and get those two big gates working properly.'

Lynn walked away shaking her head. She looked toward the heavens but the ceiling of the guest house was in the way. But it mattered not, as she wondered if God had sent this unlikely homeless swagman with a dog, and now with a laptop computer, to help her through these tough times. In her mind she noted that stranger things have happened in past thousands of years.

With a cup of coffee in her hand and Bluey's nudging head to stroke, she relaxed in her lounge chair and thought back to that day three years ago when she returned from a shopping trip into Goulburn City, only to find a note her husband had left for her, which ended with, 'Goodbye.'

This devastated her from that moment on. For days, weeks and months on end, she would lie awake at night-time staring at the ceiling for hours and hours, praying that this mental torture would come to an end, eventually sobbing herself to sleep. She asked herself, what did she ever do to deserve this? She had one boyfriend in her life and she married him, a good looking man with charm to burn, who turned out to be a useless no-hoper. Being brought up in the church she prayed to God, a God, any God that would listen — but it wasn't happening. The line was down for maintenance — that is, until now. Jack Kelly walked into her life, willing to work for hardly any money. Would he hang around for a while or suddenly be up and off?

She didn't know these answers, but one thing was for sure: Jack was beginning to inspire her. Now he was getting the build-ing certified. *That's going to cost money and I don't have one extra dollar to spend. I'll have to talk to him about that.*

Things were passing through her mind at the speed of a rac-ing car. She again wondered if God was doing his duties through Jack, as she was now getting the help she needed. She also remembered the words of the local minister when he couldn't answer an awkward question: 'God works in mysterious ways.'

For now she would put her faith in Jack. If he up and left with Bluey suddenly, then Sergeant O'Leary could have the place along with the loutish burnout vandals.

Coffee time was over; Lynn gave Bluey a dry dog biscuit while she continued on with her never ending job, but out the front Jack had finished repairing the two main gates that give access to the driveway. Now these gates could be locked for the first time in years; another tool to use against the hoons.

Lynn's friend Molly from the Uniting Church arrived at 5.30 to pick up Lynn and Jack, and then the three of them would travel into Goulburn City for late night shopping. Jack had left Bluey over with Col to spend the night with Goldun, Col's dog. Fifty metres down the road parked on the side of the road was a bright red tow truck, and behind that a twin cab ute. Leaning on the front of the tow truck was a fellow in black overalls and a cap. Jack waved to this fellow as he walked to the car. The fellow waved back.

Lynn saw this and said to Jack, 'A friend of yours?'

'Yes, somebody I met down at the park.'

Molly and her passengers drove away and when her car was well and truly out of sight the fellow standing beside the tow truck pulled out an operational radio and spoke into it. 'Right-o boys, move in and secure the front gate. The rest of you know what you have to do.'

Five men came out of the twin cab ute and headed for the guest house. One closed the big double driveway gates, locked them and remained standing there. Three of them stopped in the foyer while the fifth one went down to the kitchen area to protect the food and drinks. The only person allowed in would be Tom or the guest house boarders.

The cars started arriving and straight away there was a sense in the air that something was different here tonight. The double gates that never worked were now closed and someone was standing there. Three more cars arrived and parked in the street with the occupants getting out and carrying their skateboards. The ten of them grouped around the small gate on the footpath.

Tom showed up and drove into the double gated driveway; he'd never seen these gates closed before. He got out of the car and walked over to the person standing there. 'Who are you?' he asked.

The answer was elementary. 'I'm the security guard; the gates are staying locked tonight.'

Tom was hostile. 'Yeah well, I live here stupid, now open the fucken gates.'

The security guard looked at the photo that he had in his hand, and then looked back at Tom. 'Sorry Mr Cowdery, but you'll have to park on the street.'

'Is that so? Well I'll park right here then.'

The security guard replied. 'Ohhh, I wouldn't do that if I were you Mr Cowdery.'

'What do you think you're going to do about it?'

The security guard pointed down the street, saying, 'You see that tow truck?'

Tom looked.

'If your car's still parked there in two minutes that truck will tow your car into our compound in Goulburn City. It will cost you five hundred dollars to get it back.'

Tom gave him a mouthful. 'You dirty rotten mongrel.' He got in his car, reversed back onto the street (doing a burnout in the process) and parked in front of Col's place.

Col saw him park there and said to his wife, 'Gee I'd love to blow that car up.'

His wife said, 'If we were still living in the Middle East and on loan to the American Army I'd help you do it.'

'Yes I know you would, so for now we'll cop it sweetly. But you know something honey, I've got a feeling that all this will come to an end soon.'

They had a little embrace as their memories went back thirty years to when they were both in the Australian Army.

Tom rallied his mates. 'Come on, let's go.'

The others all followed to the guest house, carrying their skateboards under their arms. They were stopped in their tracks as three very big men in uniforms were standing in front of the doorway. One of them said, 'Yes, can I help you?'

Tom said, 'We're going in there.'

The guard answered Tom as he looked at a photo. 'You can go in Mr Cowdery, but the rest of you can't. As a matter of fact you can all get going now, we don't want you coming here or hanging around here. Now get!'

Tom went in, and then he turned to his mates and said, 'Well come on, don't take any notice of these idiots.'

The burnout vandals moved forward, but the big men standing in their way now produced batons in their hands. A couple of the girls said to their boyfriends, 'Let's go, nobody wants to get hurt.' They all turned and meekly walked away, even though they had weapons in the shape of skateboards.

Tom was heading for the kitchen, then he spotted him. 'Bloody hell! There's one of the bastards here too.'

'Yes Mr Cowdery?' asked the big man in the black uniform as he put Tom's photo back in his pocket.

'I want some food and drinks.'

'You can have one drink and one sandwich.'

Tom yelled his answer. 'I live here and you don't tell me what I can do in my place.' He took six cans of Coke out of the fridge and turned to leave.

The security guard grabbed Tom by a handful of hair and knocked the cans out of his hand. He then let go of his hair and said firmly, 'You can have *one* can, Mr Cowdery.'

Tom got away from close proximity and yelled, 'Stick it up your arse, you Maori prick.'

The big security guard thought it was funny and laughed and laughed as Tom ran down the old dance floor and out the front door to re-join his mates, who were now driving away. Tom got in his car and tore away, burning rubber and fishtailing his car down the street in what looked like a desperate attempt to catch up to the last car in his view. Where they would go was anybody's guess.

Col and his wife were sitting on their front porch. Col said to his wife, 'I'll be darned, Jack said he was going to put a stop to it but I didn't believe him.'

Back inside the guest house the security guard picked up the Coca-Cola cans and placed them back in the fridge. He walked over to a table where six guests were playing cards and stood there watching. One of them said, 'That's the worst mongrel young man I've ever seen.'

'Ahhh there's plenty more like him around,' replied the security guard.

Later on in Goulburn City, the shopping was over, and after the ten bags of supplies were in the car the three of them decided to take in one of the latest blockbuster movies at Cinema Plus, a brand new complex in the main street. And what an enjoyable experience it was too, but all good things come to an end; at 10.30 the trio began the thirty minute journey back to the outpost and the Claremont Guest House.

Halfway home the mobile phone in Jack's pocket vibrated. A text message from Covert Security. *All clear on the western front.*

Jack sent one back: *Bail out.*

The boss of Covert Security rounded up his men to leave. Another successful job completed, but they would do this again next Thursday night.

Molly's car turned off the Hume Highway and was travelling past the Bushranger Hotel, which was in darkness. Lynn said, 'My stomach turns when we round this corner and turn into our street and see all those hoons there.'

Molly turned that corner and not a car in sight.

Lynn couldn't believe her eyes, and became quite excited.

'Wow look at this, where are they? They're all sick, they're all sick ... you little beauty.'

After pulling up Jack said, 'Now I know why you wanted me to go with you, to carry all these groceries inside.'

Lynn and Molly laughed, and then they went and made the coffee and added some cake, with the three of them enjoying some nice conversation. Thirty minutes later Molly was ready to leave when young Tom came in, and it made her get-going all that much quicker. She couldn't stand the sight of him.

After Molly left Tom said to his mother, 'Was that your idea or his to chase all of my friends away?'

Lynn looked puzzled. 'What on earth are you talking about? Jack came to Goulburn City with us tonight. We left here at 5.30 and haven't been home all that long.'

Tom went on with the big whinge. 'Security guards everywhere, we weren't allowed in, couldn't get any drinks, I've had enough, as soon as I can find somewhere else to live I'm going.'

'Like I said the other night, you'll be doing me a favour, so the sooner you go the better.'

His mother's answer must have hurt because he stormed off without having his normal feed and drink.

Lynn asked Jack, 'What did you do?'

'That bloke I waved to as we left owns a security firm in Canberra.' Jack went on to explain what they did then he added, 'We'll do the same thing next week — maybe that will deter them. You said I could it.'

'Yes I know, and I'm glad you did. It was so nice to come home on my only time out and not have those monsters here.'

The next morning, Jack collected Bluey from Col's place, then it was a walk down to the park where the dog would have his usual run around before heading back to the guest house for breakfast. After that it was time to continue working on the front fence.

Bill Scanlon would be coming down for the weekend and his arrival time at Collector was expected to be around four-thirty; Jack had already booked him a room. When he arrived and signed in, Jack gave him a tour of the old building and showed him the things that he would be doing. He also explained Lynn's situation, living on the financial edge and bringing up a mongrel of a kid who wouldn't help and belonged to a gang of car hoons that terrorised the streets three or four times a week.

At five-thirty they walked to the Bushranger Hotel, taking Bluey with them. Bluey stayed in the bar with his usual female handlers, while Jack and Bill went into the restaurant to indulge in a t-bone steak. Later they engaged in darts, snooker, booze and healthy conversation while Bluey finished his night under the television chewing a nice juicy bone. They'd had a good night and eventually made their way back to the guest house. At 11 o'clock it was time for a final coffee, when Bill asked, 'What's all that noise?'

'That's the burnout vandals, let's go and have a look,' replied Jack.

They walked out the front and watched. Bill couldn't believe what he'd witnessed here. After fifteen minutes the hoon cars drove away, racing around the whole perimeter of the historical outpost before disappearing into the night — that is, except one. Tom drove into the front yard. He walked past Jack and Bill without saying a word and went to his room.

'Is that the young man you told me about?' asked Bill.

Jack replied, 'That's him all right. He's got a real chip on his shoulder, but one of the strangest things I've noticed is that he's quite friendly with the police sergeant from Goulburn City.'

'You know yourself, Jack ... we get this in Sydney too, but we stomp on it straight away so it doesn't get out of hand. This sort of thing wouldn't even last a week up town, we'd impound the cars or crush them up for scrap. Hasn't anybody here tried to put a stop to it?'

'The residents ring up the police but apparently nothing happens.'

The air was full of burning rubber as Jack closed and locked the front doors for the night. Tomorrow Jack and Bill would spend the day sightseeing in the National Capital, Canberra, before attending the Saturday night Country Rodeo Championships, and what a spectacular event it was too. Cowboys, cowgirls, marching teams, country bands with singers — and of course, the horses and bulls that provided the contest.

Sunday morning after breakfast, Bill produced some papers that give the history of those in the burnout gang. Jack had sent Bill electronic photos of all the cars and their number plates. Jack began reading the printout document, then he said, 'Hmmm, that's interesting; the kid Dittman has a suspended license.'

'You know him?'

'Yes we had a run-in, inside the foyer.' Jack told him how it happened and what he did. Bill laughed at the entertaining story about Anthony Dittman as Jack continued. When he got to the part when he tipped half a tin of white paint over the front of his suit, he said, 'Then I put the hose on the bastard.' Bill burst out laughing with that big loud laugh that he has. All those at the tables including Lynn were all looking, but of course they couldn't share the joke with them. Jack also explained the chain of events that followed with the police and lawyer Lamberton's visit.

'So Mr Dittman is one of those that wants to buy the place?'

'Yes, along with the police sergeant, Top Game Real Estate and the owner of the Royal Hotel in the city.'

'And you don't know what the project is that the State Government is talking about.'

'No, it was just something that lawyer Lamberton said to Lynn in passing.'

'Well Jack, I'll see what I can find out. Another thing I've noticed is that all the hoon cars have CB antennas — that means that they can talk to each other while their having fun. Now, Tom's car doesn't have one — probably can't afford it — but if we had a CB scanner we could listen into their conversations. How does that sound?'

'That sounds terrific Bill.'

'Okay, I'll send you down one, plus an infrared telescopic camera. We need pictures of the hoons in their cars while their doing burnouts and street racing. It takes single shots and video in the dark and it's only as big as the palm of your hand. When I get time, I'll see if I can find out where Lynn Cowdery's husband and girlfriend live.'

At 10.30 that night, Lynn came over with a plate of biscuits and two coffees; they were certainly getting the royal treatment.

Bill said to Lynn, 'Any chance of a steak and eggs in the morning?'

'Yes.'

Then Bill said, 'I have to leave here at 4:30, is that too early for you?'

'No, that's not a problem, I'll have it on the table at 4.00 am.'

'Wow, thanks a lot,' answered Bill.

Jack then said, 'I'll have one too Lynn, and I'll pay for both of them.'

'You're not going with him, are you Jack?'

'No, when he leaves I'll go back to bed for a while.'

She smiled as she walked away.

'Nothing seems a problem for that one, eh Jack.'

'No, she's one hell of a decent woman, she works her guts out all day to try and make a living out of it. She pays me two hundred dollars a week.'

'Well, Donny King won't make much out of this job then.'

They both had a good laugh as Jack continued. 'I'm going to fix this place up for her, she doesn't know it yet — we'll have to wait for the right time.'

The cars were back, racing around the perimeter road at high speed, but after that most of the noise was taking place right outside the guest house. Again they went out to watch and after a while Bill said, 'It's almost as if this place has been singled out for most of the noise, doesn't it?'

'Yes, it looks that way,' answered Jack.

The cars then left the area, but not before doing a circuit of fast racing around the perimeter of the outpost, their usual way of winding up their twenty minutes of fun.

'What do you think Bill?'

Before Bill could answer a utility drove by, heading towards the Bushranger Hotel. Bill said, 'That ute's in one of the photos.'

Jack replied, 'I took that photo right there. Sergeant O'Leary from Goulburn City Police got out of it … his name's not on that printout as the registered owner.'

'Maybe the registered owner is in it now and it's just a coincidence that it drives by here at this moment. Okay Jack, we've got plenty of food for thought. You'll get the scanner and camera on Wednesday, then you can play Sherlock Holmes undercover.'

Jack had a little laugh at that and said, 'It's an honour to be given the title of the world's greatest detective.'

Now it was Bill's turn to laugh.

THIRTEEN
The Battle of Claremont

On Monday morning, Bill Scanlon had reached the outskirts of Sydney's southern suburbs as Jack was getting out of bed for the second time. A cup of coffee and it was back to working on the outside of the guest house. Tom told his mother he was leaving; her reaction was, 'You little beauty, I'm going to throw myself a little party.'

On Tuesday morning Tom packed himself a bag and walked out without saying anything. At morning tea, Lynn told Jack that she was worried about him and indicated that she mightn't sleep tonight. What advice could Jack give? He'd had no experience bringing up kids, let alone a mad one, but he did have one thing to say. 'You know, with the attitude that he's got, how long you think he's going to last with another family before there's a blow up?'

She answered. 'Yes, you're probably right ... thanks for giving me your opinion.'

In the meantime, Tom had arrived at his new place of living. Fifteen minutes' drive south of the outpost on the Federal Highway was a large property. It comprised of dairy cattle, two thousand head of sheep and a large market garden. Tom had befriended a teenager the same age as himself and his father owned the property. This farm hired seasonal workers and had rooms for rent, but at the moment there was nobody there.

Young Jerry Baldwin had asked his father if he could help a friend of his out whose mother was giving him a hard time, and the mother's boyfriend was always punching and kicking him. The father talked it over with his wife and they decided, yes — he could come and live in one of the rooms as obviously he was living in a terrible situation. They were only too happy to help out. They knew most of the outpost's community as they attended the Uniting Church and Mrs Baldwin knew Lynn as they grew up together.

She said, 'I've known Lynn all my life and she's always been a lovely person, but the arrival of a new man in her life could certainly change all the dynamics of a mother-son relationship.'

Mr Baldwin said, 'After lunch I'm going to drop into Col's place — he lives somewhere near the old guest house — and see what he's got to say about Lynn and her new boyfriend.'

A knock on the door told them that their son's mate had arrived. They went out and greeted Tom with a warm welcome, then took him to his room where he placed his small travel case on the bed. Mr Baldwin said, 'Come and have a drink and we'll explain the rules.'

'Rules?' said Tom in a shocked voice.

'Yes, if you're going to stay here you have to abide by the rules, just simple things. Jerry has to abide by them, and so the same will apply to you. Breakfast's at 7.00 am, lunch is at 12 and dinner is at 6.00 pm. You've got to be home by 10.00 pm, if you're not then don't come home. I get up every day at 4.30 am to start my day's work as I have a big property to run and I won't have you coming home at midnight and waking me up. Do you understand?'

'Yes,' answered Tom.

Mr Baldwin continued. 'Now Tom, what will you have to drink?'

'Just a Coke.'

'We don't have Coke in this place. If you want Coke you'll have to buy your own.'

Tom asked, 'Where's Jerry?'

'Jerry's out working. He comes in at lunchtime, and you can talk to him then.'

'But I won't be here at lunchtime, I've got to go into Goulburn City. I'll have to see him when I get home in the afternoon. So I'll see youse then.' Tom went to walk away.

'Oh Tom, there's one more thing before you go. When do you get paid?'

'Next Wednesday.'

'Okay, next Wednesday you give us two hundred dollars.'

Tom couldn't believe his ears. 'Two hundred dollars! What for?'

'That's your rent. One hundred dollars per week.'

'But then I'll only have two hundred left.'

Mr Baldwin had the last word. 'Well, that's what it's going to cost you to live here.'

Tom walked away, and then drove off, burning rubber and fishtailing his car on the beautiful manicured gravel driveway that led to the highway, much to the disgust of his new landlord. Tom was on his way to do what he did every day, and nobody seemed to know what that was exactly.

Jason said to his wife,' I've got a bad feeling about this, dear.'

She answered. 'Yes, so do I.'

After lunch, Jason Baldwin pulled up opposite the Claremont Guest House in front of Col's place. Col was sitting on the front porch reading a book and enjoying a beer. Jason walked up the pathway; Col seemed to be so engrossed in the book that he didn't see him coming. Jason said, 'Is that all you've got to do these days?'

Col looked up and said, 'Well I'll be! How are you? It's been a while since you last graced my doorstep, so what brings you out this way?'

'Look mate, I need some information and I think you'd be the right person to ask.'

'If I can help, so be it.'

'The young guy Tom that lives with his mother in the guest house. Well, he came out to my place looking for a room to rent because his mother keeps picking on him and his mother's boyfriend keeps bashing him and verbally abusing him.'

Col replied, 'Is that what he told you? Now I'll tell you what he didn't tell you.' Col explained it like it was; he showed Jason a video of what the car hoons do, as he and his neighbours had been quietly collecting video evidence of the goings on in the street.

At the end of their long conversation, plus two beers and a meat pie each, Jason said to Col, 'Well, he certainly played me for a sucker.'

Col asked, 'What are you going to do?'

'Nothing for a week, I'll play along and see how it goes. In the meantime I'll go across the road and have a talk with his mother.'

Jason and Lynn had a cordial conversation about Tom, and at least for now she knew he was in good hands; she'd be able to go to sleep tonight after all. They decided that Tom would not know that this conversation took place.

Tom had been at the farm for a couple of days and for the moment, he was living within the rules of his new landlord.

Jack received the scanner and the infrared telescopic camera via an Aussie Post van and couldn't wait to try them out. After dinner he was like a little kid with a couple of new toys. The scanner was battery-operated and had a set of headphones with conversations being recorded on a hard drive. The infrared telescopic digital camera was an interesting one. The lens was no thicker than a broom handle and one hundred and fifty millimetres in length. The camera part was not much bigger than a credit card and was fifty millimetres in thickness. Again, everything could be recorded on a hard drive. He slipped the scanner onto the front of his belt, and then put the headphones on. The camera was in a soft bag with a long shoulder strap that he placed over his head.

At 10.30 Jack was ready to go outside and do some experimenting with the scanner and camera. Standing in the paddock beside the guest house that was covered in trees and bushes, he turned the scanner on — and after turning the volume up he began picking up voices. After a while Jack figured out that the conversations that he was listening to were from transport truck drivers talking to each other.

He switched on the infra-red telescopic camera and put it up to his eyes. Wow! A cat sitting on Col's back fence could be seen in pitch black darkness as if it was the middle of the day. He zoomed in and took a photo of its head.

The end of the street ran into dense bushland before it turned right; the road then ran along before running past the park and disappearing into the new homes area. He aimed the camera into the bush at the end of the street. A couple of owls high in a tree was a beautiful sight. *One of God's immaculate bird creatures,* Jack thought as he took their photo. A possum in another tree was seen walking down the tree to the base and began frolicking on the ground with another.

The animals suddenly ran away in haste as a white utility reversed into that part of the bush right where the road turned. *Ooo,* Jack thought. *Why would anybody reverse into that area this time of the night? A couple of young lovers?* But on zooming in, the head he was looking at was that of Sergeant O'Leary. *What the hell's he up to? Maybe he's doing some surveillance work himself — after all, he is a policeman.*

Jack turned the camera to video and at the same time took

cover behind one of the large bushes that was there. Then the cars started arriving, firstly racing up and down the street, before singling out the guest house for special treatment. For ten minutes the hoon vandals burnt rubber; the noise was like you would experience in the pit stop at the Bathurst 500. While Jack was filming all of this he was also rotating the dial of the CB scanner to find the bandwidth that the cars were working on, to find out if they were talking to each other.

He finally found it. They were laughing hysterically as they zigzagged across the road then a voice over the top said, 'All right, close it down and get the hell out of there, a police car's on its way out here.'

'That voice,' said Jack, 'is Sergeant O'Leary's?' He swung the camera back down into the bush. There he was, talking into a CB handset. 'Holy mackerel, he's not doing any surveillance work; he's telling them what to do. The police sergeant is behind it.'

Sergeant O'Leary hung up the handset and drove out of the bush, turning left in the direction of the park at slow speed. Thirty minutes later a police car drove around with its blue lights flashing away, and then it disappeared back the way it came. Justice had been served the Goulburn City Police way.

Jack went back inside, happy with what he'd achieved with the camera and scanner. He made himself a cup of coffee and sat at a table. Lynn had finished her work for the night and came over with a plate of biscuits and a coffee of her own. She saw Jack come inside with the headphones on and something in a small shoulder bag and wondered what he was up to. But of course, he wouldn't be telling her; instead he said, 'I was doing a bit of bird watching when the cars showed up. I didn't see Tom's car amongst them.'

'He's probably got no petrol,' replied Lynn, but she had no idea of the 10 pm curfew that he was under.

Bill rang up at smoko the next day to tell Jack that an undercover policeman was coming down to stay at the guest house for the weekend. His job was to observe the behaviour of the hoon vandals and report back to him. Jack told him what he'd witnessed last night and everything was recorded. Bill said, 'Well, that confirms a connection as to why the police from Goulburn City won't arrest these lawbreakers. Good work Jack, I'll talk to you soon.'

On Thursday night, Covert Security were all in place by 5 pm to prevent Tom and his mates from entering the guest house should they come by. And come by they did, with Tom leading the pack — but on seeing the tow truck and the guard at the locked gates, they disappeared as quick as they came, finishing up at the southern end of Goulburn City where the main food centre was located around a well-known tourist attraction called The Big Merino. This concrete sculpture of a sheep was as big as a double-storey house, and was popular as a backdrop for those wanting to have their photos taken. The area was a bonanza for the businesses here, as up to 200 local young people regularly met up in the massive car park, socialising and enjoying each other's stories and company — and along with that comes food and drinks. There was never any trouble here as the police had a zero tolerance policy. It's funny how the police could keep a tight rein on things here but couldn't care less what happened at the Collector outpost.

Tom hadn't turned eighteen yet, so when his mates decided to go to the RSL Club in the main drag he headed back to the farm, arriving there at 10.15 pm — too late to get in. He would have to sleep in the car. The Indian summer they were having at the moment was quite warm, but it was just the opposite at night where the temperature would drop to zero degrees. Tom had never been in the boy scouts to learn the motto, 'Always be prepared' — and it didn't take long before he realised he would have to go home for the night.

Lynn, Molly and Jack arrived back at the guest house after their night of shopping and entertainment in Goulburn City. After unpacking the groceries it was time for coffee and cake. While this was going on, young Tom walked in, surprising the three of them.

Lynn said to him, 'Hello son. Are you homesick already?'

He never answered, just continued on toward his room.

Jack remarked. 'He's so lucky to have a mother like you. Anybody else would have said, "What are you doing here?"'

Lynn gave the only answer she could give. 'I know he's a mongrel of a young man, but he's still my son, and I don't want anything to happen to him. One day hopefully, he'll grow up and we can put all of his bad behaviour behind us.'

In the morning Tom left early, arriving back at the farm just in time for breakfast. After that Mr Baldwin said, 'Tom, where's that two hundred dollars?'

Tom replied, 'I can't pay it this time, I'll have to pay it next dole day.'

'Okay mate,' answered Mr Baldwin.

Tom went to his room for a while and at 10 am drove away to do what he usually did, burning rubber as he went. He put his foot flat on the accelerator. Mr and Mrs Baldwin rushed out onto the front porch after being startled by the loud sound of Tom's car. They held hands as they watched this burnout monster virtually ploughing up their 150 metre long gravel driveway, with those spinning wheels sending rocks, stones and dust into the air and onto the beautiful manicured lawns. Tom added insult to injury by fishtailing the vehicle from one side to the other. As he turned onto the highway and headed north, he was laughing gleefully to himself as he punched the air in a lust of excitement, as if he'd accomplishment something — something that only he would know.

Mr Baldwin said to his wife, 'Well love, it looks like Col was right about him, a completely useless bludging lout, but at least we gave him a chance.'

They went back inside holding hands.

By late morning dark clouds were beginning to gather, and by mid-afternoon it was raining lightly. When Tom arrived back at the farm that night it was 9.30, and the tempo of the rain had increased to quite heavy. He parked his car and began the walk to the porch and the front door. There were no outside lights on, and as he reached the front steps he noticed an object on the lawn. He had a closer look: it was his travel case and beside it were his clothes, shoes and best coat.

'Dirty bastards,' he yelled as he gathered everything up. He threw his soaking wet belongings on the back seat of his car, then he went and sat behind the steering wheel and had a bit of a sob. He was still a boy but didn't know it. Eventually he started the car and drove away, this time in a proper manner. It was back to the guest house — another humiliation.

On Friday afternoon, the undercover cop from Sydney arrived and booked in for two nights; he would be going home sometime Sunday morning. He was disappointed Friday night, as the hoons never showed up, but Saturday night he got twenty minutes of 'exciting video'. Jack also got some good recording of Sergeant O'Leary talking to his drivers and urging them on.

On Sunday morning, the undercover cop left for his trip back to Sydney and after lunch Jack took Bluey down to the park for a run around. Because the weather had been unseasonably hot, the cricket club put a match together at short notice and it was taking place in the southern end of the park. Jack could see Col officiating as match referee. Bluey was given his freedom and he bounced away at full speed to search every nook and cranny while Jack lay down on the park seat to doze.

Fifty metres away danger was lurking on the road in the shape of one of the car hoons; he dialled his mates, who must have been nearby. 'Yeah, the arsehole's lying on the park bench. If we're going to get him now is the time. Okay, I'll wait until you get here.'

One by one, five more members of the hoon vandals arrived. The hoon vandals gathered at the back of the last car, they were all carrying large shifting spanners.

Young Dittman said, 'Right, let's get the bastard,' as they walked with purpose towards a sleeping Jack Kelly on the park bench seat.

The ever-alert Bluey galloped to the park bench seat and a couple of very loud woofs had Jack awake; an instant decision saw him on his feet and running hard with Bluey right behind him. Now which way to go? He headed towards the cricket match with the hoon vandals ten metres behind him, chasing hard and yelling obscenities at the same time.

Col spotted Jack and Bluey running toward him with the vandals in hot pursuit. 'Jack's in trouble, let's help him,' he yelled.

The cricketers grabbed stumps and balls and headed towards the running Jack Kelly. The vandals were getting closer to Jack but then they spotted the cricketers coming towards them with raised cricket stumps — now the rules of the contest had suddenly changed. A couple of cricket balls were lobbed behind Jack and struck a vandal in the head. He stopped and bent over, holding his head.

'Let's get out of here,' yelled young Dittman, who could see that they were totally out-numbered. They turned as one to race back to the safety of their cars. The cricketers chased them right back to their cars and watched them speed away.

Col said to Jack, 'It seems like you've made some enemies.'

Jack replied, 'As Sergeant O'Leary said the other day, I've trod on a couple of toes — I'm going to have to watch myself in the future. If you blokes hadn't been here today I might have been in real trouble, thanks a lot fellas.'

'No worries Jack, glad to help,' seemed to be the consensus. The cricketers continued on with their game while Jack and Bluey returned to the guest house.

Back in Sydney at the start of the working week, Bill Scanlon had found the address of Lynn Cowdery's runaway husband and his live-in lover, the one he'd met in the Bushranger Hotel. Bill was having a quiet day so he decided to knock off a couple of hours early to do a bit of private investigating.

He drove to Sydney's southernmost suburb, a happy place called Heathcote. After locating the house he parked fifty metres away on the opposite side of the road beside a park. Bill was driving a police surveillance vehicle; just a plain looking car with two roof racks on the top and a couple of spotlights attached. But the spotlights were actually digital cameras that could move in all directions. Inside the car, a large screen was part of the dashboard and attached to a computer with a hard drive for recording everything. A remote handset with a built-in joystick operated the cameras.

Bill turned everything on and zoomed in to cover the front yard and half the road. From this moment on, everything that appeared on the dashboard screen would be recorded. Many cars went by in both directions. Plenty of people were walking about, and in the park some youths and their girlfriends were playing a game of badminton.

With surveillance work you could never tell how long you'd have to wait to get results. Bill had picked this time because working people came home from work between three and five in the afternoon. After thirty or forty minutes a very attractive lady walked out of the front gate and onto the footpath, carrying a boy about eighteen months old. She placed him on the ground where he began walking around. Bill watched with interest as they played together as only a mother and son could.

A car pulled onto the side of the road and stopped in front of the house, with a man getting out of the passenger side door carrying a work bag. This man waved to the driver of the car as it drove away, and then he walked toward the lady on the footpath; they embraced and kissed. Bill zoomed in as close as he could to record shots of the three of them. After five minutes of playing with the boy and laughing and joking, they held hands as they walked through the front gate and out of sight.

Bill was thinking, *What a beautiful family unit*, and the descriptions that Jack had given him matched perfectly. This was them all right. *It couldn't have worked out any better if I'd scripted it.* He started the motor, drove onto the road and paused in front of their house recording it as he went by. 'Mission accomplished,' he said to himself as he turned the cameras and computer off.

He would ring Jack tonight and tell him, but for now it was time to drive back to North Sydney and spend some quality time with Marree, who was also about to finish her shift at St Vincent's Hospital.

Bill and Jack had a busy week talking to each other on their mobiles about what had happened and what was going to happen. A secret raid on the hoon vandals had been organised for Saturday night and it was expected that all the youths in the hot rod cars would be arrested. Because of Sergeant O'Leary's association with them, Goulburn City Police would be kept out of it.

Bill had found out through a State Government bureaucrat that a precious metal mine was going to open a little to the west of the outpost, making whoever owned the guest house a lot of money. It was assumed that Sergeant O'Leary, with the help of his hot rod friends, would put enough pressure on Lynn to sell the guest house to him. If Jack hadn't come along when he did, his plan may well have succeeded.

Across the road at Col's place, Col was having a meeting with eight close friends that lived in the outpost. After watching Jack being chased by the vandals, they decided that enough was enough. What if they weren't playing cricket the other day, and the hoon vandals had caught Jack? What they were going to do, kill him? They'd already threatened some of the more vocal residents that they'd burn their houses down if they didn't stop whingeing.

Col's last words were, 'We can't wait any longer to tackle these monsters, but we'll do it so that we don't implicate ourselves. Don't challenge them head on — we'll do it in the dark, guerrilla style, then they won't know who we are. Okay, we all know what we have to do, now let's do it.'

Over the next four days they made up two sets of road spikes, and next Saturday night they would put them to good use. The plan was to attend a bogus party in Canberra on Saturday that would extend into the night. A good friend of Col's was sympathetic to the problems they were having with the burnout vandals, and he offered to hold a noisy party so that they would have an alibi as to their whereabouts on Saturday, should they need it.

They would drive back to the outpost at 10 pm, and park just off the highway. From there they would make their way through the heavy bush on one of the trails that come out near the park. With dark clothing and balaclavas on they would lay in wait for the monsters and inflict as much damage to their cars as they could. Then they would quickly disappear into the night and back to the highway to their cars, driving back to the party for final drinks and possibly staying the night. Hopefully, with a bit of luck they shouldn't have any injuries. Their thinking was if the police won't do anything, the least they could do was to give Jack a bit of a hand — but of course, they had no idea that a secret police raid was also going to happen at the same time.

Bill arrived at the guest house after lunch on Saturday; he had to be there when the raid was on and was given the job by Sydney Command to be in charge of it. In the meantime Jack and Bill would go into Canberra and do some sightseeing. At 6 pm they had dinner at the Black Mountain Tower Restaurant before arriving back at the guest house at 8 pm. Now they would just wait the next few hours until things started to happen.

At 9.30 Jack locked Bluey in his kennel with a nice new bone that he purchased in Goulburn City on Thursday night just for this occasion. At 10 pm Jack went and brought the scanner out of his room while Bill went out to his car, came back with a briefcase and put it on a table that was down near the front of the building, away from all of the guests that were playing cards and watching television. Bill and Jack sat on the kitchen side of the table as if they were watching the television on the inside of the front wall; from where they sat, there was six metres to the front door.

At about the same time the Queanbeyan Police had silently moved their unmarked cars into predetermined hiding positions in the bush and behind buildings, while Col and his would-be gang of commandos were making their way through the bush and were about to come out near the park. For the moment they would stay amongst the trees until the burnouts started.

Bill received a text message to say that the Queanbeyan Police were in position and the operation had begun. He sent back an acknowledgement. Bill had a portable police radio and a handset, but at the moment it was radio silence. A special digital band was being used so that the Goulburn City Police wouldn't know that anything out of the ordinary was happening.

At 10.45 pm a 'cockatoo' spotted Sergeant O'Leary's utility

driving past the Bushranger hotel, turning left on his way to his little hiding place in the edge of the bush. A few minutes later, a second call: 'Here they come.'

Jack turned on the scanner and the hard drive recorder. The eight hoon cars including Tom turned into the street and started burning rubber. Sergeant O'Leary could be heard urging them on. 'That's it Dittman, give it to them, you're doing a good job tonight.'

Col and his boys had the road spikes ready to go on the west-side road; the idea was to let four cars go by then pull the spikes across the road, catching the second four cars. The other four cars would get caught on the park side when they sped along there, before they turned the corner where Sergeant O'Leary was hiding.

After ten minutes the vandals raced up and down the street at high speed. Now they would do what they always did: turn left and circumnavigate the whole of the outpost as some sort of hoon finale.

Col's plan worked out to perfection. They let four cars go by and pulled the spikes across the road on pre-attached ropes. With Sergeant O'Leary talking to them and wrapped up in their own excited stupor, the second four cars hit the spikes one after the other, resulting in all tyres being deflated. Two lost control and ran off the road while the other two stopped only to be attacked by the would-be commandos. With baseball bats they smashed the front windscreens before reaching in, grabbing the CB handsets and ripping them out. The occupants just froze at this level of violence.

It was then into the bush to do the same thing to the other two cars. One driver tried to do something, but two baseball bats put an end to that, and he was shown no mercy.

Col's commandos ran off to get to the other side of the park before the remaining four cars reached the road spikes. The cars were closing in and one by one they hit the spikes. The first two received four flat tyres each and instantly ran off the road, one deep into the bush. Col raced after that one. He smashed the front and rear windscreens, then he tore the radio handset out. He recognised young Dittman and couldn't resist giving him a brutal punch to the side of his head; the hoon slumped in the seat. Then Col went and did the same to the other car.

The third car copped the same treatment while the fourth car only lost his front tyres before he stopped, but before he could move his windscreen was shattered by a baseball bat and the CB handset pulled out of the car — ending any communication with Sergeant O'Leary. A sharp pick was swung into the remaining two back tyres, and then the bloke with the pick left it sticking out of the hood as a souvenir.

As far as Col was concerned the job was over, and he led the way back through the bush towards the highway. Once there they climbed into the two cars that they'd arrived in and headed back towards Canberra to finish the bogus party.

The Queanbeyan police moved in and rounded up the hoon vandals — including Tom, whose car had four flat tyres and a smashed windscreen. An unmarked police car blocked Sergeant O'Leary's exit from the bushes. Two policemen escorted him out of his car.

'I'm Sergeant O'Leary from Goulburn City Police, it's my job to catch these people!'

'Yes, we know who you are. You organised the last raid and tipped them off, now come with us.'

They put him in their car and drove down to the guest house, taking him inside.

Bill had been joined by the Queanbeyan police chief and they would interview Sergeant O'Leary. The Queanbeyan police brought in the handcuffed hoon vandals one by one, including Tom, keeping them just inside the front door. The guest house patrons were watching this real live entertainment.

On seeing her son in handcuffs, Lynn quickly walked down to

berate him. 'You silly thing, how do you feel now that the police have got you? I hope they lock you up.'

Bill said to O'Leary, 'Well Sergeant, what have you got to say for yourself?'

'I'm not saying anything; I'm trying to put an end to all this street racing and moronic behaviour.'

Bill replied, 'You've had twelve months, and what have you done? Nothing by the looks of it. Turn that thing on Jack.'

It was a recording of the CB radios tonight. Sergeant O'Leary went white in the face as he listened to his own voice urging the hoons on.

Bill continued. 'Now Sergeant ... we can keep this in-house, so it's up to you. We just want to know why.'

The sergeant bowed his head looking at the table, and after a minute's silence he lifted his head and said. 'I suppose it was greed. I wanted to buy the guest house because in the near future a mine is going to be developed not far from here. This is the only accommodation in the area, so whoever owns it will make a lot of money as it would be full all the time with workers coming and going especially in the construction phase.'

Bill was typing up something and passed it over to Sergeant O'Leary when he finished, saying, 'Read it then sign it. This will only go to senior command, nobody else will know. You've been a policeman for forty years with a good record; I think you're allowed one mistake.'

He reluctantly signed it and passed it back to Bill.

The Queanbeyan police chief said, 'Sergeant O'Leary, you can go now — and good luck Sir.'

The sergeant meekly got up out of his seat and walked away a dejected figure, leaving the guest house to walk down to the end of the street where the white ute was parked in the bushes. He would be driving out of his little hideout for the last time.

Bill said, 'Bring the young mongrel over here.'

'I'll get him,' said Jack.

Tom, in that defiant-to-the-end voice, said, 'I don't want to talk to him.'

The policeman looking after him said sternly, 'Get yourself over there before I drag you over there like a dead sheep.'

Tom went over. Bill said to him, 'Well Tom, is your life of crime over? If it is I'll let you go, otherwise you go back over with your mates and you'll soon be on your way to the Queanbeyan lockup. You'll be in court on Monday morning and a disqualified driver by lunchtime, then your car will be crushed up and sold to the Port Kembla Steelworks for scrap.' Bill was waiting for an answer. 'Come on Tom, what's it going to be?'

Tom began whingeing, 'My mother drove my father away and now she's trying to drive me away.'

Bill opened a folder that was sitting in front of him and pulled out some photos. 'Is this your father?'

Tom picked it up and looked at it, then said, 'Yes.' Bill then gave him the rest to look at. After thirty seconds Tom asked, 'Where did you get these?'

Bill answered, 'I'm a policeman. Do you know the woman in these photos?'

Tom looked at them and said, 'Yes, she lived here in Collector for a while.'

'You see Tom, your father was having an affair with this lady behind your mother's back. Your mother didn't hurry him away — he ran away with that lady. That's their baby boy in the photos … that little boy is your step-brother.'

Tom was frantic as he looked at the photos two or three times, then it hit him like a tidal wave; he broke down and began crying hysterically.

Lynn came running over and said, 'What are you doing to him?'

Bill said, 'I'm trying to keep him out of jail.'

Then she spotted the photos of her husband on the table and moved in closer.

'I'm sorry Mrs Cowdery, but if you don't want to know anything about your husband I urge you to don't look any further.'

It was too late; she perused those photos as if her life depended on it. 'The dirty bastard,' she said. 'That woman walked past here every day for months ... she lived somewhere past the park, I saw him talking to her a couple of times.' She looked Bill straight in the eyes. 'Where is the slimy mongrel?'

'Sydney.'

Lynn put the photos down and started to cry, then she gave Tom a hug; it was probably the first hug in a very long time.

Bill powered on. 'Well Tom, what's it going to be? Are you going to be a good boy from now on or are you going to jail? The meat wagon's about to leave.'

Tom said in a panic, 'Can I have a second chance? I won't do any more street racing or burnouts and I'll help Mum.'

Bill asked him, 'Now you've got to get a job. Will you get a job?'

'Yes, yes, I'll get a job, I'll get a job, and I'll do anything.'

Bill had to hear him say those words. 'Okay Constable, take the cuffs of him and let him go. Then take the rest of them to Queanbeyan and lock them up.'

Anybody could see that Lynn was emotionally upset, but she put on a brave face and said, 'I'm putting on a cup of coffee for everybody.'

All the police sat down at the table while Lynn and Tom walked down toward the kitchen — she had her arm around him as they disappeared through the door. Ten minutes later it was coffee and toasted ham sandwiches.

It was a hell of a two hours but everything turned out good. The only thing that saved Tom was that he was a minor, and that allowed Bill a bit of discretion. All the police were discussing it amongst themselves, all talking at once. The Queanbeyan police chief said to one of his men, 'Jerry, you radioed in that there were other people involved here, what was that all about?'

'Well, they actually took a bit of our thunder. When the cars began their run down the mountainside I saw six or seven of them preparing road spikes. As the spiked tyres brought the cars to a halt they tore into them with baseball bats smashing their windscreens. I held my cover, and then they just disappeared. We soon picked up the drivers, and when we got around to the other side, the same thing had happened there.'

Did you get a good look at them?'

'Yes — they were all dressed in black with balaclavas and gloves. Nothing more to say.'

'Okay, we'll leave it that way,' said the chief.

Jack had something to say. 'I wonder who they were. It's funny how it worked out. After twelve months of harassment the residents decided to fight back on the very same night that a secret police operation was also put into action.'

Bill said to the policeman in charge of the tow truck, 'Here's a picture of young Tom's car. When you move them, can you put this one in front of the paddock next door? That'll give him something to think about for a while.'

They all laughed.

The Queanbeyan police were about to go. Bill shook hands with all of them and thanked them for their cooperation. 'Any time,' they said. They'd enjoyed the coffee and the toasted sandwiches, and now it was time to return to their own base in Queanbeyan, a beautiful town on the eastern side of Canberra.

Later, Bill was talking to Lynn about her husband. Lynn said, 'I'm going to see a solicitor this week and start divorce proceedings. Then I'd like to see him one more time to tell him what I think of him, and hand him the summons papers myself. I'm sure Tom would like to say something to him as well.'

'Lynn, when you've got the papers, tell Jack — we'll make it happen.'

'Thanks Bill. You know, the first day you showed up here I said to myself, "That bloke looks like a copper" … the haircut, I suppose. When I mentioned it to Jack he said, "No, Bill's a funeral director from Western Sydney".' Bill burst out laughing and that got Lynn going as well. Then she asked. 'Is Jack a policeman too — you know, one of those undercover cops you hear about?'

'No, Jack and I have been mates for a long time. Believe it or not, Jack's a swagman — he just walks around the country picking up jobs like this one. Eventually he'll leave here and go somewhere else.'

Her face suddenly drained of all emotion and at the same time he realised he shouldn't have said that; he quickly added, 'But that won't be for a long time yet.'

Jack had been talking to one of the Queanbeyan policeman and when he left Jack came and sat down, while Bill decided to call it a night after what he said had been a big week.

Jack said to Lynn, 'Well mate, you won't be bothered by the cars anymore.'

'No, thanks to you. Bill said you'd be leaving here soon.'

'I won't be leaving here until this place is spick and span and capable of filling every room. Did Bill tell you why the sergeant wanted to buy your place?'

'No.'

'Well there's a mine going to be built not far from here, and you're the only person that's got any accommodation in the area. In a couple of years' time this place will be full — you'll be able to charge three times what you charge now, and you'll have so much money you won't know what to do with it. What do you think of that?'

'I don't know what to say.'

'Don't say anything, just enjoy it when it happens. Oh, there's going to be a few more people coming to give me a hand, I hope you don't mind.'

'No I've got complete trust in what you do … but I don't have any money to pay anybody, let alone buy materials.'

'You don't have to worry about that Lyn, we'll put it on the slate.'

Jack had had enough and decided to hit the sack while Lynn continued sitting there, pondering the events that happened today. She was satisfied that Jack wouldn't be leaving here in the foreseeable future.

At breakfast time Bill and Jack were talking about the men in black.

Bill asked. 'Got any ideas as to who might have organised that little guerrilla force? Anybody stand out at all? The curiosity's got the better of me.'

'No, they all seemed pretty upset about the car hoons. Could have been any one of them or all of them.'

Jack could see that Bill wanted to find out just for the sheer fun of it, and over the next week or so he would do some prime snooping.

Bill left after lunch for the four and a half hour drive back to Sydney — but not before he had a good talk to Tom. His car was parked next door to the guest house on the vacant block of land. All the tyres were flat and the windscreen was smashed, plus there were several dints in the top and the bonnet.

For Tom, to see his pride and joy standing there in that state was heartbreaking for him, but then he didn't care about the problems he and his mates were causing with out of control street racing three or four times a week late at night. He walked around a dejected figure. His friends were all in jail; their cars were taken into Goulburn City for crushing prior to being sent to the steelworks for smelting.

During the week, two expert business consultants arrived from GD Constructions to do an assessment on what was needed to turn the guest house into a moneymaking venture. Simple things like a Coca-Cola machine and solar panels to heat water — make money out of one and save a lot of money on the other. With thirty rooms at full capacity the potential was certainly there.

A week later, all the work began. At times there were twenty people involved, from painters to simple gardeners, with half the labour coming from the Collector unemployed. After two weeks the work was completed. Tom joined in, helping the many contractors that were there, much to Jack's surprise. They thought he was a site trade assistant, but when they found out he was doing it for nothing they were impressed. So much so that the top painting contractor from Goulburn offered him an apprenticeship, which he accepted.

Jack had one more thing to do before it was time to leave the Claremont Guest House and continue walking in the footsteps of his grandfather, and that was to get Lynn and Tom to the Sydney suburb of Heathcote so Lynn could personally serve divorce papers to her runaway husband. Jack had one of his team leave a rather new looking Ford Falcon station wagon for this purpose. Somebody would pick it up and take it back to Sydney when the trip was over.

Lynn had the legal divorce paperwork in her hand now and was looking forward to the drive to Southern Sydney. Her brain was still in denial over Jack leaving and wouldn't even contemplate the thought of it, although one little part of her brain kept repeating those words that Jack had said — words that she didn't want to hear. 'I won't be leaving here until this place is spick and span and capable of filling all of those rooms.'

Now she was looking at such a place.

The drive to Heathcote would take about four hours and they had to be there no later than 3 pm. Jack knew exactly where to go, so it was easy to judge the time of arrival with a couple of stops along the way for coffee and hamburgers. They pulled up in front of the house, matching it up with a photo. Jack then reversed the station wagon back two houses and parked; now they would just wait in hope that Mr Cowdery would come home from work, just as he did the day Bill took those photos. A look on the dashboard clock said ten past three.

Time moved on — and right on 3.30, Mr Cowdery's live-in lover came onto the footpath with the male toddler and began playing with him. Lynn's heartbeat began to accelerate.

Tom said, 'There's the bitch.'

Jack smiled at the unfolding scene. Bill had shown him the surveillance video, and what he was looking at now was almost a carbon copy. Five minutes later a car passed by and stopped in front of the house. Mr Cowdery stepped out of the car carrying his work bag; he waved to the driver as he drove away. He was clearly heard to say, 'See you tomorrow.'

Lynn said, 'I'm feeling a bit nervous about all of this.'

'Well I'm not,' said Tom. He was out of the car, walking with long venomous strides towards his father, who was now giving his lover a hug and a kiss. 'Hey you,' yelled Tom. 'I want to talk to you, you dirty rotten fucken mongrel.'

Both of them were taken by complete surprise and turned together as one. Tom punched his father twice in the face, knocking him to the ground. His lover started screaming while the toddler was showing signs of instant stress.

Tom looked down at his father and screamed, 'You arsehole, I never want to see you again.' Then he spat on him, a great big green golly landing on his face. Tom then walked back to the car.

Lynn was on the scene now with the divorce papers in her hand. 'Here are some papers from the courthouse; I'll see you in court.'

Mr Cowdery looked up at her from the ground, and as he took the papers from her said, 'I'm sorry Lynn.'

Mr Cowdery's lover said to Lynn in a nasty voice, 'You've got a nerve coming here; get back to your old boarding house.'

'Yes, I intend to,' replied Lyn. 'But before I go there's something I want to do.'

'And pray tell, what would that be?'

Lynn didn't even answer as she viciously punched her right on the nose, and at the same time grabbed two handfuls of that beautiful waist-length black hair and dragged her to the ground by it. Then she put the boot into her, striking her around the stomach and chest area followed by one good stomp on her face. Lynn headed back to the car, punched the air with her fist and said loudly, 'Geesus, that felt good.'

Mr Cowdery was sitting up now and he saw Jack standing there. 'What do you want?' he asked.

Jack replied, 'Nothing, I'm just making sure your little boy doesn't run onto the street.'

'Oh, thank you. Tell Tom I deserved that.'

Mr Cowdery got to his feet and helped his lady to her feet before picking up his little boy, who was in a very distressed state. The three of them then disappeared into the property. Jack went back to the car, started the motor and reversed before doing a u-turn and driving away, heading in the direction of the major road, hoping that nobody took the number plate particulars.

Twenty minutes later they turned onto the six lane Hume

Highway that would take them almost all the way back to the Claremont Guest House — and for Lynn, home sweet home. During the journey Jack was thinking about Lynn's attack on her husband's lover. It just goes to show that even the most placid person can arrive at an act of violence given the right circumstances — and the trigger here was, 'Get back to your old boarding house.'

They arrived back in Collector at 9 pm. Molly looked after the guest house for Lynn and she went home at 11 o'clock. Jack had a late night telephone talk to Bill and filled him in on what happened. For the two of them, they were satisfied that another chapter in the book of somebody's life had been successfully closed. Today brought some sort of finale, a conclusion, to the many things that had happened since that first day when Jack booked into the Bushranger Hotel. There was nothing keeping him here any longer. The East Coast Swaggie would be leaving on Saturday to continue walking in the footsteps of his grandfather. The sheep farm on top of the mountain had been contacted and they would be expecting him any time over the weekend.

In the meantime Jack and Bluey would spend some quality time together exploring the outpost more closely, and doing things like chase the stick down at the park, walking for ages to find a rabbit to chase without much luck, and sitting on Col's front porch with a beer and a pie — and a bone. What a great time they had.

On Thursday, Jack washed all his clothes and freshened up the swag. Lynn saw the little tent pitched on the front lawn and Bluey was asleep in it — so was Jack. They looked so peaceful, the man and his dog. Later she spotted all his clothes hanging on the line out the back. It was obvious, even to a blind man, that he was getting ready to leave; the moment she dreaded wasn't far away.

At 3 pm Jack pulled the little tent down and folded it all up, rolling it into the swag, ready for Saturday. Thursday night shopping went ahead as per normal although Lynn was unusually quiet as a little bit of anxiety was creeping in.

Arriving back at the guest house and after Molly had left, Lynn waited until Jack and she were alone, she said, 'I suppose I shouldn't ask, and you've heard me ask this question before. Who are you, Jack Kelly? You've got a friend who's a policeman and he's got more clout than our own police force in Goulburn City. You roam the countryside helping people that are down on their luck, but who are you, who do you work for?'

Jack didn't quite know what to say — for the moment he couldn't tell her, so he said something that he'd heard Donny King say many times: 'Lynn, I work for God — he or she tells me what I have to do. I take my orders from God.'

She looked towards the heavens and the boarding house ceiling, closing her eyes. She knew that her prayers had been answered. Jack heard her say in a whisper, 'Thank you God.' She opened her eyes as a couple of tears exited the corner of her eyes, and rolled down her cheeks.

'One more sleep to go,' Jack said to himself as he walked across the road to pick up Bluey after his overnight stay with Col's dog Goldun. On the way back he stopped to look at the Claremont Guest House. He liked what he saw. From a shambles of a building to a modern looking version of the same building, Lynn would now be able to make a living out of it. At the same time the homeless of Sydney had made some money. Jack had helped somebody who was rock bottom down on her luck. He'd done the community thing and ended the street racing, and in the process put an end to some lethal police corruption in Goulburn City.

On Friday evening Lynn organised a surprise party for Jack that left him a bit humbled. Fifteen people were there from the outpost to share a meal and some good conversation, along with a bit of bring-your-own drinking.

The party finished at 11 pm — for Jack it was bedtime. About 11.30 and lying in the dark, he was feeling pretty satisfied at how things had ended up here, and he began to wonder what sort of adventure he would be walking into when he left here tomorrow.

A soft knock on the door startled him. He got off the bed and opened the door. It was Lynn, dressed in a beautiful nightie and looking quite radiant. His first thoughts were, *I don't think I've seen her look as good as this before.*

'Jack … I'm sorry to bother you, but I was wondering if I could sleep with you tonight. I mean, I may never see you again and I just thought I'd like to be close to you before you go.'

Jack was silent and expressionless. She saw the shocked look on his face, then realised that she may have misjudged Jack Kelly and made a terrible mistake. She said, 'I'm sorry Jack, I didn't handle that too good did I? Now you're probably thinking I'm just a tart, throwing myself at you when you've been such a gentleman … but with all the things that you've done for me I just couldn't help it. Now I can see I've made the biggest fool of myself.'

Jack's big smile came over his face as he spoke. 'You know Lynn, you haven't made a fool of yourself, and tonight you look so attractive. I've also noticed lately you've been improving the way you look, like losing a little bit of weight. Those couple of new dresses you bought in Goulburn City look good on you and the hour you spent in the hairdressers added the final touch.'

Lynn interrupted with a nice smile. 'And I thought you never noticed.'

Jack continued. 'You're going to need to look like this when you're running this place with a staff of three or four when all thirty rooms are occupied. Like I said, you are attractive and it's not that I don't want you — if I was anybody else, any other male, we'd be on that bed and into it. But I have a reason why it can't happen. The best I can do is make you a proposition. You go and change into a pair of jeans and a t-shirt, and I'll do the same. You can come and sleep in my bed with me.'

A big smile came over her face. 'I'll go and change,' she said.

While she was gone Jack changed his clothes, when she came back they closed the door and hopped into bed together. A kiss on the forehead with a bit of holding hands was all that was going to happen here tonight.

At 4.30 am Lynn's mobile phone alarm started beeping; it was time for her to go, but before she left she pressed her lips to his, just for a few seconds, then left to begin her work that goes with running the guest house.

After lunch Jack put his swaggie uniform on — it was time to go.

Bluey, on seeing Jack with the big coat and hat on, barked excitedly before running around and around in circles. He rolled over and over along the old dance floor, then began chasing his tail before racing out the front and onto the lawn where he sat down like the Egyptian Sphinx, waiting for Jack to come out. He knew they were leaving.

Jack had the leash in his hand and now clipped it onto Bluey's collar. Lynn gave Jack a big hug with a tear in her eye and they said goodbye to each other — and although he didn't expect it, Tom came out and said goodbye. He would be starting work as an apprentice painter very soon.

Col and his wife were leaning on the front fence and Jack walked towards them. The mobile phone in his pocket vibrated; he pulled it out, stopping in the middle of the road. It was Bill with a very interesting message. They talked for a minute, until Jack put the phone away and continued walking over to Col and his wife.

He had a final chat with them and said as he shook Col's hand, 'Well, Captain Colin Robert Lucas, Australian Special Forces, it's been a pleasure to know you.' He turned his attention to Col's wife. He shook her hand as well saying, 'Goodbye, Lieutenant Anne Sanders, Australian Security Intelligence Organisation, Beirut 1993.' Jack turned and began to walk away, and then he turned back and said, 'By the way, your little secret's safe with me.'

They had a final wave as Jack continued on. Col said to his wife, 'I wonder who that guy really is?'

Anne replied, 'Could be one of what we used to be, on assignment … look how we started off.'

'You're right about that, but somehow I completely trust the guy.'

'So do I, he really is one of a kind.'

Inside the Bushranger Hotel, Jack said goodbye to all those who were there and thanked the publican for all of his hospitality. He gave Jack a nice healthy bone all wrapped up and tied with a red bow to give to Bluey some time later. Then it was time to move on.

Walking away from the historical hotel, he couldn't help thinking about his grandfather who left the outpost behind to walk to his next destination, a sheep farm on top of the mountain called Laredo — and now he was walking in the actual footsteps of his grandfather. It was uplifting and made him feel real proud.

Ten minutes later a police car passed him by and stopped ten metres further on. It spooked him a bit and he thought to himself, *I wonder what he wants; I don't think I'd be the flavour of the month at the Goulburn City Police Centre after the recent investigation. And at the moment I'm a sitting duck on the side of the road.*

The cop got out of the vehicle; it was the young policeman that came out to the guest house to investigate him after he painted the Dittmans. Constable Gatton walked up to Jack with a friendly smile and said, 'Hey there swaggie, I heard you were leaving.' He extended his hand as a gesture of friendship, which Jack accepted.

They had a cordial conversation for ten minutes then Jack asked him, 'How's your boss, Sergeant O'Leary these days?'

The constable replied, 'The Police Tribunal in Sydney ended up charging him with corruption. We don't know what his sentence will be but he deserves what he gets. He's an embarrassment to all honest police. It's taken a big toll on his health, though — he's lost 7 or 8 kilos. He told me you're an undercover cop.'

'I'm no cop, but my mate is — he's high up in Sydney. So there's a lesson for you as you grow up: don't get too greedy — and no, you don't have to book your mother to be a good policeman.'

Constable Gatton laughed at that, and then said, 'Can I give you a lift somewhere? I'm going up the mountain about ten minutes away, that might save you a bit of a walk.'

'Sure,' answered Jack, and with that the three of them got into the police car and drove away.

Ten minutes on, they stopped at a farm. Jack and Bluey continued on while Constable Gatton went into the property with a bundle of papers under his arm.

Thirty minutes later, the top of what seemed the steepest part of the mountain was now behind them as the graded gravel road and land began to level out, and after a further fifteen minutes of walking a farmhouse came into view on the left side, although it was still a fair way off. Plenty of sheep were chewing grass just inside the fences and there were lots of old ploughs and farm machinery congregated in an area beside the main drive, with some very modern looking tractors. Then he saw it: the antique truck that was often parked in front of the Bushranger Hotel.

'Ahhh, so this is where farmer Roy Bron lives.'

Inside the farmhouse, Roy's wife June was preparing afternoon tea. She opened the wood fired oven and removed the baking tray, revealing a dozen freshly baked scones. She placed six of them on a large plate, cut them in half and coated them with their own farm-made butter, cream and home cooked blackberry jam, then placed the two halves back together. June took them out the front and placed them on the table along with a couple of cups of Billy tea.

Jack couldn't see any of this going on as he approached the boundaries of the house, due to the small trees, shrubs and bushes that surround this secluded area — but he sure could smell those scones. 'Wow,' he said to himself. 'Something smells pretty good here.'

A cockatoo in a cage was singing out, 'Dad, Dad, come on Dad.'

The table with the scones now came into view, and seemingly there was nobody around. June had gone down to the work shed to get Roy for afternoon tea. They always called each other Mum and Dad.

'Come on Dad, the hot scones are on the table.'

'Right-o Mum, just wait until I get this bolt in.'

The front gate was open and it looked like it hadn't been closed for a long time. The open gate invited Jack in; he said to the scones, 'I don't mind if I do,' as he began picking them up, leaving one on the plate. With two hands full of scones, he was in haste to get away from here.

Roy and June came into the house through the back door. Roy went out the front to their cosy secluded afternoon tea area. The white cockatoo squawked quite loudly on seeing Roy, then it started talking to him as he sat down at the table with one scone on the plate. 'Hello Dad, Hello Dad.'

When June arrived one minute later, she said to Roy in a raised voice, 'Why you guts, you've ate all those scones already!'

Roy protested, 'But there was only one there. I can see the crumbs of where the other one may have been all right. A bird or an animal's been here and took away your good cooking.'

Roy started to laugh and that made June angry. She was looking up in the air at the birds flying around, then she walked out to the middle of the road — about 500 metres away she spotted Jack and Bluey, and Jack had a swag across his back.

'Yeah, a two-legged animal got them all right.'

She walked fast into the house and came back carrying a shotgun. Roy, in his haste to stop her doing something stupid, couldn't get out of the chair and slipped onto the ground. Now in the middle of the road with the shotgun pointing towards the heavens, she yelled, 'Now you're gonna get it.'

June touched the hair trigger as she brought it down, discharging it. *Boom!* The force of it put her on her back with the shotgun on top of her. Roy was there now and took the shotgun off her, helping her get up onto her feet. He could see the now-running Jack and Bluey disappearing in the distance. Roy took June by the arm in gentlemanly fashion and said, 'Come on Mum, let's get the other six scones.'

She replied, 'What about that thieving swagman bastard up the road?'

'Well, he must have been hungry or he wouldn't have stolen them. Think of it this way love, what if he hasn't had a feed in a week? Then we've helped a fellow human being out. My mother kept a diary on the unusual things that happened along this road — we might get it out tonight and have a read — but one thing I do know, the last time a swaggie dropped in here was 1950.'

June went back inside and prepared the remaining six scones. Now, after an exciting mid-afternoon on a usually boring Saturday, they would get to enjoy their afternoon tea and scones.

Jack and Bluey walked until the sun began losing its heat

— and then he saw it, the big sign on the front gate: 'Laredo'. This was his destination. It was a very long driveway, and then they came to some buildings that were in worse condition than the old guest house had been. Surely this once magnificent property had fallen on hard times and was now left in the past. The next building was pretty good and he knocked on the door that said 'Office'. There was no one there. He explored and a little bit further up the rise was a very nice colonial residence with beautiful gardens and surroundings.

A ring on the front doorbell was answered by a middle aged woman. She smiled and said, 'Mr Kelly, it has to be you … we don't get many visitors, so on hearing the bell I said, "Ahh, our guest has arrived". Come in and bring your dog with you, I'll get my husband.'

'Thank you,' said Jack.

She disappeared as Jack dropped the swag and backpack onto the quarry tiles of the entry area. She came back saying, 'He'll be here in a moment. In the meantime I'll put a cup of coffee on.'

When the station manager arrived he introduced himself and his wife as Timothy and Jewel Dowd. They sat around the table with coffee and biscuits, although Jack wasn't hungry after eating four scones (and Bluey one).

'So Jack, you've come to shear one sheep.'

'Yes, my grandfather worked here in the 30s, during the Great Depression. I'm walking in his footsteps. If I could shear one sheep and have my picture taken I'd be forever grateful.'

'Well Jack, the sheep aren't ready to be sheared at the moment and that won't happen for another six weeks, but we can set it up so that it *looks* like you sheering a sheep. We've got plenty of old fleeces to put on the floor and it will look like you're in full production.'

Jack laughed and said, 'If you do that for me I'll do a day's work for you.'

'No, there's no need for that, I'm only too happy to help. Come and I'll show you where you can sleep tonight.'

They went back to the office, where behind that was a fully self-contained flat. 'There you are mate, you'll be safe and sound in here. Come up inside at about 5.30 and have dinner with us, don't forget to bring the dog with you. Our dogs are allowed in but for tonight we'll keep them separated. Tomorrow we'll see how they get on together. Keep your eye on the fire, and before you go to bed fill it up with wood and you'll wake up to a nice warm room.'

'Okay Timothy, and thanks for your hospitality.'

'No problem Jack, I'll see you at dinnertime.'

The sun had disappeared and it was beginning to get dark; Jack turned the outside lights on as he and Bluey walked up to the farm house. During dinner Timothy said, 'So after this Jack, where do you go?'

'Canberra. My grandfather went there after leaving here and got a job on a dairy farm for a couple of months before moving on.'

'A lot of dairy farms have disappeared from that area, all being replaced with housing.'

'Yes, I'll have to see what's on offer when I get there.'

'Look Jack, for what it's worth I'm going to Queanbeyan come Monday morning and you're welcome to come along if you like.'

'Gee, that's an offer I can't refuse, thanks a lot mate.'

While they were having dinner the TV was on in the background; the news was over and now the weatherman was doing his bit. 'Well viewers, the beautiful warm weather we've been enjoying of late is about to come to an end. A cold front is rapidly moving in. Cold strong southerly winds and heavy rain are forecast sometime in the in the next twenty-four hours. Heavy snow is already falling in the Snowy Mountains and don't forget:

if you're thinking of heading down that way, make sure you take your chains with you. That's all for now. I'll be back at 11 for an update.'

Jack and Bluey settled into the flat for the night with Bluey booking a spot in front of the fire. Jack gave him the bone that the publican's wife had gift wrapped. *What a beautiful thing to do,* he thought, as Bluey gave that bone all of his attention.

The next morning after breakfast, Timothy said to Jack, 'Let's take your dog down to meet my dogs. I've got four: two cattles and two kelpies. If they get on we'll let them run together.'

They approached the pens. Bluey walked up to the wire, while Timothy's dogs were sniffing out Bluey. There was no bristling hair and all their tails were wagging, so things might be okay. Jack gave Bluey his freedom and removed the leash. Timothy let one of his dogs out. It was a cordial meeting with no problems at all. One by one they came out and within a minute they were all playing together.

The farm had an old army Jeep and Timothy took Jack on a tour of the property and gave him the history of it. 'It's now owned by two Sydney solicitors who are just sitting on it, hoping the land value will go up so they can cash it in. They run ten thousand sheep, and that pays for everything plus there's a nice healthy profit.'

Jack watched as the dogs sorted one sheep out and herded it up a ramp and onto the shearing floor. Once inside, one could see how this place in its heyday held pride and place over all others — until the world wool price collapsed. It never regained its former glory.

It was a simple matter to get the photo. Timothy set it up and his wife took it with Jack's digital camera. The end result was certainly convincing to anybody looking at that photo. Jack definitely looked like he was shearing that sheep.

Overnight the weather changed dramatically with a strong cold southerly wind blowing, and rain was steadily falling. Jack said goodbye to Jewel Dowd and at 10 am Timothy, Jack and Bluey set off for Queanbeyan and Canberra. The rain was consistent as they travelled down the Collector mountain and made their way to the Federal Highway. Now and again there were big patches of sleet but when it hit the road it disappeared. The next landmark was Lake George and already the steep hills that surrounded the perimeter were beginning to loom. The rain had been replaced with falling snow. In the distance there were flashing lights, and as they got closer they could see that four lanes of the highway had come to a halt. Police, rescue vehicles and ambulances were attending what looked like a nasty accident.

Timothy said to Jack, 'I don't like the look of this, I think we'll go back. We need chains to go any further, and that's why these cars have crashed.'

'When you stop, I'll get out and do a bit of walking.'

'But Jack, it's not safe to walk in this weather, you don't know what you could be getting into.'

'I'll be right,' answered Jack.

'Okay mate, good luck with the rest of your journey.'

They shook hands and said goodbye. Timothy ran his vehicle across the dividing lines, turning around and heading back in the direction of Laredo, while Jack and Bluey continued walking on towards Canberra. The snow and sleet had stopped for the time being and there appeared to be a lull in the wind.

The police and tow trucks had their hands full sorting the accident out, as the vehicles were in gridlock for a couple of hundred metres and more were banking up. A sign was in place: 'Highway Closed', due to snow and ice on the road. Jack was a couple of hundred metres past the accident site when the snow really began to tumble down.

One of the tow truck drivers noticed Jack in the distance and said, 'Hey look, it's an old fashioned swagman going for a walk in the snow.'

His mate laughed while one of the policemen said, 'I think I'd better report this, in ten minutes that bloke could be in a lot of trouble. The next shelter is ten kilometres away.' He got on his radio and reported what he'd seen, describing Jack as looking like an old fashioned swagman with a dog.

A call went out to all the ambulances and rescue vehicles asking if anybody could pick up a homeless individual that had been seen walking along the shores of Lake George and take him to safety. The rescue agencies radioed back that they were too busy at the moment; likewise from the ambulance service.

The dispatcher had one more call to make. He dialled the number. A person on the other end of the line picked up the phone. 'Jenny Collins speaking.' Jenny was the boss of the Salvation Army Headquarters in the National Capital. There they had a medical facility with their own doctors and nurses, and an ambulance.

'Hi Jenny, this is Jeff Clark.'

'G'day Jeff, I haven't heard from you for a while, but I've been listening to your dispatches on and off today and it sounds like you're pretty busy.'

'You can say that again. That's why I'm calling you. I remember you saying that your ambulance would be available if we ever got stuck.'

'Yes that's right.'

Jeff went on to explain the situation.

'Okay Jeff, we'll go and pick him up, but first we'll have to fit chains on the wheels. I'll call you when I've got something to tell you.'

'Okay, thanks a lot mate.'

Two male nurses who were also paramedics were assigned to pick up this homeless individual before something happened to him. It would take twenty minutes to fit the chains and prepare the ambulance for this pickup in atrocious weather conditions.

With the full force of nature's fury getting fair dinkum, Jack realised he should have gone back to Laredo. Now he was soaking wet and freezing; his teeth began to chatter and Bluey began to whimper.

Twenty minutes further on, he spotted the travellers amenities. The building was like a big lean-to with sides, it was dry and it gave some protection from the rain and snow but not the wind. He tied Bluey to a post so he couldn't run away, then he took some wood from a barbecue nearby and placed it in a pile inside the lean-to. His little gas fire would supply ignition, but it took five minutes as the wood was wet. He got more wood, then went to get more; but as he went to pick it up he had no power in his arms. He was shivering that much he didn't know what was happening, and he wondered how cold you had to be before you died.

Jack staggered back to the fire and sat down beside it, and then he lay down on the concrete floor and passed out.

The ambulance had now been prepared and was ready to leave. They drove away with flashing lights on, showing due respect for the snow, rain and visibility. Coming into the Lake George area, the ambulance crossed the median strip and travelled north on the two southbound lanes, which were devoid of traffic due to the accident and gridlock. There were two places of shelter along here, which were basic travellers and picnic amenities. They stopped at the first. Nobody there. They would now drive to the second, twenty minutes away.

Approaching the northern amenities area, Jake Anton the driver said, 'I can see smoke, looks like he got a fire going.'

'That can only help his cause,' said his partner in reply.

They drove into the area and there he was, apparently lifeless beside the fire. Jake was talking into the radio. 'Jenny, we've found him, and there's a dog as well. He's unconscious but he managed to make a fire. We'll go and check him out then I'll get back to you.'

'Okay Jake,' answered Jenny Collins.

A quick check of his pulse was a positive, and the stethoscope indicated a strong heartbeat.

Back at the Salvation Army's Headquarters, which was commonly called the compound, Jenny Collins noticed a photo that was leaning against a box of CDs at the back of her desk. Donny King had sent it with a note attached: 'The East Coast Swaggie will be in your area soon. Could you please keep a lookout for him? Let me know when you spot him. D King.'

The picture was of Jack and Bluey walking away from the Bushranger Hotel as he set off for the sheep farm. She picked the photo up to have a closer look; two words came into her mind: *I wonder.*

It took the two paramedics half an hour to get Jack out of those cold wet clothes and into a thermal suit, then redress him with dry clothes out of the cold weather kit. During this, all Jack did was groan and talk deliriously. They placed him on a stretcher and put him in the ambulance, covering him with blankets.

'Hello Jenny, we've got him in the ambulance, what about the dog?'

'What's the dog look like Jake?'

'It's a big blue cattle dog.'

'And what does *he* look like?'

'Tall, slim … quite muscular, like he's done plenty of body building. Great big cattle coat, large sun hat along with a backpack and an old fashioned swag.'

Jenny thought to herself, *There's no doubt about it, it's him all right*. 'Jake, bring him here. Mark will check him out before you take him to hospital, and bring all of his things plus the dog.'

'Okay Jenny, you're the boss. Over and out.'

Bluey had been patiently sitting there while all of this had been going on; maybe the warmth of the fire had a pacifying effect on him. Firstly, Jake and Owen had to befriend the dog. Would he bite or play up? There was only one way to find out. Jake walked over nice and slow and crouched down on his haunches. He put the back of his hand out — Bluey smelt it, and then licked it. Jake put his hand on Bluey's head and patted it, then walked over to where the leash was tied to the post, undoing the double bow and saying, 'Come on boy.'

They walked to the back of the ambulance in tumbling snow and a cold wind that had a chill factor of minus five degrees Celsius. Owen opened the door. 'Up you go.'

Bluey took one big leap, sat down beside Jack and licked him on the face. In a good sign, Jack's hand came up, found Bluey's head and gave it a bit of a rub.

'Gee, look at that will you — it seems like the dog is talking to him. I wonder what he'd be saying?' said Jake as he closed the door.

Owen replied, 'If dogs could talk he'd probably be saying, "It's all right mate, I'm here with now, I'll look after you".'

As they reversed out of the tourist amenities car park Owen said to Jake, 'The dog is pretty placid; it was almost as if he knew what we were doing.'

'Yes, that's the way I saw it too.' He picked up the radio handset. 'Hello Jenny.'

'Yes Jake?'

'We're leaving here now.'

'Okay Jake, over and out.'

FOURTEEN

The compound

After leaving Lake George, the ambulance crossed the border into the Australian Capital Territory. The Salvation Army's compound consisted of a small twenty-bed hospital, with fifteen one-bedroom motel type units plus half a dozen houses along with a chapel and administration buildings. The whole area was beautifully landscaped with a tall brick fence around the perimeter — hence the name, 'The Compound.' The snowstorm was relentless, with the southerly wind becoming more ferocious and the snow getting heavier. Canberra had never seen weather as bad as this before. When it wasn't snowing, it was pouring torrential rain.

Jake drove the ambulance through the open gates and parked under cover at the hospital. Mark the medico was waiting and examined Jack in the back of the ambulance. He had to make a decision. If Jack's condition was serious he would have to go into the city hospital — otherwise he could recuperate here. After five minutes Mark said, 'It's a typical case of hypothermia. We'll keep him here; you fellows got him in the nick of time. He'll be okay in a week's time, maybe a little longer. Put him in unit 11.'

One of the workers was assigned to look after Bluey until Jack was back on deck. This fellow did a terrific job, treating Bluey like he was royalty. A couple of times a day he would take him into Jack's room and leave him there for an hour or so, just so the dog could reassure himself that Jack wasn't going anywhere. Whenever Bluey was let off the leash for a bit of free range time, they knew where to find him: curled up on the front door mat of unit 11.

After three days Jack was coming out of his nature-enforced slumber, as his body returned to normal. Coincidently, the National Capital snowstorm began to subside with the wind dropping and the occasional coming out of the sun. A couple of days after that, the doctor declared Jack could get out of bed if he felt like it but he would spend the next two weeks here to build up his strength.

Jack's recovery was swift from that point on. Reunited with Bluey, he began joining in with the activities that go with living in the Compound. One of the families living here were the Worthingtons: Mr and Mrs, along with their eighteen year old daughter Genelle and her boyfriend Ralph. It wasn't hard to see that Genelle had the looks and shape of any one of Australia's top models. Jack thought to himself, *Gee, she's an attractive one all right. Ralph's a lucky man to be holding her by the hand.*

A relationship developed with this family and Jack enjoyed their company. At one of their midweek functions, Jack sang a popular hymn that was well received, as were all the other people who sang songs and played musical instruments. Some also told little stories and others recited poetry. The night finished with tea, coffee and biscuits.

Sitting opposite Jack were the Worthingtons, Jenny Collins and her husband, plus the medical staff. Jack had noticed on and off during the evening Genelle Worthington was continually staring at him, and it sort of made him feel a little embarrassed as she was sitting with her boyfriend.

The table was abuzz with plenty of conversation and happy laughter. Jack felt a foot rubbing his leg, and that foot belonged to Genelle, who had a slight smile on her face and was keeping determined eye contact. He kept his composure and continued the table conversation while Genelle continued to rub his leg with her foot. Eventually the evening finished with Jack saying, 'Good night everybody.'

Genelle had an extra big smile on her face as she said, 'Good night Jack … pleasant dreams.'

From that moment on, Genelle went out of her way to run into Jack. In the afternoon Jack would take Bluey for a walk toward Black Mountain, and she would come too. He changed it to a morning walk, but she spotted him leaving out of the front gates and ran after him, calling out, 'Wait for me.'

Jack was treating Genelle's interest in him as nothing more than a schoolgirl crush on the teacher. He wouldn't be offending her, or encouraging her — but aspirations of the devil weren't far away as a little voice in his head kept saying, 'Go on Jack, use the opportunity … you'll be long gone in a couple of weeks, never to see her again.'

But his own voice of reason was leading a fightback, saying, 'No way, I'm not leaving here with all these people hating me, they've all been so good to me. And what about Kate? I'm not about to let her down.'

Over the next three days, Genelle's pursuit of Jack went up a notch as she openly visited Jack in his unit and began following him around everywhere. While all of this was going on, Genelle's boyfriend complained to her mother that Genelle was acting strange and cold.

The mother said, 'I'll have a talk to her and find out what it's all about.'

The following day Jack was walking across to the auditorium when Genelle pulled up in her car beside him. 'Come on Jack, let's go for a drive to the main shopping centre, we won't be long.'

Against his better judgement he thought, *Ahh, can't see any harm in it.* So he walked around to the passenger side door and got in. They reached the main shopping centre but Genelle drove on, taking the main thoroughfare and bridge that crossed over Lake Burley Griffin. She made a right hand turn that followed the shore of the lake west, eventually coming to a stop at the rowing club and parking on the lawn. The sailing club was next door and plenty of yachts were moored there, making the area a very nice view.

Genelle said, 'I hope you don't mind. I like to come here and just look into the waters of the lake. I guess it gives me some sort of inner peace.'

'No, I don't mind, I'm not doing anything anyway,' replied Jack.

Genelle moved toward Jack and put her arm around him. 'I like you Jack, I can't help it.'

As he turned to look at her she gently pressed her lips to his. Jack lost the plot as he responded like any normal male would. His hand began undoing the buttons on her blouse, then he spread the blouse, exposing those lace-covered breasts.

My God she's so beautiful, he thought as his hand moved into the fondle position. Genelle closed her eyes and relaxed back into the seat in anticipation that Jack's hand was about to close onto one of her breasts.

Then a voice inside his head began to talk — it was Kate's. *What do you think you're doing?* Jack snapped out of his lustful trance and moved away. 'I'm sorry Genelle, I don't know what came over me.'

She replied quite crossly, 'Well, I'm not sorry. I like you, I wanted you to touch me. Is anything wrong with that?'

'No, but you've got a boyfriend and I've got a wife. There's a fine line between what's right and what's wrong, and I think we're doing the wrong thing here. Now maybe we should do the buttons back up.'

He leaned over, closing the blouse and redoing those buttons back up. She was disappointed at the rebuff, but she would live to fight another day.

They went to the clubhouse kiosk and purchased an ice cream each, then went for a walk along the shoreline of the manmade lake before returning to the car and driving away. They recrossed the bridge and drove back through the main shopping centre before arriving back at the Compound. Jack got out of the car where Genelle had picked him up.

From the windows of the administration building, Genelle's mother happened to notice Jack exit the car — she would talk to her daughter soon.

Late in the afternoon Jack was taking Bluey for his walk; there was no sign of Genelle. Then from a distance he heard her call out, 'Hey Jack, wait for me.'

He stopped and waited then they continued on the walk together. Thirty minutes later they returned to the compound; Genelle's mother watched them come through the big gates and it was obvious her daughter was spending just a little bit too much time with swagman Jack Kelly.

That night Mrs Worthington had a talk to Genelle about her infatuation of Jack. Firstly she denied it, and then admitted it. She got cranky and said, 'I'm eighteen years old and I'll do what I want. I'm old enough to make my own decisions.'

Mrs Worthington tried to talk some sense into her daughter. 'Darling, you've got a boyfriend who's a real decent man and only two years older than you. He's got a good job and that's what you need in life. Jack's a decent man all right, no doubt about that, but he's twice your age and has a wife, and they live in Sydney. He's leaving here soon and we'll probably never see him again.'

Genelle was defiant. 'Well, while he's staying here I'll continue to see him, and when he leaves here I might go with him.'

'Darling, you can't be serious, he could have lost his life in that snowstorm. He sleeps under the stars and hitchhikes everywhere with that dog. Every day he's surrounded by danger ... that's no place for you. Now come and give me a hug and let's hope that all this turns out well.'

The next couple of days Genelle continued to chase Jack at every opportunity. Eventually Mrs Worthington told Mr Worthington, then they had a meeting with the administration. They came up with a plan that would see Genelle given duties away from the Compound — possibly Goulburn City or a large rural town to the west of Goulburn City called Yass. Jack was on their agenda too, but they waited until the Worthingtons had left before discussing Jenny's idea, which got their approval.

It was early evening; the perfectly-tuned hollow chimes filled the air in the administration building for ten seconds before the clock struck eight bells in succession. Jenny Collins picked up the cordless phone and pressed in the numbers. The dial tone ended abruptly as a female voice on the other end said, 'Hello, Kate Kelly speaking.'

'Hello Kate, my name's Jenny Collins, I'm the Salvation Army Supervisor at our Compound in Canberra. Your husband's been staying in one of our units, recovering from hypothermia as a result of getting caught in a sudden snowstorm on the shores of Lake George.'

Kate interrupted. 'Yes, I was worried when Donny King notified me as to what happened, but I've been assured he's okay and in very good hands.'

'Well, you'll be pleased to know he'll be leaving here in another week or so to continue on his way. Now, what I'm ringing you about is another matter. There's a family that live here at the Compound and they have a daughter that's eighteen years old.

She has a boyfriend but since Jack's been up and around she's sort of given her boyfriend the cold shoulder as she openly pursues your husband with vigour. Nothing's happened between them but it's pretty obvious what her intentions are, and this is a most attractive young lady. I imagine a normal man would be quite vulnerable — especially when he hasn't been with his wife for six months, if you get my meaning.'

Kate replied, 'This sort of thing is always in the back of my mind, along with bashings and accidents. You sort of hope and silently pray that nothing happens until this thing is over.'

'Kate I want to ask you a question: how would you feel about coming to Canberra for twenty-four hours?'

Kate's answer was, 'You're not suggesting what I think you're suggesting, are you?'

'To put it bluntly Kate, yes.'

'What about the rules? If Donny King finds out the challenge is over, the homeless won't get that money.'

'Kate, we want that money too, but we feel it's worth a chance if we work in complete secrecy. I'll meet you at a designated spot, you change into a Salvation Army uniform, and your car will be safely locked up overnight. I'll drive you into the Compound at, say, 4 pm. In the morning I'll pick you up before daylight and take you back to your car where you re-change your clothes and nobody knows the difference. What do you say?'

A short moment of dead silence, and then, 'You know what Jenny, I'll see you tomorrow afternoon at 3 o'clock.'

They talked for another ten minutes getting all the details right before signing off.

Back in Sydney, Kate was having a restless night. Tomorrow would be an exciting day for her, full of secrecy and intrigue — plus the thought of seeing Jack for the first time in six months had her heart pounding like a sixteen year old about to go on her first date. She hated telling lies, but spun a story saying she had to visit the Big Lake Hotel at Lake Illawarra to get some details of a job that they might be doing, and while she was there she would do a bit of sightseeing and come back the next day about lunchtime.

In the morning Kate left about 10 am for the long drive to the National Capital. A couple of rest, revive, survive stops at the big truck eating houses had the trip going well. After four hours she passed the Goulburn City onramp and three quarters of an hour later reached the next major landmark: Lake George, which had been empty for the last thirty years. It was just a massive grassy plain surrounded by hills, patiently waiting for the rain to come again. Kate was thinking that the good thing about Lake George was it signalled that her destination was about thirty minutes away.

In due course she reached the outskirts of Canberra. The old drive-in theatre was the rendezvous; before long she spotted it and pulled off the road. The Salvation Army bought the property when drive-in theatres reached the end of their popularity. It was an investment they were just sitting on, even though there was an office that they used occasionally.

Before long, a vehicle pulled up alongside Kate. She got out of her car to meet Jenny Collins. They had a hug and got down to the business at hand. Jenny unlocked the big gate and both cars were driven inside with Kate parking in what was once the restaurant. They went into the projection box where Kate changed into a complete Salvo outfit, hat and all — according to Jenny she looked the real picture. It was time to go. Kate closed the gate after Jenny drove out, then she joined her in the car. The compound was ten minutes away. Kate took a big breath and slowly exhaled; she asked Jenny, 'Does he know I'm coming?'

'No, I'd say he's in for one hell of a shock.'

'I'll say,' replied Kate with a big smile on her face.

Jenny drove her car into an estate full of buildings — this was the Compound. She stopped beside unit 11 and said, 'We're here.'

Kate's nerves were on edge as she got out of the car carrying a small case. They walked to the door; Jenny inserted a key into the lock and opened the door, they both walked inside. Running water could be heard — obviously the shower. Jenny quietly said, 'I'll ring you at five in the morning, we have to leave here before daylight. And tell Jack I'll look after Bluey.'

'Sure thing,' said Kate. Jenny left.

Kate scanned the inside of the unit; it was nice and tidy. Jack's swag and backpack were on the floor, and a bright picture was on the wall beside the bed, adding a bit of nice personality. The sound of running water ceased. Kate's heart was nearly jumping out of her chest as the excitement grew. She faced that picture on the wall, so when Jack came out of the bathroom all he would see would be the back of her.

The door of the ensuite opened with Jack stepping into the room. He immediately spotted the Salvation Army uniform and was taken aback. In a stern voice he said, 'I thought I told you –'

Before he could finish the sentence Kate turned around interrupting him, saying, 'Yes, Mr Kelly?'

On seeing his wife standing there, Jack was completely paralysed; no words would come out, and then a word did come out. 'You!'

His lifeless face turned into that Rock Hudson smile, while Kate extended her arms with a come-and-get-me smile from ear to ear. They were two metres apart as Jack made a dash toward her. Kate was on the move too and when they came together it was oh so beautiful. Jack took her around that slim waist and picked her up off the ground, lifting her over his head, and then he placed her back onto the ground where they embraced again. The bed was nearby so it was a simple matter to fall onto it.

Kate flicked the towel off Jack, and how it had stayed on this long no one would ever know. Jack's hands were searching out forbidden places while Kate was doing some investigations of her own. Their hungry lips were glued together, but to take their reunion to the next and ultimate level, Kate slid onto the floor and quickly removed all of her clothes, dumping them where she stood. She dived back onto the bed and into the arms of her husband.

They hadn't seen each other for close to six months, so a moment of intimacy was long overdue. They would put that six months of separation into one passionate session. The passion would flow as their bodies became one. What started out as gentle lovemaking was now hard, fast and vicious — until a rush of pure ecstasy brought it to a sudden and breathless end. The heavy breathing began to subside. They would lay there holding each other, sleeping solidly for the next four hours.

It was 8.13 pm when they extricated themselves back into the world of reality: a beautiful hot shower together, some toasted sandwiches and coffee, sitting on the two seater lounge watching TV and just enjoying their short time together. They talked about the things they missed doing, especially taking the boat out and the thrill of horse racing — but the main thing was just being part of Sydney Harbour and all of its wonders. They turned the light off at midnight, wrapping themselves around each other, knowing only too well that this would come to an end around 5.00 am when the bedside phone would ring to wake Kate up.

Sure enough, Jenny Collins dialled the number of unit 11 right on time. '*Oh no!*' exclaimed Kate as she unwrapped herself from around Jack and picked up the handset.

'Morning Kate, I'll be around in thirty minutes ... sorry to wake you up, I know you must want to sock me.'

'No Jenny, I wanted to sock the telephone.' They had a bit of a laugh then Kate said, 'I'll see you when you get here.'

'Okay Kate, see you then.'

Kate got out of bed straight away without even thinking about it. She was wide awake now and headed to the shower, her second one in nine hours. It was quick, hot and beautiful. She got herself dressed back into the borrowed Salvation Army uniform and waited for Jenny to come. She heard the car coming and the headlights lit up the room as it turned around. Kate kissed Jack goodbye, saying those precious words, 'I love you honey,' with Jack repeating those same words to her.

Kate was out the door and into the back of Jenny's car, lying down on the back seat. She stayed there until they reached the old drive-in theatre. Jenny opened the big gate and drove inside. She relocked the gate before continuing on to where Kate's car was parked. They walked in darkness with a torch to the projection box, where Kate changed back into her own clothes — now she was ready to leave. They talked for a couple of minutes before sharing a goodbye hug. Kate thanked her before backing out of the restaurant, giving a final wave goodbye before she drove out of the old drive-in theatre to begin her journey back to Sydney Harbour.

As Kate turned left into Northbourne Avenue she noticed in her rear view mirror Jenny getting out of her car to relock the gates. Kate and Jenny would remain good friends from this moment on and would go on to spend many good times together in the future. It was still dark as she did a u-turn to head into a northerly direction and was now on her way home.

When Kate reached the grassy shores of Lake George the first signs of daylight were emerging. The cloak and dagger James Bond mission was so far a success — now she hoped that the pain in the neck Donny King wouldn't find out. In due course she passed the one-time Goulburn City outpost of Collector, and saw the sign with the arrow that said, 'The Bushranger Hotel'

She said to herself, 'Ahh, so that's where it is.'

A while later the Federal Highway joined into the Hume Highway, the main drag from Melbourne to Sydney. Next stop would be Goulburn City itself, and breakfast at a famous tourist attraction and truck stop called the Big Merino. She would arrive home somewhere around lunchtime.

Meanwhile, back at the compound Jack was awake now; he'd gone back to sleep after Kate left. Kate's unexpected visit was fleeting indeed — it was almost unbelievable, so much so he wondered if it really happened or was it a dream. He looked at the pillow where her head had been and noticed the dint. Then on the floor, a pair of stockings. Kate had left a souvenir behind.

'Yeah ... it was real all right,' he said to himself as he punched the air.

Kate's sister Sharon, who happened to be spending some time at the Kelly home, was there when Kate walked inside carrying a bag of groceries that she'd picked up at the local supermarket. Sharon made some coffee, which they enjoyed with a couple of pieces of cake out on the back balcony overlooking the harbour. Sharon asked her about her little trip and of course Kate made up one little story after another, eventually saying the job at the Big Lake Hotel wasn't large enough for their company.

Kate was full of energy and cooked the roast that she came home with. The young policewoman arrived home and sat down straight away, saying, 'Wow, isn't this something.' She and her husband were full of praise for this most luxurious of meals, suggesting Kate take more days off work to be their cook. Usually they would all do bits and pieces, but tonight Kate did all the cleaning up by herself, then sat down with a bottle of Sydney Heads Sparkling, insisting everybody else have a full glass too. This was unusual behaviour by Kate, and Sharon — who was a psychologist and an expert in human behaviour — noticed the permanent smile on her face.

In the morning Kate was at it again. She made everybody's breakfast and declared that she wasn't going to work today, and it was also a free day for Sharon.

During the morning Sharon said to Kate, 'Well? Are you going to tell me about your little two-day trip?'

Kate replied, 'What do you mean?'

'You know what I mean,' answered Sharon.

'Yes, I could never fool you could I?'

'No, but whatever you did it certainly gave you a lift ... you're virtually jumping out of your skin.'

'Sharon, I'm sorry if I told you some little white lies yesterday but I went and saw Jack and we spent the night together. I left Canberra before daylight. If Donny King finds out we've blown the challenge then the homeless won't get that money.'

'Well, your little secret's safe with me. I'm glad you did it — that will give the both of you a bit of extra strength for the next four months.' They had a hug, then Kate went and got the vacuum cleaner out while Sharon took a book out onto the balcony and relaxed on the banana lounge.

Back at the Compound, Genelle — who was a trained nurse — decided to accept a job in Yass as it was closer than Goulburn City. That way she would be home earlier to see Jack, or so she thought. They put everything in her way; there was always somebody hanging around Jack or he wasn't there.

What was left of the week seemed to disappear so quickly. On Sunday afternoon Jenny Collins put on a barbecue for Jack, and all those who could get away from their duties were there to say goodbye. He had fully recovered from the effects of the snowstorm and come Monday morning, the East Coast Swaggie would continue walking in the footsteps of his grandfather.

Jack made a speech, thanking firstly the two fellows who rescued him from the snowstorm, then everybody else who played a part in it, then finally the people who made him feel so welcome since he came here.

During the afternoon, Jack had a nice conversation with Genelle. She acknowledged the fact that maybe she'd acted from her heart but couldn't control it. 'There's something special about you, Jack, that I won't forget in a hurry. I realise that I'm only half your age but I don't care about that, I just wanted to be with you. My mother's right, I do have a good boyfriend and my mother and father are the best, so I'm pretty lucky. But when you leave here tomorrow I'm going to miss you and your dog, so you take a piece of me with you.'

Jack replied, 'I know I'll think of you often and put it down to one of the nicest things that has ever happened to me. To be chased by the most beautiful young lady in the National Capital is quite an honour in itself.'

Jack walked Genelle back to the main group and ushered her over to where her boyfriend was standing. He shook Ralph's hand and said, 'Now you two, if ever I should come back here again I would expect to see you holding hands, okay?'

They both answered at the same time. 'Okay.'

Jack then went and mingled with all the other people. Bluey was roaming around and had no trouble eating all the meat scraps that came his way; he was having his own party.

The barbecue was over with everybody helping to clean up and put everything back in its place. Jack then went and put the leash on Bluey; it was time to take him for his final walk from the Compound. As he left the front gate, there was a voice from behind. 'Hey, wait for us.'

It was Ralph and Genelle holding hands. *Thank Christ for that*, thought Jack.

That night, Jack rang Kate and they talked for an hour. Before signing off Jack asked Kate to send Jenny Collins a cheque for $5000 to pay for his stay at the Compound.

In the morning, he took the time to clean up the unit, making sure it was left in the same condition as it was when he moved into it, although he vaguely remembered what it looked like then. At 11 am Jenny Collins pulled up outside the unit. Jack and Bluey got into the car and they drove away. Half a dozen people were waiting at the gates and they clapped as they drove through. Jenny was taking Jack to the old drive-in theatre, where he would continue walking in his grandfather's footsteps.

Back in his swaggie uniform, the East Coast Swaggie said goodbye to Jenny Collins for the last time. Jack and Bluey exited the car and began to walk south along Northbourne Avenue, the main drag into the commercial centre of Canberra.

FIFTEEN

After the compound

August is the last month of Australia's winter. It was 11.30 am and the wind blowing off the Snowy Mountains was cool to say the least, but there was no comparison to the day when Jack walked into the snowstorm — at least that was all behind him as he continued on with the mission at hand. His immediate destination was the Federal Parliament House; Jack wanted to have a look at the building and watch the politicians for maybe an hour or so.

As was usual, when dressed in his big coat and hat with a swag on his back and being accompanied by a large blue cattle dog on a leash, Jack was attracting a lot of attention as he walked on.

A police car travelling south in the centre lane was a couple of kilometres behind Jack. Sergeant Banks was driving, and with him was constable Don Watts. Sergeant Banks said to his deputy after spotting Jack and Bluey in the distance, 'Hey, what have we got up here Constable?'

Constable Watts soon found what he was talking about. 'It looks like another swaggie hobo, Sarge.'

'That's exactly what it is, and we'll run this one out of town too. He won't be going anywhere in a hurry, he'll hang around the commercial centre bludging money. When he pitches that tent in the park we'll give him a couple of days to get settled then we'll evict him.' They thought this was funny and laughed. 'Then we'll take him down the Hume Highway to that submarine tourist attraction and throw him out there.'

'Do you think that will be far enough away, Sarge?'

'Yeah, that will do. We can't have these unclean swaggies con-
taminating the air of her Majesty's Royal National Capital, can
we?'

'Definitely not, Sarge.'

At that very moment the police car levelled up. They both
had a good look at Jack and made eye contact. Jack was quick to
respond by tipping his hat and bowing with a big smile.

Constable Watts said, 'Ooh this is a cheeky one Sarge.'

'Yes it looks that way. You know what? I'm going to really enjoy
our next meeting with this no-good has-been.'

To get to Parliament House, Jack and Bluey had to pass the
old Parliament House, which was now a tourist attraction. At
the moment, the spacious front lawns were occupied by a bunch
of Indigenous protesters demanding land rights. A standoff had
been in progress with the ACT police, with both sides giving
each other the stare. The police had tried the rough stuff with
worldwide condemnation. The protesters were living in tents,
cars and old caravans and declared they weren't leaving until they
got the return of a slice of land that belonged to them. Four police
cars were parked on the street, keeping an idle eye on things. The
Australian government was trying to negotiate with them, and
for the moment they were being left alone. Maybe it was reverse
psychology: ignore them and they might go away. But people with
nothing to lose tend to hang on a bit longer. One big sign read
'Aboriginal Embassy', and another 'Land Rights Now'.

Jack's hair was getting a bit long and it had been three days
since he'd had a shave. He only stopped to have a look as a matter
of interest, but one of the protesters came over to the big front
gates and said, 'G'day brother, you coming in for a cup of tea?'

Jack looked at him, then looked around very cautiously. Just up
the road a lone TV camera was set up aimed at the scene; police

in their cars were strategically placed on the road. Something was telling Jack, *Don't go over that line.* If the police got new orders to forcefully vacate those protesters, then all hell would break loose out here.

The smile on the lanky-haired protester probably made up his mind for him. 'Ohh yeah, right-o. Thanks mate,' said Jack as he walked over the boundary line.

'What's your name brother?'

'Jack Kelly, and this is Bluey.'

'Nice to meet you Bluey.' He gave Blue a pat on the head as they walked toward a group of about twenty people crowded around a very big barbecue plate covered in food and being heated by a gas cylinder. Another ten people were spread out around the spacious front lawn, sitting on chairs, while some young boys and girls were happily playing a game of Monopoly.

'All right everybody, this is Jack Kelly, he's come to give us a hand in our fight for land rights.'

'Where you from Jack?'

'Sydney Harbour, fellas.'

'What tribe are you from Jack?' somebody called out from around the fire.

Jack didn't know what to say but something came out. 'Ahh, uhh, yeah, the mob from Botany Bay.'

'That's them ones that give those First Fleeters a bit of a piz-zling a long time ago,' came from another protester, adding a bit of historical narrative into the conversation.

They were all so friendly, shaking Jack's hand and patting him on the back. It reminded him of Donny King's ambush that night in the Citadel, and he wondered what he might be getting himself into.

All the warm greetings eventually subsided as he was handed a cup of coffee before sitting down just away from the hotplate, which was throwing out a fair amount of beautiful heat that certainly took the chill out of the winter air — at least for those in close proximity. Jack sat around with all those occupiers exchanging stories, simply enjoying all the conversation. Bluey was having fun with two young people but he never took his eyes off Jack.

The old Parliament House was now a museum into Australia's political past. A lot of people worked here, and while the protest was going on, the workers come and went as if there was nobody on the front lawn. It was open to the public in way of guided tours, but as tourist buses pulled up the sight of those land rights protesters could be quite intimidating — it usually resulted in the buses driving away.

The afternoon got colder and colder as night started to close in and Jack had a decision to make: stay or go. After talking it over with the leaders of the activists, he decided to stay for a couple of days. He pitched the little tent over in the corner and joined the others around the fire. There appeared to be plenty of food and he would be putting in his share of money while he stayed here.

About 8 pm they were joined by another group of twelve supporters, among them a young Indigenous man and his very pregnant wife. It was one of those things where people's chemistry seemed to click together perfectly. His name was Brian Smith and his wife's name was Ruthie.

Jack and Brian hit it off straight away and they talked until 10 pm. Jack thought he was an interesting story, having travelled all the way from Burke, a country town in the far west of the state where he was the local rodeo champion. His job there was mustering cattle and jackarooing. Brian and his wife arrived in Canberra four weeks ago to attend his auntie's funeral, who died after a long illness. His uncle invited him to stay with him for as long as they liked, so they decided to stay, but it all depended on whether Brian could get a job. And that wasn't their only problem. After driving all the way from Burke, when they came to Canberra a copper on a motorbike pulled them over and slapped a defect on the car; now he couldn't drive it and had no spare money to fix it.

Sitting near Jack was a sixteen year old Indigenous lass — a very attractive one. Those pearly whites sparkled whenever she smiled and those big brown eyes were certainly showing more than a passing interest in Jack.

Jack went to bed in the one man tent. Bluey decided he'd have a bit of comfort as well and slept around Jack's feet, who was thinking, *This is much better than that night in the road base dump — here I've got company.*

Those occupying protesters stayed around that barbecue fire all night, singing and laughing; to his ears it was so beautiful to listen to.

In the morning it was freezing at five degrees. Breakfast was toast and there was plenty of it along with tea or coffee. No alcohol was allowed; if it was found it was poured out. The sixteen year old, whose name was Gabriella, brought Jack a plate of toast and a big mug of coffee. It was almost as if she was waiting for him to come out of the tent.

Jack sat down on a chair away from the others and it wasn't long before Gabriella placed a chair beside Jack and started talking. A little time later Brian Smith came out of one of the caravans that he'd stayed in. He collected some toast and joined Jack and Gabriella, carrying on with the conversation that began last night.

After a while Jack said to Brian, 'You know what mate? You see that yellow crane hovering over the buildings in the commercial centre?'

'Yes I see it.'

'That means there's a pretty big construction job going on

there. What do you say you and me go for a walk down there and see if we can get you a job?'

'If you think that's a good idea Jack, I'll go with you.'

'All right, as soon as we finish all this toast and get cleaned up we'll head off.'

At 10 am Jack and Brian began the walk to the city centre. Gabriella volunteered to mind Bluey until they got back. At the construction site, all the workers were outside on the street and at the moment were attending a union meeting. A union organiser was standing on the back of a tabletop truck, stoking up his members. The gates of the site were locked had two burly security guards standing on the inside, blocking any unauthorised entry. It was a massive site where a lot of old buildings had been demolished and there were plenty more to go. A sign on the front fence read 'BIG Constructions (Aust)'.

Jack pulled out Bill's mobile phone and dialled a number. He also put the phone on speaker so Brian could listen too. 'Hello Carol, this is Jack Kelly, how are things going up there?'

'Oh, Mr Kelly, this is a surprise you ringing me! Yes everything is fine, we don't have any problems at all.'

'Good to hear that — now, I need a favour, I'm in Canberra and there's a building company here called BIG Constructions. I want you to see if you can find out the name of the site manager and his phone number. I'll call you back in ten minutes.'

'Okay Mr Kelly.'

Jack and his new friend were standing well away from the fifty or so union members. At times the meeting was quite rowdy and entertaining, even though they couldn't quite clearly hear what was being said. When Jack rang Carol back, he got the information that he needed. The site manager was an engineer named Harry Kennedy — he already knew Harry well. He dialled his personal office number and waited.

'Hello, Harry Kennedy speaking.'

'Hi Harry, this is Jack Kelly.'

'Jack, old friend! It's been a while since we had a beer, how can I help you?'

'I've come to see you as I need a favour.'

'Whereabouts are you?'

'I'm outside on the street near the union meeting.'

'All right Jack, I'll come and let you in then we'll have a talk.'

Jack and Brian moved up to the small gate. Harry came over to the gate, then the security guard opened it up. Jack and Brian walked on through. Jack and Harry shook hands then a voice from the back of the truck in a loud voice said, 'You know what Kelly, you and him make a good pair.'

Harry laughed; Jack turned to look at the union organiser and now recognised this fellow. 'Hello Todd, looks like you don't have any work for your members, ha ha!'

Harry, Jack and Brian walked to the office where they sat down.

'Now Jack, in the past you've helped me out a bit, so now it's my turn to help you if I can.'

'Harry, this is Brian Smith, his wife's expecting their first baby and he's looking for a job. He comes from Burke where he's a horseman and a jackaroo. As you can see he's a nice style of a bloke and he's not afraid of a bit of hard work. I think he'd be a real asset to have on the job.'

Harry asked him a few questions then took him to the main office, where the office girl helped him fill out some forms. Harry came back and sat down. 'So what brings you to Canberra, Jack?'

'I'm having an adventurous holiday with no set agenda.'

'So how long do you think you'll be here?'

'Oh I don't really know,' replied Jack.

'Well, as you can see, I've got a problem with the men. When they come back to work Brian can start, on one condition: you start with him. I'm short of a foreman at the moment — if you can help me out for a month I would really appreciate it. We've got a job in Wagga Wagga that's coming to an end in four weeks' time, and then we'll start transferring the two hundred workers from there over to here.'

Jack replied, 'I've got a dog. If the dog can come to work with me you've got a deal.'

Harry asked, 'Is the dog in the union?'

'No, but I am.'

They both had a laugh and shook hands.

Now Jack would have to fill out the forms. Harry filled him in on the industrial problems that they were having at the moment, especially with this union official that had arrived from Sydney two weeks ago. After listening for ten minutes Jack said, 'I'll go and have a talk to them.'

They worked out a strategy and Jack left the office, walked out the gate and headed towards the union meeting. Sydney-based union leader Todd Munday was really singing a song. 'So what I'm proposing, fellas, is that we go home and meet back here in another fourteen days. That will give them something to think about, and if they keep refusing our demands we'll do another fourteen days and keep on doing this until they do come to the party. Will somebody move it that way?'

A voice from the back said, 'I'll move it.'

Then Todd asked, 'Do we have a seconder?'

Jack interrupted. 'Now before you second that motion, I think you should listen to what I have to say.'

All eyes turned to look at Jack. Todd Munday got nasty at this intrusion at a vital stage of the meeting, he shouted, 'Hey Kelly, you got nothing to do with this meeting! Now fuck yourself off, this is union members only.'

Jack replied, 'Yeah and I'm a member of the union, here's my card.' And with that he leapt up on the back of the truck. 'Fellas, my name's Jack Kelly, I own a company in Sydney called GD Constructions. I'm going to be working here for a couple of months as a foreman. Now, it's your right to tell me to go if that's what you want, or you can hear me out — it's up to you. I'm only trying to do what's best for you.'

A voice in the crowd called out, 'Okay Jack, but make it quick.'

'All right, thanks. When you all started here, a site agreement was reached with wages being $100 over the going rate for the district. Everything was going fine until Todd showed up. The company agreed to another $50 but that wasn't enough for Todd, so now you've been on strike for three weeks and he's proposing another two weeks. From right now, the company is willing to add another $50 to the total, making it $200 over the going rate for the district — which is pretty fair when you think about it.

'I've also been advised to tell you that if you reject it, then you may as well look for work somewhere else because you'll never work on this site again. In four weeks' time there's a job in Wagga Wagga that's coming to an end, and the workers that are working there will be transferred here ... and there's two hundred of them. Now, these blokes are not going to care if you're on the job or not, they'll just come here and take over so the site will be open for business.

'So there it is fellas. You can take the $200 extra to the rate and return to work tomorrow morning — you can all work Saturday to help catch up on the money you've lost — but if you decide to stay out then don't bother coming back, it'll be too late. That's all I've got to say, thanks for listening to me.'

Jack jumped off the back of the truck and walked back inside the small gate, standing there as Todd Munday lost control of the meeting. Chaos broke out as the union members started fighting amongst themselves. A big fellow beside the truck yelled out, 'All those who want to return to work in the morning, come over to this side of the road. All those who don't want to come back to work, stay on the other side.'

Three quarters of them crossed the road, so it was obvious that there would be a return to work in the morning. Todd Munday looked a forlorn figure standing on the back of the tabletop truck, watching his union members walking away except for half a dozen of his loyal supporters. Munday was thinking. *Curse you Kelly, I'll get you one day.*

Jack went back inside and told Harry, 'They're coming back in the morning.'

'You little beauty! You're a genius Jack, I watched the whole thing from behind the venetians.'

Harry gave Jack a mobile phone and the keys to one of the utes; now he had a set of wheels. 'Where are you staying Jack?'

'Up there at the old Parliament House.'

'Christ, with the protesters.'

'Yeah.'

'You always did like a bit of excitement, eh Jack?'

'You could say that.'

'Okay Jack, leave it with me — I'll find you somewhere to stay.'

Jack and Brian drove away in the company ute and went for a bit of a sightseeing tour on their way home to the old Parliament House. Bluey was happy to see Jack, as was young Gabriella. She slid her hand inside his arm and escorted him to the barbecue plate. Brian's Ruthie met her man with a kiss and they walked away holding hands.

At 6 pm a van arrived with pizzas, KFC and a hundred bottles of soft drink. Jack received two phone calls: one from Harry Kennedy to say he had found somewhere for him to live, and another from Bill. They had a good talk and when Jack told him where he was right now, that big laugh of his boomed through the speaker of the mobile — he couldn't believe it. Then Bill said he was coming to Canberra for the weekend; they sure would have plenty to talk about.

While they were having dinner Jack said, 'Hey Brian, we'll leave here in the morning at 6.30.'

Brian wasn't impressed. 'That early, Jack?'

'Yes, your honeymoon is over mate. That job is going to last a couple of years and you will make more money than you've ever made before. If you do the right thing by Harry, when this job is over he'll take you with him to the next one, you've got the chance. By the way, when's that baby due?'

'Next Sunday, if she makes it that far. It looks like she's about to drop it any tick of the clock.'

'Oh well, we'd better hope and pray. Gee this chook's nice.'

Gabriella had filled Jack's plate up chock-a-block and he sure was enjoying it, and Bluey was helping out consuming the chicken scraps.

At 8 am the Black Mountain Aboriginal dancers put on their paint and entertained everybody for about an hour; they were great, as were the four didgeridoo players. The TV cameras recorded the whole performance; no doubt it would find its way onto TV screens in the near future.

It was 11 o'clock when Jack went to bed but before he left his newfound friends he said, 'Tonight will be my last night here, fellows. Brian and I will be starting work tomorrow and I'll be staying down on the site. But I'll still be coming here to mix with you, so you haven't seen the last of me yet.' He handed over two hundred dollars to go towards their treasury coffers.

At 1.30 am the policeman in charge of keeping law and order noticed something: there were only two protesters around the fire and they were sound asleep. Perhaps this was the moment the police were waiting for. He made a phone call; the organisation moved into action as approval to drag out the protesters was granted. Six carloads of police silently pulled up on the road to join the others, who were waiting for the order to attack. The thirty police, all in riot gear, were now poised.

A taxi drove by and upon seeing the police all over the road the driver sounded his horn so he could proceed on by. It woke one of the protesters, who were shocked to see all the police. He grabbed a cow bell and started ringing it. Almost immediately the protesters were on their feet and running toward the gate.

One of them woke Jack up. 'Jack, we need a hand ... the police are getting ready to attack us.'

Jack raced to the gate and a mass pack was formed. A TV cameraman came out of nowhere and began recording everything as the police moved their line closer. The Channel 7 chopper was overhead taking an aerial view of the whole thing, which was now being broadcast live around the National Capital. A television reporter with a microphone in his hand was describing the scene. 'Now as you can see, the police are ready to launch an attack to end the illegal occupation of the Old Parliament House by Indigenous protesters.'

Before he said another word a policeman shoulder-charged him, knocking him rotten, and said, 'Now take your camera somewhere else.'

But the reporter didn't move, and all of this captured by another camera. A Federal staffer woke the Prime Minister, who watched the TV for one minute then phoned the police chief. She was yelling into the phone. 'For Christ's sake, don't attack the protesters until we finish all the negotiations! I certainly don't need any bad publicity, especially when I'm already behind in the polls.'

'Yes, Prime Minister.'

The police charged the gate and the protesters waited. No sooner had the two sides collided and began wrestling, a whistle sounded. The police backed away after getting new orders.

The disappointed policeman said to his men, 'Let's get out of here, back to the station.'

They all reluctantly returned to their vehicles and drove away. The protesters cheered as one, thinking that they'd had a somewhat of a hollow victory — but the elders knew somebody had intervened here, stopping the bloodshed that would have happened. Jack went back to bed, but most of the others stayed around the fire talking about what might have been.

In the morning Jack and Brian drove down to the building site to start their first day on the job — everything went according to plan. Jack's accommodation was a three bedroom flat on top of one of the shops that had yet to be demolished. Bluey was given two jobs, one being site mascot and the other being assistant night watchman.

From that moment on, things seemed to fall into place. Bill arrived for his weekend stay and both he and Jack spent some quality time catching up on each other's stories whilst inspecting some of Canberra's world class tourist attractions.

Brian's Ruthie gave birth to a beautiful baby, arriving a couple of weeks late. Jack was honoured when Ruthie said, 'I'm going to call him Jack, after you.' Brian's car had been repaired, and the police lifted the defect notice — now he had his own set of wheels.

Time, as it does, had silently moved on and with the arrival of fifty workers plus a couple of foreman from Wagga Wagga, Jack realised it was time to say goodbye to BIG Constructions. He also took note that from the moment he accepted the invitation to have a cup of coffee with the Indigenous protesters on that cold morning at the old Parliament House, six weeks had gone on by.

On Monday morning Jack put on the big coat and hat, then the backpack and swag, and now he was ready to continue walking in the footsteps of his grandfather. He mightn't have worked on a dairy farm as his grandfather did, but he was sure he would have got his ancestor's approval for the things he did while he was here.

Bluey started barking when he saw him in the coat and hat and began to chase his tail before Jack shot him with his make-believe revolver. 'Bang bang.' Bluey dropped down, rolled over onto his back and put his legs straight up in the air. Jack patted Bluey's belly, keeping right away from that big red sploshy tongue that was urgently looking for a face to lick. Jack put the leash on Bluey and now it was time to go.

They walked away from the three bedroom flat that was on top of the old butcher's shop with a touch of sadness; this had been their home for a short while, and Jack was in his element here amongst the concrete trucks, the sound of circular saws and jackhammers — a place where you'd meet three or four different people every day.

Jack walked to the site shed where Brian Smith was having a morning smoko and said goodbye. They shook hands and had a bit of a hug. Brian had a few tears running down his face as he said, 'Thanks for what you did for me, Jack; I don't know how to thank you.'

Jack gave him a card and said, 'You can ring me on that number after Christmas, and then we can have a talk.'

'Okay Jack, goodbye.'

There was a final chat with Harry Kennedy, and after thirty minutes when all the goodbyes were over Jack handed back the keys to the ute and the mobile phone. It was time to start walking to the old Parliament House to say goodbye to the protesters.

Twenty minutes later he was nearing the big gates of the

protest site. After six weeks the only change here seemed to be the weather; spring had sprung and the air was noticeably warm.

The protester that he met on the first day that he came here spotted him and came running over. 'Hello brother, you coming in for a cup of tea?'

Jack looked around. The four police cars were still there along with the lone TV cameraman that was hoping to get some juicy footage of confrontation, but it wasn't happening at the moment. He looked back at the protester and answered his question. 'Bloody oath.'

They had a hug and walked over to the barbecue plate. Young Gabriella came over and said, 'I've missed you Jack.' She took him by the arm and asked, 'What would you like?'

Jack replied, 'One of those snag sandwiches would do.'

She raced over to the hot plate and soon had it made along with a cup of coffee. They sat down with the others, who were now well away from the fire, talking and just having verbal fun. After an hour Jack thought it was time to leave.

Gabriella said, 'You know Jack, my father said that if I found a fella that I liked, I could marry him … and I've found you.'

Jack replied, 'That's all right Gabriella, but your father wouldn't like you marrying an old codger like me.'

She answered, 'I'll ask him. Hey Dad, Jack wants to marry me!'

Jack replied in a surprised voice, 'Is that your father?'

'Yes.'

Then Gabriella's father said, 'She's all yours Jack, you'll be doing me a favour, take her with you when you go — then I won't have to feed her or buy all those nice dresses and high heel shoes anymore.'

'Well … I'll come back tomorrow and we'll talk about it,' replied Jack.

Gabriella caught Jack by surprise and instantly plonked her lips onto his, giving him a bear hug at the same time. 'Eeeee,' she screamed with joy. 'The man of my dreams, I'm going to tell Mum.' She ran away to one of the caravans.

Jack seized his chance and said to the others, 'Okay lads, I'll see you later.'

'Okay Jack, good luck on your walkabout.'

He put the swag and backpack on, took hold of Bluey's leash and hastily exited the front lawns of the old Parliament House, turning left and walking south in the direction of the new Parliament House.

Five minutes later Gabriella came back to where Jack was sitting. She looked around then asked, 'Where is he?'

One of them said, 'He's gone back to work.'

She ran out to the front footpath and looked both ways — Jack wasn't in sight. She stomped her foot on the ground and angrily said, 'Damn it!'

Her father and his fellow protesters all had a good laugh.

Jack and Bluey continued on, and he was thinking that of all the places he'd been, the one place that eluded him was the new Parliament House — but as he was this close, he would use the opportunity to have his first look. Bluey might be a problem but he said to himself, 'I'll worry about that when we get there.'

The walk continued, and it would be another twenty minutes or so before they would arrive. Suddenly Bluey began to hang back; Jack turned around to have a look.

'Oh no, he's having his morning crap. No, no! Bluey, not here, wait till we find a tree to hide behind, come on, come on.'

Jack was pulling on the lead but Bluey wouldn't budge. His back was arched, his tail was up and the first steaming hot stool was about to be delivered to the beautiful green lawn.

A police car was travelling around the curve. Sergeant Banks said to Constable Watts, 'There's that bludger, Constable — I knew we'd catch up with him.'

Constable Watts answered, 'Yeah that's him all right, and look what his dog's doing.'

'Hoo hoo hoo, we'll have ourselves a bit of fun here Constable.'

Jack spotted the police car slowing down. *Oh Geesus, how unlucky can a bloke be*, he thought as the police car stopped right beside him. Bluey's production of doggy doo resulted in a nice big brown pile, and now he was ripping the daylights out of the lawn with his paws, such was his exuberance after doing what comes naturally.

The police approached. The first to speak was Sergeant Banks in true textbook style, and even if he found a bloke in the process of murdering his mother-in-law it would still be the same. 'Good morning Sir, how are we today?'

Jack answered with the innocence of a Catholic Church choir boy. 'I'm fine thank you.'

'Now Sir, I'm a bit concerned about your dog. Soiling of Her Majesty's lawns attracts a fine of a thousand dollars, unless you as the owner cleans it up.'

'It's not my dog,' replied Jack.

'Did you hear that Constable? The dog's not his!' Both police laughed hysterically. Sergeant Banks continued. 'Well Sir, whose dog is it?'

'I don't know, it's a stray.'

'Okay, so, when did you find it — the animal, that is?'

'I didn't find it, he found me.'

Both police burst into hysterical laughter once again. Jack's blood began to boil and he was thinking, *I'd love to pick up that pile of warm dog shit and shove it down your face, ya skinny bastard.*

The laughing stopped. The sergeant pulled out his notebook and said with a smirk on his face, 'Now pick up that pile of dog shit and take it with you and I won't book you, what do you say about that?'

'I'd say that's very generous of you, Sergeant ...'

'Sergeant Banks.'

Jack thought to himself. *Ah well, if I gotta do it, I gotta do it.*

And Sergeant Banks, with that fixed smirk on his face, was eagerly awaiting what Jack was going to do next. Constable Watts opened the door of the police car and came back and gave Jack a plastic bag with a black police logo on it — much to the disappointment of Sergeant Banks, who was enjoying watching Jack squirm.

Jack said. 'Why thank you Constable ... ahh ...'

'Watts.'

Jack looked at him and said as he lifted his hat, 'Constable Watts, you are a gentleman and a scholar Sir, thank you.'

The loud sound of a car coming up the road all of a sudden attracted the attention of Banks and Watts as they turned to look. It was a souped up hot rod with four youths on board, two of them hanging out of the windows, who yelled as they went by, 'Pigs, pigs, dirty rotten pigs!'

Sergeant Banks said strongly, 'There's those louts we're looking for, let's get them.'

Jack was instantly forgotten as the police car sped off to chase the louts in the hot rod. He'd already placed his hand in the bag and picked up Bluey's doggy doo; he would throw it in the next bin that they came to.

The roads around this area were complete circles with on and off ramps, and after Bluey and Jack had been walking for about five minutes Jack could hear that hot rod coming and the police car right behind it with its siren blazing and lights flashing. They passed Jack at high speed; the police car was beginning to overtake the hot rod. Both cars disappeared around the circle.

Jack heard a couple of thumps like the two cars colliding, then a screeching of tyres as breaks were applied. The police car had forced the hot rod into the gutter, making it stop.

One minute later Jack could see a gang member laying on the footpath up ahead, unconscious with handcuffs on. The other three were putting up one hell of a fight. One of them had Constable Watts in a headlock from behind; Watts was headfirst in the driver's side door of the police car, while the other two were attacking Sergeant Banks behind the police car.

Jack tied Bluey to the front bumper of the police car, dumped the swag and hat while the plastic bag of doggy doo went onto the bonnet. He came up behind Constable Watts' assailant and punched the lout viciously in the small of his back. The lout screamed blue murder and relaxed his headlock on Constable Watts as Jack gave him a second one in the same spot. Constable Watts extricated himself from the car doorway and punched the lout in the face. Jack threw the bag of doggy doo under the front seat, grabbed the lout and said to Constable Watts, 'Get the handcuffs on him.'

Jack went to give the sergeant a hand and they soon had it under control with the four louts being sick, sore and handcuffed. Jack put the swag, hat and backpack back on, unhooked Bluey from the bumper bar and silently slipped away as two paddy wagons arrived to take the troublemakers to jail. A tow truck arrived to take the two cars back to the police storage area.

Sergeant Banks said, 'Thank heavens that homeless bloke showed up when he did or otherwise we might have been in trouble, eh Constable?'

'Yes he certainly saved my bacon. I'm going to thank him …'

They looked around; Jack was nowhere to be seen.

The new Parliament House where the Government of Australia

sits is located on the top of a hill appropriately named Capital Hill. The building was a magnificent piece of architecture with views overlooking the whole of the city of Canberra. Jack and Bluey walked up to the front foyer and watched through the clear glass doors. People were coming and going and in general it was pretty busy, with a lot of security personnel keeping an idle eye on things. Jack took Bluey around to the side of the building where there were bike racks, enough to house a hundred of them, but only ten were being used. Jack tied Bluey to one, gave him a pat and said, 'Lay down boy.'

Which he did. After another reassuring pat on his head, Jack walked back to the front foyer and through the automatic sliding front doors of Parliament House. He was met by a security guard who said, 'Yes Sir?'

'I'd like to watch Parliament for a while.'

'Sir, you can watch it all day if you like.'

The guard called two other men in uniforms to remove the backpack, swag, hat and coat off Jack before running an electronic scanner over them. 'You can't take anything past here,' Jack was told.

They took the articles to a cloak room, when they came back they gave Jack the ticket. Then it was usual airport type security: emptying your pockets onto the moving belt and picking them up after going through the human scanners. Jack was given the green light and proceeded to the gallery stairs.

There were only a hundred people watching in both galleries, so there was heaps of room. He selected a seat in the front row directly behind and overlooking the Prime Minister, and sat down.

The speaker, Mr Rory Henkins, would have made a good Ned Kelly lookalike if his beard was black. *What a pity*, thought Jack. The leader of the opposition, a short fat man with a face like an owl, was whingeing, yelling and crying all at the same time — and he never took a breath for ten minutes. He finished his address whilst looking at the Prime Minister saying, 'Now why don't you do the right thing by yourself, your party and the people of Australia by resigning or giving us a date for an election? Your useless Government has to go — you just don't get it, do you Ms Prime Minister?'

The speaker interrupted: 'The opposition leader's time has expired.' But the opposition leader ignored him and kept on ranting. The speaker brought his wooden mallet down twice — *Bang! Bang!* — with such force that it would have done the Chief Justice of the High Court proud. The speaker yelled at the top of his voice to the opposition leader. 'Sit down or I'll call the sergeant at arms and have you thrown out.'

The opposition leader sat down red-faced while the members seated behind their leader all booed at the same time. The speaker ignored them, then he said to the Prime Minister, 'Would the Prime Minister like to respond to the opposition leader?'

She got to her feet, her blue hair flowing behind her like Superman's cape. Jack thought, *Gee, they've got a blue rinse set down here too.* A reference to the rich old women in Sydney when he was a kid growing up. They used to dye their hair blue as some sort of status and to hide their greying hair. 'Yes Mr Speaker,' she said, 'I would like to say something. Who'd want to respond to drivel like that?'

The speaker responded. 'I don't think I could find anybody to do it.'

Before the Prime Minister sat down she pulled a face and poked her tongue out at the opposition leader, who got to his feet protesting at this unladylike behaviour from the nation's top leader.

Outside the building, a group of Hell's Angels had just arrived to stage a demonstration. They were protesting new federal laws that would severely restrict their freedom and hamper their illegal activities. The legislation would be introduced into the house and debated sometime this afternoon. Bluey was quite happy to have a sunbake and a bit of a doze while waiting for Jack to come back, but the noisy arrival of twenty or so Harley chopper motorbikes spooked him to the bone.

The Hell's Angels were in no mood to be nice; they ran a barricade and rode onto the beautiful front lawns and gardens. They were doing doughnuts and tearing it up. The head of security ordered all guards out onto the lawns to stop this surprise invasion, leaving the entry foyer temporally unmanned. Bluey soon had the knot undone that shackled him to the bike rack, and set off to find Jack. He approached the sliding doors, which opened when a gentleman came out. Bluey was in like Flynn; he walked through the scanners and got a clean bill of health. His bloodhound nose told him that Jack went up the stairs. On reaching the landing he spotted Jack and walked up to him, jumping up and licking his face.

'How in hell did you get up here, you blue bastard? Oh well, it doesn't matter, you're here now so come on, settle down.'

Bluey sat down on his rump but he could see over the safety partition down into the chamber. Jack took hold of the leash and gave him a pat around the neck. One of the TV cameramen spotted the dog's head watching the debate; he alerted the TV director, a Terrence O'Brien, who ordered one camera be kept trained on the dog and the bloke it was with. The four cameramen and director O'Brien were having a chuckle amongst themselves at the attendance of this most unlikely spectator.

The opposition leader continued attacking the Prime Minister. 'Yes Mr Speaker, the Prime Minister should do the honourable thing and resign forthwith. Women should be at home having babies, doing the cooking and ironing, and not trying to do a real man's job in this Australian Parliament.'

The Government MPs began booing and hurling abuse at the opposition leader and those sitting on the other side. Parliament became an abuse feast as the speaker lost control. Both sides lifted the level of personal vulgar abuse to an all-time high record. The speaker was trying to regain control. 'Quiet,' he yelled.

Bluey began to howl, but the howl blended in with the noise of the parliamentarians. The speaker brought the mallet down twice. 'Quiet, quiet.'

Bluey began to bark, backing the speaker's call for silence.

'Silence in the chamber, and that means you too dog.' He paused. '*Dog?* Get that dog out of here!'

The chamber burst into hysterical laughter as all the politicians looked up and there was a dog leaning over the gallery rail, barking its head off at them.

Jack said to Bluey as he took another grip on his leash, 'Come on mate, let's get out of here, I think we've just worn out our welcome.'

The TV cameras followed the East Coast Swaggie as he left the gallery — then it was down the stairs, out of the exit door and back into the foyer. He casually picked up his clothes, backpack and swag from the cloak room, walked through the sliding doors and out of the building.

Back in the House of Representatives, the speaker had finally restored law and order, saying, 'Thank you, thank you all. Now we can get on with the next item of business.'

With the Hell's Angels ripping up the front lawn with their motorbikes, Jack and Bluey slipped away unnoticed. The big church half a kilometre away was testing its bells after doing some maintenance work, and it seemed to bring some sort of finality to Jack's visit to Australia's Parliament House.

Man and dog walked on, heading south, and after an hour they managed to hitch a ride in the back of an old caravan being towed by the Petersons, an old couple on a caravanning holiday — probably their last they did before old Father Time caught up with them. Jack's destination was a river town called Mildura, situated in the northeast of the state of Victoria. Jack's grandfather, when he left Canberra, made his way there to work on farms picking fruit.

The road they were travelling on skirted the base of the famous Snowy Mountains and after some hours they stopped at a roadside cafe for afternoon tea, before continuing on and arriving at a camping ground beside the mighty Murray River, long after the sun had gone down. Jack thanked them for the lift and when he said he was leaving, they wouldn't have a bar of it. They put the annexe out and Jack was invited to sleep there the night, with Bluey curled up beside him.

Breakfast was bacon and eggs, and what a luxurious treat that was, while Bluey had to settle for a tin of dog food out of the backpack. At morning tea Mr Peterson pulled out a large map and together they worked out a possible route that would take him to Mildura, a distance of 600 kilometres. The Petersons talked Jack into staying one more night, and after lunch they spent the afternoon exploring the colossal Hume Dam that towered above their campsite.

In the morning after paying for his keep and exchanging telephone numbers, Jack and Bluey caught a water taxi to the New South Wales river town called Albury, the major centre of the area. A beautiful city of trees, spacious parks full of flowers and shrubs.

Boy, this is one immaculate town, he thought as he transferred to the local river ferry that would take him to the next major centre: the historical town of Echuca, 230 kilometres away. Even though it was dark, from the moment the ferry pulled into the jetty you could feel and see the 150 years of history right in front of you, when this place was the biggest inland river port in the nation. For Jack it was like stepping back in time — what a beautiful feeling that was. They went and found the local caravan and camping ground; they stayed in the little tent for the night and in the morning did some exploring and looked at some of the sights.

At lunchtime they walked down to the dock area, picked up some takeaway from one of the many food shops and took it across the road to the local park, sitting down at one of the wooden picnic benches. Bluey enjoyed his two pieces of raw fish and a pork sausage and washed that down with a big drink of water from a tap that was nearby just inside the fence. There was only one other person in the park and he was sitting at the next bench seat, eating an ice cream and reading the national newspaper.

Jack gave Bluey his freedom and he bounced away at full speed before coming back and lying down. Jack got talking to the gentleman on the next seat and a cordial conversation followed. He seemed to know the history of this beautiful place and they talked for a long time.

He spotted Jack's backpack and swag and said, 'Looks like you're living on the road mate.'

'Yeah, I'm on my way to Mildura, I've got a week's work on a fruit farm, then I come back here and continue to make my way back home in time for Christmas.'

'Where do you live?'

'Sydney.'

'Hmm, you've certainly travelled a long way just to do a week's work on a farm in Mildura. You won't find many people doing that, eh?'

Jack could see the puzzled look on his face and explained the reason behind his journey, and the story of his grandfather.

'Wow,' said the bloke when Jack was finished, 'I've never heard anything like that story you just told me.'

While they were talking Bluey went for another run-around, and when he came back this stranger starting playing with him. After about ten minutes he said to Jack, 'Gee, I like this dog mate, he's a beauty.'

Jack was thinking, *Don't pick up a stick and wave it about, he might chew your hand off.*

He was puffing when he sat back down, then he introduced himself as Dick Canaan. 'You know Jack, it's so nice to meet a person who's fair dinkum. We've been talking here now for two hours and you haven't whinged once. Look, I'm a trucking contractor; at the moment my truck's being loaded. In the morning I'm taking that load to Mildura, I live there, and there's room for you and your dog if you want it.'

Jack replied, 'I don't know what to say, except to say I accept.'

They shook hands and had a bit of a laugh. Dick said, 'I'll pick you up here tomorrow at 7 am, it's a long way.'

They talked a while longer, then Dick left while Jack went back to the camping ground and re-erected the little tent for another night's stay at Echuca.

Jack and Bluey had an early rise, and were at the park and sitting on that seat before 7 am. The truck pulled up a few minutes later; When Dick got out, Bluey spotted him and took off in instant gallop. Dick put his hands out as if to say to Bluey, 'Come on boy, I'll catch you.'

Bluey leapt through the air and collided with Dick, knocking him over backwards onto the grass, and before he could get up Bluey sploshed his big red tongue over his face. Dick was laughing that much he couldn't get up; when he did he said to Jack, 'What a way to start the day,' as his handkerchief came out and he headed to the tap to wash his face.

Jack said, 'Better your face than mine, Dick.'

Dick laughingly replied, 'Glad to oblige Jack, glad to oblige.'

They walked towards the fully laden semi-trailer and Bluey let out a couple of woofs in anticipation of the truck door coming open; when it did he jumped up and got in all by himself.

Dick said, 'Christ he's keen.'

It wasn't long before they were all safely aboard. The powerful diesel engine roared into life and the semi moved away to join the traffic before finding the Murray Valley Highway.

SIXTEEN

Arriving at Mildura

It was 1 pm when they reached the outskirts of Mildura. The owner-driver of the semi-trailer, Dick Canaan, drove the vehicle off the highway and into the massive truck parking station situated beside the roadhouse. Refuelling and eating was the paramount thing here. Bluey was sound asleep in the middle of the big front bench seat, all curled up around himself. As the truck came to a jerking halt he opened his eyes, sat up to have a better look and instantly began to bark.

Jack said to Dick, 'I wonder what the hell he's onto.'

Dick replied, 'Something's sure spooked him all right.'

Bluey was looking around everywhere while he continued to bark, then he went into a howl. Jack put his arm around him and patted his belly, at the same time saying, 'It's all right mate, it's not the full moon yet ... and I'll make sure the dog catcher doesn't get you today, okay?'

'He might have had a nightmare Jack; he's been asleep for about two hours you know.'

'Yes, I suppose it's possible Dick ... anything's possible.'

Bluey finally settled down and the three of them got out of the truck with the intention of going into the roadhouse to have something to eat. Dick had seen dogs in there before so he went in first to talk to the manager, as he knew him well. After five minutes Dick came back out with the all clear to bring the dog in.

The manager seated them near the rear entrance, away from everybody else. He placed a large mat for Bluey to sit on, then tied a thin rope on his collar and attached it to an anchor point about two meters away, just to make sure the dog couldn't roam around. A young waitress came over and took their orders. As she walked away Jack called out, 'Something for the dog while you're at it, Miss?'

'Okay,' she answered with a big smile on her face.

An hour later and after pigging out it was time for Jack and Bluey to leave. Jack shook hands with Dick, thanking him for the lift.

Dick then gave Jack a business card. 'Jack, you told me you were staying here a week or so, and then you're going back to Echuca. It's going to take me that long to organise another load … maybe it might work out, you never know. If it does I can drop you off there, so give me a call the day before you're ready to go.'

'Okay Dick, I'll do that. And again, thanks a lot mate.'

The manager, sensing Jack was about to leave, came over and untied Bluey. Jack took hold of the leash and was standing there in his swaggie uniform. The manager said, 'You know what? Dick's brought many a hitchhiker in here over the years, but none as interesting as you. As a matter of fact I've never seen anything quite like you before. Sometimes this place is full of misfits due to the fruit picking season, but you'd take the prize.'

Jack just put on that charismatic smile and said, 'Mr Manager, in another week's time you'll never see anything like it again either.'

'Oh what, the St Vincent De Paul's going to rehabilitate you and put you on the road to normality?' He laughed sarcastically.

Jack's mood changed, he saw red and just for a few seconds wished he had that tin of white paint with him, then he felt like giving him one good punch in the face, resulting in an instant thick lip or a bloodied nose — either one would do. He was beginning to think like a bikie, do it just for the fun of it, but he managed to keep his cool and said calmly, 'In a week's time I'll be hitchhiking back to where I come from so that I'll be home for Christmas. My time here will be over, never to wear this outfit again.'

'And where is home?'

'Sydney Harbour.'

The manager just stared without saying anything more. Jack paid his bill and thanked him for looking after Bluey, giving him a fifty dollar tip, but never said goodbye to him before departing the roadhouse.

After Jack left the manager sat down with Dick and said, 'Where in the streets of hell did you find him?'

Dick replied, 'Echuca. I kind of like him, and I think I'm a pretty good judge of character. Look, he even gave you a tip — when did you ever get a tip?'

'Never.'

'Well, there you go.'

Jack and Bluey had a twenty minute walk to the main shopping area, then another fifteen minutes through that space. They covered the main walk and were now approaching the commercial section in the main street. As Jack walked along the footpath, all eyes were upon him. This tall, scruffy looking gentleman swaggie with the big hat, long cattle coat, backpack and swag being escorted by a very big blue cattle dog on a leash was certainly giving the shopping population something to talk about.

A hotel came into view that stood out like a beacon. It was 125 years old and had been restored to its colonial glory; it looked absolutely magnificent. A lot of men were sitting outside the hotel at tables enjoying a drink and conversation. Some of these tables sat right beside the footpath boundary.

Jack stopped at the first table and looked at the three blokes that were there. 'G'day fellas, I was wondering if you can tell me where the local camping ground is around here.'

One of them answered, 'Yeah, sure thing mate. Keep walking the way you're going and when you reach the traffic lights, turn right and keep on walking, you'll come to them. There's two there right beside the river. Don't take the first one, he'd take one look at you and shit himself, and you can't take your dog in there. The second one would be more to your liking and you can take your dog in there.'

'Thanks a lot mate,' answered Jack as he tipped his hat and continued on.

The second table only had one person sitting there, drinking a beer and nibbling from a plate of cracker biscuits and small squares of cheese. Jack noticed he was wearing a black cowboy hat and a distinctive and unusual western shirt. As he walked by the next table, four men were sitting there with an average age of about twenty-five years. One of them said to the others, and Jack heard it quite plainly, 'Where do these grubs keep coming from? The place is full of these homeless bastards. If I had my way they'd be locked up the minute they showed up here.'

Jack was out of earshot now as he walked along the footpath; the four guys continued talking.

'How many are coming tonight?'

'Looks like about ten,' one of them replied.

Another one said, 'Better make that nine, I'm not going.'

'Oh? And why not?'

'The missus has given me one month to straighten my life out: stop drinking excessively, no more gambling and become a family man or she's going to take the kids back to Albury and divorce me. The last time we wrecked that camping ground with the down and outs she found out and told me if it ever happened again she wouldn't be waiting the four weeks she'd be gone the next day. I'll be at home with her.'

The lone drinker at the next table was all ears but he kept on nibbling the cheese and sipping his beer; he was in his own little world, it seemed. He pulled out his mobile phone and began to text a message.

The pressing of the keys seemed to irk one of the four drinkers. He spoke angrily to the lone drinker in the black hat. 'Why don't you take that mobile phone somewhere else mate?' This guy was pissed and looking for a fight.

The lone drinker ignored him.

'Hey you,' he raised his voice much louder as he stood. 'Look mate, I'm going to come over there in a minute and shove that phone right up your arse.'

Two hotel bouncers had spotted the aggressive boozer and before anything happened, they grabbed him from behind and threatened that if he didn't settle down they'd throw him out.

'I'm already out, stupid,' he said to the two bouncers.

'Not while you're sitting at those tables you're not, now either quieten down or go.'

'Yeah,' said the boozer, 'I'd like to run into you some dark night.'

'What about in front of your place tonight, say 10 pm?' answered the hotel bouncer.

The boozer replied, 'I'll be there waiting for you,' then he sat back down.

The lone drinker put his mobile phone away and continued sipping his beer, while the two bouncers walked away.

The table of four were about to disband with a final word. 'Okay, we'll meet at the corner at 10.15 then we'll go and do it right.'

The one who was having trouble with his wife said, 'Don't forget I won't be there.'

The aggressive boozer said, 'While we're there I'm going to cut the nuts off that dog.'

'Hey that'll be something to watch, won't it?' said one of them.

They were all laughing hysterically as they left the table and walked away.

Meanwhile, Jack had arrived at the camping grounds and went into the office to book a site. Joe's Camping Ground was a two star rated enterprise, while the one next door had the highest rating, a six. It looked a picture with its high security fence all around, along with its CCTV cameras, beautifully manicured lawns and flower beds. Joe's, on the other hand, looked like a camping ground on Struggle Street; the state it was in left a lot to be desired.

At the same time at the Colonial Hotel, the lone drinker was on his feet and walking, seemingly going in the same direction as Jack. Down to the traffic lights, around the corner and after a fifteen minute walk he finished up at the camping grounds by the river. He passed the six star rated site and came to the one next door: Joe's.

Joe was an Italian migrant who came to Australia in 1950 when he was eighteen years old. Joe worked on the building of the Snowy Mountains Hydroelectric Scheme for the next ten years. When the job came to an end he came to Mildura to pick fruit and ended up buying the camping ground. Twenty years later, another camping ground was allowed to start up beside Joe's, where no money was spared; before long, Joe's Camping Ground began to slide down. Joe turned eighty-three last week, and with failing health he and his wife were about to retire — it was only a matter of getting the right price, and then they'd buy a unit in the Mildura Rest Home.

The lone drinker from the pub walked into the office/shop and asked the elderly lady, 'A bloke with a dog came in here. I wonder if you could tell me where he is.'

'Certainly Sir, he's on the other side of the shower block facing the river.'

'Thank you.'

Walking past the shower block, he could see Jack and the dog looking into the water. Bluey heard him coming and gave off a couple of woofs. Jack turned to face this gentleman, whom he immediately recognised as the bloke from the hotel with the unusual shirt and black cowboy hat. The lone drinker stopped short of Jack and said, 'Hi, I saw you walk by the hotel a little while ago.'

'Yes, I'd know that shirt anywhere,' replied Jack.

'After you passed by, the four blokes at the next table were discussing something between themselves and some of it concerned your dog. Those blokes are coming down here tonight to wreck the camping ground and beat up everybody here, and one of them is going to ... ah, to use his own words, cut the nuts off that dog.'

Jack replied, 'Now, I don't think I'd like that idea.'

'The thing is, sometime tonight, eight or nine guys pissed as parrots are going to walk in here and trash this place, and while they're at it their going to target your dog. I'm telling you this so you and your dog can get the hell out of here. I don't like to see animals getting hurt.'

Jack replied in a worrying voice, 'What about all these other people that are here, and the two old spaghetti owners? Wouldn't it be better to notify the police and let them handle it?'

In reply the lone drinker said, 'Look, it's very important that the police don't find out. This thing happened six weeks ago and no charges were laid. The police were called and arrived forty minutes later. Everything here was wrecked and twenty people found themselves in hospital for up to a week.'

'Cripes,' said Jack, 'thanks for telling me, I'll bail out for the night.'

Satisfied that the dog would be safe, the lone drinker walked out of Joe's Camping Ground and back towards the way he came.

Jack had a quick think. *Why would he say it's very important that the police don't find out? Maybe there's another Sergeant O'Leary out this way too … crooked police, that would be the only reason somebody would say a thing like that.*

The one thing that Jack couldn't do was walk away and leave all these fruit pickers to be ambushed — and it wasn't in his nature to walk away from a fight. He could see half a dozen guys standing around a caravan; he would go and talk to them.

'Hi fellas, I'm Jack Kelly. I've booked in to stay a week or so to pick a couple of boxes of fruit. Were any of you guys here when a bunch of thugs attacked this place five or six weeks ago?'

One fruit picker answered. 'Yeah, all of us. The whole thing lasted five minutes, most of us were asleep. About 11 o'clock they cut the tent ropes and when we tried to get out they punched and kicked us. There were about ten of them wearing balaclavas and they carried cricket stumps as weapons. Suddenly one of them yelled, "Come on, let's go," and they all ran away up the street. When we got to the footpath they were getting in cars and driving away. A little time later a couple of ambulances arrived and began treating the injured. Much, much later the police arrived and took statements. You know what mate, nobody was found and they all got away with it.'

Jack said, 'Well there's a good chance that the same thing is going to happen again tonight.'

One fruit picker said, 'Well, I'm getting out of here, I missed two weeks of work last time because of those people.'

Jack replied, 'I don't like the way these fellows operate and I'd like to help the people of this camping ground. Before you run away, just give me five minutes of your time. We can beat these guys at their own game. They don't know that we know they're coming, so we can catch them by surprise — just as they caught you by surprise last time.'

The fellow who wanted to run off all of a sudden had a change of heart and said, 'You know what, mates? We might be able to pull this off. I'd love to get some revenge on those gutless bastards. What about it fellas, at least this time we'll go down fighting eh?'

'Yeah, bloody oath, we'll get stuck right into them,' they all answered.

'Okay mate, how are we going to do this?'

Jack answered, 'Well, we're going to need weapons at least the equal of what they've got, like a cricket stump.'

'We can do better than that, there's a heap of old tent poles one and a half metres long in the store room.'

'Okay,' said Jack. 'What's the lighting like after dark?'

'Very good.'

'All right, we'll have to leave the lights off and wait. When they show up, we'll put the lights back on. See how many other people you can recruit, but we've got to keep it a secret. I'll go and have a talk to Joe about it and see what else we can muster up, and don't hang around in big groups in case they have a spy next door or across the street or somewhere.'

Jack's meeting with Joe was cordial, and Joe admitted he was terrified of another attack — although they didn't target him or his wife or the buildings, next time it might be different. Jack told him what he was planning to do and he gave his consent, saying, 'He would stay and help too.'

Joe was horrified when Jack told him what they were going to do to Bluey, so at 9 o'clock they would lock Bluey in one of the brick storerooms. Inside the main storeroom the old tent poles were there, along with plenty of empty ice cream containers and six four-gallon drums full of something.

'What's in the drums Joe?'

'Sump oil, I do my own oil changes.'

'Can we have some?'

'Sure, you can have the lot.' He did the catholic cross on his chest.

Jack walked around the camp talking to all the males. In the end they had twelve would-be soldiers. They put a plan together that should work. Two 'cockatoos' would be placed 400 metres down the street; they would ring Joe the minute they saw them coming, then Joe would quickly walk around telling the fruit pickers, 'Showtime.'

The empty ice cream containers would be full of the discarded sump oil and placed strategically with the idea to throw the oil into their faces, forcing them to close their eyes. Four fire extinguishers filled with powder would provide a bit of extra firepower should it be needed. The lights were normally turned on at dusk, but tonight they would be left off as per the plan. They had a team meeting in the amenities block away from prying eyes; everybody knew what they had to do. Under the cover of darkness the tent poles were handed out and the containers of oil placed into position. At 9 pm the two cockatoos walked up the street, and now the hardest part of all — to wait.

The fruit pickers, working for half wages to make a living, were at first reluctant to fight back but were now keen to get on with it. There was one last thing to do, and that was to lock Bluey in the brick storehouse, and everything was set.

Fifty metres past the eastern boundary, Jack noticed a car pull up on the other side of the road and turn its lights off. He went to the backpack and took out the police infrared scope and camera. Near the front boundary and hidden behind a bush, Jack lined up the car and its occupant. The driver was sitting behind the steering wheel, watching the camping ground through binoculars.

One of their cockatoos, Jack thought. *I'll have to close him down.* He returned the scope to the backpack, then walked towards that parked car. The person in the car was watching Jack with interest as he approached. The car window was down.

Jack bent down and said, 'Sorry to bother you mate, but I wonder if you could spare a cigarette.'

The answer was short and sharp. 'No, now ping off you bludger.'

Jack was persistent. 'Ahh, come on mate give us a smoke.' Jack's eyes quickly searched the front of the car. The cricket stump was right beside him and the balaclava was also there. 'Orr come on mate, give us a smoke.'

'Listen, you filthy bludger, piss off.'

'I'm not going until I get a smoke.'

The bloke in the car said, 'Right, you asked for it.' And with that he opened the car door, so fast Jack was lucky to avoid it. No sooner was the guy out, he was swinging wildly. Jack ended that with his favourite shot: a massive punch to his stomach. Jack closed the car door and let him get half of his breath back, then forced his arm up behind his back and added a hammer lock to march him toward the camping ground. He was snorting and protesting at the same time, but there was nothing he could do; he'd underestimated Jack, and it was too late now.

Inside the camping ground, two fruit pickers helped Jack get him into the store room. They taped his mouth up, then bound his hands behind his back and sat him down in the corner, finally tying his feet together. Jack found a bucket and put some sump oil in it; a four-inch paintbrush made it complete. Jack said to young Tommy Noble, 'If he moves or tries to make noise, paint his face with that oil then tip the rest over his head.'

'Okay Jack.'

At 10.15 things started happening. Two cars stopped up the street with the occupants getting out and walking the half a kilometre to their objective. They passed the two cockatoos who were well hidden from passers-by, but from their position they had a good view of the road and surrounding area. The phone call was made.

Joe went and alerted the fruit pickers with, 'Showtime.' Then he went to the light switch to wait for the signal from Jack to turn the lights on. Nobody was sure where they would strike first, but it was assumed it would be like last time and that's where they waited.

They weren't disappointed. The eight men with cricket stumps in their hands and balaclavas covering their faces stepped into the camping ground, which was in total darkness. With the poor street lighting behind them, to the hidden fruit pickers the invaders stood out like big black gorillas. It would take ten to fifteen seconds for their eyes to adjust to the dark. They attacked the first tent by cutting the ropes; when the tent collapsed they used the cricket stumps to inflict injury to anybody who might be inside. The fruit pickers moved in with the oil, throwing it at their heads and hoping to catch their eyes. Jack gave the signal to turn the lights on.

The gutless thugs never knew what hit them and it was all over in less than a couple of minutes. They were surrounded by angry fruit pickers extracting revenge with the tent poles, giving them a hiding. The elder fruit picker said, 'All right you guys in balaclavas, on the ground.'

Two wouldn't go down but after a couple of savage hits with the tent poles they joined their mates on the ground. The invaders were outnumbered, outmanoeuvred and never had a chance. All covered in sump oil, they looked a pretty sorry lot.

Jack said, 'Leave their balaclavas on while I get the other one.'

He was still sitting in the same position that Jack left him in, with the young fruit picker standing there with the brush full of oil in his hand. 'He nearly copped it a couple of times Jack.'

'Okay, thanks a lot Tommy — now we'll take him down to join his mates.'

Jack cut the tapes off him and dragged him to his feet. He attempted an escape but Tommy painted his face and eyes with sump oil, putting an end to that. Half blinded with oil and with that hammer lock back on, Jack forced him to walk and threw him onto the ground with the others, where he landed on more sump oil.

Jack spoke. 'If they attempt to make a run for it or try to remove the balaclavas, get into them. I want the police to see them like this.'

Just like last time the ambulance arrived; one policeman then showed up. He came over and introduced himself as the Mildura Police Superintendent.

'All right you blokes on the ground, sit up.' He pulled out his gun and threatened to shoot anybody who tried to run away, then he saw the one that Jack had manhandled; he never had a balaclava on. 'What are you doing here?'

He was a policeman. 'I was doing some undercover work and got caught up in all of this.'

Jack interrupted. 'Yeah, that's why you had a cricket stump and a balaclava with you wasn't it?'

The superintendent looked at Jack, then looked back at the policeman on the ground. 'Okay, for now you stay there.'

The ambulance officers moved in, removed the balaclavas and began treating their injuries. The police superintendent spotted another policeman; he just shook his head in disgust.

A police car and the paddy wagon arrived. The superintendent said to them, 'It took you long enough to get here, probably got lost somewhere eh?'

There was no answer.

Then he said, 'When the ambulance people finish their job,

take them to the police station and lock them up for the night, we'll sort it out in the morning.'

'All of them Sir?'

'Yes, all of them,' he barked.

A large crowd of spectators had gathered on the footpath, watching with interest. After forty-five minutes and their injuries now treated, the camping ground invaders were handcuffed, loaded into the paddy wagon and taken to the Mildura lockup.

The superintendent said to the fruit pickers, 'Okay boys, you can put those poles away now. I know you were acting in self-defence, but I want to talk to all of you in the morning. We'll make one statement then you can all sign it, so I'll see you all then.'

With that he left the scene of the crime and drove away.

In the morning the police superintendent was back and got the statement he was looking for, bringing an end to the violence at Joe's Camping Ground that was caused by a group of blokes who hated homeless people — and low-paid fruit pickers fitted into that category.

After interviews at the Mildura Police Station, the perpetrators were all charged and released on bail. The two policemen were suspended from duty until after the court case — then their futures would be decided.

The Mildura Show was on next weekend, spread over four days. Jack had been invited to attend a small ceremony where the mayor would hand Jack the keys to the city for his charity work. This would bring some sort of premature finality to the challenge of 'walking in the footsteps' of his grandfather, even though he still had to make his way back to Sydney Harbour for it to be complete. But first, a couple of days picking fruit on a farm about a twenty minute drive out of town.

The bus would be leaving at 6.30 in the morning to take the fruit pickers to their jobs; Jack would be going with them. It was low pay and you had to work pretty hard to make a living out if it — nonetheless, while the season lasted there were plenty of takers.

A hot bowl of Uncle Toby's Oats in the morning, courtesy of Joe's wife Maria, then it was off to catch the bus. Thirty odd people plus one dog were waiting when the bus pulled up. When Jack and Bluey stopped to pay the five dollar fare the bus driver said, 'Sorry mate, no dogs allowed.'

Jack ignored him and paid the five dollars, then he shoved a $20 note into the driver's top pocket and walked to the centre of the bus and sat down, while Bluey lay down in the aisle.

The twenty minute trip was jovial and landscape was beautiful and green. On arrival at the farm the foreman showed Jack around and explained to him what he had to do. Two days' work would be enough here to inherit a small pay check to send back to Donny King as proof of being here.

Back in the National Capital, Sergeant Banks and Constable Watts had taken delivery of their now-repaired police car that had been with the panel beaters for a bit over a week. The policing duties were such that Sergeant Banks remarked to his deputy, 'Well Constable, we've had a pretty good day today, eh?'

'You can say that again Sarge, it sort of makes you want to come to work doesn't it?'

'Yes, it sure does.'

Towards the end of the shift, Sergeant Banks began sniffing the air around him.

Constable Watts asked, 'What's up Sarge?'

'I don't know, I thought I smelt a strange smell. You know, like the smell of oil on the engine or something like that.'

'Oh yeah?' remarked Constable Watts.

With their shift over and back at headquarters, they lifted the bonnet to check the engine. The engine was spotless.

'Ah well,' said Sergeant Banks. 'It looks like I imagined that smell. All right Constable, I'll see you tomorrow.'

The next day turned out to be a busy one. Banks and Watts never had time to scratch themselves. The police radio never stopped giving them jobs. One minute they were on the south side of the city, the next they were on the north side. About 2 pm a call was received, instructing them to go to one of the southern shopping centres to help break up a nasty brawl — every available police car was being despatched to the area. They were twenty minutes away, and halfway there Sergeant Banks began picking up the scent of that smell again. He looked at Constable Watts again and asked, 'Are you sure you haven't got dog shit on the bottom of your shoes?'

Constable Watts looked at him, then bent forward and picked up his feet one at a time to have a good look at the soles. 'No, it's not me Sarge, there's nothing on my shoes, but I can really smell it now!'

Sergeant Banks pulled the police car over to the side of the road and stopped. He got out of the car and bent down to look under the seat. As his head got closer he remarked, 'Yeah, something died here all right, it's putrid ... bloody panel beaters.'

Sergeant Banks got down on his knees and was now looking at what looked like the corner of a plastic bag. He dragged it out and stood up, holding it at stretched arm's length, he pulled a face as he said, 'Whewww, that stinks ... whatever it is.'

Constable Watts noticed the police insignia on the bag. 'Hey! That's the bag I gave to that homeless swaggie to clean up his dog's mess.'

Sergeant Banks could see maggots swimming in Bluey's dog

shit, which had now turned into liquid. 'Oooohhh,' he yelled as he more than urgently flung it into the centre of the road.

A car travelling in the opposite direction ran over it, striking it in the perfect spot. It compressed the bag, which exploded — splattering liquefied dog shit and maggots all over Sergeant Banks, Constable Watts and the police car.

'That swagman bastard,' yelled Sergeant Banks. 'Just wait till I get my hands on him.' He turned to face Constable Watts. 'You see what happens when you help his kind? You had to give him that plastic bag, didn't you? Now because of you we're standing on the side of the road covered in dog shit and maggots.'

'I won't make that mistake again, Sarge.'

'No, and I'll make sure of that all right.'

The police radio was blaring away. 'Car 77, Banks and Watts, where are you? You should have been here by now. Do you copy? Sergeant Banks, pick up the handset.'

'Banks here, we're almost there, Banks out. Come on Constable, get in and let's go.'

They gritted their teeth and drove away at high speed with the siren blazing and the lights flashing under the utmost uncomfortable of conditions. They would surely have a good shower tonight.

Jack had finished his two days of fruit picking and the foreman gave him a cheque. They shook hands, and then he went and collected Bluey and boarded the bus for the trip back to the camping ground.

Wednesday was a relaxation day for Jack, with the working part of the challenge over. Bluey and Jack sat beside the fast-flowing, mighty Murray River, watching the river traffic go by. Mostly holiday-makers in motorised houseboats, but there were also river ferries and the odd restored paddle wheeler.

Jack began thinking of the weekend coming up. Bill and Marree would be flying in on Friday afternoon, and Saturday they would attend the Mildura Agricultural Show with him. The Show normally wasn't on at this time of the year as the big wet washed out the previous date, then kept on raining, but eventually they settled on this weekend and so far the weather had been fine for the last six weeks.

After lunch, Jack took Bluey for a walk. With his swaggie uniform on, they headed in the direction of the Big Truck Parking Station and Eatery.

Opposite, at the Colonial Hotel, two of the four guys were sitting at their usual table that was right beside the footpath. One of them said to the other, 'Do you see what I see?'

'Yeah, I do. Let's get the slimy homeless mongrel.'

Two tables away, the mystery man in the cowboy shirt and black hat was sitting there sipping beer while reading the *Daily Telegraph*. He couldn't help but hear what they said.

The two waited until Jack and Bluey were almost out of sight, then they upped their glasses of beer, emptying the contents. They left their seats as one and walked across the road, getting into a white twin cab utility.

The mystery man paid close attention to the twin cab as it drove away. A short time later he downed his beer, left his seat and walked down the street got into a brand new Range Rover. He started his four wheel drive and slowly made his way after the twin cab utility.

Jack had reached the truck stop and continued on, oblivious to the danger that was lurking not far behind him. The two pub drinkers were following from a long distance, watching Jack through binoculars, while the mystery man was stalking them, also with binoculars.

There wasn't a lot of traffic, only the odd truck and some cars in bunches every now and then. A branch road led off the main thoroughfare and Jack took this road. Half a mile later the land flattened out and it was clear except for one clump of trees that appeared to be full of birdlife. Here, Bluey would be able to have a run in the open paddocks and maybe he could chase one of those brown bunny rabbits, if he could find one. At the moment they couldn't get off the road; a large gutter had been dug beside the toad as testament to the amount of water that flowed here during the big wet. A further 50 metres on, the gutter ended as the road went into a gradual slope. They would get around it there.

The two guys in the twin cab began to move in; now was the perfect time for them, as this area was isolated. The vehicle idled up to Jack and was now only a couple of metres behind. Jack suddenly realised that a vehicle was close behind him; he turned to have a look as it came to a halt. The two guys jumped out and by the time Jack saw who it was, it was too late — they had him surrounded with his back to the ditch, which was nearly one metre deep. Bluey started barking; he knew when danger was near. The two guys were in a ten to two position and stood about a metre and a half away.

Meanwhile, the mystery man in the Range Rover had entered the branch road. He stopped his vehicle and put his powerful binoculars up to his eyes, quickly surveying the situation. He opened a bag that was sitting on the seat beside him and pulled out a double shoulder holster; he slid his arms into the straps and at the same time did the buckles up. He then took two .38 revolvers out of the bag and placed them into the holsters. He drove on at the speed of a turtle and at the same time, pressed a pre-set button on his mobile phone.

'Yeah, you'd better get out here now as quick as you can. Three kilometres out of town there's a lane that turns left off the main road called Woods Lane, you'll find me there. Don't put your siren on.'

A few seconds of silence, then, 'Right.' Call ended.

Jack's heart was pounding as he realised he was in for the fight of his life against two very big men. One had a black eye — he said to Jack, 'Remember me?'

Jack replied, 'Yeah, how could I forget you? You were going to bash up people while they slept. You're a real brave bloke, aren't you?'

Then the other one said, 'Because of you I might lose my job, and you're going to pay for that.'

Jack answered, 'Well, you can only blame yourself can't you? And I've got no time for corrupt cops.'

The one that Jack was talking to got nasty. 'Why you arsehole of a homeless bum, what gives you the right to judge anybody? Don't answer that because it doesn't matter — before I deal with you I'm going to kill that dog of yours right in front of you, now what do you think about that?'

At that instance he produced a knife. Before Jack could answer a flock of white cockatoos left the clump of trees, viciously fighting with ear piercing squeals. Both assailants lost their concentration and looked up. Jack dropped Bluey's leash and brought up a vicious kick, catching the corrupt cop on his arm and knocking the knife out of his hand. He followed that up with a do-or-die punch to the left side of his jaw. The corrupt cop staggered back two paces and landed on his back, hitting his head on the road.

His mate came up behind Jack, but before he could do anything Bluey sunk his teeth into the fleshy part of his leg and wouldn't let go. He was screaming and screaming and trying to kick the dog off, but Bluey stood firm. Jack turned around and punched him in the face as hard as he could, then gave him a punch on the left side of his jaw followed by one to the right — he collapsed to the ground in Ga Ga Land and didn't move.

The mystery man had silently approached. After getting out of the Range Rover, he crept along the side of the twin cab.

Jack was getting his breath back and giving Bluey a pat when he heard, 'Goodbye dog.' It was the crooked cop; he'd managed to roll onto his side and pulled out a hidden revolver, and now he was going to shoot Bluey.

An intervening voice: 'Drop that gun now.'

The crooked cop turned his revolver in the direction of the mystery man and fired, but he missed and the bullet went through the windscreen of his own twin cab. The mystery man fired two shots into the crooked cop, killing him instantly.

'You okay mate?'

'Yes,' replied Jack. 'I don't know where you came from, but I'm sure glad you did.'

The other one was still on the ground but very conscious of what was going on. The mystery man was walking around with a revolver in his hand and another in his shoulder holster. He stood over the crooked cop's mate and pointed the revolver at him. 'You were going to shove my mobile phone up my arse the other day, weren't you?'

He lengthened his arm as if to take aim before he fired. A thought flashed into Jack's brain. *Shit, he's going to kill this bastard too.* The bloke on the ground was looking into the barrel of the mystery man's revolver — it was being aimed right at him. He couldn't talk and then he began to shake violently before emotionally breaking down. His mate was lying in a pool of blood on the road no more than two metres away and now he thought it was his turn to cop a bullet.

The mystery man barked, 'Turn over, lay on your stomach and put your hands behind your back.' He was slow to move so the mystery man viciously kicked him in the ribs and yelled, 'Well, go on!'

He moved pretty quickly after that. The mystery man placed his revolver back in its holster and put his hand out to Jack. Jack accepted the gesture and it was a very strong handshake indeed. He introduced himself as Steven.

'We've been watching this lot for a couple of months now,' said Steven, 'and I have a feeling that this episode will bring it to an end.'

A video camera recorded the action from Steven's Range Rover; it was disguised as a spotlight. Steven went and got a Nikon camera out of his vehicle and began taking photos of the crime scene; he asked Jack to stay in the same position where he took a dozen photos from different angles.

A minute later a police car came down the road and stopped. It was the police superintendent, who took over the investigation at the camping ground. He pulled his mobile phone out and ordered an ambulance and the paddy wagon. He then took Steven a short distance away where they had a private conversation. The ambulance arrived and picked up the body of the crooked cop and treated the other man's leg wound, where Bluey had gnawed on it; they also gave him a tetanus shot. The paddy wagon arrived and the prisoner was placed in the caged section prior to being transported to the Mildura lockup.

The superintendent said, 'Well Jack, you seem to be in all the action around Mildura.'

Jack replied, 'Yes, it seems that way but my number was up today. He was going to shoot me and Bluey for payback for my involvement in the ambush at the camping ground. Steven came out of nowhere and saved my life ... but in doing so he had to kill that man.'

'You know, we don't have any sympathy for crooked police. Look mate, Steven and I are going out for dinner tonight — we'd like you to come along with us, compliments of the Police

Integrity Unit. You'll have to make a statement but you can do that tonight. Do you have any nice clothes?'

'Yes, I have two pairs of jeans.'

'All right then, we'll pick you up at 5 pm.'

'Okay,' replied Jack. Bluey was certainly all spooked up at the moment — his hair was bristling to say the least — and Jack's nerves were also on edge after witnessing the most violent of acts. He said, 'I don't mind a fight but this sort of thing is out of my league.'

Steven replied, 'Come on Jack, I'll drop you off at the camping ground.'

After the events of the day, for Jack it was a day he'd rather forget so a few beers tonight was just what the doctor ordered. He had a beautiful shower and a shave and got dressed up for the occasion. Joe and Maria were dog-sitting Bluey, giving Jack a bit of freedom.

Steven and the superintendent arrived right on 5 o'clock. Jack sat in the back of a brand new Holden Monaro sports car, and he was thinking as they drove away, *Gee, this is a nice car*. The CD was playing some country music; ironically the title of the song was 'The Bushranger Hotel' and it was very interesting indeed.

Eventually they arrived at the tourist town of Brigadoon, and it wasn't surprising when they stopped at the Restaurant Motel. This place was five star and it sat overlooking the mighty Murray River. As they walked Jack was thinking that this place was too good for the homeless East Coast Swaggie, but what can you do when someone else is paying the bill?

The hostess showed them to their table, which was situated beside the big glass windows, giving a clear elevated look of the river. There were many jetties and a large wharf where some house boats were parked. This restaurant catered for river traffic and as Jack and his two police friends sat down another houseboat full of customers pulled in and tied up at one of the jetties.

While Steven and the superintendent were having a conversation, Jack's mind went back to the dangerous events of today. If it hadn't been for the intervention of an observant and alert undercover police operative, he would have most certainly been shot to death by the crooked cop in an act of revenge. Whenever he felt down or when things seemed to get too tough, he would think of Kate — and watching a man being shot to death today, even a bad man, was very hard to stomach. He wished that she was here to hold his hand and give him that reassuring cuddle, indicating that everything would be all right.

Looking through the restaurant window at the river and the houseboats tied up at the wharf, it reminded him of that night at the Cruising Yacht Club in January. They'd arrived at the club a little early — so, arm in arm, they'd walked along the marina jetty, stopping to look at the maxi yacht, *An Incredible Time*. She'd looked so beautiful stretching and rising on her lines in co-ordination with the harbour swell.

Then there were those words from Kate inside the restaurant. 'So, Jack B Kelly, when you go for that walk in the footsteps of your grandfather in two weeks' time, you make sure you're back home in time for Christmas. When I look down Lighthouse Lane on Christmas Eve, I'll expect to see you walking back up and into my arms.'

He remembered his own words in that emotional scene in front of his friends, Bill, Marree, John and Cher: 'Honey, when you look down Lighthouse Lane on Christmas Eve, I'll be running back up it and into your arms, no doubt about it.'

Tears were flowing out of his eyes and running down his face. Steven lightly bumped the superintendent with his elbow to alert his attention to Jack, who appeared to be in some sort of trance. Steven said. 'You all right Jack?'

Jack came back to reality. 'Oh, sorry about that fellas ... good memories have come back to say hello.' He took his handkerchief out to dry his eyes and face.

Steven asked, 'What's she like Jack?'

Jack replied, 'Bloody beautiful.'

The waitress came and they ordered their dinner and drinks, with the drinks coming back straight away.

The superintendent had something to say. 'Look Jack, we'll tell you our story then you can tell us yours. Do you have a problem with that?'

'No I don't,' replied Jack.

The superintendent continued. 'My name is Allan King, and Steven is my son. We belong to the Police Integrity Unit — that is, we investigate crooked police. Steven and I are a team; we trust each other and get results. Rumours got around about corrupt police activities in Mildura and we were sent here to find out the extent of it. I replaced the previous superintendent who'd been here for twenty years, and some of the police here gave me the cold shoulder for it. We'd already identified half of the sixteen police in the command, but you uncovered the number one of it all — the bloke that Steven shot today.

'Steven just hangs around anywhere groups of blokes go: pubs, motorcycle clubs, football clubs, that type of thing. We'll be here another couple of months then we'll disappear to do it all over again somewhere else. Now, we're always on the lookout for that special person who doesn't mind a bit of danger and can look after themselves, and we think you fit that bill nicely. Jack, would you be interested in learning the specialist trade of "undercover cop"?'

Jack said nothing for about half a minute. Then he smiled as he said, 'Allan, Steven, I'm really flattered that you've offered me a position in your team. Steven saved my life today and I will always remember you guys ... but, I'm not the person you see in that hat and cattle coat with a swag and dog on a leash.'

Steven interrupted. 'Well there you go, you sure had me fooled! Another reason to consider our offer, you have got the perfect resume.'

Jack pulled out his wallet and removed a business card 'GD Constructions' and gave it to them. 'I own that company. We turn over 50 to 100 million dollars a year.' He went on to explain the reason behind his journey. 'My time here ends next week, and then I'll swag my way back home. Keep the card, we'll keep in touch — you never know what can happen in the future. If ever you come to Sydney you can stay at my place. There's a water cruiser parked in the shadows of the harbour bridge, you can't miss it.'

'Well Steven, he didn't reject it, he's left the door open.'

Jack laughed as the food began arriving and at $80 a head it certainly lived up to its price tag. Steven and Allan only drank light beer, while Jack continued on with the Crown Lager.

After dinner it was darts and snooker with Jack winning all the games, then it was time to say goodbye to the five star restaurant 'Brigadoon' and head back to Joe's Camping Ground.

Before Jack got out of the Monaro Sports Pack he said, 'For what it's worth, my best mate and his wife are flying in tomorrow night. He's a detective with the Sydney CIU, maybe you'd like to meet him? We're going to the show on Saturday.'

'Sure, we'll catch up with you sometime Saturday. Oh, and by the way Jack, it's important nobody finds out that we're father and son ... and more importantly, that Steven's a policeman.'

'My lips are sealed,' replied Jack. The two policemen drove away while Jack went into the shop to collect Bluey. Maria was watching television while Bluey was stretched out on a mat kidding to be asleep, but he had one eye open and his tail was bouncing up and down on the carpet. Joe came into the shop and asked Jack if he would like a Vienna coffee. How could he say no?

It was 11 o'clock when Jack left the shop and right at the same time ten backpackers from Europe showed up, wanting somewhere to sleep the night. Joe put them in an old double-decker bus that he'd converted to bunks and they all happily piled in there.

Waking up to the sounds of outboard motors and happy laughter was a blessing after the violent acts of yesterday. He looked at his watch: almost 8 o'clock. He'd slept well and so had Bluey, who squeezed in beside him. Jack purchased a tin of dog food and a hot bowl of Uncle Toby's Oats, and joined the newly arrived backpackers on the riverbank for breakfast. Judging by the amount of happy noise these young men and women were making, they were having the time of their lives. Later, the backpackers all disappeared for the day, while Jack volunteered to do some maintenance work for Joe and Maria.

Bill rang at 6 pm to say that the ten seater plane had landed and they would be at Joe's Camping Ground in ten minutes. Jack was waiting on the footpath when Bill and Marree pulled up in their rented car. After a bit of handshaking and hugging they went to the shop and had a coffee and some doughnuts. Bill gave Jack a programme of the events and a timetable of the section he would be taking part in at the show tomorrow. For the first time the East Coast Swaggie would be part of a publicity campaign highlighting homelessness, along with a drive for money. After the ceremony, the TV cameras would be watching Jack as he made his way back home to Sydney Harbour.

After coffee Jack took Bill and Marree to his tent beside the river. He said to Marree, 'Well, what do you think of that?'

She answered, 'You know what Jack? You'll never ever catch me sleeping in a thing like that.'

They all had a good laugh together. Jack introduced Bluey to Marree and she shook his paw saying, 'Well I never, a handshaking dog! What an amazing thing for an animal to do … and you found it on the side of the road?'

'Yes,' answered Jack.

In due course Bill and Marree left to book into their motel; they would meet up again tomorrow at the Mildura Showground.

In the morning Joe gave Jack and Bluey a lift to the showground as he had some business to do nearby. It was 10.30am as Jack and Bluey neared the front entrance after a 200 metre walk. Bluey began to bark quite excitedly, just as he had when they stopped at the truck parking station on that first day in Mildura. Jack thought that maybe he could smell animals or something.

They approached the ticket sellers for admission; a fellow in a white coat walked in front of him and gestured with his hand. 'This way Mr Kelly.' He led him to a door and opened it.

Jack said, 'I'm willing to pay.'

'Not today you're not, enjoy yourself.'

They walked through the door and into the Mildura Showgrounds. Jack in his swaggie uniform was getting plenty of stares from the show goers, and there was a huge crowd out to enjoy everything synonymous with show culture. Carnival rides, food stalls and sideshow alleys. He could hear the squeals of young ladies from the Big Dipper on the other side of the ground. Bluey sat on his hindquarters, put his head in the air and began to howl. He took off and began towing Jack with a lot of strength as if he knew where he was going.

Then Jack spotted it. There stood a very large tent with a big sign: 'MacGregor's Dog Show'. *I get it. No wonder he knows this place*, he thought. At the front of the tent there was an admission box with a young lady selling tickets. Jack walked up to it and pulled out twenty dollars but Bluey beat him there. Up on his hind legs he put his head through the grill. The young lady calmly said, 'Hello Prince, I thought you ran away.'

She patted him on the head and he licked her on the hand. Bluey looked at Jack before putting himself back on all fours.

Jack said, 'One please.'

The ticket seller answered, 'The show's almost over and I'm not going to charge you anyway. You go on in, I'm sure they'll get the surprise of their lives.'

'You might be right about that, thanks a lot,' said Jack.

He pulled the flap of the tent back, entered and closed it behind him. Bluey was in a towing mood again and pulled Jack toward the front. There were about forty people watching the dog show, which was taking place inside a small circular arena bordered by a knee-high partition, while the seats were placed in a semicircle with a couple of aisles. Jack sat down on a spare seat in the front row. Bluey started barking very loudly, so much so the dogs in the show stopped performing.

Mr MacGregor was the ringmaster and carrying a tiny whip; he looked in the direction of Bluey. Mrs MacGregor breathed in heavily, placed her hand over her mouth and said, 'It's Prince!' The silent prayers she said back at the road base dump had been answered.

Jack undid the clip on the leash. One big bound and Bluey was over the partition, joining the other dogs. All of a sudden these dogs were running around at very high speed. It looked like it was part of the normal show as everybody stood up and clapped as one. Mr MacGregor didn't stop them running, especially with the happy crowd, but eventually he blew his whistle twice. The dogs stopped running and stood up on their hind legs like humans, one behind the other.

The ringmaster fired a pistol loaded with caps. He yelled out, 'Hey.' One by one as the gun went off, the dogs rolled onto their backs as if shot dead, including Bluey/Prince, who was the last one to fall over. Mr MacGregor was standing in the centre of the ring; with a wave of the whip, the dogs ran to one side where they stood up on their front legs. In human terms this would be considered a handstand. Next they ran to the opposite side and chased their tails collectively, before finishing in the front where the dogs all laid down and rolled over and over. One sharp crack with the whip and a 'hey' the dogs ran to some cages at the back where Mrs MacGregor was ringing a bell. When they ran inside she closed the doors. Inside the cages there were dishes of raw meat but Bluey wasn't going anywhere near there anyway — he came back to Jack and sat down like the Sphinx. Jack put his leash back on.

The audience were on their feet and clapping after a most enjoyable performance by man's best friends. When the clapping was over Mrs MacGregor joined her husband in the centre where they both did a bow to the audience. The dog show performance was finished and the paying public began to leave, while Jack stayed where he was. Mrs Mac came over and introduced herself; then Mr Mac came over and said to Jack, 'Thanks for bringing my dog back.'

Jack replied, 'I didn't bring your dog back, he brought himself back.'

Mr Mac said, 'I'll take him now.' He went to grab the lead but Bluey flared up and snapped at him, growling quite viciously.

Jack said, 'The dog doesn't seem to like you for some reason.'

Mr Mac answered, 'It doesn't matter, it's still my dog and if I have to go to the police I will.'

He had another go at grabbing the leash, but this time Jack grabbed his arm and said, 'You know something? I've never had the pleasure to thump an old bastard, but the way you're going it looks like you'll be the first. Call the police and see if I care.

It'll give me a chance to tell them you dumped the dog beside the Hume Highway. Then I'll tell the RSPCA that you left the dog without sufficient food, shelter or water. After that I'll take out a full page ad in the major newspapers, telling them what you did to one of your own dogs. Then we'll see how much the public likes your dog show after that.'

Mr MacGregor said, 'Now, now, there's no need to be like that! We can come to some sort of an arrangement.'

Jack replied, 'Yes and I'll tell you what that arrangement is. I've got some business here and the dog is part of that business. I have to walk into the arena as part of a promotion. The TV cameras will be recording it for the news tonight. Now, sometime this afternoon I'll bring the dog back and the dog will decide what he wants to do. If he wants to stay with you I'll walk away; if he follows me out of the tent, then you accept it, okay?' With that Jack added, 'I'll be back about 2.30. Remember, the dog decides.'

He pointed a finger at them as he turned and walked away. Mrs MacGregor was standing there with her mouth wide open, while Mr MacGregor pulled out his mobile phone and rang the police. He was one hell of a proud Scotch man who hated to lose — his decisions were final.

Because of all the police corruption the station was undermanned due to the suspension of six policemen. When the desk sergeant picked up the phone, sitting at the desk nearby was the superintendent, the one that Jack had dinner with the other night. He heard yelling from the other end of the line. When the phone call ended he said to the desk sergeant, 'What was all that about?'

He handed the superintendent the sheet that he'd just filled in. After reading it, the superintendent burst out laughing. Sitting on his desk in front of him was a copy of this morning's local newspaper, *The Mildura Mail*. The headline read, 'Welcome The

East Coast Swaggie' and below was a large picture of Jack and Bluey. The superintendent moved the paper closer to the desk sergeant and said, 'Missing cattle dog, huh? Have a look at that and tell me what you think.'

The sergeant replied with a smile on his face. 'Sir, I do believe we've found our suspect all right.'

The superintendent replied as he stood up and put his cap on. 'I'll handle this one.'

He walked out to his police car and drove away in the direction of the showground. On arrival he parked in the police car park that was just inside the perimeter fencing, then he headed to the dog show tent. Mr MacGregor was waiting and invited the superintendent to a chair at a table where they both sat down. The superintendent pulled out his little black book and started asking questions. 'Now, when did you discover that the dog was missing?'

'A couple of months ago.'

'Did the dog escape from its cage?'

'No.'

'So, the dog was running wild and didn't come back?'

'Not exactly.'

The superintendent was thinking, *Hmmm, I don't think I'm going to get the real picture here, he's avoiding the questions already.* He said to Mr MacGregor, 'I'll go and find this bloke with the dog. Oh did you post a reward for the recovery of the animal? You said he was a very valuable dog, put any ads in newspapers or the internet?'

'No.'

'You didn't do anything like that at all?'

'I just said that didn't I?' replied Mr MacGregor in a raised voice.

The superintendent was thinking to himself, *Wow, This bloke is the most arrogant arsehole I've ever had the pleasure to meet. I'd love to lock him up just for the fun of it.*

Superintendent Allan King left the dog show tent and began looking for Jack and Bluey. He spotted them in the stand watching the horse jumping and trotting races. Jack saw him coming and waved; Allan waved back, and it didn't take him long to climb the steps and take a seat beside Jack. They shook hands, then Allan gave Bluey a pat on the head. He pulled out his little black book for the second time today and said to Jack, 'Is there anything you want to tell me?'

Jack answered with a question of his own. 'Did the Scotchman ring you?'

'Yes, he's made a complaint that you somehow acquired his dog, a very valuable dog, and he wants it back.'

Jack replied, 'If I stole his dog why would I go anywhere near that dog show, let alone walk into the tent and let the dog off the leash? Bluey raced into the ring and did exactly what he was trained to do. When it ended Bluey came back and sat down with me, so I put his leash back on. When MacGregor came over he attempted to snatch the leash and Bluey snapped at him. I told him after I faced the TV cameras I'd come back and the dog could decide who he wants to be with.'

Allan said, 'I can see who the dog wants to be with right now. So how did you know he came out of this dog show?'

'I didn't. Perhaps I should go back to the beginning. Six months ago I was hitchhiking south, just north of Goulburn City on the Hume Highway. Roadworks had been going on and a road base dump had been established. I stayed there the night in my tent.' Jack told him the whole story. 'Coming into Mildura, Bluey went totally ballistic, barking and howling. When we walked towards the showground today he started doing it again and when we got inside he towed me along. As soon as I saw the tent of the dog show, I knew that this was his home. I think he's been mistreated somewhere along the ways.'

'Okay Jack, this is what it looks like. The Scotchman says he lost the dog two months ago. You say you found the dog six months ago walking along the side of the Hume Highway north of Goulburn City. So it looks like it could be your word against his.'

'Not really Allan, I've kept a diary from the time I left home. I've got the number plate of the truck that picked me and Bluey up and dropped us off at the Bushranger Hotel. I can give you the phone number of the publican there, and you can talk to him.'

'All right Jack, this afternoon I'll come down to the camping ground and we'll go through your diary, get our facts and figures right. I'll go back to the Scotchman now and tell him I've interviewed you. At 2.30 pm the three of us will have a civilised talk. Four, actually — his wife should be there too. I'll see you at the dog show tent this afternoon; don't go in there without me.'

'You're the boss Allan.'

Police Superintendent Allan King left to go and talk to the Scotchman again before returning to the police station.

A stage had been set up just inside the trotting track and this is where Jack would be presented to the people of the city. A large banner read: "Welcome to Mildura, East Coast Swaggie". It was nearing fifteen minutes to midday.

Jack said to Bluey, 'Come on mate, we'd better find our way back to the main entrance before they start the march without us.'

Bluey replied: 'Woof woof woof.'

Back at the main entrance, the people taking part in the march were being organised into their positions. The Salvation Army Band took up the front position while Jack and Bluey would follow with the two ladies who had been shadowing Jack most of the way, one on each side. Then it was Bill and Marree followed by VIPs, councillors, would-be politicians and charity organisations. A large crowd had built up, watching the proceedings with interest. The bandmaster came over to Jack and was having a bit of a chat when his mobile phone went off.

'Okay we're all set here, we'll leave right now. Ready Jack?'

'Ready as I'll ever be.'

With that the band struck up and away they all marched. People love to hear an old fashioned brass band and as they moved on, the spectators moved with them — and when they reached the main arena those people went up into the stands, now nearing full capacity. The short quick blaze of orchestrated publicity and the story in this morning's newspaper certainly had a lot of people wanting to get a glimpse of this modern day swagman and somebody else's dog.

Marching into the arena was quite a buzz, not only for Jack but for Bill and Marree — and the two Salvation Army ladies, as they were the ones who had organised this little ceremony, which looked like being a huge success.

The mayor was waiting to present Jack and Bluey to the people. He was all dressed up in his mayoral robes, looking a bit overdone. He had a big smile on his face that went from ear to ear. It was so fixed, it looked like it had been painted on. He looked a lot like Tibet's exiled leader, the Dalai Lama. The band stopped playing when all those in the official party were on the stage. The mayor shook Jack's hand and gave Bluey a pat on the head before taking to the microphone.

'Ladies and gentlemen, I give you the East Coast Swaggie: Jack B Kelly. This individual has just swagged his way from Sydney Harbour to Mildura, walking in the footsteps of his grandfather who came here in 1934 during the Great Depression looking for work. By being here today, The East Coast Swaggie has secured a payment of five hundred thousand dollars to help homeless people. Along the way he struck up a friendship with a stray dog, and now they're inseparable.' Several other people made speeches and then it was Jack's turn.

'Thanks everybody for inviting me here today, it's good to see the people of Mildura supporting their local show after the big wet in this part of the country. I've been here about a week and I've really had more than my fair share of excitement. I've just concluded a few days' fruit picking on a farm not far from here, just as my grandfather did in the 1930s. When his work here ended, he swagged his way back to Sydney Harbour. The Great Depression was over, and unfortunately World War Two had just begun. Sometime next week my time here will also be over, and I'll be leaving your wonderful city and country hospitality behind. I have to be home by a certain date — if I don't make it my wife might divorce me. Love you Honey!'

Bluey began barking quite loudly as the mayor presented Jack with the keys to the city. 'There you are Jack; the City of Mildura is yours until you leave here next week.'

'Thanks very much Mr Mayor,' from Jack as a final handshake for the cameras followed. Then Jack waved the two large golden keys above his head to the applause of the spectators. The Salvation Army band played as the participants of the Welcome East Coast Swaggie Ceremony began to break up. The mobile stage was towed away, and the show resumed with the running of a trotting race.

Bill, Marree, Jack and Bluey went into the barbecue tent. Lunch was a steak with extras — and as usual, Bill had two. At 2.30 it was time for Jack and Bluey to return to MacGregor's Dog Show. The police superintendent was waiting outside. Jack and Allan shook hands, then with Bluey the three of them went inside the tent.

A simple negotiation with Mr MacGregor turned into a

shambles. His Scotch temper mixed with yelling and screaming — nobody could get a word in, he wanted his way or the no way.

Eventually Allan said loudly and forcefully, 'Enough, enough!' He pointed to the MacGregors and said, 'You two and Jack along with the dog, 10 am tomorrow at the police station. We'll sort it out down there.'

Jack, Bluey and Allan left together; they walked to the police car where Allan said, 'Let's go and get that diary of yours.'

At Joe's Camping Ground, Jack opened his locker, removed the little black book and gave it to Allan, who looked at it and said, 'Police issue.'

'Yes that's right,' replied Jack.

They went and sat beside the river, going through the pages. Allan wrote down all the information that he needed in his little black book then said, 'I'll go and make a couple of phone calls and catch up with you in the morning at the station.'

Jack said, 'Bill and I are having dinner at the Hilton Motel tonight about 7 o'clock — maybe you'd like to join us, I'm sure Bill would love to meet you. Oh, and I haven't told him about the incident or about Steven.'

'All right Jack, I might just do that. What'll you do with the dog?'

'Joe's wife Maria looks after him, she reckons me and Bluey are her Mafia bodyguards.'

Allan laughed at that as he walked away towards the road and the police car. Half a dozen fruit pickers came out of the shop virtually blocking Allan's path. He happily said, 'I hope you guys are leaving those tent poles locked away.'

'Yes, we won't be needing them anymore … but Superintendent, if ever you need a hand we'll pull them out again.'

Allan replied, 'Well that's very nice of you to offer your services, but I'll let you know when. Enjoy the rest of your day.'

Bill and Marree picked Jack up just prior to 7 o'clock and duly arrived at the restaurant right on time. Marree decided she would stay sober, allowing Bill to catch up on some good old fashioned guzzling — a pastime he was very good at. Allan arrived a little later and Jack introduced him to his friends. As was expected, the two policemen got on like a house on fire, having a wonderful exchange of conversation that continued right on through their meals until the conclusion of their night with the party breaking up at 11 o'clock.

In the morning Jack and Bluey walked into the police station at 10.00 am. The Scotchman was already there. He went to pat Bluey, but Bluey wasn't having any part of him — he snapped and growled.

The superintendent said to Mr MacGregor, 'It's easy to see the dog hates your guts, what have you got to say about that?'

'Nothing.'

'Now, I told you to bring your wife with you, where is she?'

'I handle all matters to do with business and family.'

Allan got nasty. 'And when I'm investigating a legal dispute I'm bound by the integrity of the law, and inside this building you'll do as I say. This matter won't go any further until your wife shows up. Now get out.'

Mr MacGregor yelled, 'You're the worst copper I've ever met.' He stormed out and drove away.

That outburst had entertainment value for those inside the police station, as they had a good laugh at the Scotchman's expense. Thirty minutes later he was back with his wife, and the dispute settling procedure began.

Of course the police had rehearsed what was going to take place here; it was just a matter of asking questions from a sheet and writing down the answers. The separate sheets would then be studied, allowing the police to come to a decision; it wouldn't take long at all. The problem was Mr MacGregor. He answered his own questions, and when his wife was asked a question he would butt in to answer for her, taking over the whole process — much to her frustration.

Allan decided to put an end to it. 'Sergeant, take Mrs Mac-Gregor into the other room and ask her those questions there.' Mr MacGregor protested vigorously, and Allan warned him one last time: 'Shut up or leave.'

In the meantime Jack and Bluey were in the crib room enjoying a cup of coffee and a biscuit respectively. Jack had already made a statement, and of course Allan already knew the facts. Twenty minutes later the interview was over. Jack was called back into the room — the superintendent was about to deliver his verdict.

'Well, gentlemen and Mrs MacGregor, this is how it will be. Mr MacGregor could be charged with abandoning Prince twenty kilometres south of Moss Vale in New South Wales on the Hume Highway almost seven months ago, whereupon Jack stumbled onto the dog. The dog followed him as he walked along the side of the busy roadway and they became friends. It was just sheer luck or coincidence that MacGregor's Dog Show and the end of Jack's journey both came together here. Mr MacGregor abandoned the dog, never wanted to see it again.'

Mr MacGregor screamed at his wife, 'Why you bitch! After all the things I've done for you and this family and now you betray me! After this things are going to change in our lives.'

She interrupted him. 'They've already changed, Scotty. There's a plane leaving Mildura tomorrow at midday for Bankstown and I'm going to be on it. I'm going home and packing. I'm not enjoying this or you anymore. Remember, I own half of the dog show and if you try to stop me I'll go and see a solicitor.'

'Just wait till we get back to that tent, Lassie.'

Allan had something to say. 'To keep the peace I'll come back to the tent with you while your wife collects her things. She can stay the night at my place with my wife and we'll make sure she gets on that plane tomorrow.'

The Scotchman went into a rage and yelled, 'I wish I'd never seen this place and one thing's for sure, I'll never come back here again.'

When Mrs MacGregor said she was flying to Western Sydney Jack wondered, and now he asked her, 'Do you live in Sydney?'

'Yes,' she answered.

'I live in North Sydney.' Jack gave her a business card and said, 'Give me a call after Christmas. Maybe you'd like to see your favourite dog.'

The Scotchman stormed out got into his car and drove away, talking to himself.

As was expected, the police said Jack could keep the dog. If Mr MacGregor wanted to take it further he would have to take Jack to court. For the moment they wouldn't be laying charges against the Scotchman for abandoning his dog; they would wait and see how things played out. The superintendent drove away with Mrs MacGregor and headed for the dog show tent at the showground, so she could pick up her things in peace and get away from there without her husband's harassment.

In the meantime, Jack and Bluey were making their way back to Joe's Camping Ground. Bill and Marree were coming around to Joe's to attend the camp barbecue at 5.30 and after that they joined in with the European backpackers for a sing-along on the banks of the mighty Murray River, and that ended at 10.30 pm.

In the morning, Bill picked Jack and Bluey up at 11.00 am and drove to the airport. Mr MacGregor was already there in the terminal lounge, waiting for his wife to show up. A little while later she did, accompanied with the police superintendent's wife in a police uniform — she was a copper too. Mr MacGregor came over to her while she was talking to Bluey and asked, 'Can we talk before you go? There's something I want to say.'

'All right,' she replied.

They walked away; he faced her, taking her by the hands and said, 'Lassie. I'm sorry for my actions lately and all the other silly things that I've done. Last night I couldn't sleep, my brain was working at 100 miles an hour. I can't stand the thought of losing you, and I realise just how precious you have been to me in the past ... and you're even more precious to me now. I'll do anything you want, I'll get down on my hands and knees and beg, but please don't walk out on me ... please be there when I get home.'

Jack's entourage couldn't believe their eyes; here was this proud Scotchman down on his hands and knees, looking up at his goddess with tears running down his face, begging for forgiveness.

'Please, please don't walk out on me.' He was wailing like a poddy calf that had just lost its mother.

Mrs MacGregor went down on her knees — then they hugged each other, kissing and crying. Jack sensed that Bluey wanted to go and join them so he unclipped his leash. He took two big bounds and began licking both their faces. Mr MacGregor began patting Bluey and he put his arm around him. 'Prince, I'm sorry I let you down so badly. I don't blame you for running away.'

Waiting passengers and airport terminal personnel gathered around to watch this exhibition of raw emotion between two older people and a dog. An announcement came over the PA system: 'Southern Airlines Flight 11 to Western Sydney will be leaving in fifteen minutes, please board the aircraft.'

Mrs MacGregor said to her husband, 'I'll see you when you get home.'

She gave him a final hug then gave Bluey a big squeeze as she dragged herself away, going to the ladies room to wash those tears away. Bluey came straight back to Jack to get his leash back on. Allan's wife walked Mrs MacGregor out to the ten seater plane, Jack shook hands with Bill and gave Marree a hug, and he wouldn't see them again until Christmas Eve, some five odd weeks away. A final call to board the aircraft saw all ten seats occupied. The engines had been warming up for ten minutes, ensuring correct operating temperature.

Mr MacGregor stood silently on the side of the tarmac not far from Jack and watched as the aircraft taxied to the far end of the runaway, making a u-turn before stopping. After a minute or so the all clear was given to take off by the control tower. Right on midday, the twin engine aircraft began to move away. Captain Kevin Drake opened up the throttles, reaching full taxiing speed. Kev pulled back on the stick and the aircraft rose majestically into the air. Mr MacGregor was still waving when the plane became a disappearing dot.

Jack was thinking, *Gee, this arrogant Scotsman has learnt plenty of lessons in the past few days … I really felt sorry for him, watching a beaten man beg. Bluey felt it too, otherwise he wouldn't have gone anywhere near him.*

Jack and Bluey then left the airport and walked back to the camping ground, while Mr MacGregor sat in the coffee lounge pondering the last thirty-six hours. He was possibly thinking that the five day drive back to Sydney was going to be long and lonely.

Sitting on the bank of the river just as it got dark was a pleasant experience, made even better when an old fashioned paddle wheeler loaded with passengers powered on by. Wild ducks were swimming just in front of Jack, and in the middle of the waterway a flock of pelicans were searching for a feed. He pulled Bill's phone out of his pocket and pressed in the numbers belonging to truckie Dick Canaan — could he be so lucky? The dial tone rang a couple of times, then, 'Highway Trucking Co.' Jack recognised his voice.

'Hello Dick, this is Jack Kelly.'

'G'day Jack, I've been watching you on TV lately, you're quite a star.'

'Ahh, thanks a lot Dick but I'd prefer not to be a TV personality, I'll be glad when it's all over.'

'You still looking for that lift to Echuca?'

'I sure am.'

'Well, be up at the trucking station on Friday at 8 am, we'll have a cup of coffee then be on our way.'

'Gee thanks a lot Dick, I'll see you then.'

'Okay Jack, goodbye for now.'

With the lift organised and three days up his sleeve, Jack would spend his time doing whatever he felt like doing at the time. But one thing was for sure — he wanted to mow Joe's Camping Ground and chip the edges. That in itself would be a pretty big job.

Joe and Maria had formed a strong friendship with Jack and Bluey, so they organised a monster goodbye barbecue for them on Thursday afternoon, right beside the banks of the mighty Murray River — they'd catered for fifty people and there were already thirty people there. When the fruit bus pulled up at 5.30 pm all the pickers went straight to the barbecue and began eating almost immediately after a hard day's work, and that suited them just fine. Six people came in from next door while Superintendent Allan King and his son Steven arrived. At 8.00 pm the Danish backpackers that were staying in the double decker bus brought out their guitars and sang a number of ABBA songs. They did some musical backing for Joe and Maria who sung the Italian favourite, Volare, and they were oh so good too.

It was such a beautiful send off for Jack and when he made a thank you speech to this wonderful bunch of people, a few tears ran down his face — but life goes on. He said a final goodbye to Allan and Steven then helped clean up, and at 10 pm it was all over. Tomorrow he would be on the first leg of his journey back to his home, Sydney Harbour.

In the morning Jack was up early. He had a beautiful hot shower, thinking he wasn't sure when his next one might be. Maria brought out a bowl of hot Uncle Toby's Oats and some meat leftovers for Bluey. He dismantled the tent, putting everything into the various pouches pockets and bags. He put the big coat and hat on then the backpack and finally the swag. He'd already paid his bill, and with Bluey on his leash it was time to go.

One last look at the muddy waters of the river at Mildura for both of them, as a mother duck with five ducklings paddled on by, bringing a pleasant finality of some sorts. As they approached the shop, Joe and Maria came out. Joe hugged the daylights out of Jack while Maria was doing the same to Bluey.

Then Joe said, 'I feel like I'm losing my son.' It was Joe's turn to shed a few tears, he said, 'Sorry,' as he dried his eyes with his hanky.

Maria gave Jack a hug and now it was her turn to blubber. She managed to say, 'Goodbye swagman, I'm going to miss you and your dog, goodbye.'

Jack looked at his watch. It was 7.30 am, and he would be at the trucking station right on time. 'You know Joe, Maria, I've a feeling we'll meet up again someday.'

Joe replied, 'I hope so Jack, I hope so.'

Jack had written his address and phone numbers on a piece of paper — he handed it to Joe and said, 'Give me a call after Christmas if you want to.'

Joe looked at it and said, 'You little bewdy.'

'Come on Bluey, we gotta go.' And it was a goodbye to Joe's

Camping Ground as Jack and Bluey began the walk that would take them up to the main street, on their way to meet Dick Canaan. The hotel wasn't open yet but somebody was sitting on the step near the footpath — he recognised the black hat and cowboy shirt. It was Steven.

Jack stopped and said, 'You're all by yourself mate.'

'Yes, I thought I'd sit here and watch you as you walk by on the start of your journey back home. That first day you came here you talked to a couple of guys at a table, and then you walked on. I was surrounded by corrupt police. You organised those fruit pickers to fight those bastards and won. I won't forget you, Jack Kelly from Sydney Harbour.'

Jack replied, 'You know Steven, I won't forget you either — you saved my life.'

'It was a pleasure Jack; now continue on your way mate.'

'Goodbye Steven.'

Jack and Bluey arrived at the truck station at 8 am; Dick was waiting. They shook hands and Dick said, 'Come on, you can bring the dog in.'

They walked into the near empty food hall and sat in the same place where they sat before. The piece of carpet was there along with the short length of rope attached to an anchor point. Jack tied the rope onto Bluey's collar. They didn't have long to wait as the manager came over with a tray: two mugs of coffee and half a dozen slices of thick raisin toast.

The manager also had something to say. 'Jack, the first day you came here I was pretty rude to you. After watching your story unfold in the newspapers and TV, I realise I'm not half the man you are, and I'd like to apologise for my behaviour.' He extended his hand.

Jack stood up and accepted the offer saying, 'There's no way you could have known, so no hard feelings.'

'Anyway, I won't be so quick to judge people in future. Dick said you were all right, so again mate, I'm sorry. Enjoy your coffee, it's on me.'

Half an hour later they walked out to the truck. Bluey had a look around, sat on his rump and had a big howl. Jack put his arm around his belly and patted him at the same time. 'That's it mate, get it out of your system, there's no more dog shows for you. It's Sydney Harbour, here we come — so you might have to learn to swim eh?'

Dick opened the truck door, Bluey stopped howling and with a bit of coaxing he jumped up into the cabin, followed by Jack and Dick. Dick hit the starter button, pulled the gear lever into drive, opened the throttle and the fully laden semi-trailer slowly moved away.

SEVENTEEN

Heading home

The beginning of the journey back home had just begun. Firstly, the five hour road trip to the river port of Echuca, where Jack said goodbye to truckie Dick Canaan. The next day it was the ferry ride against the river current. The sun was setting when the ferry docked at the parks and garden town of Albury, the major centre on the river.

After spending the night in the local camping ground, a courier company keen to get some free publicity delivered Jack into Canberra, a journey that took four hours and skirted the base of the beautiful Snowy Mountains. They stopped at the old Parliament house. The protest was over. Australia's High Court had intervened after pressure from the United Nations, but a condition toward a settlement was that the protest had to end with the 'embassy' being dismantled — talks were now ongoing. Everything here was back to the way it was, prior to the arrival of a bunch of Indigenous protesters who occupied the front lawns for six months. They just wanted to be recognised for who and what they are, and for the return of a small parcel of land that was stolen from them by a foreign power over two hundred years ago.

Jack was thinking, *Wow, to look at it now the whole thing could have been a mirage, but if it was then I was in it ... it was certainly a pleasure to meet those people and to spend some time with them.*

It was time to move on with the next stop being the Compound, where the courier driver and Jack parted company. Jack thanked him for the lift and with Bluey he walked through the main gates. Genelle Worthington came running out of the administration building. 'Jack, Jack, I knew you'd come back for me.'

He couldn't help but flash that big smile of his as she melted into his arms with vigour. Again he thought, *What a beautiful creation of femininity she is.*

Bluey jumped up and began licking her face. Genelle let go of Jack and began playing with Bluey, who was now off the leash and running at full speed in a circle. The more she spurred him on, the more things he did.

Jenny Collins came out and joined them saying, 'I wondered when you'd get here.'

Before she said another word, Bluey finished his run by jumping up at her, almost knocking her rotten, but she managed to stay on her feet and gave him a hug — narrowly avoiding that big red sploshy tongue that was eagerly searching for a face or a neck, the ultimate prize for a happy dog.

In the morning Jenny Collins drove Jack to Collector and the Claremont Guest House. On the way Jenny said, 'Genelle's broken it off with Ralph, you know — the poor bloke's shattered. She says she wants to play the field for a while and do some different things without being tied down. Her mother's not happy about it, but what can you do?'

Jack replied. 'I don't suppose you can do anything about it; she's the one who makes the choices under the guidance of her parents. It's all about experience, and one day it all falls into place.' He instantly remembered that morning when Genelle took him for a little drive and they parked at the rowing club beside Lake Burley Griffin — how could he forget it? She certainly showed that day she wasn't about to settle down with Ralph any time soon.

The forty-five minute trip ended with Jenny parking out the

front of Claremont Guest House. Bluey started to bark, so Jack let him off the leash and opened the door of the car; he raced off toward the front foyer and disappeared inside.

He found Lynn in the dining area where they had a happy reunion, with Bluey wanting to lick her face, while she was talking to him like a baby. 'Come on, I'll get you a biscuit.' Bluey followed her into the kitchen and came out carrying a dry dog biscuit, taking it to his spot under the television. *Now I wonder where he is?* She'd hardly thought the words when she turned around — Jack and Jenny were halfway down the old dance floor. They had a hug then Jack introduced her to Jenny Collins. They sat down with coffee and biscuits and shared some enjoyable conversation. After an hour or so Jenny said goodbye; she would be returning to the Compound to carry on with her duties there.

Lynn said, 'I've been watching your story on TV. You were at the Mildura Showground receiving the keys to the city. When that was over they did a five minute story on you. They showed the business you run, the house you live in ... and your wife, she's beautiful. Now I understand why I had to wear jeans to bed that night.'

Jack laughed and said, 'Well, I didn't disappoint you; we had our night in bed.'

'Yes we sure did, and now that I know the full picture I feel so proud to have met you and shared a tiny part of your life. And boy, I'm sure glad your grandfather swagged his here in the 1930s.' She reached across the table taking Jack by the hands. 'How can I ever thank you for changing my life — and more importantly, Tom's?'

'You've already thanked me, just to look at you now: a picture of health and happiness, no worried look on your face wondering where your next dollar's coming from. If anybody needed a break or a bit of a hand in life, you qualified. I get enjoyment out of the results.'

'And you told me you worked for God.'

Jack smiled and said as he pointed a finger at her, 'How do you know I don't?'

Lynn had the last word. 'I guess I'll never know. You know, when you showed up here my husband had been gone three years. Three years I worried myself sick over that selfish man, not knowing where he was or why he'd left, and all the while he was having himself a time and a half while I was in misery. If you and Bill hadn't searched him out I might have spent another ten years in misery. You'll be pleased to know my divorce came through uncontested four weeks ago. I thought of you and Bill all through that day, I was so happy. But the thing that makes me laugh even now when I think about it is when Bill left after coming here the first time. I said to you, "That bloke looks like a copper", you innocently said, "Nahh, Bill's a funeral director from Western Sydney".'

They both laughed and laughed. Lynn continued on with her work and Jack gave her a hand, while Bluey stretched himself out under the TV to sleep for a couple of hours.

At 4 o'clock Jack put the coat and hat on and took Bluey down to the Bushranger Hotel. He thought he might have a beer with the farmers and workers that congregated there after a hard day's work — he was well acquainted with them all — and he also wanted to say goodbye to the publican. When he walked in, everybody stopped doing what they were doing and just stared. Then they all started talking at once, wanting to know this and that. Questions were coming thick and fast — he didn't know which one to answer first. Then they wanted to shake his hand, all at the same time.

The two schooner-drinking ladies soon had Bluey doing all those tricks, much to the amusement of the hotel patrons. The publican disappeared out to the kitchen, coming back with a bone. When Bluey spotted it that was the end of the tricks as far as he was concerned. He took it to his favourite spot under the television.

A familiar voice behind Jack said, 'Hey swagman, my wife wants to know where those scones are.'

It was farmer Roy, the owner of the antique truck parked outside; he'd obviously been doing some Jacky Frost detective work since Jack was last in here. Jack turned to look at him, that big charismatic smile coming across his face as he said, 'Farmer Roy, you can tell your wife at dinner tonight while you're having your possum soup and your kangaroo leg fritters that those scones were the best I've ever tasted, and it was a pleasure to snitch them.'

Everybody had a good laugh at that.

'And you know what else? I reckon those scones had to be worth five bucks each, but I'm going to pay you double.' Jack shoved a fifty dollar note into Farmer Roy's top pocket. 'Now that'll be the first time she ever made a profit out of a batch of scones, just make sure you give her that note.'

This was a happy time in the Bushranger Hotel with all those around clapping and cheering.

Unbeknownst to Jack, when he walked into the Bushranger Hotel, sheep farm manager Dittman and his hoon son Anthony where driving by and spotted him with Bluey. Mr Dittman made a u-turn and parked near the hotel. He said to his son, 'Come on, let's get this over with.'

They walked in through the swinging doors with purpose; the happy crowd went quiet. Bluey stopped chewing while the publican mumbled.

This is all I need, Jack thought. *Looks like I might I get a fight today after all.*

Dittman was a tall imposing figure, and the vibe he gave off instilled fear into those he came into contact with. He really wasn't welcome in this place at all. Mr Dittman looked at Jack and said, 'I'd like to talk to you Mr Kelly, and at the same time talk to everybody. Now, I know that all of you people here hate my guts, and after having a good look at myself, I don't blame you. Sometimes you can get so full of self-importance that it distorts your judgements, so when somebody does you an injury the easiest way out is revenge. My son's just got out of jail as you all know, and he's still got a court case coming up. Now I have to take responsibility for that.

'This started just after Easter when Anthony went to the guest house to visit his mate Tom. He came home a short time later covered in paint and grass clippings. He told me a bloke wouldn't let him in, threw paint over him then knocked him down and threatened to kick his head in. My boy's nineteen, so what do I do? I want revenge for what somebody did to my kid when he's old enough to take responsibility for his own actions. I was in my brand new suit about to go to an important meeting in Goulburn City. I said, "Take me to this bloke and I'll sort him out". When we got to the Boarding House, sure enough there he was, up the ladder painting. I yelled at him and copped the paintbrush in the eyes and mouth … Jack Kelly threw me down the steps and onto the lawn where he tipped half a can of paint over my suit. Right there and then I wanted to kill him. Then he put the hose on me and told me to get going or I'd need a dentist. I wanted revenge at any cost.

'When Anthony lost his licence last January, he kept driving. What did I do? Nothing. I never told him not to drive that car or took the keys off him. I was told he was terrorising the neighbourhood late at night in his car, I still did nothing. Then he got caught in the police raid that night. He lost his car — a car that I paid for. Then I realised that I'd failed as a father. I was the one that was out of control.

'Mr Kelly, I'd like to thank you for coming to Collector to show us the way, the right way. You certainly made me see the light. I've been attending anger management classes in Goulburn City as I do want to be part of this community. I want to be able to come in here after work and laugh and joke along with you while having a meat pie and a beer. You all do it, why can't I? So Mr Kelly — Jack, if I may call you that — I won't be proceeding with that legal claim for a new suit. Revenge is not the way to go; it was my fault so I'll cop it on the chin.'

He put his hand out as a gesture of friendship. Jack accepted and they shook on it. Half the bar gave Dittman a bit of a clap for a pretty courageous speech, while the other half reserved their judgement. Bluey sat on his rump and gave a bit of a howl, creating a lot of smiles.

'Now Jack, I'd like to buy you a beer.'

Jack, Mr Dittman and Anthony went to the bar and came away with a schooner each. They selected a table away from everybody else, sat down and had a reasonable sort of a conversation. When Jack finished his beer he shook hands with both of them, wished them a Merry Christmas and decided to go. He said goodbye to everybody as he knew his chances of coming back here were slim indeed. He saved the publican for last, shaking his hand and saying, 'Well goodbye mate, it's been great to know you. When I first came here you showed me what country hospitality was all about, and I won't forget that.'

'Goodbye Jack — I've a feeling that this is goodbye, and for what it's worth, how could I ever forget the first day the East Coast Swaggie walked into my hotel and left his mark on this community like no other? Take care mate.'

They both shed a tear as Jack walked away, collected Bluey and headed back to the guest house. They were almost there when Col came out of his place with Goldun on a leash.

'Hey Jack, I'm going down to the park, do you feel like coming to give the dogs a run?'

'Yeah sure Col, it's good to see you again mate.'

'You too Jack, you too.'

Bluey was all over the female labrador and she was certainly enjoying the attention. With their freedom given, Bluey and Goldun had the time of their lives. Eventually they came back and lay down exhausted. The sun had disappeared over the mountain when Jack and Col had arrived back at their abodes, and according to the clock in the guest house foyer it was 6.30.

A little surprise awaited Jack once he was inside. A select group of people were sitting at a table away from the guest house patrons. Col's wife Molly was there, so it was obvious Col would arrive after he put Goldun in the yard. Lynn was all dressed up for the occasion; young Tom was there in a different frame of mind. They gave Jack a bit of a clap as he approached the table and was invited to sit down on the end. Lynn took Bluey over to the TV where a bowl of milk and a bone awaited him. The early conversation centred on Mildura; it was obvious the TV reports for the nightly news had all these people more than interested in the exploits of the East Coast Swaggie.

Lynn hired a group from Goulburn City called 'We'll Come And Cook Your Dinner'. And what a feed it was — an old fashioned baked dinner. Molly brought one of her daughters along to look after the guest house patrons. To supplement the baked dinner they finished with country homemade wild blackberry pie and ice cream.

At 8 o'clock Lynn made a speech which ended in, 'I honestly don't know how I can ever thank Jack enough for the way in which he changed my life and Tom's. Jack, I'll be forever grateful.'

At that stage, overcome with raw emotion, she had to sit down. Tom came to comfort her as she uncontrollably cried tears of joy.

She came up for air laughing and crying at the same time; she managed to say, 'Darn it now I've messed up my mascara.' It was a happy ending with all those there giving a little clap.

In due course the visitors drifted away and at 11 o'clock it was Lynn, Tom and Jack. Finally, Tom went to bed — leaving just the two of them. They talked until midnight. Jack said goodbye to Lynn before taking Bluey out to the kennels and locking him up, then it was back to his old room for one final sleep.

The two ladies that had been shadowing Jack from the time he left Sydney Harbour would be arriving to transport him to Moss Vale for a meeting with Kyle Walker. Lynn and Jack had a hug then loaded everything into the car, including Bluey. One final wave to each other as the car moved off and it was goodbye to the Claremont Guest House, the Bushranger Hotel and the Goulburn City outpost of Collector.

Lynn stayed on the footpath, watching the car as it disappeared around the corner. She was feeling sad and lonely as she walked along the old dance floor back to the kitchen, pondering Jack and Bluey disappearing out of her life for a second time. But she was soon smiling again as she remembered how her life was before this swagman in the big coat and hat walked in here looking for a job. To look at the guest house now, it was certainly a miracle of some sorts — God or not.

Beside the dryer on the bench Lynn noticed a white envelope. She opened it and took out a beautiful Christmas card. Lynn opened the card and Christmas bells began to chime. The words were simple. *Merry Christmas to Lynn and Tom, from Jack and Bluey.*

She never expected that, and then she felt something else in the envelope. It was a GD Constructions business card with a phone number underlined in red. A message read, 'Give me a call in the new year.'

She smiled as she said, 'You can bet on that, Jack ... you can bet on that.'

The trip to Moss Vale would take a little over an hour. They passed the Goulburn City onramp and fifteen minutes later Jack noticed the road base dump coming up. *Boy, what a day and a night that was*, he was thinking, then the memory of it all slipped into the past.

The two ladies dropped Jack off at Kyle Walker's place; he would be staying the night there. Tomorrow Derek Dunn would pick Jack and Bluey up and take them down the mountain to Lake Illawarra.

Jack and Kyle had a lot in common, both helping people down on their luck. They had a lot of things to say to each other and their meeting was good. Kyle showed him around the organisation, inspecting the shelters and the six farms that they had in the area. A barbecue that night added the final touch and brought the evening to an end, but not before Jack told him that the fellow that was picking him up in the morning belonged to the Hell's Angels Motorcycle Club. Bill had found him and asked him if he'd like to do it. Derek jumped at it, but he didn't know that Bill was a policeman.

The next morning over breakfast Kyle Walker said, 'You know that day I dropped you off on the highway in the middle of nowhere?'

'Yes,' replied Jack.

'Well I didn't sleep for a week worrying about you, wondering if anything had happened to you, and now you're going off with a Hell's Angel bikey. Doesn't it worry you what those people get up to? Before you get to your destination anything could happen to you.'

'You know Kyle, in any organisation there's always good and

bad. Derek seems to be a good one, but I'm very much aware of who and what they are.'

'Well, I sure hope you know what you're doing.'

Two beeps on a car horn was Derek's calling card. It was good-bye to the Walker family. Jack shook hands with Derek before the bikie gave him a real brotherly hug.

Derek said, 'Well, you've sure had an adventure all right. I've been watching your story on TV, you're becoming quite famous.'

'It's the last thing I want.'

All of Jack's gear went into the boot while Derek made friends with Bluey and put him on the back seat. A couple of horse floats went by, loaded up with thoroughbreds. Jack remarked, 'There must be a race meeting on somewhere.'

'Yes there's a meeting on at Bong Bong today and I was wondering if you'd like to go. You can stay at my place tonight and I'll run you down the mountain in the morning.'

'Sounds good to me, as long as the dog's not a problem.'

'No, the dog's fine, so let's do it. Bong Bong here we come!'

The country horse racing track with the peculiar name was about forty-five minutes away, situated on the approaches to the wealthy Southern Highlands town called Bowral. The journey seemed to go so quick and as they could see their destination up ahead, they both agreed it was an amazing sight. Cars lined both sides of the road and cow paddocks had been turned into organised parking. Further on, at least one hundred tourist buses were parked in a large area. As the racetrack came into view, all that could be seen was a lot of human activity. It was 10 o'clock, so obviously it was an early start in this neck of the woods.

This picnic meeting was the largest in Australia, with its reputation preceding it. Well-documented over the years via TV news bulletins and newspapers, Bong Bong was an experience like no other. Thirty thousand fun seekers flooded into Bowral this particular weekend every year to party, feast and booze, testing the town to the limits. Late night vandalism was a bit of a problem, but other than that it was an economic bonanza for the pubs, clubs and eateries. After the pilgrims left on Sunday, one might be mistaken for thinking that Cyclone Teddy Bear had passed over.

Derek drove past the main entrance to the course and continued on for five minutes until they came to an estate, where he pulled up in front of a new looking house. 'This is where I live, Jack.'

Jack took his gear out of the boot while Derek looked after Bluey. They went into the property; two Harleys were parked there, including the one with the side car. The backyard was fully secured and Bluey was given his freedom — he bounded away to do a thorough investigation. Derek showed Jack where he would be sleeping; in the meantime a cup of coffee and some cake would go all right. Derek rang for a taxi and twenty minutes later it arrived to deliver them to Bong Bong picnic races, five minutes away by car.

Jack was thinking as he got out of the taxi, *Geesus! This reminds me of the football match at Shellharbour, a massive crowd of people enjoying themselves in a carnival atmosphere.* Bong Bong was built around a hill, and at the moment this hill was covered in human beings living out of their Eskys. There were sixteen races with eight of them being trotting races. So a race every twenty minutes: one thoroughbred, then one trotting.

A meat pie stall attracted Jack and Derek's attention; they bought two each along with the standard can of Coca-Cola and went to watch the first race, which was won by the favourite — much to the delight of this massive crowd, who were still yelling and screaming five minutes later.

The first trotting race was next. They watched the trotter's parade then Derek said, 'I think I'll back the number ten, gee it looks good and it's got *back me* written all over it.'

Jack replied, 'If looks win the race then that horse is over the line, but it doesn't always work out that way.'

'Sounds like you know a bit about horse racing.'

'Yeah a little bit, but you back whatever you want. Don't let me sway you one way or the other because I know nothing about these horses.'

Derek backed number ten and got a good run for his money — although after looking the winner all the way up the straight, another horse claimed it right on the line. Derek was happy even though he lost. 'That was worth ten dollars just for the fun of it! You not going to have a bet, Jack?'

'No, I'm just enjoying being here.'

Six races had been run when the course announcer launched an appeal for an amateur trotting driver for race eight. Jack opened his race book and had a look at the conditions. He thought to himself, *I reckon I'd be qualified to drive that trotter.*

The appeal for a driver came over the public address system for a fourth time. Jack said to Derek, 'Let's go down and see what's going on with that trotting driver ... I might be able to help out, but only if they can't find somebody else.'

At the office Jack wasn't well received at all. Dressed in his swaggie uniform the clerk was quite sarcastic as he told him to *wait over there*, while he served two other men who were dressed in suits, hats and ties. While that was happening, two other fellows came along to talk to the clerk. Standing there they began talking.

One asked the other, 'I wonder if they've found somebody yet.'

'Doesn't look like it, otherwise they would have contacted us by now.'

Jack interrupted them. 'Are you the gentlemen looking for a driver?'

'Yes,' said one.

Jack replied, 'If you can't find somebody, I might be able to help you out.'

'Look mate, we're getting a bit desperate, what are your credentials?'

Jack pulled out his wallet and produced a card and a folded piece of paper. 'This is my trackwork license and this is my trial permit.'

They looked at them with one of them saying, 'Okay, you'll do Jack Kelly.'

The other one said, 'I've seen you on TV! You're the bloke that's walking around Australia for charity, it's nice to meet you.' He put his hand out and Jack shook it. 'My name's Kev Newman, I own the horse. And this is the trainer, Mal Brooks.' Jack shook hands with him.

'So let's go and see the stewards,' said Mal.

And they all walked away down towards the stables. Jack was interviewed by two stewards and was given the green light to be the substitute driver in race eight. While they were getting prepared with colours, clothes and safety equipment, Jack asked, 'What happened to the driver Kev?'

'Friday night's a curse here at Bong Bong — they all go out and drink themselves stupid. Even though twelve hours may have passed since your last drink, if you don't pass zero alcohol test one hour before the race you're not allowed to drive — and that's what's happened to our driver. That's what makes it so hard to suddenly pick up a freelance driver.'

The horse was being paraded by a young female attendant. Derek said, 'I'm going to put fifty dollars on you Jack, because you're number ten.'

Jack replied, 'Put fifty on for me and I'll fix you up later.'

'Okay Jack.' Derek headed off in the direction of the betting ring while Jack was being introduced to the horse.

Mal said, 'Jack, believe it or not, you're on the best horse in the race, but because an unknown is driving — that's you — the horse has blown in betting from 3/1 to 10/1. There are two drivers in the race that you have to look out for. These two fellows are very good drivers and they'll do anything to win, and I mean anything. They're brothers and they work together. Now, this horse has two sprints and sometime during the race you'll have to go around the field and sit beside the leader. When you do the brothers will protect their territory — they'll drive you off the course or try to box you in. You can't miss them. One's in all black colours and the other one's in red.

'Good luck Jack, we'll see you after the race.'

Jack took his seat in the sulky and grabbed hold of the reins just in time to join the others out on the track. A parade down the straight followed by a one lap warm up, then it was time to get up behind the mobile barrier, which was beginning to move away. The trotters were all travelling nicely in their gait as they picked up speed. The blue light came on and, *'Racing'* — down to the winning post and two laps of the course to go.

The race was on in earnest up front, as the amateur drivers all wanted to be in the lead. Jack, being out of the worst barrier, just ambled his horse from the mobile start and dropped it back to last. He'd watched his trainer Vic in Sydney do this many times so he knew how it worked. Several drivers tried to improve their positions, but the brothers always seemed to be in their way, forcing them to sit three and four-wide until they snagged their horses backwards to get a better position a bit closer in.

Jack was sitting three lengths last on the fence to avoid the stop-start tactics of those up the front, which would make any horse unsettled. Another driver got trapped three-wide by the brothers and couldn't drop in anywhere, so he'd have to come right back to last. Jack sensed this and moved his horse into the two-wide line, and the horse that was coming back eventually sat behind him on the fence. One of the brothers moved his horse around the field fast and took up the running, while the other one would do his best to balk anybody coming from behind, helping his brother win the race in the process.

With 600 metres left to go, Jack gently pulled his horse into the three-wide line and gradually worked his way around the field in an attempt to get to the position outside the leader. If he could do this successfully, he should have plenty of power left for the final 200 metres.

The red-shirted brother was waiting as Jack's horse invaded his space. He bore his horse out, forcing Jack three and then four-wide. Jack had no choice but to give his horse full rein and a cut with the whip. When Jack's horse ran straight past him, Red Shirt got so angry he struck Jack across the back twice with his whip. It didn't hurt that much but a thought did come into Jack's mind: *I'll get that bastard later.*

Jack's horse reached the position beside the leader just before the final turn came up, thanks to a brilliant burst of acceleration. Now the horse came back and settled beautifully. Like Mal said, he had two sprints in him, and there was one left. Around the bend and into the final straight, he could hear the spectators chant and yell. At 100 metres to go, they were neck and neck. The black-shirted brother began to urge his trotter on, flogging it.

Jack was waiting for the 50 metre mark before giving his horse full rein. The black-shirted brother could see this and turned his whip to Jack, striking him twice on the shoulder. Jack had his whip in the right hand. He turned toward the driver beside him and whipped him on the chest and neck. The look on the brother said it all: somebody dared to fight back. Jack gave his horse full rein; it bolted away and won by six lengths.

He was thinking, *I might have won the race but stewards don't like violence, it's against all the rules of racing ... they might promote the 3rd horse as the winner. One thing's for sure, there will be an enquiry.*

The numbers went into the frame and everybody ran to the TV monitors to watch replays of the race. It soon became the talk of the racetrack. As Jack brought his horse into the winners stall, a large crowd of punters began to clap. As the black-shirted brother brought his horse into the 2nd place getter's stall, the same group booed and began to yell obscenities at him. Soon the placings were confirmed, subject to an enquiry. Jack drove the horse into the middle of the track where he posed for a photo — a memorable one at that — and then it was back to the stables. They put the horse in his stall alongside the other horses.

The two brothers came looking for trouble. One of them said, 'You dirty rotten fucken mongrel, we're going to –'

Before he could say another word Jack thumped him in the stomach. The other one moved in. Jack grabbed him by the ears and hit him with a classic head butt, then tripped him over. As his head went down Jack punched the back of it with a nasty blow. Jack then walked away. Seven or eight people witnessed all of this — including Derek, who'd arrived just in time. 'Need a hand Jack?'

'No thanks, I think it's all over.'

Jack went into the driver's room to change back into his own clothes; one of the stewards came in and said. 'Jack, you'll have to come into the steward's room, you and the brothers.'

'Okay, the brothers are in the stables fighting each other.'

'Hmmm, interesting, I'll go there now.' The steward walked into the stables; the brothers were looking a bit dejected. 'Right you two, into the stewards' room.'

'We're not going anywhere!'

'Suit yourself, if you don't go they'll disqualify you for years.'

He walked away. They knew they had to attend and reluctantly walked into the room. Jack was already sitting down, and the brothers were seated well away from him. There were four stewards and one security man — obviously he was there to keep the peace if things got out of hand.

The chief steward began. 'You know why you're here so I won't bore you with a lot of talk. The first thing we have to decide is whether your actions denied the chances of the other runners. After watching a reply of the race a couple of times, the stewards deemed that no other runner was interfered with, so the all clear was given to pay.' The chief steward paused before continuing. 'In all my time as a steward I've never seen such disgraceful action. Now let's have a look at you, Barry Blackman. When Mr Kelly made a slow run around the field you came out underneath him, which is all right, but then you continued to veer your horse out in order to take him out of the race. Luckily for Mr Kelly his horse was good enough to out-sprint you, but not before you struck him twice with your whip. What have you got to say for yourself?'

'Nothing.'

'Good. You can go now but you'll never drive a horse at this venue again, ever. Goodbye. Mr Colin Blackman, you've been in trouble here before. Again you attacked another driver with your whip. What have you got to say for yourself?'

'I'm sorry Sir, it won't happen again.'

'That's what you said last year. Well, we are suspending you for thirteen months — that means you can't drive at this meeting next year. Now beat it.' Colin Blackman left his seat and walked out. Mr Kelly, we haven't met you before, so what have you got to say for your actions?'

'Well, after being forced off the track and being struck by the first brother's whip, when I got to the position outside the leader the second brother got his whip on me. It hurt, and I just naturally responded to protect myself.'

'Okay Mr Kelly, we're giving you a warning — don't you ever do it again.'

'No Sir,' answered Jack.

The chief steward continued. 'Mr Kelly, I would like to say it's a pleasure to have you here today. We've all seen your exploits on TV and in the media and appreciate the work you do for homeless people. Also, the way you drove that horse today was absolutely perfect. Off the record, I would have done the same thing that you did to that brother.'

They all laughed, Jack shook hands with all of them and said goodbye. Derek was waiting patiently outside the steward's room, and he gave Jack five hundred dollars. Jack gave him back one hundred dollars, saying, 'That will pay for the petrol tomorrow.'

Derek reluctantly took it. They went and met up with Kev Newman and Mal Brooks in the Bong Bong bar and had themselves some wonderful conversation over a couple of beers and a barbecue steak each. The four of them went and watched a few more races, then it was time to go. Derek and Jack hailed a taxi back to Derek's place.

The next morning after breakfast Jack, Bluey and Derek got into the car and began the start of the hour long drive to Lake Illawarra, and the Big Lake Hotel. It was 9.00 am when they drove past the Bong Bong racetrack. The party was still going on but on a much smaller scale. Two thirds of the motor vehicles had gone, while the hill in the centre of the course stood out like a beacon, covered in litter. The cleaners would earn their money, sometime later today or tomorrow.

Twenty minutes on they came to the Robertson Pie Shop on top of the escarpment. They just had to have a meat pie, didn't they? On leaving, the road followed the rim of the mountain, giving a wonderful view of Lake Illawarra in the distance.

Thirty minutes later they arrived at the kiosk on the southern shoreline of the lake's entrance channel. Jack and Derek had a final cup of coffee. They shook hands before saying goodbye. Derek drove away to return to his home in Bowral, the number one town on the Southern Highlands.

On the northern side of the lake entrance, opposite the boat ramp in the two-storey townhouse, Jack's ex-girlfriend Chantal knew that he was working his way back home, re-visiting the places that he'd stopped at on the way to Mildura. Like everybody else she'd been watching the nightly TV coverage each night. She still had feelings for Jack, she couldn't hide that — after all, Jack was her first real love, and she regretted her act of stupidity that ended with Jack breaking off the relationship. *But he must still like me, otherwise he wouldn't have come here to visit me in the first place. He could have just kept on going and I wouldn't have even known that he'd been here.*

Last night's news bulletin had him at the Bong Bong picnic races — would he stop here or pass on through? Chantal was feeling nervous and at the same time anxious — she was hoping that he would drop in and say hello. Her boyfriend Bozz was better now and they had a good relationship, but Jack had that special place reserved in her heart.

She was sitting in the deckchair on the second-storey balcony, occasionally scanning the walkway on the bridge to check the pedestrians walking north. She went downstairs and made a mug of coffee, bringing it back up and relaxing back in the deckchair. This time she had a pair of binoculars; now she could do the job properly. Twenty minutes later with the coffee mug drained, her eyelids began to get heavy. She put the binoculars down and dozed off.

Back on the southern side at the kiosk, after having a good talk to the owner, Jack said goodbye and began the walk to the northern side. Jack and Bluey came to the steps that led to the bridge walkway, made their way up and once there continued on. Nothing had changed here, only the month. February had turned into December. He stopped to look; the birds were still in their own groups, and the pelicans still had the high ground on the hill beside the channel where it was standing room only. The drink-straw birds were doing some worming and a couple of big black swans were majestically swimming by.

Continuing on and after talking to a couple of fisherman and passing quite a lot of pedestrians, he stopped right in the middle of the northern channel just as he did on the first day that he came to the Big Lake Hotel in February. He pulled the binoculars out of his pocket along with the phone. He punched in the numbers of Chantal's phone before lifting up the binoculars to scan the shoreline. Firstly the boat ramp, then across the street to Chantal's townhouse, onto the balcony and — bingo. Jack pressed the green button, not knowing what sort of a reception he would get.

When the phone on the balcony table began to ring Chantal jumped a foot in the air. She got her bearings and pressed answer. 'Yes, Chantal speaking.'

'Hi, this is Jack Kelly. I was wondering how you're doing?'

'Hello Jack. Funny, I've been thinking of you lately.' Her heart was thumping loud and clear; she was trying to act in a casual way, but underneath she got totally excited when she heard that voice. 'Probably because you're on TV every night. Is walkabout nearly over?'

'Yes, a bit over a week and I'll be home.'

Chantal had her binoculars on him and said, 'Well, you'd better come down and have a cup of coffee.'

Jack could see that she was looking through binoculars so he gave her a wave. She had a happy smile on her face as she waved back.

Jack and Bluey continued on towards the end of the bridge, and as he did he noticed that the personality had returned to the land beside the King Prawn Club. The Surf Club Carnival was back and judging by the amount of people roaming around, it was doing good business. Down the steps to the edge of the lake channel and one minute later Jack and Bluey walked up the steps to the door of Chantal's townhouse and strolled inside. They had a friendly hug then Chantal said, 'So you found yourself a dog.'

'Yes, this is Bluey.' Bluey sat on his rump and put his paw out so Chantal could shake it; she also gave him a pat on the head.

'Gee, what a beautiful dog he is Jack, where did you find him?'

'I didn't, he found me and I couldn't persuade him to leave.'

While they were talking Chantal made some toasted sandwiches and coffee. She fed Bluey some cooked rissoles and biscuits. After lunch Jack and Chantal took Bluey for a walk over to the northern side of the lake entrance, where they let him run wild on the vast open spaces of yellow sand. They walked along the beach for a couple of kilometres or so, stopping to look at the crashing waves occasionally. The white-tipped water was strong as it ran up the beach in front of the waves until momentum ran out, and then ran back down the slope to re-join the ocean. Bluey was having a fantastic time running at full speed through the water, which was up to half a metre deep. The surf and sand was a new experience for him; he had to chase every seagull that landed in his vicinity on the sand that seemed to have no end to it.

That night Jack and Chantal went to the King Prawn Bowling Club for dinner, before going into the dance hall section. The regular band was still there, entertaining the club patrons with their twanging guitars and synchronised singing. During the break the band leader came over to their table and said to Jack, 'I remember you singing a song here a while ago.'

'Yes,' said Jack. 'That was last February, believe it or not.'

'Gee, it seems just like yesterday. How about singing us another one?'

'Yes, I can do that.'

'Okay, after the break we'll sing one song then I'll introduce you, then you come up onto the stage.'

'Right-o, I'll be there.'

After the break the band struck up again with plenty of people getting up and dancing. When the song ended the band leader announced, 'Ladies and gentleman, all the way from Sydney Harbour, just so he could sing a song to you — give a big hand for Jack!'

A big round of applause followed as Jack left his seat and took to the stage. They talked for a couple of minutes, getting the scale and notes right — then it was a one, two and three and it just happened. It was a beautiful ballad that was on the hit parade called 'Gee it's great to be back here.'

And what a good piece of music it was too. They lowered the lights to make it intimate; the sound effects, the stage lighting and that voice of his made him look like a superstar. Chantal was thinking it was a nice song, not like the other one that was titled 'You don't mean that much to me.' That one didn't fit into her brain at all, especially after their break up years ago.

The applause was consistent as Jack made his way back to his seat. They wanted more, but that was it.

Later on Jack and Chantal walked around the carnival to look, content watching the people enjoying themselves. They indulged in a strawberry banana split and a beautiful cappuccino before walking back to Chantal's townhouse opposite the boat ramp. Jack spent the night on the couch in the lounge room, while Bluey had to settle for the tiny backyard.

At 10 o'clock in the morning, Jack was back in his swaggie uniform. He said goodbye to Chantal and began the ten minute walk with Bluey that would take him to the Big Lake Hotel. Walking through the commercial centre he heard someone say, 'Hey there's that bloke that was at the Bong Bong races. He's walking all over Australia for charity.'

Two young ladies came running out of the real estate office to get an autograph. Jack signed both of them with their names and the words, 'Jack Kelly, The East Coast Swaggie.' One of them stole a full-on kiss right on his lips while the other one took a photo.

He continued walking on and was suddenly surrounded by people of all ages wanting autographs, asking questions, and getting their photos taken with the swagman and his dog. They moved into the safety of the Tom Thumb Park, where Jack tried to accommodate the wishes of all those people as best he could. After another two hours he'd finally made it to the Big Lake Hotel. He didn't intend to stay, he just wanted to say g'day — but they wouldn't let him go, so he consented to stay the night. Jack made a phone call; the two Salvation Army ladies would now pick him up in the morning to take him to Bundeena.

Bluey would stay at Ernie's father's place and Jack would also stay there the night. Harry Bush the publican shouted Jack dinner that night, and all the Big Lake Footballers from the 'Summer Grudge Match' were invited along too; they sure had a lot to talk about.

During dinner Harry Bush said to Jack, 'In a couple of weeks' time I'm going for a holiday to America.'

Jack replied, 'Oh yeah, that's funny isn't it ... before I came here in February I'd just got back from a holiday there, a very imposing place.'

'So I'm told. We'll have to have a talk when I get back.'

'I'll look forward to it.'

Jack also had a talk to serial pest Shorty; although he was still a pest he wasn't as bad as he used to be, according to the bouncer. He spared a thought for Kelly Marsden, the lady from Newcastle, who came to attend her sister's wedding at Shellharbour, arriving a couple of weeks early to 'have a look around and a bit of fun'. She was a decent one all right. The day she left, Jack carried her bags out to the car. A simple goodbye hug at that time created some emotional heat and steam — maybe it was a good thing that she'd gone.

At closing time Jack said goodbye; Ernie drove him home to his parents' place, much to the delight of Bluey. In the morning he said goodbye to his hosts, and stepped into the car driven by the two Salvation Army ladies. They would deliver him into Bundeena, where he would spend the night.

The one hour drive through the pristine bushland of Australia's first national park seemed to go so quickly. Arriving at the petrol servo he said goodbye to the two ladies before they drove away; this would be the end of their mission, but he imagined that he would be seeing them again, very soon.

Nice Christmas music was coming out of the servo and Christmas decorations covered the pumps. Jack would be meeting the ferryman Mal Hodge shortly but first he would have to have one of those bacon and egg hamburgers — better make that two with a large coffee, and a tin of dog food.

After meeting Mal when the ferry came in, they went down to Mal's house just past the shopping centre — Jack would be staying here tonight, while Bluey would have use of the big backyard. In the morning Jack and Bluey caught the 9.30 ferry across Port Hacking to Cronulla. Jack shook hands with Mal and waited thirty minutes for Bill's courier mate to arrive. He would deliver Jack and Bluey to George Street, Sydney, right on 11 o'clock.

Bill was waiting on the footpath when the courier van drove into the reserved parking space and stopped. Jack and Bill had a talk for a few minutes and now it was time to walk this last 200 metres. In his swaggie uniform and Bluey by his side, they began walking.

Strategically placed TV cameras were recording their every move. Circular Quay was the waterfront base for the Sydney Harbour ferries, along with the overseas shipping terminal — and it was straight ahead. Jack hated to think of what was waiting for him when he finally arrived, but already he could see signs of human activity. A large crowd was waiting and began clapping and cheering as Jack, Bill and Bluey approached. He acknowledged them with a nod and, 'Thanks very much.'

What a sight. Hundreds and hundreds of people standing wall to wall on the ferry terminal patio, waiting to catch a glimpse of the East Coast Swaggie and Bluey, the 'Wonder Dog'.

A guard of honour funnelled them across the road, and the immediate spectators began following Jack like he was the pied piper of Sydney. Jack didn't know it but he was being directed towards the Opera House, and it became obvious to him that this was the final destination. There was still a ten minute walk and up to now he hadn't seen anybody that he knew. The Salvation Army had sentries set up every ten metres to act as a guide, and this went all the way to the welcoming dais.

The Opera House came into full view; Jack was looking at a spectacle in itself. It suddenly swept into his brain: he was the one all these people had come here today to see. The big banner hanging above the massive glass windows of the Opera House said it all: 'Welcome Home to Sydney Harbour, East Coast Swaggie'.

He never expected all of this and felt a bit humbled and embarrassed at the same time. Now he had to walk through another guard of honour that went all the way up the steps. The Salvation Army Band began playing 'For he's a jolly good fellow' as the popular duo of Jack and Bluey began the final walk through two rows of immaculately dressed Salvation Army Soldiers. Reaching the dais steps, a female in a Salvo uniform ushered Jack up the steps with a sweeping hand. She said, 'Up the steps, thank you Sir.'

Jack's infectious smile exploded across his face; it was Marree. They had a little hug then Jack said, 'Gee it's good to see you mate, where's Kate?'

'I think you know the answer to that one.'

Jack looked across the harbour to the north side, in the direction of the Kelly mansion. Then he looked back at Marree and said, 'You're right, that's one question I shouldn't have asked.'

It was up the steps to the dais and the awaiting Donny King. They shook hands, then Jack shook hands with the Lord Mayor of Sydney, the irreplaceable Clover Moore. She said, 'Congratulations Jack, and welcome home to Sydney Harbour.'

Television personality Robbie Hinds was acting as host; he walked up to the microphone as the clapping crowd went silent. 'Ladies and gentlemen, I'd like you to give a big welcome to the East Coast Swaggie, Jack B Kelly. He's just returned to Sydney Harbour today, after walking in the footsteps of his grandfather for the past ten months. As you can see he's looking a bit rough around the edges and his clothes are a bit tattered, and I'm sure he's got plenty of stories to tell us. We look forward to hearing some of these in the near future.'

Robbie Hinds went on for another five minutes before handing over to Donny King, who talked for ten minutes on the things that led to the challenge; he then congratulated Jack on completing the journey. Mayor Moore then presented Jack with a cheque for 500 000 dollars made out to Sydney's Homeless

Peoples Shelter as the prize for completing the challenge as per the rules. She also acknowledged that a further 200 000 dollars had been raised following Jack's much publicised trip back from Mildura — and they expected more to come.

Now it was Jack's turn to say a few words. He firstly thanked all the people for coming and giving away their free time on Christmas Eve in the middle of the day just to support him. He spoke for a further ten minutes before saying, 'Merry Christmas.'

He stepped back waving both hands above his head as the very large crowd of 4000 people erupted into happy applause. Jack noticed that Donny King had lost a lot of weight. His big fat face was now full of hollows and he wondered if he was sick. Jack waved the people goodbye, who instantly added cheering to their applause. As he turned around he noticed the pilot boat coming into the jetty on the western side of the Opera House. John Steed was standing on the front; it was time to go.

Jack asked Donny King if he was coming over for Christmas lunch. He answered, 'Yes, Kate had already asked me.'

Clover Moore handed Bluey's leash back to Jack, and together Jack and Bluey left the dais and walked towards the pilot boat. Richie sang out, 'Hurry up, we want a beer!'

Jack laughed and replied, 'Is that all you think about?'

'Bloody oath, beer and women.'

In his big coat and hat, along with his backpack and swag combo, Jack descended the stairs. Bluey wasn't keen on the water and tried to hang back. Jack shook hands with John Steed, then Richie and said, 'Ah gee, it's good to see you guys.' He introduced Bluey. Bluey sat on his rump and put his paw out so that John Steed could shake it.

'Wow, what sort of a dog have you got here Jack?'

'I picked up a good friend along the way, man's best.'

Jack gently picked Bluey up and lifted him over the gunwale, where Richie took over and lowered him to the floor of the cockpit. Jack climbed aboard; Richie started the motor and reversed along the side of the Opera House until the pilot boat reached the open waters of the harbour. A bit of throttle and some starboard rudder soon had the Pilot Boat moving in the direction of the Kellys' private jetty.

A television crew in a launch was following the pilot boat. Ten minutes later they pulled into the private jetty and it was time for Jack and Bluey to get off — they were home.

On the jetty Jack was living up to his nickname, the East Coast Swaggie. Still in his swaggie uniform and three days without a shave, he was beginning to look a bit like one of Sydney's homeless.

'Thanks for the lift John, will we see you tomorrow?'

'I'll be there.'

'All right mate, I'll see you tomorrow, we'll talk then.'

Jack knew Kate would be at the lane; his heart began anxious pounding. He looked up and there she was. John Steed kept hold of Bluey's leash; Jack was running up Lighthouse Lane while Kate was running down. When they met they clasped each other in a double bear hug. Emotions were running high with tears running down their faces as their hungry lips met time and time again. A TV cameraman followed Jack up the lane and was recording everything. John Steed let go of Bluey's leash and the Wonder Dog raced away to join up with Jack and his new mother. Jack and Kate took a breath; Kate said, 'So this is the dog.'

'Yes,' answered Jack, Kate patted his head and Bluey responded by licking her hand. The pilot boat was leaving; Jack and Kate waved to John and Richie, and then Jack shook hands with the TV cameraman, who then walked back down Lighthouse Lane to get back on his launch — his assignment was over.

Kate picked up Bluey's leash and the three of them walked up the lane, then through the security gate and into the house. Jack now took off the tattered coat and hat that had served him well; he threw them outside the door along with the tent swag-combo. Kate made lunch and gave Bluey a steak all cut up along with a bowl of milk. He ate and drank like it was his last feed.

Kate said to Jack, 'There's something you ought to know.' She had a beautiful smile on her face, and Jack had noticed that the lovely skin around her cheeks was showing the most radiant glow. She took Jack around the back with both arms, and he clasped her around her back. Kate said, 'I'm three and a half months pregnant.'

Jack was speechless for a few seconds, and then he said, 'You mean that one little encounter at the Canberra Compound did the trick?'

She replied, 'Yes but that was more than just one little encounter — I'd never experienced anything like it.'

'No, neither had I.' Jack grabbed her around that slim waist, raised her high above his head and said excitedly, 'You little beauty.'

Then he placed her back on the ground. From this moment on, the first day of the rest of their lives would now begin.

It's been seven months since the East Coast Swaggie returned home to Sydney Harbour. Christmas and the New Year came and went with the usual celebrations.

Sadly, Donny King, the powerhouse worker for Sydney's homeless, passed away in February after a short battle with liver cancer. Ironically he'd never smoked or drank at any time in his life. The 'pain in the neck', as Jack described him, will surely be missed by those who live on the streets of Sydney.

On a much happier note, six weeks ago Kate gave birth to a beautiful baby boy who they named James B Kelly, after Jack's dad. Their family was now complete.

Other than that, not a lot has changed in the lives of the Kellys. They still take to the harbour every chance they get. Kate can be seen doing the things she loves to do, like organising the food, making the drinks, keeping up a full supply of coffee and generally fussing about. New arrival James B Kelly lies in his blue bassinet, happily taking in the movements around him. Up on the flying bridge, Jack was at the helm driving the Powermaran amongst the harbour activities, zig-zagging between the sailing boats and dodging the ferries. For Jack, life couldn't get any better than this.

Adopted wonder dog Bluey has settled into his new life on Sydney Harbour and now occupies the co-pilot's seat — he's also the lookout. If another boat moves in a bit close he starts barking at it. Jack pats him on the head and says, 'Good on ya mate.' Two minutes later he's barking at another one. Kate made him a Nimitz style sailing hat, and had a pair of Elton John sunglasses custom made to suit his head. So it can be rightly said, that on a chosen day in Sydney Harbour, Bluey would be the best dressed dog.

Our story began in the early hours of a Friday morning amongst the tranquil surroundings of Sydney Harbour, the greatest natural harbour in the world, where the coastal gulls with their never-ending chirping constantly patrol the waterways on endless flights to nowhere. Where the massive white sails of the Opera House stand out in the darkness like the beacon of architecture that it is, and where the tall buildings mirror themselves in the water. And all this overshadowed by the colossal Sydney Harbour Bridge, a truly amazing icon of engineering.

It wouldn't be too hard to imagine that in the early hours of a given Friday morning, an electronic alarm clock is sounding to awaken the occupants. Fingers probe in the darkness to turn the cursed thing off. Jack B Kelly rolls onto his back and breathes out heavily, then turns toward his wife Kate, who is sleeping peacefully beside him, then asks the obvious question. 'You awake Honey?'

'Yes,' came the sheepish reply.

'Then let's go,' they declared as the team of Jack and Kate Kelly head off to the Powermaran and Sydney Harbour to do it all again.

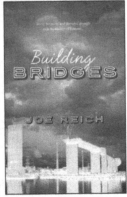

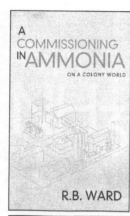
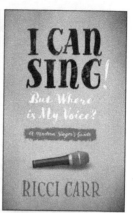
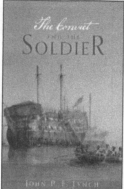
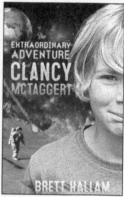
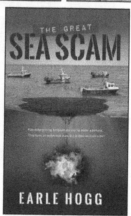

BEST-SELLING TITLES BY KERRY B. COLLISON

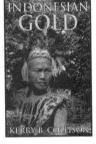

SID HARTA PUBLISHERS

Readers are invited to visit our publishing websites at:
http://sidharta.com.au
http://publisher-guidelines.com/
Kerry B. Collison's home pages:
http://www.authorsden.com/visit/author.asp?AuthorID=2239
http://www.expat.or.id/sponsors/collison.html
email: author@sidharta.com.au

Purchase Sid Harta titles online at:
http://sidharta.com.au